TIME-CROSSED LOVERS

Amy Robbins was vaguely aware of a mad swirl of color, then a flood of blackness. When they stepped out of the time machine, things looked exactly the same. The newspaper was dated Saturday, November 10.

Three days in the future!

He *was* H.G. Wells. She was certain now he was telling the truth, certain he loved her!

Then the banner of the *Chronicle* caught her eye:

CAREER GIRL MURDERED
FOURTH "RIPPER" STYLE SLAYING
HAS POLICE BAFFLED

And her body convulsed with fear. There was no mistaking the victim's photograph and its identifying caption:

AMY CATHERINE ROBBINS

Time After Time

a novel by
Karl Alexander

A DELL BOOK

Published by
Dell Publishing Co., Inc.
1 Dag Hammarskjold Plaza
New York, New York 10017

Dell ® TM 681510, Dell Publishing Co., Inc.

ISBN: 0-440-18804-0

Reprinted by arrangement with Delacorte Press
Printed in the United States of America

First Dell printing—October 1979

For Mary Ann

This novel is based on a story idea by Karl Alexander and Steven Hayes.

The author also wishes to thank David Spector, Michael Scheff, Nicholas Meyer, Jacqueline Tunberg & William Tunberg for their advice, criticism & support.

London, *circa* 1893

PROLOGUE

The gentleman got off the train at the Mile-End station early in the evening and quickly walked to the street, a tight smile on his face. He had a thin, yet handsome visage that did not quite match his muscular frame and athletic stride. He wore a bowler tilted forward at a rakish angle to enhance his appearance.

He crossed the street, a black leather bag in his gloved hand, and was careful not to slip on the wet cobblestones. A cold, heavy mist was rolling up from the Thames, and he could hear the foghorns in the distance. He breathed deeply and did not shiver, for over his well-cut dark suit he wore a fine lamb's-wool cape that kept out the chill. Except for a slight headache, he felt very well indeed. Yes, it was good to be back in the East End if only for a short while, and the weather suited his need for discretion.

He signaled for a passing hansom. The two-wheeled carriage stopped, its wheels skidding in the wet. He sprang lightly into the passenger seat and leaned forward, his dark, glowing eyes alert for the once-brazen and now downtrodden. He did not foresee a problem, for the district had not changed. Odors of stale petrol and dead fish wafted up from the docks. A mantle of damp suet covered everything, diffusing even the brightest of the gas-lit streetlights.

The gentleman had the cabby take him to the north end of Commercial Street where the sloven of gin shops and flophouses began. He paid for his ride, then moved off into the night, his stride jaunty, his mouth wet with anticipation. As he neared the dismal corner of Folgate and Commercial streets, he saw a drab harlot emerge from a low-life pub, huddle into her dirty, threadbare coat and walk dejectedly toward him. He studied the tart from the vantage of an alcove. Her face was pinched and sallow, her eyes dull, her teeth rotten. Her belly was swollen from malnutrition. The gentleman's heartbeat quickened, and he nodded imperceptibly.

He was about to call her over when he saw her look back, then hunch over and hurry away. Something was wrong. He stepped out of the alcove. The reason for her distress was a bobby crossing the street to follow her. The gentleman smiled again. He would shadow them both.

He watched her run past the coal-blackened buildings, hurry by Spitalfield's Market, then turn onto White's Row. He pursued, surprised that she had the strength to move so quickly. When he reached the narrow street that stunk of foreign vagrants, he saw her dart into an alley. The bobby kept going straight, and the gentleman allowed himself a dry laugh. So much for the bobby.

The narrow, filthy passageway twisted behind factories like a dry moat, and the gentleman found that he had to labor to keep up with her, but that was fine; it only increased his desire for the sweet slime of the alley slut. When she reached Houndsditch Road, she doubled back into a maze of side streets that seemed to lead nowhere. But the gentleman was familiar with the area; all he needed was an occasional glimpse of her slight figure to keep on the trail. He moved too rapidly and quietly to be accosted by the few beggars and thieves shut out in the damp freeze. Even the boldest would have been intimidated by his powerful arms and shoulders, anyway.

Finally, he saw her stop and lean against the dank brick of a building, her chest heaving. While she worked to get her breath, he slipped across the street to make it appear that he was coming from the other direction. He looked up and saw that he was near the corner of Fairclough and Berner streets, and he could hear the rattle of the District Line carrying citizens more fortunate than the harlot past this, the sinkhole of London. Then he approached, letting his footsteps ring with a hint of authority. He saw her listen, then look. She quickly straightened her clothes and forced her best smile. He stopped close to her and returned the expression. He noticed hope in her eyes that had not been there a few moments ago. Then she wet her lips and made a small, uncertain gesture with her head toward a high wooden gate that served as the workers' entrance to a garment factory.

The gentleman quickly looked in all directions, turned back to her and nodded. He allowed her to take his hand and pull him through the gates into a narrow courtyard bordered by brick walls. He heard singing, and as they crossed the small space he looked up and saw that the voices came from the second story of the building next to the factory. A socialist workers' club meeting was starting—the members were singing the "Internationale."

They reached the back end of the factory. She led the gentleman down several steps into a cloistered area where the walls were lined with commercial-sized dust bins, some of them filled with the remnants of cheap material. He hesitated and inspected the place very critically. Once satisfied that the cloister was ideal, he smiled. He was certain that no one would interrupt them.

From his waistcoat, he removed an ornate gold pocket watch and opened it. Also a music box, the small timepiece began playing a French lullaby, and painted on the inside of the lid was the likeness of a beautiful, dark-haired young lady. The gentleman gazed at the portrait, then carefully placed the watch on a concrete ledge above a dust bin.

The harlot faced him, opened her coat and pulled her dress and three petticoats up to her waist. She wore nothing underneath. He shuddered with pleasure at the sight of her shaved pubis just below the slightly distended belly.

"Five bob and you can do what you like, sir," she whispered above the second chorus of the "Internationale."

He said nothing and handed her a gold coin. She gasped with surprise, stepped back and quivered. He chuckled. No doubt, a guinea was the most the harlot had ever received for her favors. He knew she would have accommodated him for a few shillings, but he liked it better this way. The unexpected extra money made the tarts suddenly warm and loving, the way mothers were when they got flowers on their birthdays.

This one was no different. While he pulled down his trousers, she gratefully kissed him. She tasted foul, but wasn't that the way women were? He welcomed the rancid kiss. His breath quickened. He felt her hands on his thighs. He could wait no longer.

With a guttural sound, he spun her around hard, lifted her skirts, bent her over and roughly entered her from behind. She emitted an agonized groan. For a guinea, she must think the pain exquisite, he mused.

He used his hands to guide her hips until she was in rhythm with his thrusts. Then he noticed that she was moving with him eagerly, her head arched back, her breath coming in quick gasps. He smiled. She was going to have an orgasm. That was fine, that was the way it should be, this, the first time.

He threw his head back and hissed through his gritted teeth. Then he closed his eyes, relaxed his muscles and let go of his feelings. His mind raced. From the blackness emerged colors and forms. The harlot writhing against him became his sister, and her beautiful face was twisted with desire despite the innocence of the lullaby. God, how he loved her. He wanted to be with her for the rest of his life. How could they say it was wrong? How could they punish him? He would run away with her to a foreign country. They would marry and no one would know. Their life together would always be like this, it would always feel this good. There would be no others—not for either of them. There was no need. They were one. . . .

What was that she was whispering at the height of her passion? There *had* been others? He was *not* the first? She had lied to him all along? She had *not* saved her precious maidenhead for her true love?

The pastel forms in his mind took on shades of red and black, and he grunted as his climax began, his hands fumbling in his coat pockets underneath his cape.

"Touch me, sir, touch me!"

The harlot reached behind her to take his hands, but they weren't there. She groped for them, waved around for them, whimpering frantically, her body already starting to jerk spasmodically.

He was the first and only. With one hand he grasped her hair and snapped her head all the way back. *He was the first and only.* With the other he cut her throat from ear to ear with a postmortem knife.

The singing ended, and the gentleman released a deep breath in a long, continuous sigh. His headache was gone. Then he proceeded to cut up the harlot's corpse, his hands working the knife with considerable speed and expertise. When he finished, he carefully placed her parts in an empty dust bin and arranged them in a mock pose of horror. Then he stepped back to view his work, his shoes sloshing in the half inch of blood that now covered the floor of the cloister. He turned one hand a little to the left, then admired his composition much like a sculptor who was carving a bust.

Satisfied, he returned his watch to its pocket and attached the chain to his waistcoat. He started to leave, but stopped at the head of the steps to listen for a moment. The socialist workers applauded a speaker, and then all was quiet except for the murmured voices of the meeting.

The gentleman quickly crossed the courtyard and hurried through the gate out into the street. He heard horse hoofs on the cobblestones and the telltale squeaking of the springs of a hansom. The cab stopped at the end of the block, and he saw someone get out of the carriage and walk briskly into the building, perhaps late to the meeting. He smiled at his luck, ran to the cab, hailed it and jumped inside. The cabby flicked his reins, and the horse trotted away.

Once the hansom turned onto Brick Lane, the gentleman sensed that he was out of any possible danger and relaxed. He basked in the triumphant feeling that always came over him after a murder and his concomitant sexual release. His body tingled inside as he pictured the encounter. The harlot had been so willing and excited that he deemed her worthy of the creative collage he had constructed out of her bloody parts. Yes, it had been one of the most satisfying experiences for him, ever. Perhaps the best. The afterglow would keep him happy for weeks, maybe months. And when it ended, then he would return to Bethnal Green or Shoreditch.

The only problem was the police. After the news of this one got about, there would be another public outcry demanding his arrest and execution, probably the most massive response yet. Scotland Yard detectives would swarm around the East End for a long time. He would have to be very careful and selective in the future, a fact that he did not relish.

Perhaps it was time to leave England. He could certainly afford it. Yes, that might be a solution. Although once he killed again, people would know where he was. His style was definitely not commonplace. Perchance he would go to southern France where the women were coquettish and the police inept. He smiled and imagined using his knives on some dark-haired courtesan under a moonlit night on the beach at St. Tropez.

He heard another train in the distance, and the sound brought him back to reality. He reached down, opened his bag, took out white rags and a bottle of cleaning fluid. He meticulously scrubbed the bloodstains off his hands and shoes, then noted with satisfaction that there weren't any on his clothes. He attributed that fact to his talented hands and surgical knowledge.

The hansom stopped in front of the Whitechapel station. The gentleman got out fully composed, paid the cabby and quickly walked inside. He bought a ticket for Mornington Crescent and listened patiently as the clerk told him he would have to transfer from the District Line to the Northern at Charing Cross. He already knew.

What the gentleman didn't know was that the bobby who had originally followed the harlot had arrived at the intersection of Fairclough and Berner streets just as he was leaving. The bobby had become suspicious, had investigated and had found the harlot's remains in the cloister at the end of the courtyard. He had summoned his fellow officers, who responded quickly after hearing his brief report. Seven minutes after the gentleman boarded his train the cabby positively identified him to the police. And five minutes after that the station clerk confirmed his identity and revealed his destination. Within the hour Scotland Yard had the "H" Division mobilized and was on a prowl of their own.

ONE

Number 17 Mornington Place was a tall and narrow brick house with a well-kept yard bordered by a hedge and an iron-railing fence. With its three-gabled roof and dark-brown trim, it looked like all the other residences east of Regency Park between Euston and Camden Town. The streets appeared similar, too, for they were well laid out and at night were always crowded with lively, energetic people who liked to mingle in the gas-lit haze visiting or going on errands, despite the fog and the extremely cold weather. Discomfort could always be outweighed by a wool scarf, a heavy coat and the good fellowship of neighbors strolling to and fro. Besides, the warmth of a snifter full of brandy was never more than a short distance away inside a friendly pub.

The tenant at 17 Mornington Place was in love with the neighborhood, perhaps because for the first time in his twenty-seven years he was living in a decent borough north of the city and was free to do as he pleased. Recently he had purchased a new Raleigh bicycle equipped with the latest in safety brakes, and every night he leisurely rode through Mornington Crescent and absorbed the sights, sounds and smells. Then he turned those impressions into controversial, hence popular, articles for which he was paid a decent living wage.

This evening he had decided to look in Regent's Park, which always had been a good environment for source material in the past. He had pedaled all the way to York Gate on the narrow Outer Circle and the well-kept, familiar beauty of the green lawns and low overhanging trees softened by the constant mist had not even registered on him. He seemed to be within a dense fog of his own creation. When he reached the curved finger of the park's placid lake, however, he suddenly recalled delightful summer afternoons of boating with sophisticated female companions, a bottle of chilled French wine, bread and cheese; the memory made him realize that he had not been able to curtail his own inner excitement and allow himself to become the detached, yet passionate, observer that Londoners were so used to reading. It was as if he had bicycled five miles from Mornington Crescent with blinders on. He hadn't even felt the cobblestones which normally were a constant source for jolts, sore muscles and new bicycle tires. He cursed his own lack of concentration, then laughed. The reason was obvious. Later that night old friends and former classmates were coming over, and—great Scott—did he have a surprise for them.

He wouldn't have been out bicycling on this evening at all except that Mr. Hastings—the intrepid editor of the *Pall Mall Gazette*—had asked for three more articles by the end of next week. Yes, he was definitely behind in his work, for he had been devoting more time than usual to an obsessive scientific project in his obscure private laboratory. He had also been spending more money than the articles—no matter how well received—had been paying. So it was imperative that he find material and find it quickly.

He leaned forward, tensed the muscles in his small but lithe and energetic body and pedaled faster, for the road ahead was strangely deserted, and he needed human subjects for human articles.

The mist was turning into a light rain. He wiped his handsome angular face dry with a large handkerchief. Wetness had caused his thick, dark-brown walrus mustache to droop over his mouth. He imagined it made him look like an expatriate Russian bohemian living in Paris, so he rode no-handed for a short distance and used both hands to twirl the mass of hair back into a stylish shape. He reminded himself that he was fresh out of mustache wax and should pick up a jar the next time he was near the chemist's.

He rounded a turn, passed the Hanover Gate to the park and saw a very tall, thin and stately gentleman walking an equally tall and thin brace of Borzois. Perhaps an article about the striking physical (and psychological) resemblances between the owners and their pets would do. He chuckled at the thought of receiving irate letters from royalty and commoners alike who happened to own bulldogs or basset hounds. The only problem was that he would not have time to research the various and sundry breeds and species of animals that humans liked to surround themselves with. Oh, well. Perchance that was material for a more leisurely time.

He steered around a cart carrying milk cans, and as he passed he noticed that the horse pulling the cart suddenly lifted his tail and deposited a pile of feces in the middle of the road. A common enough occurrence, he thought, but what about the poor wretches who clean it up day in and day out? How did they (eastern European immigrants, no doubt) feel about the eccentric excesses of the Duke of Clarence, for example? Was there humor in that? No, the subject was much too verisimilar and socially realistic for the cyclist's romantic tastes. And he had no desire to imitate the venerable Charles Dickens. So he would just have to keep looking.

But after another mile of laborious pedaling, the

cyclist had seen nothing more of interest and finally decided to stop. He left the Outer Circle, turned north on Prince Albert Road, then coasted down a hill that curled through great stands of elm and maple. He wheeled to a halt in front of the Regent's Inn, a gathering place for couples returning from vigorous walks through the park. He went inside for a pint and took a table near the great stone fireplace. Bayberry logs were ablaze and radiated a great deal of heat from the hearth. He removed his scarf and blazer, then loosened his tie.

He sipped his beer and looked around the room, listening for the spark of an idea. He saw a couple seated in the corner and his intuition told him to observe them more closely, so he turned in their direction. They held hands, and he overheard them exchange mutual complaints about the fact that too many people used Regent's Park despite the November cold. The cyclist wondered where they had all been when he had ridden through.

"What we really ought to do, love, is spend your next holiday at the seaside," suggested the wife. "Even the fishermen won't be about."

The husband concurred. "Being out of season, the rates would be cheaper, too."

The cyclist's face wrinkled up into a broad grin, and his brown eyes sparkled. He pulled a note pad and pencil out of his knickers and began scribbling. Why hadn't he thought of it before? The seashore was his favorite of all places within a half day's train ride from the city. He recalled—more with relief than pain—a weekend he had spent there a year ago January. He had gone with his wife-and-cousin, Isabel, to recover from a mild attack of exhaustion and tuberculosis. He had been teaching biology at the time, and Isabel insisted that he give up his dreams of becoming a great writer and inventor and devote all of his time to his job and marriage. She had become the champion for everything that he detested and demanded that he choose between her and his radical ideas and unrealistic goals. He had chosen himself, then. Now he emitted an ironic chuckle and penned a working title: "How to Go to the Seashore Married on Friday and Return to London a Bachelor on Monday."

He put his pencil down, drained his beer, leaned back and sighed. He might even get all three articles out of that experience. Add Isabel's knickknack-collecting aunt and a former student with both suffrage and seduction on her mind, and he just might have a whole damned book!

He was about to purchase another pint when he thought better of it and pulled his watch out of its vest pocket to check the time.

"Good *Lord!*" He exclaimed. It was half-past eight, and his guests were due to arrive anytime after nine! He grabbed his coat and hurried from the pub.

He leaped onto his bicycle and furiously began pedaling toward home. Almost immediately he came to the hill that a half hour ago he had so casually coasted down. He worked his legs hard and strained to increase speed, but the twisting grade was unusually steep. His breathing became labored, and he began perspiring under his clothes despite the chill. Uncomfortable, he hoped that his exertion would not ultimately result in pneumonia, a disease he had feared ever since an opposing grammar school rugger had kicked in his frail chest and collapsed his lung.

In spite of his intense physical effort to accelerate, he never got his bicycle moving much faster than a crawl. He hopped off reluctantly and pushed the Raleigh the last few yards to the top of the hill. As he walked, he frowned and wondered why bicycles were so primitive. They *could* be manufactured with gearing mechanisms designed to alter the revolutions of the wheels. Other machines were. Better yet, perhaps they could be outfitted with a lightweight power source such as an adaptation of the Daimler-Benz internal combustion engine developed by the Prussians.

"Hmmmmm," he uttered. Maybe he'd start working on that soon. The idea seemed infinitely more simple than his current invention. He grinned, remounted the bicycle and quickly pedaled back through the park toward Mornington Crescent. The devil with articles on the seashore! Once his project came into his mind, he grew excited all over again and could think of nothing else. He had finished the device in his laboratory that morning, and he could hardly wait for the reactions of his friends. True, the contraption needed testing, but still the occasion made him feel extremely proud and self-fulfilled. Despite a subsistence-level childhood and a beloved mother who always held the Bible over his head as a philosophic truncheon, despite his failure at apprenticeships, his chronic tuberculosis, his poor record at the university and the suffocating effects of his first marriage—despite all this he was going to change history. Tonight his friends would be the first to know, and eventually the faculty at the Normal School of Science just might want to bestow an honorary degree on a former student who had been sent down seven years ago.

H. G. Wells got off his Raleigh in front of 17 Mornington Place, wheeled it through the gate and left it leaning against the side of the house under the archway.

"Mr. *Wells*," exclaimed the punctilious Mrs. Nelson as he hurried into the kitchen. "Where on earth have you been?" She folded up the *Daily Mail* she had been reading, placed it on the table behind her, then automatically poured a cup of tea, rose and handed it to him. She returned to her chair, crossed her legs and patted the bun of silver hair atop her thin and handsome face.

Then she critically appraised him with her keen blue eyes and frowned. "You shouldn't be gadding about on that machine of yours in weather like this."

"The weather's always like this," he replied to his housekeeper, then took a large gulp of tea.

"But a man in *your* condition—"

"I've never felt better in my entire life."

She shook her head and sighed. "That's what Mr. Nelson said. The day before he died, God bless him."

H.G. ignored her remark and drained his cup. "Is anyone here yet, Mrs. Nelson?"

"No, sir." She looked up—her eyes sparkling—and added with a touch of sarcasm, "Of course, if your friends are like you, we can expect them to be late, can't we?"

"If it's fashionable," he retorted with a smile. Then he placed his cup and saucer on the counter near the kitchen sink and turned to leave the room.

"I've laid out a sweater for you," she said affectionately. "There's a chill in the drawing room."

"It's *not* a drawing room, Mrs. Nelson, it's a *library*."

"Call it what you like, sir, but the fact is—"

"I'll put another log on the fire." He left the kitchen.

Mrs. Nelson returned to her *Daily Mail*, but couldn't concentrate. She shook her head, inadvertently smiled and looked up at the beamed ceiling. She violently disagreed with every opinion Mr. Wells had ever voiced to her, especially his views on religion and marriage. What was it he had said? Oh, yes. Ninety-nine percent of all marriages either end in revolt or passive endurance. And: If God exists, how could he allow nature to be so mindlessly cruel? Wasn't that condoning torture? When she had disapproved of his divorce, he had laughed and pointed out that if he were not single, she would not have a job. To her further consternation, he took delight in saying that there might be hope for the country after all if more conservatives like Mrs. Nelson ended up working for radicals like H. G. Wells. Still, being the man's housekeeper was the most challenging and exciting thing that had ever happened to her.

She poured herself more tea and hoped that Mr. Wells would approve of the canapés. She had spent the entire afternoon toasting bread, cutting it into small wedges, then spreading it with her own special cheese mix, relish and sausage. She sighed. Given the hour and the company, he would probably be more interested in the wine.

Which wasn't altogether true. For after adding three logs to the small fire that burned on the hearth, H.G. took one of the artistic little canapés off the pewter hors d'oeuvres tray, tried it and found it delightful. As he munched, he saw that aside from the canapés, Mrs. Nelson had laid out a handsome bowl of fruit, cheeses, bread, silverware, fine crystal glasses and several bottles of a passable French claret. Candles burned behind the spread on the sideboard, and he smiled with pride and admiration.

He inspected the rest of the room and saw that his housekeeper had made it look bright and comfortable despite the lack of rugs, decent curtains and abundant furniture. The one settee had been freshly covered, the two red velvet chairs cleaned and the imitation Chippendale desk polished.

H.G. was ecstatic. Mrs. Nelson had given the room both a dignified sense of order and an air of warmth and comfort. She had transformed it from a place he used only to read into the perfect haunt for a scientific romantic such as himself. The room was now the ideal setting for his gathering of friends and the occasion of his revolutionary announcement.

He knew that his friends would be pleased and surprised, for some of them hadn't seen him since the university days when he was subsisting in a messy and grimy West End basement room on the meager stipend of a pound a week. Ah, Mrs. Nelson! he thought. What a wonderful woman. He hoped that she would be his housekeeper forever. Besides, what would a household be if everyone always agreed? How could a person learn anything?

He was tempted to rush back into the kitchen and kiss her on the forehead, but he didn't want to embarrass her, and he was late enough already. He hurried upstairs and changed into gray tweed trousers and his comfortable Norfolk jacket. Then he brushed his dark-brown hair and critically inspected himself in the mirror. He grinned as usual, for he liked his face; he felt that his sharp yet subtle features complemented his devotion to writing and inventing. And someday he had no doubt that his affable countenance would attract a charming, sophisticated and intelligent woman; an *emancipated* woman—both on the boardwalk and in the boudoir.

With a flourish, he ran a comb through his mustache and was ready.

The guests began arriving shortly after ten o'clock, trickling in from various affairs they had attended earlier in the evening. Mrs. Nelson took their coats and hats and hung them in the hall cupboard, wondering why Mr. Wells—or anyone else, for that matter—would want to impress gentlemen she suspected were bohemians or libertarians. Nevertheless, she remained polite and courteous and showed the guests into the drawing room *qua* library where Wells greeted them warmly. Then she closed the door to the room and gratefully went to bed, for it was almost eleven, and she was very tired.

In the library there was a brief interlude of awkward small talk about the post-university years, the guests realizing that whereas their careers had taken them steadily upward, Wells's grip on the bottom rung of the ladder seemed tenuous at best. Optimistic and bubbling with enthusiasm nonetheless, H.G. passed the canapés around, then poured the wine and handed each guest a glass along with a personable remark. Then, with a sweeping gesture, he directed them to make themselves comfortable. They occupied the settee and chairs and began sipping the claret. Since he had only enough furniture to seat five, H.G. remained standing, but that was fine with him. He could dominate the conversation.

And so the evening began.

H.G. paced near the fireplace liberally drinking his wine. H. Ronald Smythe, now a myopic economist doing research for the Queen, was making a long-winded comment about the frivolity of fiction. H.G. listened patiently and waited. His slim and dashing figure moved gracefully, yet was poised, for he always spoke with his entire body. His dark eyes never left Smythe's face.

"Fiction has always been falsehood, and I would even say that it encouraged crime," said Smythe. A half glass of wine had dulled his already pedestrian wit so that he didn't realize he was speaking too loud and repeating himself.

"I was never aware that books committed crimes," said James Preston, a barrister who intended to run for Parliament. "I always thought that *men* were the culprits."

Everyone chuckled.

"Well, I should like to hear our host's comment," said Smythe, now the color of his maroon bow tie.

H.G. half turned. His voice was thin and reedy, but confident nonetheless. "First, may I compliment Ronald for his tenacious ability to put up with the Queen's unegalitarian views on finance?"

The guests laughed, now completely at ease.

"We were discussing fiction and crime," the portly economist remarked dryly.

"So we were," replied H.G. "So we were. I'm not sure about the connection you've made, Ronald, but I would agree that it is a crime some things get published." He paused for another laugh. "It is also a crime that some things don't." His eyes sparkled. And then he launched into his discourse slowly, realizing now that his guests were comfortable, he had to put them in the right frame of mind for his announcement or they would deride him.

"We all want a world free from social injustice and moral systems which give man less credit than the gorilla from which he ascended." He paused to light an Upmann cigar.

Only mildly interested so far, the surgeon, Leslie John Stephenson, continually leaned out of his chair to take wedges of cheese and canapés from the hors d'oeuvres tray. Famished, he didn't stop until he realized he had eaten almost half of the food by himself. Always concerned about his appearance and dress, he dabbed at the corners of his brooding mouth with a linen napkin, then inspected himself. There were several crumbs of cheese and toast on his lap. He carefully brushed the offending bits of food off his trousers and into the napkin, which he folded into a precise tricorn and placed on the table. Then he took a moderate sip of wine, sighed, sat back, stroked his cleft chin and listened.

"You speak of crime, my friends," H.G. continued. "Crime exists because the British monarchy and the Church hierarchy oppress most of the people and let a privileged few do as they please."

"Are you implying that the Queen and the Bishop of Canterbury are criminals?" Preston asked.

"Only that they do not know any better," H.G. replied, then added, "Although in my view, Queen Victoria has sat upon men's minds like a great paperweight for almost one half a century. A rational man of intellect just might consider that the greatest social crime in recent history."

When the laughter died down, Stephenson cleared his throat and interrupted in a soft and musical voice that had a touch of cultured melancholy. "It doesn't matter what kind of society we live in. Crime will always exist."

"Not if we have a society where all men are well fed and free enough to adhere to a modern ethical system."

Stephenson smiled thinly. "The only way that will ever happen is if you lobotomize entire populations."

The guests chuckled at Wells's expense, and H.G. recalled that while playing for the university's cricket team, Stephenson used to bowl with reverse spins so the hardwood ball would bounce into the legs of opposing batsmen. Obviously, he had learned to think and speak in a similar fashion.

"My dear Stephenson," said H.G., "don't you look forward to a day when you could read *good* news in *The Times*?"

"What's the difference? You, yourself, have already cited the Queen's inadequate justice system. *And* the absurdity of a religion telling you what to eat and how to behave! If justice, itself, is amoral, then why have it? If some criminals avoid punishment, and there is no God in heaven with a final retribution, then bully for crime! Let men do as they please. Their comeuppance will occur when they turn their backs on the wrong person."

H.G. was momentarily at a loss for words. Stephenson had scored telling points just as he used to when he and Wells were opponents in the school's Debating Society. Stephenson had been a formidable adversary then and clearly hadn't lost any of his talent for making his sharp-edged cynicism sound palatable. But H.G. wasn't exactly faint-hearted when it came to arguments, either. His eyes narrowed, and he focused them on Stephenson, then decided to use his persistent, rhetorical approach to regain the upper hand.

"Don't you feel that we should instill morality in people, John?"

"Why?"

"To preserve order."

Stephenson laughed. "There *is* no order, Wells!"

"Then what about the sanctity of human life or don't you believe in that, either?"

"I work in a surgery, Wells. People come and go. They are born, they become sick and they die." He leaned forward and lowered his voice so that it sounded even more melodious. "The most I ever know of my patients is what condition their organs are in. I'm like a damned mechanic who makes repairs on a carriage, only I have blood on my hands instead of grease! The ultimate question, Wells, is can you fix it or not? How long can you keep the wheels turning and the heart pumping?" He paused and leaned back again. "Now what is so bloody sacred about that?"

H.G. blushed. "Nothing. If you phrase it that way."

The others laughed, then buzzed with excitement.

"I do believe that the most literate among us has just lost his first debate," Smythe said gleefully.

Wells glared at Smythe. "Not entirely, Ronald. I would agree that there is no consistency in justice or moral systems today, but we *do* have science and technology. Ultimately, they will replace belief in God and the Queen. They are the hope for the future of mankind. They will lead to mass enlightenment. And *they* will be the retribution we all seem to think is so elusive."

Stephenson frowned and drained his claret. He could not immediately think of a response, for aside from his medical education and experience, he did not have a thorough knowledge of technology or any speculation as to where it might lead. For the moment he remained silent, as he had been forced to do during most of his childhood by his dictatorial father.

Meanwhile, H.G. recovered his poise and continued pontificating. "In less than a hundred years, there will not be any more war or social ills *or* crime. Our world will be a progressive Utopia where *everyone* will be free to pursue the noble experiments of the mind and the delightful pleasures of the flesh." He paused to look at his guests and saw that they were all listening intently, even Stephenson and Smythe. He imagined that he was addressing the combined faculties of Oxford, Cambridge and the University of London; to a man, the eminent body of scholars hung on every word he uttered, for they knew the drama of a brilliantly delivered lecture.

He was in fact leading up to something momentous, and he saw that realization in the expression of the guests who thus far had stayed out of the dialogue. Harper, the psychologist, had his eyes closed and his fingers pressing into the bridge of his nose in order to concentrate more keenly. And Grinnell, the visionary science teacher, was continually nodding his head and stroking his manicured beard.

But then Stephenson interrupted again. "I find nothing *noble* about the human condition, H.G. And there certainly isn't a damn thing delightful about a human soul imprisoned in human flesh. Furthermore, there is no indication anywhere in medical science that the future will be any different."

Smythe nodded in furious agreement.

H.G. smiled at his adversary, for now he felt that he definitely had the upper hand. "I sympathize with you, John. Having to spend your days surrounded by the sick and the dying. Human beings that you wished you could help, but can't because medical science is still in its infancy. You were born before your time. We all were."

"What the devil are you getting at, Wells?" Stephenson involuntarily ate three more hors d'oeuvres. "More predictions? They won't help you win an argument."

"I'm not interested in debating with you, John," H.G. lied. "I'm merely saying that by the late twentieth century the human condition will be a happy and fulfilling experience for everyone on earth."

"Can you be more specific?" Stephenson asked sarcastically.

"Pick any year you like past 1950," H.G. replied with rancor and a magnanimous gesture. Then he puffed on his fine Cuban cigar.

Smythe could no longer contain himself. He rose unsteadily. "Excuse me for sounding utilitarian, Wells, but you could describe Armageddon in—in, say—1984, and it would still mean nothing to us."

"That you have limited yourself to the dreary confines of present-day London is no one's fault but your own, Ronald."

"Well, what do you suggest we do?" Smythe asked. "Petition the Pope for an encyclical on reincarnation?"

Much of the laughter was directed at Wells, and Smythe acknowledged it by turning and nodding like a lame sea gull.

H.G. ignored Smythe, but there was no question that the spell he had worked so hard to create had been broken. He was irate and wondered what he should say next when suddenly it occurred to him that he didn't need any mood or dramatic tension to build up to his announcement. Thus far, the debate had satisfied his love for polemics, but this wasn't just another gathering of old classmates who used to argue philosophies and political movements in the teahouses of South Kensington. This was the most important meeting of his entire life.

All he had to do was explain. And explain he would.

"Come now, H.G.," said Preston, his face now flushed from three glasses of wine. "Why did you *really* invite us here this evening? *Surely* you had more on your mind than to have us witness a renewal of verbal broadsides between you, Smythe and Stephenson." He paused to light a cigarette. "If not, I must say quite candidly that my undergraduate days have been finished for quite some time—as have been yours—and that I must take my leave. I have a full day tomorrow." He half rose.

"Sit down, James," said H.G., appearing much calmer than he really was, "and prepare yourself." Deep in thought, he slowly paced three more circles in front of the hearth before taking a deep breath, looking up at his guests and pressing on.

"My dear friends, we have all learned that everything has length, breadth, thickness and duration. Duration—or time—is the fourth dimension, would you agree?"

There was general assent, although Stephenson and Smythe were guarded in their agreement.

"Our conscious lives take the form of a fall or a flight along the spatial dimension, time, but at any one moment we can *perceive only* three dimensions. Yet we all know that the totality of our being is from birth to death. Hence, we are four-dimensional creations. What we see from moment to moment is only a *section* of our reality."

"You still haven't given anyone a ticket to your so-called Utopia," said Stephenson.

Wells wanted to reply bluntly, but merely smiled again and let the remark pass. "If time is a kind of space, then *why* can't we move about in the fourth dimension as we do in the other three?"

"We do," said Smythe. "At the pace that we call minutes, hours, days, weeks and so on."

"What if we could speed up or slow down the pace?"

"Impossible," said Stephenson. "Time dictates to us the speed of life and that is the way it is."

"Did we study science to be satisfied with the way things are or to investigate the unknown?"

Harper and Grinnell both agreed with Wells. Stephenson, Smythe and Preston made quips about the state of H.G.'s finances and sanity, although none of them made any moves to leave.

The argument continued for hours, with short breaks for more food and wine. Wells savored every minute of the discussion, for he was doing what he loved—using words and logic to convince the skeptical. To the cries of "Impossible," he smoothly cited the recent fruits of science's labors: Edison's talking machine, the practical electric bulb (he already had several installed in his laboratory), the Daimler-Benz internal combustion engine, Marconi's wireless transmissions and—praise the Queen—London's new electric underground railway.

"What *isn't* possible, gentlemen?" Wells spread his hands, then cut and lit another cigar. He noticed the clock on his desk. In another half hour the sun would be rising. They had talked all night.

"What isn't possible?" said Stephenson tiredly. "Traveling into the past or future isn't possible."

H.G. swung around, eyes bright and piercing despite the late hour. "What were you doing eight years ago, John?"

"Studying medicine. What does that prove?"

"What was your first lecture class?"

"Anatomy."

"Can you picture the face, stature and mannerisms of your professor?"

"Certainly."

"Can you close your eyes and see the drawings and charts of the human body?"

"Definitely."

"Can you recall the first cadaver your class dissected?"

"What *are* you getting at, Wells? Of *course* I can! My memory's as good as anyone's!"

"Then your mind has just traveled through time. Fait accompli." H.G. smiled, then administered the coup de grace. "And if your mind can do that, why not the rest of you?"

The guests murmured to each other.

Stephenson was on his feet exclaiming, "It's against *reason*, Wells!"

"Perhaps. But so is defying gravity. You *do* know that more than one man has risen over five thousand feet above the earth's surface in a balloon, don't you?"

Stephenson started to speak, then sagged and thought furiously. Ten years ago, who would have thought of an electric light bulb? Or a talking machine? One hundred years ago, who would have thought of a camera? Or a gramophone? Technology did appear to be developing faster and faster. Maybe Wells was right about a Utopian future with a contented population. His theories *seemed* sound.

Smythe had the floor, and as he spoke he gestured triumphantly. "Doesn't this all sound suspiciously familiar? Much like a collection of absurdities Wells published in the *Journal* five years ago?" He turned and addressed H.G. "What did you title that piece?"

" 'The Chronic Argonauts.' "

"Oh, yes," Smythe continued. "Wasn't it about a young man who traveled through time encountering great civilizations in the future? What a lot of simplistic rubbish that is! Give up this thinking about a time machine, Wells. It's a *waste* of time, and it doesn't suit you."

H.G. cleared his throat and smiled smugly. "I haven't just *thought* about a time machine, gentlemen, I have constructed one."

TWO

The uproar of voices from downstairs awakened Mrs. Nelson. She listened for a moment and could hear Wells's muffled tones and then another uproar. She looked at her clock on the bedside table: 5:15 A.M. She frowned. The man has no sense at all, she thought. No sense and no breeding, despite his educated ways. Him and his cronies will have half the neighborhood up before long. Humph! If Mr. Wells didn't have the consideration to tell his guests when to leave, then she would tell them herself. She got out of bed and quickly donned a gray, floor-length robe over her blue nightdress.

As she started downstairs, she shook her head. She just didn't understand the man. He could be so nice and thoughtful, so kind and generous, then turn right around and spout his radical and blasphemous ideas until all hours of the morning. No doubt the former qualities could be attributed to the guiding hand of Mr. Wells's mother, who kept the family together, Mrs. Nelson thought. The latter were undeniably part and parcel of his irresponsible father, who was always away playing in semiprofessional cricket matches. Not to mention the schooling that planted the spurious seeds of Darwinism, socialism and other irreligious notions in poor Mr.

Wells's impressionable mind. She sighed. Perhaps some day soon she could induce the vicar to drop in for some tea; *he* might be able to talk some sense into the young man.

When she reached the bottom of the stairs, she heard sharp knocking on the front door. Who could that be at this hour? If there were more of Wells's scruffy friends about, she'd send them packing soon enough. She yanked open the door. The fog had lifted, and she had to shield her eyes from the rising sun.

"Mr. Wells is not receiving any more guests this evening, gentlemen," she said haughtily to two hard-looking but sheepish men. They removed their hats and straightened their ill-fitting suits. She was about to slam the door in their faces when one of them flashed a badge.

"Morning, mum. I'm Inspector Adams. Scotland Yard. I apologize for the hour, but is the man of the house about?"

After Wells had made his announcement, the guests had leaped up and begun bombarding him with questions, the most vociferous being Stephenson. H.G. had never seen the man so excited. His eyes had glazed over and his shouting went beyond the bounds of decorous behavior. Wells imagined that Stephenson was acting very much like a converted disciple to Catholicism. And why not? The time machine would nullify death and, he mused, hopefully the existence of God, too.

When his guests had calmed themselves, H.G. endeavored to explain. He kept his account as simple as possible, realizing that he had been studying and testing the concepts of time and fourth-dimensional geometry for years. His friends hadn't, and he wanted to convince them irrevocably.

He began. "Gentlemen. Atoms rotate through the

solar system just as the solar system rotates through the universe. The universe also turns while it travels at the speed of light through space.

"What I have discovered is that both the past and the future exist *permanently* in our universe, but our consciousness sees only '*now*' because it has been conditioned to do so—perhaps by nature's dictatorial need to maintain order.

"Time planes, or spheres, are *adjacent* to the one we now find ourselves in, and they function according to the laws of the Gaussian coordinates. In other words, our particular time dimension is merely an electromagnetic field. Swirl, if you will.

"What I have done is constructed a machine which juxtaposes fields of energy, creating friction. The result is an ever-increasing and magnifying series of chain reactions which *lift*, or literally *rotate*, the machine out of one time sphere and into another. Acceleration will keep the machine and its occupant above all time spheres in a conscious but vaporized state. You may go into the past or the future at will."

"How do you know which is which?" asked Grinnell.

"If you rotate to the west, you gain yesterdays. To the east, you accumulate tomorrows." H.G. drained his glass of claret and poured more.

"And if you go north, you'll find Scotland, and south, you'll end up in the Thames," remarked Smythe sarcastically. "I say balderdash!"

"Quiet!" snapped Stephenson. He turned to face H.G., his eyes wide and glistening. "Does the device *work*, Wells?"

"Theoretically. I have not tested it yet because I have been concerned with the re-entry problem. Although this morning I installed what I term the Interstices Vaporizing Regulator. Hopefully, it will automatically keep passengers above the time spheres if it detects danger."

"What danger?"

"Well, you wouldn't want to stop off in the middle of a pestilence or a war."

"Doesn't the time machine stay where it is?" queried Grinnell perceptively.

"Of course it does, but in a thousand years England may have sunk, and this house may be on the bottom of the Atlantic. In such a case the IVR would sound a warning, take over the controls and guide the passenger to the nearest safe landing date." He paused. "In addition to the IVR, the machine has another safety feature. The Rotation Reversal Lock. This device automatically returns the machine to its starting date after the completion of a voyage unless overridden." (He did not show them the special key which would shut off the RRL.)

"But why would you want the damned thing to return?" asked Stephenson.

"What if you were injured during flight and incapable of fending for yourself? Wouldn't you want the time machine to take you back home?"

"You mentioned that the machine stays where it is during a trip," commented Grinnell. "I'm not sure I understand. Could you explain how that is possible?"

H.G. smiled. "It moves only along the *fourth* dimension. It *always* occupies the same space, but if it is not in today's space, then you may find it in yesterday's space or tomorrow's."

"Then it does indeed disappear?"

"Of course. *For* the duration of a particular jaunt through time."

The guests murmured.

"In a fortnight I shall want you all present for the maiden voyage."

Suddenly, Smythe was on his feet again. "The maiden *voyage*? Come off it, Wells!" He laughed derisively. "If you persist in these discourses, the only trip you'll be taking is to Bedlam!"

"Hear, hear!" Preston concurred, nodding his head and clapping his hands.

But before H.G. could reply, Mrs. Nelson opened the hall door and stuck her head into the room.

H.G. turned. "Yes, Mrs. Nelson, what is it?"

"Scotland Yard is at the door, Mr. Wells."

"What the devil?" H.G. exclaimed with surprise. Then he briefly faced his guests. "If you will excuse me, gentlemen."

As soon as he had left the room, his guests were out of their seats, talking excitedly and moving spasmodically around the room.

Stephenson quickly started for the door that led to the kitchen. Before he arrived there Smythe intercepted him with the air of a foreign minister who is bewildered over the sudden defection of a staunch ally.

"John!"

Stephenson turned.

"You *haven't* taken Wells seriously, have you?"

The surgeon frowned impatiently at the distraught economist. "If I have?"

"Well, *I'm* beginning to think that he's gone stark, raving mad."

"Wells is no more insane than you or I."

"But surely you don't believe a time machine possible!"

"Of course I do." He smiled thinly. "Is not necessity the mother of invention?"

Smythe took off his glasses and rubbed his tired eyes. He put his spectacles back on, raised one finger and was about to ask a penetrating question. But he never uttered the words.

Stephenson was gone.

At the front door beside Mrs. Nelson, H.G. listened impatiently to the detectives as they wearily and methodically explained the nature of their visit. He was reminded of his brief and unpleasant tenure as a drapery apprentice when the foreman was spelling out why he had to account for every minute of his time during the day.

When Adams was finished, H.G. replied with unusual venom, for he detested the presence of a unilateral authority. "That is absolutely ridiculous, Inspector! I am not in the business of murder, and I do not entertain those who are!"

"A suspect was seen in the neighborhood, sir."

"Well, then *look* for him in the neighborhood!"

"Our instructions are to have a look inside every house in Mornington Crescent. Even *yours*, Mr. Wells."

"My good man, I have *guests!*"

"And *I* have a warrant," Adams replied sternly, then held up a writ signed by the sleepy clerk of Regent's Court just a few hours ago. He gestured to his companion. "Come along, Duggan, let's get on with it." He entered the house and went upstairs, alert for whomever he might suddenly confront.

Duggan was so large that he had to stoop under the doorframe to get inside. And when H.G. started back for the library, he found himself restrained by one huge hand. Then Duggan gently turned the much smaller man around, expertly searched him, straightened up and smiled.

"Shall I do the others here, too, sir?"

H.G. turned on his heel and strode into the library, where his friends waited. They were quiet now, having overheard the conversation at the door, and they all watched H.G. as he tried to find words that would make him appear dignified instead of humiliated. The only thing that came to his mind was to speak quietly.

He repeated what Inspector Adams had told him, then politely asked his friends to leave.

"You *must* understand that this comes as a great embarrassment to me, personally," he said, his hands strangely clasped behind his back. "Furthermore," whispered H.G., "I implore all of you to keep this evening's remarkable revelations to yourselves. I must test the device before its existence is made known to the world."

The guests murmured to each other sheepishly—some speculative, some serious. But they left the library agreed that no outside words would be uttered about H. G. Wells's claim that he had constructed an operational time machine.

And so they queued up at the front door, where Mrs. Nelson delicately (the police had humbled her considerably) handed the guests their coats and hats. Then Duggan spread their legs and searched them one by one. As only true British gentlemen could, they totally ignored the detective and accepted the frisk as if it were just another part of the evening. After all, what was a mere murder and a trifling personal indignity compared to a time machine?

When they all had left, H.G. felt more sad than angry. For months he had dreamed of announcing his discovery to a small—if not critical and influential—circle of friends. Who would have thought that the police would interrupt such a gathering? He shrugged with resignation, which was far from his usual militant stance. He could only thank God that at least they had come at the end of the evening as opposed to the beginning or middle.

He sighed and went back into the library. He poured himself the last of the claret, then sat in his favorite chair close to the fire. He stretched his legs out and stifled a yawn. It felt good to relax after standing and talking all night. His mind drifted, but before he could think of something pleasant, Mrs. Nelson came into the room. She carried a tray that held a pot covered with a cozy, milk, sugar and a cup. When she saw him still drinking wine she frowned.

"I thought you might want some *tea* while you waited for the police to finish."

He started to reply, but heard noises from upstairs. Adams and Duggan were now going through his bedroom. He scowled.

"Damn them! Do you think they'd be here if I hadn't published those articles on free love?"

"We're *not* the *only* household they're having a look in, sir." She set the tray down on the table with a bang. Free love, *indeed!*

"I wonder." He took a sip of wine, then smiled at her. He played with the ends of his mustache—a sign that he was about to say something at which Mrs. Nelson would take offense. "The next time you go to church, pray for a socialist state, will you?"

Before Mrs. Nelson could tell Wells in no uncertain terms that his salvation was in serious question, Inspector Adams appeared in the doorway, hat sarcastically in hand. He raised his eyebrows slightly.

"We're sorry to have disturbed you, sir."

H.G. slowly rose from the chair, took a deep breath and straightened to his full five feet seven inches. "You've *more* than disturbed me, Inspector, you've desecrated my fundamental human rights!"

"We'll be going, then." Adams executed a slight bow and headed for the hallway.

"Just what the devil did you expect to find, Inspector?"

Adams turned and replied, "Jack the Ripper."

Stunned, Wells sank back into his chair. Dulled by wine and lack of sleep, his brain was in no condition for analytics, but he thought hard anyway. He didn't acknowledge the departure of the detectives because he hadn't even noticed that Mrs. Nelson had left the library to show them out.

Jack the Ripper? That maniac hadn't been in the news for several years, and many experts speculated that he had either left the country or committed suicide. So what was Scotland Yard doing looking for him now in Mornington Crescent? His prowl had been the unfortunate streets of Whitechapel.

Undoubtedly there had been a murder, but why even suspect Jack the Ripper? God knows, there had been several hundred cheap imitations of the man's style in the past two years alone, if *The Times* were to be believed. But how could the police be so certain that the grisliest killer of them all was at it again? Wells shuddered. He knew that they knew. He possessed absolutely no knowledge of criminology, but he had an intelligent and innate respect for Scotland Yard. If their detectives said that Jack the Ripper was in the neighborhood, chances were, he was. Wells understood that and regretted the manner in which he had treated Adams and Duggan. He sighed again and thought that the detectives' visit was actually a blessing for he knew that his house was safe. He turned and read the clock on the desk. Ten minutes to seven. The fire had gone out and there was no more claret. It was time he retired.

Just then Mrs. Nelson called out to him from the hall by the front door. "Mr. Wells? Did Dr. Stephenson go with the others?"

"Of course he did."

"Did you actually see him leave?"

"Mrs. Nelson—"

"Why would he leave his cape and bag in the cupboard? He couldn't have left."

"The police just searched the house, Mrs. Nelson! There's no one here but you and I." Just after he had spoken, he realized that he was probably wrong. He gasped, bolted up out of his chair and hurried into the hall.

Mrs. Nelson was white with fear. She was holding up

Stephenson's cape and staring at it aghast. She glanced at Wells, then pointed to the hem of the garment. He frowned, for he did not immediately see the object of her concern.

"What, Mrs. Nelson?"

"Bloodstains, Mr. Wells."

He took the cape from her, inspected it more closely and did indeed find several brown spots on the wool. Only a person as meticulous as Mrs. Nelson would have noticed them in the first place.

He hung the garment up again in the cupboard, then pulled the leather physician's bag down from the shelf and stared at it for a long moment. When he finally moved to open it, Mrs. Nelson shrank back against the wall. He looked up at her. "Shouldn't you be fixing us some breakfast, Mrs. Nelson?"

She nodded, then put her hand to her mouth and hurried out of the hall. He watched her leave. When he heard the door to the kitchen close, he turned back to the bag, unsnapped the hasp and slowly pushed the sides apart. His heart pounded. He exhaled in a long hiss while lifting some bloodstained rags out of the bag. He dropped them on the floor and leaned farther forward. Under the rags was a collection of stainless-steel surgical knives that glittered brightly even though no direct light was hitting them. An odor penetrated his nose. It reminded him of a childhood Sunday morning when his father was butchering chickens behind the shop for the evening meal. He pinched his nostrils shut with his fingers and breathed through his mouth to avoid gagging.

There was a small tin in one corner of the bag. With his other hand he reached inside and lifted the top off the tin. He gasped, lurched back and retched several times.

The police had been right about Jack the Ripper, for the tin contained a finger, a kidney and two eyes.

Wells quickly jammed the rags back inside the bag,

snapped it shut, then stood and pushed it into the cupboard with his foot. He closed the door, turned and leaned against it. His jaw muscles worked furiously, and he thought hard. So, Dr. Leslie John Stephenson, former classmate and journeyman surgeon, had been doubling as Jack the Ripper all these years. H.G. felt cold and shuddered. Who would have known? The man always had seemed bright, articulate and socially graceful. Yet, H.G. had noticed a quiet, foreboding, even sinister quality in Stephenson that occasionally had manifested itself in the form of a brief, violent outburst. He recalled once when he'd watched Stephenson play for an unprecedented third straight handball championship at the university. Hard pressed to win, Stephenson had maneuvered his challenger into a corner, then slammed the ball so that it ricocheted off the center wall and into the man's face. Victorious, Stephenson had stormed off the court without an apology or even the traditional handshake. At the time H.G. had attributed the act to the frustrations and pressures of a student preparing himself for a career as a surgeon, not realizing until now the full and horrible import of his speculation.

It suddenly occurred to H.G. that the handball incident had happened in the spring of 1884 when he was finishing his first year at the university and Stephenson his last. Obviously, then, the 1888 murders had taken place when Stephenson was a student at the Cambridge medical school! If only H.G. had known then what he knew now. But why? What had possessed Stephenson? What kind of hideous demon ruled the inner recesses of his mind? H.G. did not have a clue.

More urgent thoughts came to mind. Was Stephenson still in the house? If so, where? How could the police have missed him? Their search had taken well over an hour and no doubt had been very thorough. True, Stephenson could have left with the others, but he never would have gotten past Duggan without his cape and bag. Maybe he had, however. Maybe he had left the cape and bag because he obviously didn't want them searched. No, the logic was all wrong. H.G. had been at the front door with the detective the entire time. Stephenson had not been there. He had not been searched and he had not said his good-byes. In the confusion and excitement, he had apparently not been missed. If he *had* left the house, he had done so by another exit.

Then how had he escaped? H.G. gasped again and slapped his hand to his forehead. Great Scott, what had taken him so long to figure it out?

He raced down the hall to the small door that led to the back stairs. He opened it and hurried down into the basement. He saw that the door to his laboratory had been broken into and was now slightly ajar. The yellow glow of an incandescent lamp shone through. Had he forgotten to turn the light off? No. The electric light bulb was too new and precious to be ignored.

He slowly crossed to the door and pushed it the rest of the way open. There was no one in the laboratory. His eyes narrowed. Stephenson was definitely gone, and he had left in a most unconventional manner.

The time machine was carrying its first passenger.

THREE

The time machine sat in the center of the laboratory, a faint bluish glow emanating from it that soon died away. To an objective eye, the device probably would have seemed squat, ugly and askew, but to its creator it was a thing of beauty.

The passenger compartment was square and stood eight feet high. It was constructed out of heavy steel plates which were held together by thousands of individually installed rivets and bolts. The sides of the machine were tapered to facilitate rotating through the fourth dimension. Small, paned windows were built in all around so that the passenger could see what historical event he might be getting into at low-velocity manual operation. Of course, at a cruising speed of two years per minute, the outside world would appear as nothing more than a blur of colored molecules as the device slipped through time in a vaporized state.

Beneath the cabin and extending three feet into the ground was the engine. Most of the parts were precisely machined stainless steel, but here and there nickel and ivory glistened alongside buffers of industrial diamonds.

The heart of the device was the arrangement of twisted crystalline bars which worked to juxtapose, concentrate and swirl the electromagnetic fields of energy, enabling the machine to spin out of and into time spheres.

Inside the cabin were the controls, which could easily be operated from a geared swivel chair. The chair turned so that the passenger would not be affected by the incredibly high-speed rotation. That amount of centrifugal force would certainly kill a man in seconds. The dials indicating years and dates did rotate with the machine, but the steering and pressure mechanisms were also gyroscopically installed so that the device could be controlled when entering a particular time plane. An emergency supply of food, oxygen and clothing was stored in an enclosed space behind the chair.

H.G. approached the time machine, his face full of wonder. He peered in one of the windows. The chair was empty, so apparently Stephenson had at least gone beyond the present. Then he dropped to his knees, opened the engine hatch and looked inside. He checked several connections (ones where the crystalline bars had been fused with metal gear faces) that he had been losing sleep over. They were intact. Then he carefully placed his hand on the Interstices Vaporizing Regulator. It was still warm, but obviously had not heated up and melted. That was good news. He closed the hatch, straightened up and wiped his hands on a rag.

He walked around to the front of the machine and tentatively pushed on the cabin door. It was locked. That left no doubt in his mind since the door locked only from the inside. Stephenson had used the machine and left it somewhere on another time plane. Since the man didn't have the special key to override the Rotation Reversal Lock circuitry, the door had automatically latched. After the prescribed ninety-second delay, the RRL had gone into operation, and the machine had returned to its home hour.

"My God, it worked," H.G. said quietly. He looked

up and smiled with pride at the shiny brass plate that he had riveted over the door just yesterday. Etched lettering spelled out THE UTOPIA, the name he had bestowed on his device. He had planned to christen it with a bottle of champagne before the maiden voyage.

Suddenly he frowned and became indignant. "He comes into my home masquerading as an old friend and a legitimate physician, drinks my claret, devours the hors d'oeuvres, picks my brain and uses my time machine! The bloody bastard! How dare he!"

But how had Stephenson been able to successfully pilot the machine? Was it that simple-minded? H.G. glanced over at his workbench and saw that his technical diagrams were out of place and had been hurriedly studied. That was how. He cursed again, then turned back to his machine.

He removed his key ring from a pocket, unlocked the passenger-compartment door, stepped inside, sat down and studied the control panel. The Rotator Control was set in the extreme eastward position, and the dials told him that Stephenson had gone to 1979. Why then? Wells frowned and thought. Early in the evening he had predicted that the world would be a Utopia by the late twentieth century, but he hadn't mentioned a precise date. He smiled grimly. Apparently, Stephenson hadn't needed one.

Obviously, the man had used the time machine to escape the police. When inside the device and at the controls, he had no doubt become befuddled, realizing that he couldn't dally over dates with two Scotland Yard detectives upstairs. So he had dialed today, then added on the first year that came to mind, which was 1979. H.G. frowned. He could not fathom the logic of Stephenson's decision, but whatever his reasoning, H.G. guessed that Stephenson hadn't gone that far into the future because he didn't want to encounter too radical a change in terms of human behavior, dress, speech and so on.

"Humph," he muttered. If *he* were right about the late twentieth century, Stephenson would be totally lost and out of place in 1979. The man would definitely have serious problems trying to adjust to a Utopia in that there would be no violence or aberrant behavior with which he could identify. Suddenly, H.G. straightened up. Good Lord, what was he worrying about Stephenson for? What about the happy and contented people of 1979? If technology had in fact freed them from the drudge of mindless toil, the oppression of conservative political systems and the scourge of poverty, then they would be an artistic and unabashed people. They would patronize and participate in music, dance, poetry, painting and other forms of culture. They would be open and honest. They would *accept* Stephenson as one of their own and they wouldn't *know*! And what if he went on another ghastly rampage as he had done in '88 and '92? If they weren't used to crime, the people of 1979 would be helpless when faced with London's most notorious butcher. There would be panic. A great deal of panic.

H.G. stared at the control panel. He had to do something. Quickly.

Suddenly angry again, he climbed out of the machine and slammed the heavy door shut. A bloody murderer using my unprecedented device to escape justice, he thought. *My* time machine that was built for and should exist for the betterment of mankind; that was *named* for a perfect human society. Then a horrible thought struck him. Had he created a technological monster? If he hadn't built the device in the first place, Stephenson would not have traveled into the future! That meant that Stephenson was *his* responsibility, and he didn't want to be accountable for what that maniac would do in 1979. It wasn't merely principles of justice and morality that were involved; it wasn't just H.G.'s personal sense of worry and outrage. It was as if he were the owner of the trading ship that had brought the black plague to Europe in the Middle Ages.

He paced and fumed and quickly made up his mind. Dr. Leslie John Stephenson might not believe in retribution, but H.G. Wells was of a different opinion. There was only one thing to do: get Jack the Ripper and bring him back.

He strode resolutely to a safe built into the wall of the laboratory, spun the combination and opened the door. He removed the fifty pounds that he kept there for emergencies, started to put the money into his billfold, then stopped and thought. What about Mrs. Nelson? It wasn't as if he were taking a trip to Africa and could mail her a few pounds from Johannesburg if she needed it. No, he had best leave her the fifty pounds. It would keep her solvent for at least six months, and if he weren't back by then . . . He shuddered.

He moved back to his workbench, put the money into an envelope, then hastily scribbled a note.

> *My Dear Mrs. Nelson:*
> *I must leave London for a while. If I have not returned in thirty days, please use what is left of this currency to help yourself secure another position.*
>
> > *My Best,*
> > *HGW*

He folded the note and put it into the envelope, hoping that its implications weren't too ominous. Then he placed the packet outside the laboratory, closed and locked the door. He moved back to the safe, reached farther in and took out some heirloom jewelry that his mother had given him for his firstborn daughter, whenever that happened. He grimaced as he looked at the precious stones. Children? There were too many in the world already. But he was wasting time.

He pocketed the jewelry, moved to the time machine, took a deep breath—desperately hoping that it would not be one of his last—and climbed inside. He locked the door, got into the chair and strapped himself in. There was no need to reset the Time-Sphere Destination Indicator, for Stephenson had already determined it: year, 1979; month, November; day, five. Alas, Wells's maiden voyage was not going to be a pleasure trip.

He synchronized his pocket watch with the clock on the control panel, quickly figuring that 1979 was forty-three minutes away. It was now 7:14 A.M. Stephenson had at least an hour and a half head start.

He engaged the series of switches that activated the engine. A low hum from below told him that energy fields were already interacting and building up to speed. He was only moments away. A small light on the control panel flashed. The machine was ready.

He sighed and wiped perspiration off his face. It still wasn't too late to change his mind. Stephenson had left out of desperation, but he, H. G. Wells, didn't have to go hurtling through time. He could remain in the present and go on tinkering, writing and dreaming. He could lead a decent, productive life without jumping off into the unknown. Hadn't his mother always warned him about being impulsive? He remembered one of the last times she had chastised him. He had refused to study for his third-year examinations at the university because he was in the middle of writing a short story. The piece was published in the *Journal*, but he lost his scholarship and was asked not to return to the Normal School of Science.

He moved to shut down the engine. He was halfway through deactivating the switches when he suddenly stopped himself. What the devil was he thinking of?

Had he put in all those years of study and research and construction for nothing? The story had been "The Chronic Argonauts" and had started him thinking about fourth-dimensional geometry in the first place! Impulsive, yes; but foolhardy, never! Besides, was not his entire *raison d'être* to chart the unknown? To do what no man had ever done before?

He abruptly scowled. He wasn't charting the unknown. A ruthless killer had already been in this chair before him. That cemented his decision. He would bring back Leslie John Stephenson or die trying.

He reactivated the switches.

When the machine was ready again, he released the brake on the Accelerator-Helm lever with a trembling hand, then gently pushed it. Nothing happened. He swore under his breath. He had been so timid he hadn't even moved it. He gritted his teeth and resolutely shoved the lever all the way forward until it locked in the flank position.

He was not prepared for *The Utopia*'s response. It very quickly picked up speed and soon was turning so fast that the blurred walls of the laboratory became translucent. At once he felt like he was falling helplessly, and at the next moment it seemed that a great invisible force was pushing him upward. He imagined that he was in the eye of a giant tornado's funnel, then became dizzy. His head rolled against the back of the chair; his stomach churned, and he felt that he was going to be sick. This definitely was not what he imagined time traveling would be; this was not the way it was supposed to happen! Had he done something wrong? Had he failed to anticipate something? Had he violated some unknown precept of the universe?

The machine continued to accelerate, and his sense of logic left him. His mind became confused, then totally disoriented. The feeling of motion changed to that of a careening, headlong rush; the physical momentum became awesome. He began to scream. He *knew* he was going to crash, explode and die somewhere in the extra-temporal fog that whirled around him. Terrified, he fought to get out of the chair as if that would do him any good. But time traveling had already weakened him so much that he did not have the strength to unbuckle the straps that held him in the seat. It was a good thing, too, for if he had left the chair he would have been thrown into the vortex and disintegrated instantly.

He whimpered and trembled as the machine swayed and jarred along its odyssey-twirl. He felt lost and doomed. Suddenly he dropped his chin down onto his chest, closed his eyes tightly and, for the first time since he was a child of nine, automatically began praying. Tears of agnostic remorse ran down his cheeks. He asked for repentance. He asked for release. Then he abruptly opened his eyes and shook his head to clear it. Now was no time to revert to religion. He *had* to regain control of himself. But it was no use. His eyelids drooped. He imagined that a blackness was coming over his body and enveloping his mind. He grew sleepy. He felt as if he were floating. Melting. There was no substance anymore. Nothing. His last conscious thought was that he was pain-lessly dissolving somewhere along the fourth dimension.

He woke with a start. The grayness had lifted and the hum of *The Utopia* was less pronounced. He rubbed his eyes and saw that the swirl around him was now a myriad of bright but blurred colors. Then he dug into his vest, pulled out his pocket watch and held it out in front of him. He blinked, then gasped and stared. Not only was the watch a myriad of bright and blurred colors, but so were his hand and arm! He looked down. So were his legs and feet! He must be *vaporized*. He quickly felt his body. It seemed no different; it was just that it was difficult to see. The principle of time dilatation at work, he assumed.

He waved his arm in front of his eyes and saw what looked like a dancing swarm of fireflies. He giggled. True, he had obviously disintegrated, yet he felt fine. He was at one with the universe!

But where was he and what time was it? Or was it any time? He strained to read the watch. First he saw a faint black outline around his hand and arm. Then he brought the watch closer to his eyes and stared at it for a long time. The colors jumped around like indiscriminate licks of flame, but eventually he made out the faint outlines of the clock hands and numbers.

He had been traveling for twenty-three minutes. He leaned back, sighed and closed his eyes so that he could think more clearly. If his calculations were correct, he would be arriving in 1979 at 7:57 A.M. So he *hadn't* died along the fourth dimension. He had merely been sleeping while his body metamorphosed into a vaporized state. He was all right!

He laughed. He was going to succeed! He bounced up and down in the chair with joy. Exhilaration and euphoria came over him, and with a religious fervor he shouted out that he, H. G. Wells, had done it. He had conquered the mysteries of the fourth dimension, and if he could do it, so could others. There was nothing left beyond the grasp of mankind. Human intelligence was infinite! Man could progress to eternity! Man was king!

"Do you hear that, God?" he exclaimed triumphantly, then immediately felt foolish. If he were in fact vaporized, nothing at all could hear him.

At 7:54 the swirl of colors began to fade into gray, and H.G. knew that the machine was preparing to drop into 1979. He got dizzy, sick and disoriented again, but it was not as bad as the first time. And when the panic started to come on, he controlled his mind by concentrating on possible problems that he could do nothing about, like a malfunction in the IVR. Or what if he had a chemical reaction to 1979 and exploded? Or imploded?

At 7:56 sharp there was a report like a loud clap of thunder. Everything went black. Wells slumped in the chair, unconscious.

The sound of distant voices and echoing feet woke him. His initial thought was that he had been in a comatose state for an eternity and was now confined in a futuristic hospital where advanced human beings were testing his nineteenth-century mind and body. A quick glance around the inside of the time machine told him that this was not so. He then critically inspected his immediate surroundings and was surprised. The control panel was cracked and faded, the once-shiny ivory switches now a dirty brown. The glass over the dials was intact, but so discolored with age that the numbers and digits were almost impossible to read. The Rotator Control was rusted and stuck in its eastward position. He would have to fix it if he ever hoped to get back home.

He turned in his chair, unlocked and opened the cargo hatch. The water had evaporated, the food was a pile of aging dust and the clothes disintegrated when touched. Something had gone wrong. He turned further and noticed that the chair swiveled with ease. The flight harness that held him in the chair was as good as new, and the Accelerator Helm Lever still glistened with the light coat of oil he had applied the day before he left.

He frowned and cursed himself. He had made an almost fatal mistake in design. He should have mounted the *entire* cabin gyroscopically in order to keep everything inside free from the devastating effects of high-energy rotation. Had he gone much farther into the future, the controls themselves might have disintegrated.

A sudden thought struck him. Why hadn't the machine appeared aged after it had delivered Stephenson into 1979?

"Hmmmmm." His forehead wrinkled up. He didn't quite understand, but he speculated that there must have been some matter-rejuvenation principle at work when moving *back* through time. That meant that he would have to think twice about ever journeying into history. When the technology of the machine did *not* exist, then . . . He frowned. That was a problem for another day. He grinned ruefully. What the devil. *This* trip was over. He had arrived safely. And what would a test flight be without technical problems?

He unbuckled the harness and got out of the chair. He immediately felt dizzy and had to sit down again. He took several deep breaths and, when he felt stronger, slowly stood. He leaned against the side of the cabin and peered out one of the windows for his first look at the future. The glass was opaque and cracked. He couldn't see a damn thing.

Muttering, he turned and unlocked the door with the special key that overrode the RRL. He certainly did not want the machine to automatically return to 1893 and leave him stranded. Then he noticed with surprise that the door handle had been recently cleaned and oiled. And when he pushed the door open the hinges did not groan and creak as he would have suspected. They, too, had been freshly lubricated. Had someone else been caring for his machine?

He stepped out into 1979.

He inspected the steel sides of the time machine. All had held up well except for the brass name plate above the door. The letters spelling THE UTOPIA had eroded into a crusted green patina. He certainly hoped that that wasn't indicative of the particular time plane he'd stepped into.

He slowly turned and found himself standing on a dais spotlighted from directly overhead. The platform was in the center of a huge circular room with high ceilings and an ornate, arched entrance way. What had become of his laboratory? Theoretically, his time machine should not have moved *except* along the fourth dimension. What had happened? Something *had* gone wrong!

He trembled. He was afraid to move, afraid to breathe. The stillness of the place made him wonder if time-traveling hadn't imploded him into his own mind so that he was *reversed* and looking at the inside of himself from farther inside. Was he dead? Was he enveloped by layers of inner imagination? A cocoon of the genius of man? There was only one way to find out. He took a small step forward and winced at the echoing sound of his footfall. Then he turned all the way around and saw that he was standing in the middle of an exhibit. His eyes widened. Behind him other strange-looking inventions were featured, the smaller ones on sculpture bases. Were they engines, communication devices, figments of his imagination or what?

In front of him in three large, glassed-in cases were a host of leather-bound original editions and framed diagrams. The only set he recognized were the ones he had drawn for the time machine. He frowned, then looked to his right. In the far corner of the room in another display case he saw the familiar covers of the *Pall Mall Gazette*, now yellowed with age. He stepped off the dais and moved in that direction, a man in desperate search of the old and the familiar. He ran into a purple velvet rope barrier that bordered the entire area. He turned again and beheld the scene.

A sign on the wall read, "H. G. WELLS—A MAN BEFORE HIS TIME."

Oh my God, he thought, have *I* done all this? Has

my laboratory become a *bloody museum*? Have I joined the relics of science past? Have my triumphs and defeats, both private and public, become antiques to be fingered and soiled by tours of schoolchildren? What do they *think* of me?

He moved closer to the center of the room to get a better view of the exhibit. He was awed and bent. His mind became confused, and then he wanted to cry. The wonder of it all, the sudden realization that he had become a famous man was almost too much for him. He wanted to crumble. What was left for him if he had seen all the fruits of his life's work at age twenty-seven? Why hadn't he thought of that possibility before so blithely hopping into the time machine? And what was worse was that almost all the books and inventions were *ahead* of him in time! He hadn't even conceived of them yet. His head ached. He felt like a slave unto himself. Were there to be no more excitements in his life? No more discoveries? Would he know everything before he did it? Maybe. Maybe not. He didn't have to investigate all these things. Suddenly he burst out with a victorious chuckle. Maybe if he *hadn't* time-traveled, then he wouldn't have gone back home and eventually done all this writing and inventing. And it *was* comforting to know that he had made it back to 1893 London. If there ever was a case of optimism maintaining sanity, this was it.

He moved back into the thick of the exhibit to examine his life's work more closely, despite his earlier reticence. He felt better and had somewhat regained his usual scientific detachment.

Until he saw an old photograph.

His eyes widened and his mouth fell open. He shrank back, put a trembling hand to his head and wanted to look away but was compelled to stare.

There was a man in the picture. A rather stout and

portly man with receding hair, heavy jowls and a multitude of wrinkles. The man wore rimless glasses and was frowning at someone. He did not look at all happy. A caption below the picture read, "H. G. Wells at age fifty."

"No!" He gasped. "No, that's not me! I *won't look* like that! I won't allow myself to!"

His exclamations echoed from the curved ceiling. There was a flatness to the sound that made the environment seem even more alien. Still, he stared at the photograph. Time machine or not, the print confronted him with the image of his own mortality. The ultimate question flashed before him. When did life end for H. G. Wells?

He looked around wildly, certain that the exhibit contained an obituary somewhere. Thank God it wasn't in large letters under his name. He didn't want to know, he didn't want *ever* to know

He sagged and felt sick. He had to get away from this place. He started for the rope barrier, forcing himself not to look at anything else in the exhibit. Instead, over the door to the room, he saw a clock that read 4:04. He stopped, frowned and pulled out his pocket watch. 8:04.

He moaned, now completely disoriented and on the verge of panic. He knew that his calculations weren't that far off, unless something drastic had happened. His laboratory was gone, the house was gone, *everything* was gone, and he appeared to be in a museum. The time wasn't at *all* right, and the displays seemed to be extratemporal mockeries of his mind. He couldn't stand it any longer! He had to know where he *was*, if *anywhere*!

He heard voices and footsteps approaching the room. The presence of those alien sounds forced him to act. He saw that he could not escape undetected, so he hurried back to the time machine, got inside and huddled on the floor.

A tour guide led a group of fifteen into the room. "Another giant figure to emerge from the late nineteenth century was H. G. Wells. Author, scientist, social critic, historian and inventor," droned the guide.

Awe-struck, Wells listened.

"Six months ago, archaeologists working ahead of London's massive urban-renewal project uncovered Wells's obscure laboratory that had been inside a bricked-up basement. And of course you all know what was found inside."

H.G. pushed the door open, then poked his head partway out of the hatch so that he might see and hear what these late-twentieth-century folk looked and sounded like.

"Ladies and gentlemen," the guide continued with a flourish, "the California Academy of Sciences and the Science Museum of San Francisco are proud to have on public display the famous Wellsian time machine!"

San Francisco! How the devil had he ended up in San Francisco when his machine was supposed to travel only along the fourth dimension? He thought furiously and soon it came to him. Of course! If archaeologists had "discovered" his laboratory and the time machine, then undoubtedly his device would have gone on a world tour for everyone to see. Or maybe the city of San Francisco had purchased the device outright, although he couldn't imagine the British Government allowing such a transaction unless the spheres of influence had changed considerably. He remembered that in the early nineties wealthy British royalty had purchased Egyptian relics and had them shipped to England. So why not H. G. Wells to America? Egypt had been weak and powerless. Was England now in a similar position? No, never. The time machine must be on a world tour.

"Of course, the enigmatic man's labor was fruitless, for the device is never known to have worked."

H.G. sat up indignantly. *That* remark was infuriating! How dare the fool say that the time machine never worked!

A small girl in the audience saw Wells and giggled. "Mommy, what's that funny-looking man doing in there?"

The guide turned and saw Wells slam and lock the time-machine door. "Hey, you! You're not supposed to be in there!"

H.G. frantically grabbed the Rotator Control and tried to force it into the westward position so that he could get out of 1979 and back to his own time. He couldn't budge the lever. He had one choice. He could go farther into the future, but he'd be damned if he'd do that, given his machine's present condition.

The tour guide was rapping on the door. "Sir, the exhibit is off-limits!"

With a cry, H.G. unlocked the door and shoved it open. It smashed into the guide and sent him sprawling. Then H.G. vaulted out of the machine, ran through the exhibit and hurdled the rope barrier. The people got out of his way, some laughing with surprise. He raced out of the room and soon was lost in a maze of hallways and corridors. He heard whistles blowing behind him as a host of security guards gave chase.

He had never been so terrified in his entire life.

At the end of one corridor he came to a fire door marked "Emergency Exit" and pushed through it. An automatic fire alarm went off which further added to the confusion of the guards, for now they had to evacuate the building.

H.G. hurried down a short flight of stairs and found himself moving past a series of basement rooms full of old display cases, broken pedestals and antique junk no longer deemed worthy of the hallowed rooms upstairs. He saw lights from the bend in the corridor, but heard no voices. He continued past the junction in the corridor and eventually saw an exit.

He went outside, then up a flight of stairs to a concrete walk. He moved away from the museum and tried to appear casual even though he heard an uproar as the guards were evacuating people out the front doors. The path led him into some trees, and once the museum was out of sight, he was relieved.

He noticed that the weather was similar to the atmospheric conditions which plagued London. The sky was overcast and a light fog was blowing through the trees, although the temperature was slightly higher and the humidity less than London's. But the air smelled funny —it lacked the distinctive flavor of burning coal. He sighed, then shrugged before frowning and reminded himself that he was on a mission of justice and mercy; whatever happened, he could not afford to indulge in the luxury of nostalgia; besides, it wasn't fitting for an inventor of his caliber.

He went down a curve of rustic steps, through a gateway and discovered that he was in a Japanese garden. He felt more relaxed and paused to admire the beauty of the flowers and the exquisite colors of the large carp in the ponds. He gently touched a bonsai tree, smiled and was somewhat reassured. Up Park (the estate where his mother lived and worked) had a garden like this one, only much smaller and not as elaborate. It lacked the arched bridges and the curious little shrines. Nevertheless, he recalled that he used to read there and write an amateur newspaper which was distributed among the domestics under his mother's charge. He managed a small smile and wiped away a wistful, emotional tear. Those were the gentle, idle days when he was recovering from the traumas of abortive apprenticeships. And those days were no more.

Suddenly he squared his shoulders and turned his back on the bonsai tree. What was it that he had just reminded himself about nostalgia? The garden was beautiful—no more and no less. He should accept that as a sign that 1979 was both an old world and a new one; a world that combined the good things of the past with the better things of the future/present which he hadn't seen yet. He did admit to himself, however, that it was nice to know that the world still abounded with flowers and trees and grass and other pastoral forms of life. He resumed walking, following a path which led around the main pond and presumably out of the garden.

A high-pitched distant whine came from behind him. He turned. The noise grew louder and rolled past him like thunder. He grimaced, put his hands over his ears and dropped to his knees. Then he looked up and to his astonishment saw a giant, metallic machine with large, sleek wings, cone-shaped engines, porthole windows and blue and white markings. It was descending through the sky, definitely defying gravity. Good God, what was this? Hadn't Icarus fallen into the Aegean Sea?

H.G. forgot his discomfort, stood and half ran (in a straight line) through the gardens. His eyes followed the huge airship until it dropped out of sight and its sound became a dull roar. He bubbled with laughter; he raised and shook his fist triumphantly. Man had been trying to fly since the days of the Greek empire. After thousands of years, man had succeeded. The immense flying machine was proof of what H.G. had been espousing all along: science and technology definitely meant ease, comfort and progress.

He laughed again. Maybe he, himself, had helped to *invent* the airship. He *must* inspect one closely before he left 1979.

He felt something nibbling at his feet and looked down. He was standing in a foot and a half of water, and carp were eating his trousers. He must have walked into the pond while trying not to lose sight of the aircraft. With an embarrassed mutter, he stepped out of the water and walked out of the garden.

He followed a walkway through expanses of grass and trees and realized he was in a park every bit as beautiful as anything London had to offer eighty-six years ago. Across a lawn children were playing with a dog, middle-aged parents were reading and lovers were sunning themselves on blankets. The sight was peaceful and idyllic. Surely he had stepped into Paradise, despite his initial panic in the museum. Tears came to his eyes once again. He was glad for the human race and longed to be part of this new world which was a definite improvement on the snarl of urban human despair in London, 1893.

He frowned. Nostalgia for the present was just as bad as nostalgia for the past. He could not continue just gawking through dreamy eyes. He had to find Leslie John Stephenson. It was urgent. Imperative. He was not going to be responsible for unleashing that twisted deviant upon the happy people of 1979.

He walked up a small hill, realizing that soon he would have to talk to someone, get his bearings, then gather his wits so he could track down Stephenson. As he neared the summit, he heard a steady clamor that sounded like a series of waterfalls, or was it gusts of wind? Whatever, the noise was alien, and he steeled himself for another marvelous sight.

From the top of the hill, he saw that the park ended and was bordered by a street. No cobblestones. But what was that *noise* coming from? He turned and gasped. A mile away was an immense, wide ribbon of concrete that curved across the horizon. It was obviously a roadway, a modern highway, for speeding along the sections of concrete were antlike machines that darted in and out, creating a ballet of technology.

H.G. grinned. How clever, he thought. Those vehicles must be descendants of the Daimler-Benz internal com-

bustion engine and piloted by average human beings,
too. Remarkable! No horses. And no feces all over the
streets to clean up, either. Good riddance.

Suddenly he saw a bullet-shaped, red, white and blue
train come over a hill and speed alongside the highway.
If he had been closer, he would have seen "Bay Area
Rapid Transit" painted on the side of the engine. The
train stopped at a platform, disgorged passengers, then
whisked away with an electric howl.

He gawked. What a train! What a beautiful, efficient,
masterful piece of machinery! Obviously it was the
grandson of the underground railway, but it did not emit
huge clouds of sulfuric fumes. What a marvel!

So this is San Francisco. Splendid. London must be
incredible.

H.G. left the park in a very good mood. He strolled
along a sidewalk, pausing to touch and admire the design
and craftsmanship of the vehicles parked along the street.
Soon he came to an intersection where a young lady sat
on a bench under a sign that read "Bus Stop." He
stopped a few yards away from her and gazed. Her hair
was long and black and had curls that spilled over her
shoulders. Her face was both handsome and soft, with
high cheekbones vaguely reminiscent of royalty and full
lips that suggested pleasure. She was wearing a loose
peasant blouse and ("My God, how marvelous!")
trousers that matched! Her skin was tan and healthy,
and her shape, outlined by the casual attire, was perfect
enough to make H.G. imagine that he had landed in the
Garden of Eden and was staring at the abstract of a
progressive Eve.

He continued gazing at the young lady, and images of
nineteenth-century sexual encounters quickly passed
through his mind. But they were only fleeting, for he

was in the future now. What would it be like, coupling with a lass ninety years younger than he? Was it still done in the same way? Were females still the extremely reticent half of the human species when it came to the act of physical love? Did they still hide their flesh under mounds of blankets, insist that the curtains be drawn and shut their eyes tightly when their sex was penetrated? Did it still take days or even weeks to get them into a bedroom or to a secluded place?

H.G.'s heart pounded and his hands grew moist. Before he left he wanted a lady like this. There had been so many disappointments in the past. Not just with Isabel, but with the lot of them. No matter how sophisticated a woman had seemed in his experience, they all reverted to either innocence or religion when sandwiched in bed with him. Enlightenment? Whoosh! None of them had ever come close. And, to tell the truth, neither had he.

His thoughts became more specific. How *easy* it would be to shed this young lady of her clothing. There were no balloon skirts and layers of petticoats and God knows how many hand traps *above* the waist to dispose of. Just the blouse and the trousers. Here, in 1979.

He swallowed hard and nodded slightly. He was determined. Aside from catching Stephenson, he must definitely try some "futurological" sex. He smiled with pleasure, not realizing that he had appeared foolish for quite a while. The young lady finally felt his gaze, turned and glanced at him, then quickly looked away.

Whistling, he jauntily came up alongside her. "Excuse me, madam." He bowed slightly. "Can you tell me where I am?"

She rolled her eyes, frowned, got up and briskly walked away.

H.G. was momentarily puzzled. He already knew that these people spoke English, so that couldn't be the problem—unless it was his dialect or choice of words. Then H.G. inspected himself and understood. His clothes were out of date. Not only that, his shoes and trousers were wet and muddy, and he could only imagine what the rest of him looked like. He must cash in the jewelry for some modern American currency, buy some clothes and make himself appear respectable.

The other side of the street seemed populated, so he figured that he might as well begin there. He started to cross the intersection, not really understanding or caring about the red light atop the green metal lamppost. When he was in the middle of the street, several vehicles came around a curve, speeding toward the intersection at forty-five miles per hour. He was looking the other way when he heard a horn blast. He spun around, gasped with horror and froze. The gleaming metallic machine was hurtling toward him. Surely he would be hit and crushed! Then he heard a horrible screech and saw black smoke billow up from the wheels of the craft. At the last moment it swerved, missed him and stopped. The young man who was operating the machine leaned out of a window, glared at H.G. and yelled:

"You *stupid* son of a bitch!"

And then the other vehicles were upon him, their operators playing a surprised and grotesque zigzag, trying to avoid him and each other. The cacophony of horns was deafening.

H.G. finally reacted. He sprinted for the sidewalk, but just then a man riding what appeared to be a very large motorized bicycle rounded the corner at high speed. H.G. dove to get out of the way, hit the pavement and just barely jerked his legs out of the machine's path in time. The edge of the rear fender caught his trailing coat and left a large rent in the distinguished tweed. A belch of fumes from the twin exhausts briefly enveloped his head and left him coughing, teary-eyed and gasping for breath.

Extremely shaken, H.G. scrambled up and fled back into the park. He hurried through a stand of trees, then crossed long, sloping lawns at a calmer pace, moving back in the direction from which he had come. He followed a little-used path down into a glen thick with trees and foliage. He sat on a rock, rested and tried to quell the anxieties resulting from his first brush with an alien technology. He told himself that the incident was probably his own damned fault since he was unfamiliar with the laws governing the mass use of machines. Then he grew annoyed, for he remembered the words of his brilliant and fascinating biology instructor, T. E. Huxley. The man had said, *You must respect the great potential power of science and treat it wisely. Above all, never place science above the realm of humanity, for there is nothing as sacred as the individual rights of man.*

H.G. sobered. When weighed against those words, his moment in the street became even more alarming. Why hadn't the drivers of those machines stopped for him? Were they careless, impatient, not properly trained? Whatever the reason, he knew that when he left the park again he would be very careful until he felt at ease with the incredible technology around him.

He got up to inspect the glen and noticed that the sun had set. Undoubtedly all the places of business were closed, so he wouldn't make any progress this night selling his jewelry.

He wondered how Stephenson was doing. Badly, he hoped, and he didn't think that was wishful thinking given his experience with those bloody machines. So Stephenson couldn't be far. If he were alive. Then H.G. shuddered. He suddenly had a feeling that Stephenson *was* all right. Anyone who could elude Scotland Yard for five years and carry on as a respectable surgeon would survive in *any* time sphere. H.G. wasn't so certain about himself.

Although hungry, thirsty, in sore need of a bath and clean clothes, he decided to spend the night in the park.

He was in no shape to test the mettle or hospitality of the San Franciscans. Since insects abounded in the glen—especially mosquitoes—he left the area and climbed the hill where he had been before. At the top, he curled up between a tree and a bush and used his shredded coat as a pillow He listened to the strange sounds of the city as night came over the park. God, what he wouldn't give for that pot of tea Mrs. Nelson had made for him just a few hours ago, not to mention a bottle of passable French claret. Not even in his unhappy, poverty-mired childhood had he ever felt so isolated and alone. Cursing, he twisted and rolled on the damp, uneven ground, unable to get comfortable.

And then another feeling settled over him like a dull ache. It was more than a sense of helplessness in an alien world. It was the fear of permanently losing his own age. He couldn't shake it.

He slept fitfully, to say the least.

FOUR

He woke with a start just after eight o'clock in the morning when the steady roar of the rush hour was at its noisiest. He rose and could not immediately see anything clearly. He rubbed the film of sleep from his eyes, then felt a burning sensation in them and assumed that it was due to a poor night's rest. Finally, the day came into focus. From his vantage he stared down at the modern highway, blinking his red eyes and feeling his beard stubble.

He frowned. The eight lanes of machines moved slowly and frequently jammed up, unlike the evening before. It was a clear case of too little road for too many machines. He glanced up and saw machines in the sky circling the highway like annoying soloists in a mechanical symphony. They weren't as big as the airship he had seen the day before, but hovered much like hummingbirds. His analytic mind quickly figured out that the sky machines were monitoring the snarl of road machines below. He grinned, for he already had a much simpler solution. Put layers of highway, one atop the other. What could be more logical? Or natural?

He stood, stretched his stiff muscles, then coughed and spit up blood. That confirmed it. One more night out

on the ground and he was sure to have a recurrence of
the tuberculosis. He resolutely left his lair, stomach
growling, hand tightly clutching the jewels in his coat
pocket. He walked down the hill, out of the glen, then
across the lawns, now covered with dew. He found a
fountain and drank long and deep, then splashed water
on his face and felt refreshed. His spirits rose a little,
and he left the park.

This time when he came to an intersection he wisely
waited for other pedestrians to materialize, then did
exactly as they did when it came to crossing in front of
the idling machines. He eyed the vehicles with a touch of
suspicion while reminding himself to keep his reactions
subdued so that no one would take undue notice of him.

One strange spectacle compelled him to stop and
stare. Workers wearing metal hats and thick orange
vests were in the bucket of a yellow crane fifteen feet
in the air attaching something to a streetlight. The
object was long and flimsy, red and green and dotted
with large silver stars. Wells turned and saw that *every*
streetlight up ahead of him was adorned with the same,
curious, elongated ornament.

Another truck was loaded with the things, and more
workers were wiring branches of holly to the bases of
the streetlights. Not real holly, for there was no pungent
odor. Imitation trees on streetlights? Metallic streamers
overhead? What had the world come to? Or was there
to be a celebration of some kind?

When he saw an upside-down, cardboard St. Nicholas
in the back of the truck, it came to him. Christmas
decorations! He'd always heard that Americans were
much more garish than their English counterparts, but
decorations in the street? All this to celebrate the birthday of an ex-fisherman who had a way with words and
philosophies? Obviously, humanity had not progressed
beyond the twelve days of Christmas. He wondered how

religion could still have a foothold in a society advanced enough to produce giant airships. Maybe it didn't. He looked at the bright decorations again. They weren't religious in nature. Perhaps all they did was announce that the season for gifts and good fellowship was at hand. But Christmas was seven weeks away, he thought. Then he smiled and approved. If the holiday atmosphere had been extended from twelve days to seven weeks, that was good. People would be more courteous than usual for a much longer period of time.

He turned and ran into a cluster of shoppers, knocking brightly wrapped packages out of a lady's arms.

"Oh, I'm dreadfully sorry!" He moved to assist the startled lady, but she shrank away from him and expressed fear. Puzzled, he stepped back, then bent to retrieve her packages.

"Get away from those!" She pushed him away, scooped up her packages and hurried off.

H.G. straightened up and stared after her. He didn't understand why the lady had been so irate. Especially since she obviously had just purchased an armload of gifts. He recalled that buying presents for others always made him feel joyful—like when he'd given Mrs. Nelson a mother-of-pearl set of combs on her birthday and she had rushed upstairs so he wouldn't see her crying with happiness. Perhaps this lady had felt *compelled* to make her purchases. If so, she would naturally feel resentful. That would explain her outburst.

"Whoosh." If that kind of behavior were common, then much of the ostentatious display of holiday good cheer in 1979 could be a ritual. H.G. frowned. He certainly hoped it wasn't.

He managed to walk the rest of the way to the heart of the city without incident, although he found his breathing more labored than usual and gradually developed a splitting headache. He attributed both ailments to a lack of food and his consumptive history. He was only puzzled by the hazy, yellow-brown color of the sky.

A half block east of Union Square, H.G. saw a sign advertising a jewelry store on the mezzanine floor of a ten-story building.

He pushed through the glass doors of the building and observed people going up what appeared to be a modern-day flight of stairs. Only these people weren't using their arms or legs! While they remained stationary, the stairs moved.

He studied the device and nodded. Obviously the moving stairs existed to augment lifts, and if machines could move people upward, why should men waste their own energy doing it when that energy could be channeled into creative phenomena? Once again H.G. approved, then felt sad that he hadn't been born into the late twentieth century and its marvelous potpourri of electronic wizardry. He remembered that he had been so thrilled when the lighting man who installed the incandescents in his laboratory had explained the rudiments of filaments, circuitry and basic electricity even though he had already discovered most of those theories for himself while designing the time machine (with a little help from the scientific abstracts published by the remarkable American Thomas Edison). Those theories, however, were no doubt primitive now.

He moved to the base of the escalator and paused. He worried about getting caught in the moving stairs, then shook off the feeling as a mere Victorian apprehension. He stepped on board and smiled. He was free to move. He raised his foot, took a tentative step and bounced upward. With three more quick steps, he felt that for an instant he'd left gravity behind, then stumbled onto the mezzanine. Aha! That was the reason for the device. A man could go up and down twice as fast as normal!

He found the jewelry store, entered and politely asked a salesman if he might discuss a matter of extreme importance with the proprietor. Eventually, a tiny man with white hair and ornate, miniature hands with jewelry approached Wells and introduced himself as Max Ince, the manager. H.G. announced the nature of his business and was led to a counter at the back of the store. Ince took the Wellsian heirlooms and began examining them under his jeweler's light, gently feeling them, carefully inspecting them from every possible angle.

H.G. watched Ince for a while, but the man proceeded so methodically that he couldn't stand his own anticipation. (Were the stones worthless or valuable?) So he looked about the store for something to divert his attention. Not far away on the counter was a display featuring timepieces. He removed one of the modern chronometers from the display. The tag read "Digital Watch." He began playing with the buttons and became totally absorbed. Occasionally, he chuckled with enjoyment.

Finally, Ince sighed and looked up over the top of his glasses. "Absolutely gorgeous, young man. I haven't seen stones or settings like these since before the war."

"*War?*" said H.G., taken aback. "What war?"

"You know," replied Ince with a pinched smile. "The war."

"Oh." H.G. realized that he would have to restrain from pursuing obvious historical matters which he knew nothing about. Perhaps, in time, he would get to a library.

Ince frowned. "If you don't mind me asking, where did you get these?"

"They were a gift from my mother. She has a post at Up Park. An associate of Mrs. Fetherstonhaugh who bequeathed her these heirlooms in the first place."

"London?"

"*Greater* London." H.G. sniffed, but not pretentiously. His nose had started to run. "How much are they worth?"

"Roughly?"

H.G. nodded.

"Around fifteen thousand dollars." Ince subtly gestured at the dirt on Wells's clothes. "But for a non-bonded sale, you would get much less."

"Whatever is fair," said H.G., relieved. "Include this remarkable timepiece and I'm ready to do business."

Ince beamed. From a counter drawer he took out a sales contract and a host of other forms which he placed before H.G. "If you'd be so kind as to fill these out, sir. And I'll need your passport, visa, driver's license and a credit card. Oh, yes, your current address and phone number, too. It'll take about a week to process your check."

"A week? Could you give me something on account?"

"With proper identification and verification, we might work something out."

"What do you mean, verification?" He ripped up the forms. "I'm not running for Parliament, I'm selling you some of *my* bloody jewelry!"

Ince raised his thinning eyebrows. "Do you have a customs declaration, sir?" he asked sweetly.

"Wait a minute! You don't think I *stole* these, do you? Good God, man, I'm—I'm an Englishman," he said weakly.

Ince turned his back on H.G. and walked into his office with the jewels. H.G. leaned over the counter and saw the little man work the keyboard of a small electric machine that looked remarkably similar to a "collective mind" invention he had made rough sketches of about six months ago. (*His* device—when he built it—would store the thoughts of great men in copper armatures and then combine the ideas by electronic impulses, the notion being that a synthesis of wisdom would enable mankind to progress at breakneck speed.) He speculated, with sudden indignation, that the machine Ince was using served a far more mundane function, that being to test the veracity of his claim.

"I say, Mr. Ince!" H.G. ejaculated. "Just what is it that you are *doing* with my heirlooms?"

"Checking them against the computers." He returned to the counter, slowly shaking his head. "And I am sorry to say that I can't find a record of them."

H.G. grabbed the little man's arm in desperation. "What could you give me for them right now? In cash?"

"Two thousand," Ince replied confidentially.

"Sold."

Ince moved back to the safe in his office at a hurried shuffle.

H.G. glared after him. "Bloody brigand!"

He left the jewelry store with an envelope containing the money in small denominations and a digital watch that he now proudly wore on his left wrist. As he went down the escalator and out of the building he pressed the buttons in various sequences, getting the time, date, year, barometric pressure and number of days left in 1979.

He rounded a corner and smelled food. His nose locked on the delicious odors, and he quickened his pace. Moments later he stood in front of a new restaurant. It was a low structure with a dark-brown roof, light-brown stucco sides and large, tinted-glass panels all the way around. The building was surrounded by pavement with white lines that sectioned off uniform rectangles where people could leave their vehicles when inside the establishment. H.G.'s reaction to the macadam lot was to cross it cautiously because the patrons of the restaurant seemed to arrive and leave in extremely short periods of time. The service must be incredible, he thought. Either that or the food eaten in 1979 must not take very long to prepare or consume. He looked up at the sign which towered over the place. It read, "McDONALD's—Billions and Billions Served."

He entered the establishment and was surprised to see that it vaguely resembled the interior of a London restaurant in 1893, only everything was new and shiny. The wallpaper was a montage of printed old photographs and lithographed street scenes. Of course! He snapped his fingers. The motif was San Francisco's Barbary Coast of the nineteenth century, and the proprietor had obviously chosen to imitate it. H.G. then wondered what purpose the decor served, for there was no mood or atmosphere to the place. People were coming and going too quickly to remember what they'd eaten, in his opinion.

He touched a brown tabletop, then a bright-orange swivel chair and marveled at their composition. It wasn't wood or metal, yet it looked like both. What *was* the curious substance? He restrained himself from investigating further, for he looked up and saw several people staring at him.

He moved to the other end of the room and stood in a line, which seemed to be proper behavior if one wanted to eat. Then he looked up and stared at a translucent menu (curiously lit from behind—the reason escaping him) because that was what everyone else in the line was doing. He read the list of items sold, and the only three words that made any sense to him were "coffee," "tea" and "milk." He had no idea of what to purchase, so he listened to how the customers in front of him ordered their meals. After hearing five such exchanges, he slowly nodded, then frowned. Yes, the language was definitely English, but the idiom baffled him. What the devil were "quarter-pounders without"?

When he got to the head of the line, he had memorized a previous order and even correctly carried out the ritual of collecting three napkins and a straw, which he stuffed into his bedraggled coat pocket.

"Yes, sir, may I help you?" said the smiling counter girl dressed in a green- and white-striped outfit.

Her clothes looked too bright and shiny to be wool or even cotton. He assumed that they were a different kind of fiber, perhaps derivative from the same glossy matter that covered the tables and chairs. Once again, he had to restrain himself. He wanted to reach out and feel the material.

"I'd like a Big Mac and fries," he said hesitantly.

"Anything to drink?"

"Tea, please."

"Here or to go?"

"Here."

He paid her with a twenty-dollar bill, humbly accepted his change and food, then escaped to a booth in the far corner of a room called "The Pirates' Den." He picked up a fry and nodded with familiarity. It was obviously a chip, and "fry" was the American derivation. But when he took a bite, he found that the fry was limp, lukewarm and tasted like undercooked dough. It was obviously not a chip, and he assumed that he had just eaten a wedge of protein, possibly manufactured from grass seed. He sipped his tea, weak by British standards, but warm and stimulating nonetheless. He regarded the tea bag as a clever little convenience—no more picking oolong leaves out of one's teeth at embarrassing moments.

On the seat beside him was the morning edition of the San Francisco *Chronicle*. He picked it up, jammed his mouth full of fries, then scanned a Herb Caen column which touted that the restaurants of San Francisco were superior to those of Modesto. He shook his head, dropped the paper and muttered with horror, "My God, what have they *done* to the English language?"

He took his Big Mac out of its box, after concluding that the styrofoam was a rubberized paper manufactured to withstand weather extremes. Perhaps modern writers used sheets of it to ensure posterity. Then he unwrapped and studied the sandwich. The aroma overwhelmed him, but this was no time to be critical. He was famished. He chomped, chewed, frowned, then raised his eyebrows.

"Ummmmm."

He took another bite with gusto. The Big Mac was exquisite. Perhaps the most delicious food he had ever eaten.

He devoured the rest of the hamburger and was about to go back and purchase another when he felt someone staring at him. He turned and saw a small boy trying to make sense out of his old-fashioned clothes and drooping walrus mustache.

"You in a commercial, or what?"

By the time H.G. found a respectable clothing store he was used to the traffic that clogged the streets and surprised that he seemed to be moving about faster than the machines. Although his ears had not yet adjusted to the downtown level of decibels, he felt light-years away from his bizarre night in the park. And there was still a smattering of old buildings in the city, reminiscent of nineteenth-century London. Their graystone façades reassured him, whereas the reflective exteriors of the newer buildings made him apprehensive. Still, he now had 1979 food lining his stomach, and once contemporary fashion draped his form, he wouldn't have anything to worry about—except Leslie John Stephenson.

He entered the clothiers and was patient with the salesman, who couldn't get over his heavy, four-button (ripped and dirty) tweeds; high, matching vest; white shirt and yellow silk tie.

"Is this what they're wearing in London now?"

"It's been a while since I left." H.G. was rapidly becoming a master of ambiguity.

The salesman suggested high-waisted, prefaded jeans, a tailored shirt with ruffles, topped off with a snap-brim hat for starters. But once H.G. learned that some men did indeed still wear suits and ties, there was no dissuading him. He selected a ready-made light-brown two-button suit with a vest, a beige dress shirt, a maroon tie and dark-brown Oxfords. The salesman was impressed with his impeccable taste.

H.G. found the dressing room too small to afford him the luxury of disrobing comfortably, and as he shed his old suit he wondered if the room had been made deliberately constricting so that potential customers would make up their minds more quickly. Whatever the case, the shortened door made him nervous, for he felt that his legs and shoulders were naked to the world. He began to perspire heavily and hated dressing under that condition.

He put on the shirt, struggled into the pants, felt for the buttons and was momentarily bewildered until he found the zipper that closed the fly in half a second. He raised his eyebrows, tucked in the shirt and moved about a little. Great Scott, what *comfort*, he thought. The trousers were not nearly as bulky as his old ones. Also, they were lined and cut to fit his shape! And the shirt— it didn't balloon out with yards of unnecessary cloth that needed blousing; it just sort of naturally draped around him as if he'd worn it for years. And the *feel* of the material was almost electric!

He slipped into the vest, quickly knotted the tie, threw on the coat and hurried out of the dressing room. He felt liberated—as if the clothes he had worn before had been designed for an elephant. The ones he had on now made him feel good and smart and sophisticated. He did a little twirl in front of the mirror and beamed. Then he twisted his mustache into shape, stepped back and admired himself—still a distinguished English gentle-man, but more important, a late-twentieth-century human being. Who said that clothes did not make the man?

He strode to the cash register where the salesman waited, hovering over the bill.

"You look very nice, sir, very nice."

"Thank you."

"It comes to $476.18."

H.G. slowly counted out the money, not yet familiar with American currency, but astute enough to realize that he was paying a damnable amount for a haberdashery. He didn't have time to complain, but it was worth a comment. "Doesn't go very far, does it?"

"Not anymore, sir."

"It isn't the pound, of course," he added provincially.

"That's for sure." The salesman laughed. "I hear they're going to devalue it again."

"The *pound*?" H.G. was aghast.

"That's right. You got any left, I'd exchange them for good, old, almighty Yankee dollars."

"Why thank you. Thank you very much."

He hurried out of the store, not bothering to take his old clothes. The salesman had given him an idea. If Leslie John Stephenson were to survive in San Francisco, then he—just like H. G. Wells—would have to have some American money. So if he had any English pounds with him, one of his first acts in 1979 would be to exchange them. Since H.G. had nothing to lose, he figured that he might as well begin hunting at the banks.

He stopped. Not just *any* bank, he thought. Stephenson may be a sexually perverted killer, but he still is an Englishman. He would choose a bank that made him feel at home. In San Francisco? He smiled. If Lloyd's had offices all over the world a century ago, surely other British enterprises must have followed suit.

He got directions to the Bank of England from a

policeman and was pleased to learn that it was located only a block off Union Square. He was awfully tired of walking.

He crossed the square with a jaunty, unabashed stride, despite his sore leg muscles. Thanks to his new clothes, he felt more at home in the late twentieth century. Above the traffic noise he heard a bell clanging that sounded distinctly alien to the honks and roars and digital click-clacks of 1979. He turned, looked and beamed. A cable car loaded with tourists rolled across an intersection and started uphill. H.G. was reassured. Despite the mighty power of the electron, a nineteenth-century relic was still functioning. He had seen schematics of the cable cars in *The Times* not too long ago. So, San Francisco has a sense of history and a little heart, he thought. Good for them and bully for me.

He allowed himself a nostalgic wave at the Union Jack hanging over the Bank of England and pushed through the revolving glass doors. Once inside, he imagined that the air smelled better. The atmosphere definitely seemed more stately.

Across the large room from the row of tellers were a half-dozen desks that he correctly assumed belonged to officers of the bank. He frowned. Something was missing. He briefly closed his eyes and drew a mental picture of the Lloyd's in Mornington Crescent where he usually conducted his financial transactions. Of course! Here, there was no exchange board on the wall behind the tellers to keep customers aware of the daily fluctuations in currency, especially on the European market. Then he raised his eyebrows. Perhaps there was no longer any *need* for an exchange board. Perhaps that information could be discovered by employing one of those small machines that the jeweler, Max Ince, had called a computer.

He sighed. Progress was one thing, but how the devil could the Bank of England deem itself British without the physical presence of the traditional exchange board? Regardless, he was going to have to consult an officer of the bank. He went to the first desk, unconsciously humming along with music that emanated from the walls. ("Follow the Yellow Brick Road"? he asked himself. Was that what the words were saying?)

The desk was unoccupied, so he waited about ten feet away near a pillar and a tall, flourishing potted palm. He was drawn to the plant, for he had never seen such a large specimen before. He didn't know that it was possible for a parlor palm to grow much taller than three feet, and here was one that crowned above his head.

When he got close enough, he saw that the plant only *appeared* to be a parlor palm. This one was a much more curious and exotic species of fauna. He gently touched a leaf, and the feel reminded him of the table-top at McDonald's. He assumed that the remarkable substance was vegetable in origin. An American sub-species of the Burmese rubber tree, no doubt, although he did not recall any such genus from his brief botany studies. It must be a modern hybrid, he postulated.

He was about to try the next unoccupied desk when a young woman who he guessed was twenty-two or -three sashayed out of a door and over to the desk. She was a little shorter than H.G. and had dark blond, shoulder-length hair with a few subdued curls. Her facial features were delicate with just enough tan to make her resemble a "Gibson girl." Her eyes were large, very brown and could be businesslike, innocent or mysterious, depending on the occasion.

H.G. gawked, but not at the eyes. She was wearing a dark-blue pants suit. True, he had seen women on the street in such interesting attire, but in the Bank of

England? In pants tight enough around the hips and thighs to suggest the *actual shape* of the *mons veneris*? His *mons pubis* began to twitch, and he blushed. He tried to keep his eyes above her waist, but that didn't help, either. Every time she moved, her well-shaped breasts moved, too, obviously freed from the constrictions of a corselet. He recalled the massive physical and psychological barriers presented by the Merry Widow. It had taken him four years to learn how to unhook the monstrous device without pinching his partners.

She felt his stare and looked up. "May I help you?" she asked in a low, melodious voice that made him shiver.

"I'm—I'm waiting for an officer of the bank, thank you," he replied in reedy tones.

She smiled and gestured at a chair alongside the desk. "I'm a bank officer. Why don't you sit down?"

"But you're—"

"I know, I know. You expected someone with an English accent, not to mention the decor *à la* California. I apologize for the plastic palms." She made a sweeping gesture that suggested inner poise and grace. "This your first trip to the States?"

To put it mildly. H.G. managed a nod and sat down. He had mentally prepared himself for technological advances before he left, but a *woman* working for the Bank of England in a management capacity? Suffrage was one thing, but who the devil was taking care of the children and preparing supper? What had become of the time-honored afternoon tryst? He thought for a moment, then logically figured that if a man could slip away from the office for a few hours, a woman could too. And his hat was off to the chap lucky enough to be caught *in flagrante delicto* with this specimen here.

He grinned foolishly and continued staring at her. Now young ladies occupied the hallowed halls of commerce, did they? He rather liked the idea, but if they all looked like she did, how could one get anything accomplished?

"Just what did you want, sir?"

He looked away, for he had just gotten a whiff of her perfume and it had done him in. He adjusted his coat and crossed his legs, trying to hide his erection. His complexion turned crimson.

Finally, he forced himself to think. He realized that if this bank were anything like commercial establishments in 1893 London, a person could not just walk in and ask for personal information, no matter how distinguished. Such information could be expected only as a casual by-product of a normal business transaction. H.G. didn't know if the same state of affairs was generic to 1979 San Francisco, but if anything, he should proceed with caution. He decided to start with the Wellsian charm. He extended his hand. "I'm Herbert George Wells." His grin was all teeth.

"Amy Robbins." Instead of shaking his hand, she placed a business card between his fingers.

Undaunted, H.G. slipped the card into his coat pocket. "Could you tell me a little about the services your bank offers potential customers?"

Twenty minutes later H.G. had applied for both Visa and Master Charge cards. Also, Amy had convinced him that if he were carrying a sizable amount of cash, he should purchase some traveler's checks. Soon after that he had almost finished signing approximately fifteen hundred dollars worth. By then she had warmed to him considerably, despite his frequent stares that became more pronounced when she took phone calls.

He pushed the stack of checks to the center of the desk for her inspection, then leaned back and massaged his aching signature hand. She buzzed through the checks, looked up and smiled.

"Okay. Now all I have to do is see some identification."

"I'm afraid that I don't have any."

She frowned.

"You see, this morning I lost my traveling companion at the museum. We were separated in the midst of, ah . . . a fire drill. He has my valise and all my papers are in it."

"That's a problem," she commented. "Very definitely a problem." Then she looked down at her desk and gave the matter some serious consideration. She had been with the bank for almost two years now and was generally regarded as the most trustworthy middle-management employee. Despite her casual nature, she performed every function by the book, much to the delight of the English-born-and-bred-and-educated vice presidents. She did so because this job was her first, and she wanted to prove to everyone that she was a capable, competent human being, in spite of dropping out of college to get married and then failing in that, too.

Against all expectations, she had come to San Francisco on her own and so far had forged her own way. And she loved her freedom and sense of independence. One might say that she coveted those conditions, for they gave her life purpose and meaning. The basis for it all was the job; she did not want to make any mistakes. And the book said, "*Always* ask for identification."

But here was a man the likes of whom she had never encountered before. Genteel. Warm. Pleasant, yet unusual. Archaic. Normally, she trusted no one, but when this man looked at her, she felt all her professional common sense go awry. For some inexplicable reason, she knew she had to have faith in him. It seemed very important.

"Well, I certainly hope you find your friend." She

smiled. "It's been a pleasure serving you, Mr. Wells." She extended her hand.

"Herbert." He sighed with relief, then took her hand and held it for much longer than a handshake. "Perhaps you would care to show me around the city. When we both have the time, of course."

"Sure. My number's on the card I gave you. Give me a call."

"A call?"

She patted the arm of Ma Bell. "*Telephone* me."

"Oh, yes, of course." He stood and hesitated. He had already subtly alluded to Stephenson, and she hadn't picked up on it. He had a horrible feeling he was going to walk away empty-handed.

"Was there something else I could help you with, Herbert?"

"As a matter of fact, yes." He brightened and sat down again. "I'm supposed to have dinner with my traveling companion. I think I mentioned that I was separated from him earlier?"

"Yes. He has your valise."

"Well, I have no idea where he is, and I thought there might be a slight chance that he was in here earlier in the day to exchange some British currency."

"What's his name?"

"Leslie John Stephenson. Step-hen-son. He's a surgeon. A rather tall and dark chap."

"Oh, yes, Dr. Stephenson was here. I guess it's pretty obvious you both just arrived." She blushed. "Anyway, if it's any help, I recommended that the Jack Tar Hotel on Geary Street is a decent place to stay. You might find him there."

H.G. smiled with immense satisfaction. "Is it very far from here?"

"Nothing's far from anywhere in San Francisco."

"You've been so very kind and helpful, Miss Robbins. Thank you ever so much." He took her hand again, only this time he kissed it. She bubbled with laughter. He stood, but he knew he couldn't just dash off. That would be rude. Besides, this girl was extremely vivacious and sensual. After the business with Stephenson was properly resolved, who knew what might happen? "Perhaps we should have lunch together in a day or so."

"I'd love to."

He leaned over to her—one hand on the desk frightfully close to her right breast—and smiled. "I found the most marvelous restaurant not far from here. Scottish, I believe."

"What's the name of the place?"

"McDonald's."

And then he was gone. She stared after him, mouth open. Neither of them immediately noticed that he had forgotten his traveler's checks.

FIVE

H.G. pushed through the bank's glass doors and once again found himself out on the street. The aura of Amy's presence still surrounded him, the result being that he glowed like the cherubic altar boy he wasn't. He strolled along, beaming foolishly and thinking about how wonderful it was to be alive. Then he walked into a parking meter, and the sudden pain in his chest brought him to his senses. He gritted his teeth, narrowed his eyes and frowned. He would have to force himself to be cold. After all, he wasn't on a bloody holiday, he was in pursuit of a depraved killer. Women and wanderlust would have to wait.

He quickened his pace, moving toward the intersection of Post Street and Grant Avenue. He dodged and vaulted ahead of the other pedestrians, his jaws resolutely clamped shut. Stephenson would soon be within his grasp, and not long after that, justice would be served.

When he reached the corner, the signal light abruptly changed, and the machines accelerated past him across the intersection as one roaring metal phalanx. Their fumes briefly enveloped him, and he recalled the unpleasantness of London's underground. Suddenly, he felt befuddled. Even if he did know precisely where the Jack Tar Hotel was, he had no idea how he was going to get there. He retreated to the side of a building, calmed himself and decided that observation was the best policy. He didn't have long to wait.

A well-dressed, gray-haired lady carrying a stack of Christmas packages leaned out into the street, raised one arm and extended a finger as if she were pointing at something strange in the sky. H.G. looked up and saw nothing but gray overcast. He frowned. Could the lady be testing the wind? Or did she have a cramp in the aforementioned arm?

A drab vehicle painted yellow with prices emblazoned on its doors stopped by the lady. An obese man rolled out of the driver's seat, approached her and opened the rear door. H.G. noticed that his cocked hat bore the insignia "Yellow Cab" above the bill.

The lady got inside and said something to the driver. He nodded, got back in the driver's seat and took off.

H.G. blushed, momentarily embarrassed by the lapse of his strong analytic processes. What could have been more logical? The squat, ugly yellow machine was obviously the descendant of the staunch and traditionally uncomfortable English hansom.

Then he pursed his lips and frowned again. So far in 1979 his view of the internal-combustion-engine-driven vehicles had alternated between admiration and suspicion. But whatever his current feelings were, they didn't matter, for he knew that he, himself, was going to have to make use of one of the modern cabs if he ever hoped to catch up with Leslie John Stephenson. He took a step toward the curb, then hesitated. He cursed himself. Now was no time for second thought. After all, if he had the courage to strap himself into a time machine, why the sudden apprehension about getting into another kind of machine? It was absurd! He should listen to his scientific nature.

He did; and it told him that he had built the time machine with his own precise hands, whereas the vehicles rushing and braking and honking and belching before him were definitely alien. He sighed. The machines could be the work of the devil for all it mattered. He was in a hurry.

He stepped to the curb. Half hidden by a lamppost and a sign, he timidly raised his arm and pointed one finger skyward.

The light turned yellow, and Wells saw a cab a half block away hurtling toward the intersection with no apparent intention of stopping. Then, at the last moment, the vehicle swerved across Grant Avenue's three one-way lanes—horn blasting—and smoked to a stop inches from H.G.'s left foot. He gasped and jumped back against the lamppost, arm still raised, finger still pointing. He glared indignantly at the driver, then unconsciously brushed off his coat with his right hand. What cheek!

The driver leaned his upper body out of the window, folded his arms over the door and placed the square chin of his bullet-shaped head between his wrists. He flashed H.G. a dazzling, derisive smile.

"You want a cab?" He pointed at Wells's upstretched arm. "Or are you bidding on a street sign?"

H.G. opened the rear door and gingerly got into the cab. He was immediately disappointed by the cheap interior, the collapsed seat springs and the odor of carbon monoxide that emanated from a perpetually malfunctioning heater. The inside of the machine was utterly *primitive*, with no handmade British touches to offset its unattractive nature. He wondered if he had selected the right mode of transportation.

"Where to?"

"The Jack Tar Hotel."

H.G. saw the driver press a pedal with his foot. The cab thunked, groaned and jerked up to the intersection.

The brief acceleration lurched H.G. forward, then tossed him back against the seat. He smiled and suppressed a giggle. The cab was obviously in disrepair. He had always assumed that the technology of the future would be clean and in perfect operating condition. Now he realized that his assumption was devoid of logic. If a hansom can rust, rot and decay, why not a Yellow Cab? He conjured up an image of all the new and marvelous things he had seen, and they were heaped into a gigantic mountain of waste. Bent, broken and twisted, the mechanical creations of man cooked under a hot sun that would eventually dissolve them. Nearby, a man of the future, wearing a dirty loincloth and holding an ancient section of pipe as a club, scratched himself and wondered what god the huge pile of junk was a monument to.

H.G. could no longer contain himself. He burst out laughing.

The driver swiveled his head around like a bald eagle. "What's so funny?"

"Nothing." He breathed deeply to stop himself from laughing. Then he became curious. "My good man, how often do you take your vehicle into the shop?"

"The garage? It was there last week."

The light changed. The driver pressed down hard, and the cab leaped forward, taking H.G.'s breath away.

"See? Really gets out and moves, don't it? You want a better pickup than this, you got to get into a race car. Like the '72 Plymouth I used to run at the track back in Decatur."

H.G. grew accustomed to the motion and speed of the vehicle very quickly, even the abrupt stops and starts that the driver made at traffic signals. Unlike his reaction to the movement of the time machine, he did not become sick and disoriented. He guessed that was true because the Yellow Cab was motoring linearly, whereas his time machine moved centrifugally and at a much higher speed. He found this ground travel pleasant, even exhilarating, and wondered if there were some law of physics which he could adapt in order to make travel along the fourth dimension more agreeable to the human physiology. Nothing immediately came to his mind, so he decided that that was a problem for future afternoons in the laboratory. Right now, the cab was idling at another red light, and suddenly he longed for more speed and maneuvers.

"How fast will this vehicle go?"

"Around ninety. Ninety-five."

"Oh, *really*?" H.G.'s eyes widened.

The driver assumed that Wells was challenging *his* cab, hence questioning *his* virility. "Yeah. Really." He grabbed a small metal device with an attached cord from the center of the dashboard, pressed it into his face, pushed a button on it and began barking. "Breaker, breaker, this is Kojak-the-Hack going west on Grant. Any CHiPs between my wheels and the deep blue? Over?"

H.G. gawked at the driver. It wasn't the device that impressed him, for he'd already seen the telephone in operation; rather it was the language. It sounded like a combination of Scottish and Gaelic with an added touch of Prussian, all delivered with an American twang. He shuddered, but not because he didn't understand what was being said. It was the noise of the intonations. The staccato burping of words reminded him of his mother heating up lard for fried bread when she was annoyed. And the rhythm of the sound—if one could call it that— was like the clamor of milk cans clanging together in a horse-drawn cart on a cobblestone street at 3:30 A.M. He closed his eyes and covered his ears.

"Negative, Hack, negative. All the CHiPs I seen is on their way to a 10-49 in Daly City. Happy RPMs. You gotta clean slate to the Golden Gate."

The driver ended his conversation, then hunched over the steering wheel and glowered at the street ahead.

The light turned green.

The driver pushed his foot to the floor, and the vehicle roared across the intersection. In eight seconds Kojak-the-Hack had slammed through the gears, and his yellow juggernaut was flying down Grant Avenue at sixty, lurching through traffic like a supercharged tank burning pure alcohol. He bounced in the seat and rode the wheel with his entire bulk, applying body English when needed. He also used his horn frequently—in most cases where a more prudent and sane motorist would apply the brakes.

At first H.G. just stared at the driver with awe and didn't know what to make of the man's antics. Then he discerned that the driver was engaged in a very *personal* activity, one that seemed vaguely familiar, yet out of place. The grunts and groans of the driver were quasi-erotic, and H.G. realized that the man was in the middle of a private, *sexual* form of ritual, and he was so carried away that he seemed to have forgotten that H.G. was in the backseat. He continually talked to his cab as if it were an enthusiastic woman bucking under his squat, sweaty frame. H.G. had read with both scientific and prurient interest about certain activities common to lonely shepherds, but never before had he heard of or witnessed lascivious behavior between a man and a machine. What would one term such an impropriety? It wasn't onanism because a machine was involved. H.G. thought hard about the conduct going on in the front seat, then coined it "technophilia." Almost immediately, the word took on embarrassing connotations, and H.G. felt like a voyeur. He blushed and looked away. True, the sensations of speed, power and acceleration were exhilarating, but in his view and experience, sexual relations brought on an entirely different set of emotions. Or was it that along with advanced technology came depersonalization? Had sex, too, become mechanical? H.G. asked himself with a great amount of dismay. The question was worth reflecting upon, but he didn't get an opportunity, for his own level of excitement was increasing right along with the speed of the cab. His analytic posture was left behind somewhere in the belching clouds of exhaust.

The driver ran a red light, then swung onto Columbus Avenue doing a good seventy-five. The tires squealed and smoked, and the cab almost turned over, but he deftly jerked the wheel back to the right, straightened out and increased speed.

"Come on, show me, baby! Come on! Faster, faster!"

H.G. was left gasping and giddy by the turn; he laughed with excitement. The continued high-speed swerves were thrilling to him, and he found that he, too, was becoming emotionally involved with the cab. He gripped the front seat with both hands and silently urged the vehicle to even greater mechanical feats.

The driver suddenly braked and turned onto Union Street. Then he accelerated again, and the cab sped up a very steep hill, every bolt and joint shuddering and straining. At the top of the rise, the vehicle shot into the air and floated for thirty feet before nosing down and slamming to the pavement. Surprised, H.G. let out a whoosh of air, then clapped his hands and knees in delight. He could no longer contain himself.

"Again!" he cried. "Again!"

The driver obliged. He did six more hill jumps and was about to attempt a seventh when the cab overheated and popped its loosely locked radiator cap. He cursed as the temperature-gauge needle bounced into the red, then stopped his beloved machine. He got out, lifted the hood and backed away as the clouds of steam billowed up and dissipated. The engine groaned and ticked.

While the cab rested, and cooled, H.G. sighed and leaned back in the seat. The wild ride had left him drained and devoid of tension. He uttered a giggle. Had he, too, just experienced "technophilia"? If so, he admitted to himself that the sensations could definitely prove to be habit-forming.

The driver closed up the hood, got back inside the cab and started the engine. He slowly pulled away from the curb, a serene smile on his otherwise blank face.

The trip to the hotel was staid and uneventful, but H.G. didn't notice, for he had his head back on the seat, his eyes closed, and was smiling. His imagination was back there rocketing off concrete summits in quiet residential areas. When he reluctantly climbed out of the backseat of the cab, he was no longer the same.

H.G. Wells had fallen inexorably in love with the automobile.

Leslie John Stephenson sat at the dining table in his hotel suite and picked at the *escargots* he had ordered from room service. Although tired, he was satisfied with the progress he had made in the short time since he'd arrived in 1979. He felt that his strong sense of survival had been renewed and honed, for after he had left the museum, it had taken him less than an hour to locate a free hot supper and a warm bed at the St. Vincent De Paul Rescue Mission on Haight Street just east of the park. And just this morning he had gotten a free ride into the city and had exchanged some of the gold sovereigns he always carried in his money belt for several hundred dollars American. Then he had purchased several outfits of clothes and was now lounging in a one-hundred-and-fifty-dollar-per-day suite high above the annoying metallic sounds of the street. He smiled. Not bad for a fugitive from Scotland Yard. And all in less than twenty-four hours, too.

He pushed his lunch away and went back to a poem

he was working on; he was impressed with the effortless way in which the modern pen with the internal source of ink moved across the Jack Tar stationery.

"An Ode to Joan of Arc"

You whom the flames twist around;
Smiling, you utter no sound.
Your mouth is hot with desire
To caress the inevitable fire . . .

He put the pen down and massaged his red-rimmed eyes. He poured himself another glass of Beefeater's, then got up from the table and went out onto the balcony. He gazed at the overcast sky and the sweep of square buildings that sloped away from the hotel. The sight reminded him of the view of Bath from the library of his family's country estate that now belonged to one of his simpering older brothers. He took a slug of gin with an angry toss of his head, then hissed as the liquor burned his throat and stomach.

Aesculapius. That had been home once. That was the name his dictatorial father had given to the estate because he was a doctor, and he had three sons who he insisted would become doctors, and he had a daughter who would no doubt marry a doctor. Stephenson, Sr., had envisioned himself as a latter-day Squire Allworthy, and once a month he would stage fox hunts, driving his intrepid hounds to the limit of their endurance, then hold forth for his friends in front of the great stone fireplace. On such occasions young Leslie and his siblings were banned from the front portion of the house, and their mother was reduced to the role of sniveling alewife.

Aesculapius. Stephenson took another gulp of gin, clenched the balcony railing and gritted his teeth. That was where he had gone home to after his first year at the university. That was where his love for his dark-haired, ivory-skinned sister had matured and flowered. That was where he had seduced her—upon the meadow behind the caretaker's house on a warm summer afternoon, the air heavy with pollen and sweet odors. He had interpreted her eagerness as a sign of true love and at the height of his passion asked her to run away with him and marry him. There had never been another woman. Just her. She replied without remorse that she was content where she was and that while she might like him at this particular moment, his passion had been preceded by others. "Who?" he cried with anguish. He learned that the caretaker had been first and that she had lain with their father—not once, but many times since.

She had unleashed a demon.

Aesculapius. Home. He took another quick swallow of liquor. The place where early in the evening that same day he had tried to kill his sister with a carving knife when he could no longer contain his rage and humiliation. He would have succeeded, too, if his father hadn't heard her screams, come into the room and beat him senseless with a fire poker.

Aesculapius. A former residence. He had been back once, interrupting his studies at the Cambridge medical school to take the train down for the reading of his father's will. A pastoral setting for a funeral. A place where he had told the vicar and his brothers that he thought it fitting that the cancer which had consumed the old man had made his death slow and painful. He had inherited nothing. His sister had not returned and no one knew where she was. The day he left, his brothers committed his mother, for she was found in the kennels groveling with the hounds.

He had nothing left but himself, his dog-eared volumes of the *Sturm und Drang*, his scholarship and his rare talent for surgical inquiry.

He would succeed and prosper.

Suddenly he hurled the glass into the sky. It sailed

a good hundred and fifty feet before shattering on the top of a building across the street. He left the balcony, went into the bedroom and turned on the color television, the first device that had truly captured his imagination and fascination in 1979. He eased into an overstuffed chair, put his feet up on the ottoman and watched the midafternoon news break.

The broadcaster matter-of-factly reported on guerrilla warfare in Africa, a famine in Asia, striking workers in the Northeast and increased crime rates in major urban centers. The weather continued cool and overcast.

The newscaster disappeared and was replaced by a blonde selling cosmetics. She was followed by a pitch for Preparation H, a plea for the Heart Association and, finally, someone offering "great deals and slashed prices on new and used cars."

Stephenson was on the edge of his chair, gawking at the tube, amazed by the quick succession of visual images. His mind had trouble sorting them out, for there was no continuity, and unlike the printed page, this form of communication did not allow for reflection. Then again, perhaps one wasn't supposed to ponder over what he saw; maybe that was done for the viewer at the source of the images. If so, that was good, and he decided to let himself be saturated.

The Pride of the Marines returned to the Friday afternoon matinee, and Stephenson was transported to the war for the Pacific. Two U.S. Marines smoked cigarettes and whispered as they sat behind what looked like a refinement of the Gatling gun. Suddenly a grenade exploded in their faces. One was killed, and the other rendered blind. Then hordes of Japanese soldiers emerged from the jungle and attacked. Whimpering with fright and panic, the sightless Marine began firing his machine gun, swinging it back and forth in a wide arc before him, guided only by his ears.

Stephenson bounced in the chair with joy, eyes wide

with excitement as the hordes of Japanese were cut down by the bursts of machine-gun fire. He imagined that he had the weapon in his own hands and was dug into the meadow at Aesculapius. His father and friends were coming for him, their horses at full gallop, their red coats and white riding breeches glistening in the sun. He fired. Men and horses were cut down instantly. But his father was up again, running for him, waving a fire poker high over his head. Another long burst of fire, and his father went down permanently, his form held together only by his clothes.

When he returned to reality, Stephenson felt relaxed and elated. He watched the maudlin ending to the war story, then turned off the television. He was extremely satisfied, for he had just seen images and affirmations to the only part of the human psyche that he truly admired and respected. Then he thought furiously. Queen Victoria (that pompous, horse-faced bitch) would never have allowed any of what he had just seen to be staged in England. So, societies must have changed drastically, allowing a man to express himself more freely, hence more violently. He chuckled. If this thing called television reflected the current state of the human beast, then he was more at home here than in his own age! He laughed cynically. The irony of it—he really *had* been born a century before his time! He could hardly wait for night to fall so he could go out on the streets and make more personal observations and conclusions. Maybe he would meet a girl. A coquettish one who knew how to please before dying with grace. He shuddered with anticipation.

He stood, stretched, then picked up his beloved pocket watch off the dresser. He opened it not to check the time, but for a reflective gaze at her likeness on the inside of the lid. He closed the watch and slipped it into the small pocket on the waist of his new trousers. He attached the chain to his wide leather belt. Then he tried on the Panama hat that he had purchased along with the stacked-heel Oxford shoes. He turned in front of the full-length mirror by the closet. The hat fit perfectly. He shifted his weight to his right foot, dropped his right shoulder, put his hands on his hips, raised his eyebrows slightly, then thrust out his pelvis. He sighed with satisfaction. He even *looked* like a 1979er. He had that same foreboding and furtive air, that same glint of sordid luxury that he had noticed in the mannerisms of some idle men he had seen on the street.

He grinned and admired his transmutation. Although landing in San Francisco instead of London had been a rude shock at first, he no longer cared. A city was a city, and so far he hadn't encountered any problems with the American language. Soon he would get a map of San Francisco and would know the streets and his way around in a matter of days. Perhaps he would learn how to operate one of those modern, machine-driven runabouts (preferably, one of the long, sleek, black models with tinted glass); then he could travel about at will, a contemporary man of leisure—free to indulge whatever whim might strike his fancy.

Suddenly, someone knocked sharply on the door to his suite.

He emitted a sharp gasp. Who was *that*? Had he ordered something else from room service and then forgotten about it? More gin, perhaps? No, he had complete control over his mind; he never forgot anything. Whoever was out there was totally unexpected and had obviously ignored the "Do Not Disturb" sign he had hung on the door handle.

He exhaled in a quiet hiss, then slowly left the bedroom and silently walked to the door. He waited and listened, his large right hand closed into a murderous fist. Maybe someone had the wrong room. Maybe they would go away.

There were five more knocks, louder than before. Insistent and pounding.

Annoyed now, Stephenson scowled at the door, his jaw muscles working furiously. "All *right*!" he shouted. "Who's *there*?"

"Desk, sir," replied a voice muffled by the thickness of the door.

"What the devil do you want?"

"It's your luggage, sir."

"*Luggage*?" Surprised, he stepped back and stared at the door, totally confused. "*What* luggage?"

"Your bags just arrived, sir."

"My *bags*? That's *absurd*! You must have the wrong party."

"You *are* Dr. Stephenson, aren't you?"

With a puzzled growl, Stephenson stepped to the door, unlocked it, then jerked it open. "Now what in the bloody name of hell . . . ?" He suddenly gasped and staggered back into the room, his jaw slack, his eyes wide with horror.

"My God," he uttered with dismay. "*Wells*?"

H.G. stepped into the room, closed the door, deliberately dropped the "Do Not Disturb" sign he had taken off the door handle into a dust bin, then calmly turned to face a trembling Leslie John Stephenson. He didn't feel angry or tense, as he might have suspected, but rather somewhat saddened to be the first one to confront Jack the Ripper. He had known Stephenson for quite a long time, and he felt uncomfortable staring at the man when they both knew that he, H. G. Wells, was an instrument of redemption, if not judgment. Yes, the business was going to be distasteful.

He moved into the center of the room and studied his

adversary critically. The first thing he noticed was the man's conspicuous attire, and he couldn't help but comment dryly, "Isn't that haberdashery a little ostentatious, John?"

"How did you get here?"

H.G. merely smiled.

"How did you find me?"

"The details aren't *really* important, are they?"

Stephenson sighed, ran his hands through his hair, then turned away from H.G. and spoke with an uncustomary softness. "Obviously, then, you know."

"You left your cape and bag in the hall cupboard," H.G. replied flatly.

"Forgive me for the inconvenience."

"I guess neither I nor any of our mutual acquaintances realized the extent to which one of us could have descended," H.G. said forcefully. "What could have *possessed* you, John?"

Stephenson stiffened, then faced Wells. "There is no explanation. And even if there were, it's no one's affair but my own."

His hand found the bottle of Beefeater's, and he held it up. "Would you care for a spot of gin, old boy? The taste isn't as sharp as it used to be, and it's frightfully expensive, but then again, it's imported. *Given* our location"—He allowed himself an ironic smile—"It's quite good, actually. May I pour you a glass?"

H.G. was taken aback at the thought of imbibing with such a creature. But the longer he stared at Stephenson —the more he considered the circumstances—he understood that accepting the man's hospitality might be a wise thing to do. Perhaps he might be able to *logically* convince Stephenson that he should return to 1893 London. After all, the man seemed rational. He grudgingly returned the smile. "I don't see why not. As long as we can be civil about this entire matter."

Stephenson crossed the room to the bar, set up two

glasses, poured them half full, set the bottle between them, then sat on a stool. He turned to Wells and gestured for him to sit down. "Now that you've come all this way, just what is it that you intend to do?"

"Take you back," blurted H.G.

Stephenson laughed sardonically, then spread his hands in a generous gesture. "Whatever *for*?"

"Do I really need to explain, John?"

Stephenson sighed, then leaned back against the bar. "I've never really liked you, Wells, but I've always respected your talents and abilities, I've always enjoyed your company. You know how to challenge men's minds. But this is not a literary circle arguing about who wrote Shakespeare's plays. Nor is it a polemical group of students discussing the merits of Bismarck versus the ineptitudes of Napoleon III." He paused. "It is you and I out of our own time—for all intents and purposes, larger than life. We have transcended mortality, hence, humanity. There are no rules for you and me. Save one—I am *never* going back to 1893. So why don't we just forget about that and discuss our unique situation like gentlemen?" He took a drink. "Can we do that, Wells?"

"We may be out of our own time, John, but we have not transcended humanity. Must I remind you that there are basic universal laws to which we will always be beholden? Such as, respect for another human being?"

"Ah, yes," replied Stephenson. "To be more specific, I took your time machine without asking your permission."

"To put it mildly."

"Well, would you be so kind as to accept my apologies? In the haste of the moment, I obviously forgot my manners." He laughed. "Perhaps I could compensate you for the trip. What does it cost to travel eighty-six years nowadays?"

"You're deliberately missing the point, aren't you?"

"What point?"

"The basic difference between good and evil!" He exploded. "We all know what it is! We all understand it!"

"Of course we do, Wells. Good is when we feel pleasure and evil is when we experience pain."

"There isn't a remorseful bone in your entire body, is there?"

"Remorse?" Stephenson laughed again. "To a world without remorse," he said, his eyes twinkling. He toasted himself.

"Whoosh," H.G. sighed with frustration. "But those murders, John! How *could* you?"

"Once I had acquired an elementary knowledge of surgery, it was really quite simple."

"But *why?*"

"I enjoyed it."

"Have you no feelings for your fellow human beings?"

He frowned impatiently. "My good man, I believe I made my position on that matter quite clear on an earlier occasion. Must I repeat myself?"

"*Murder* is *wrong.*"

"Says who? On the contrary, it has been a natural expression of human emotions since Cain did in Abel. I've never considered murder a crime."

"It is *evil!*"

"Perhaps in your view, but not in mine. It is a very functional act, as basic to human needs and desires as sexual intercourse."

H.G. was unable to reply.

Stephenson smiled and continued. "One can murder for pleasure or profit, one can murder for wealth or fame. For political, religious, social, economic or humanitarian purposes. A dictator can be assassinated just as a hated parent can be killed. The weak and the dangerous can be eliminated. And so on. Can you imagine the terrible shape the world would be in if murder did not exist, Wells?" He paused, then spoke softly. "To murder is to love, for both acts ensure that the human race will survive."

H.G. thought furiously. The man had made a persuasive case for indiscriminate murder. He had even made that vile act sound attractive, and H.G. realized that he could probe into Stephenson's psyche at will, but would never find a penitent conscience or even a pang of regret. The man's soul was not tortured at all; rather it was twisted, the basis of his *raison d'être* being that society was a vegetable garden of people to be harvested and consumed at will.

H.G. would have to win this debate with the tools of deduction.

"I'm sure that the human race would survive and flourish without the institution of murder, John," H.G. replied dryly. "And I'm also sure that the great majority of rational human beings do not share your deviant opinions, myself included. What you fail to see is that there would be no great civilizations without law and order, the foundation of which is a basic respect for the rights of others."

"I would agree with you, Wells, except for one thing—it is fallacious to assume that the vast majority of human beings are rational. And when irrationality rules the kingdom of man—as it has ever since the first Neanderthal picked up a club—then laws are made solely for the convenience of those who hold power; they are broken by those who are destined to become powerful who in turn will institute an entirely different set of regulations for *their* convenience and pleasure. The dialectic that Hegel was talking about is actually an endless historical cycle of chaos. Am I right?"

When H.G. did not immediately reply, Stephenson burst out laughing, leaned over and patted him on the back. "Go back to the nineteenth century and reread Friedrich Nietzsche, my friend. John Locke, Matthew Arnold and John Stuart Mill have softened your brain."

H.G. recoiled and slapped Stephenson's hand away. "I've had enough of this cynical nonsense! You have used my scientific achievement to escape justice! Therefore, you have damaged my reputation and besmirched my honor!"

"Well, bully for me." Stephenson laughed.

"It's a matter of principle!"

"Principle?" Stephenson sneered. "Would I be correct in saying that times have changed, Wells?"

"My good man, morality *never* changes, no matter what you say! You're returning to London to pay your debt to society!"

Stephenson stood and glowered over H.G. "You little fool! Haven't you been observing the world around you? 1979 is *overrun* with people like me. Rapists, murderers, arsonists, robbers, terrorists, *ad infinitum!*"

H.G. laughed derisively. "What rubbish!"

"You don't believe me?"

"How could I believe any of your nihilistic diatribes?"

Stephenson made a curt gesture with his hand. "Let me show you something."

H.G. followed him into the bedroom and saw him go to a large electronic box with a dark-gray screen and turn a switch.

"They call it television."

H.G. stepped back and gasped, for he was staring at an instant color picture of two people talking. So *that* was the end result of Marconi's wireless. What a wonderful, graphic, clear way to communicate. "Marvelous! Simply marvelous!"

"I couldn't agree with you more." Stephenson turned a dial once and produced an image of two men in nineteenth-century western attire facing each other, a street between them. One drew a pistol and shot the other three times. Stephenson gestured from the screen to Wells and smiled smugly.

"I believe that is an illustration of history," H.G. commented indignantly. Rage began building inside him as he realized what his adversary was up to. He clenched and unclenched his fists.

Stephenson turned the dial again. The screen showed a wrestling match where two giant men appeared to be killing each other while an unruly, obsessed crowd urged them to commit even more horrible atrocities. One wrestler threw the other out of the ring into the seats and was declared the winner. Then the scene shifted to an advertisement for a children's doll. This one was a replica of a modern soldier in full battle dress, and he was "on sale for Christmas at Zody's, only $13.95."

Stephenson laughed with delight. "They sell firearms there, too. In the sporting-goods section. What was the phrase you used the other day? *Fait accompli?*"

"You haven't proved a thing!" H.G. shouted.

"Haven't I?" he replied impatiently, then turned off the television and strode back into the living room. "This is *my* world, Wells!" He turned. "I belong here and you don't! You're a misfit and a relic of the past!"

"You're going back!" H.G. said lividly.

"I'm not going anywhere!"

"The hell you say!" He grabbed Stephenson by the arm and began leading him toward the door. The larger man obliged for several steps, then jerked his arm free and emitted an ironic chuckle.

"My good man, I do believe that *you* have become irrational." He brushed off his shirt sleeve. "Perhaps even violent. Have I proven my point now?"

H.G. growled with rage and ran at Stephenson, his arms flailing. Stephenson backed away, then suddenly strode in and backhanded Wells into the wall.

H.G.'s breath whooshed out. He had never realized how strong and physically adept Stephenson was; but then again, he had always been conscious of the rational

Stephenson, the sane Stephenson. He was not prepared to deal with the hulking menace that now stood before him.

With a low series of grunts, Stephenson moved in and took a vicious swing at his opponent. H.G. ducked and scrambled away. Stephenson's fist punched right through an oil painting and cracked the wall behind it.

H.G. dove for the man's legs, but Stephenson sidestepped and brought a knee up hard into the side of his face. H.G. crumpled, then groggily rose to his knees and desperately tried to steady himself and let his head clear. He heard derisive, scornful laughter that sounded vaguely flat and far away.

His opponent raised a muscular arm and brought one large fist down on top of H.G.'s head with all the force he could muster. Wells emitted a short cry, fell back on the rug, twitched, and then lay still.

Stephenson gazed down at H.G.'s limp form and sighed with satisfaction. So much for justice and rationality. Then he noticed that H.G. was still breathing. He frowned. He would have to remedy that. He stepped lightly around Wells and went behind the bar where he rummaged in a drawer full of barroom accessories and found a stainless-steel ice pick, nine inches long. He inspected it. The point was fine—almost needle-sharp—but the absence of a blade disappointed him, for he would be able to inflict only puncture wounds on his former schoolmate. The weapon would do, however; it was certainly more acceptable than crushing Wells's head with a piece of heavy furniture.

He moved back into the room, bent over H.G. and turned him onto his back so that he could stab into the man's eyes. He raised the ice pick, tensed his muscles and was about to plunge the weapon home when he had second thoughts. He dropped his arm, straightened up and gazed out over the balcony. He sighed. Actually, it would be a shame to kill Wells. The little man was so brilliant. After all, hadn't he made time-traveling possible? Was he not the Columbus of a new age and dimension? Hadn't Wells created the very device which had allowed him to elude Scotland Yard one last time?

Suddenly, Stephenson gasped and remembered. He slowly grinned, looked down at the prostrate Wells and nodded. Of course! When he had hurriedly scanned the boldly penned diagrams for the time machine, he had read about the Rotation Reversal Lock and the special key that overrode it. He hadn't really understood the principles then, but now it was all coming clear. *That* was how Wells had followed him! The time machine had returned to its home hour because he, Stephenson, did not have the key. Therefore, if one *did* have the key, one could travel anywhere along the fourth dimension and never have to fear pursuit. He grinned. He would take the key. He didn't have to stab Wells to death. He could leave the inimitable little scientist hopelessly mired in the late twentieth century.

His hands trembled with excitement, and he began searching through Wells's pockets. But then H.G. emitted a loud groan and began to twitch as strength returned to his form. Stephenson frowned and sat back on his haunches. There was no time. He would have to kill the little man and then find the key. What the devil, he told himself and shrugged. The end had always justified the means.

He took a deep breath and once again raised the ice pick.

Suddenly, someone knocked quickly and casually on the door.

"Maid."

Stephenson dropped the ice pick, emitted a short cry and scrambled to his feet.

The door opened, and a young girl pushed a cart loaded with cleaning utensils into the room. She saw the two of them—one prone, one upright—abruptly stopped moving and put her hand to her mouth, more in surprise than in fear. She did not immediately scream.

Stephenson had the presence of mind to shield his face with his hand so that she would be unable to recognize him. Then he rushed by her out into the hallway. He glanced back and saw that Wells was moaning and stirring. With a low curse, he turned on his stacked heel and hurried for the lifts.

SIX

H.G. opened his eyes, blinked several times and did not immediately know where he was. The room was a haze— the blue carpet merging with the off-white walls in circles of painful, distant colors. Someone was screaming, but he did not know who or why yet. He groaned and pushed up onto his elbows, still blinking. His entire body ached —unnaturally jammed up from Stephenson's pile-driving blow. When the room began to come into focus, he tried to raise his head. The compressed vertebrae in his neck cracked loudly, and he gasped at the sharp, fierce pain. He gingerly got up on his hands and knees, then slowly and cautiously swiveled his head back and forth until his upper spine finally popped and snapped back into place. He felt instant relief and was able to move freely, despite a steady, dull throb behind his temples.

He could see better, too, and then recognized that a young girl in a uniform was in front of him on her knees, her eyes wide with concern. She was gently touching his forehead.

"Sir! Are you all right, sir?"

"I've been better, thank you." He got to his feet, then saw the ice pick on the floor. "Good bloody *Christ*!" he exclaimed. A chill swept over his body, and he began to tremble. He realized that he was extremely fortunate to be alive.

"Would you like me to call a doctor?"

"No thank you."

He became more and more angry by the second. What a monstrous creature, he thought, what a base, unnatural human being. He should have known that Stephenson would stop at nothing—not even the murder of an old classmate—to avoid justice. Well, there definitely would be no more appeals to reason and rationality on his part. Not after this.

"Are you sure you don't want to see a doctor?"

"The only physician I'm interested in has already vacated the premises."

A vengeful H.G. Wells scooped up and pocketed the ice pick, then left the room.

As he rode down in the lift, he calmed himself and tried to guess what Stephenson would do. Neither of them knew the city of San Francisco, so H.G. figured that his adversary had probably left the hotel and was just aimlessly walking the streets. So, the only problem was time. How long had he been unconscious? How much of a head start did Stephenson have? Probably only several minutes since H.G. remembered that the handle of the ice pick had still been warm and stained with moisture from the man's hand when he had first discovered it and picked it up off the carpet. H.G. grinned at his perception. So much for the question of time. Then he frowned. If Stephenson had left the hotel, what direction had he gone in? There was no scientific way of telling, so H.G. decided just to follow his impulses and take whatever route seemed the easiest to negotiate physically for a man out of his own time. He could only hope that he hadn't lost Stephenson forever.

The lift came to a smooth stop at ground level. H.G. hurried out and half ran across the lobby, nimbly cutting through groups of Japanese tourists and dodging clusters of furniture as if he were an elusive halfback on a Rugby field. He went outside and darted across the hotel's circular driveway to the sidewalk that paralleled Van Ness Avenue. He looked both ways and quickly appraised the topography of the city. To the west, the street went upward in a long grade that would be difficult and unpleasant to walk. Moreover, his natural inclination was to proceed downhill, so he began moving to the east where the street sloped down to the handsome buildings of the civic center a half mile away. Almost immediately, he came to the intersection of Van Ness and Geary. The light was against him, and heavy traffic rolled up Geary Street heading south and out of the city. Had Stephenson gone north on Geary or continued east on Van Ness? Once again, H.G. looked in both directions. Geary Street was wide and brighter in that it was lit directly by the late-afternoon sun. Van Ness, on the other hand, was bathed in shadows; the buildings were taller and closer together, too, which would make a fugitive in a hurry seem less noticeable. H.G. nodded imperceptibly and crossed the intersection, continuing east on Van Ness.

Two short blocks later, H.G. caught sight of Stephenson's Panama hat bobbing above the stream of pedestrians. Thank God his intuitions had been correct!

He smiled grimly, crouched low and began running as fast as he could without bowling over the other people on the sidewalk. He crossed O'Farrell Street against the traffic and ignored the honking horns and irate curses of the drivers. Then he dodged out into Van Ness Avenue proper—outflanking a meandering mass of pedestrians—and vaulted back onto the sidewalk just ahead of another speeding phalanx of vehicles. Breathing heavily now, he raced along and finally caught up with Stephenson at the corner of Van Ness and Ellis Street where the man waited for the red light to change. H.G.'s jaws clenched and his muscles tensed. He came up behind Stephenson, grabbed him, spun him around and had the ice pick poised an inch from the man's throat. Shocked, Stephenson breathed in sharply and his eyes widened. H.G. saw the fear in his opponent's face, and he knew that he had won.

He was about to issue a command when a lady standing beside them saw what was happening and screamed. H.G. automatically turned to explain, and that was all Stephenson needed. He slapped the ice pick from H.G.'s hand, shoved the smaller man away, then turned and sprinted into Ellis Street against the light. He dodged three speeding cars and had just about reached the opposite corner when a Volkswagen bus made a fast left turn onto Ellis, accelerated and smacked into Stephenson head-on at thirty-five miles per hour. He was knocked a good twenty feet through the air before crashing down onto the pavement headfirst.

A crowd instantly gathered around the prostrate Stephenson, everyone shouting and yelling, some wondering what they should do, others (curiously detached) only there for the violence of the moment.

From the curb, H.G. watched in a daze. A large and powerful black policeman wearing white gloves hurried over to the scene from his station in the center of the intersection. He quickly dispersed the crowd, then kneeled over Stephenson, loosened his clothing, removed his own coat despite the chill and used it to cover the unconscious and seriously injured man.

H.G. felt leaden, and all he could do was stare. A sadness came over him that he did not immediately understand, for if anyone in the universe deserved to be metallically smacked down onto a rough, macadam surface, surely it was Leslie John Stephenson. Perhaps it was the manner in which it had happened. Stephenson had not been felled and maimed by another human being. He had been squashed by technology, and the vehicle that had done it just sat there waiting to be driven again. Did a man out of his own time—even one

as monstrous as Stephenson—deserve to be smitten by
an inanimate object that he didn't understand? Or was
that the way of the world, time planes or not? H.G.
closed his eyes and rubbed his aching temples. Maybe
it was the impersonal nature of the accident that made
Stephenson's fate seem so cruel and alien, for H.G. had
always regarded the miracle of life as precious and the
absurdity of death as personal. Yet here was a badly hurt
man on the pavement eighty-six years from home, naked
to machines and people alike in a futurological city. No
one here would care; no one back home would know.

H.G. suppressed an urge to burst out in sobs and
forced himself to witness what was happening now on
the opposite side of the street.

The hapless, long-haired driver of the offending vehicle walked in tight, aimless circles, spasmodically wring-
ing his hands and wondering if he'd just killed someone.
After a while, he slumped against the side door of his
weather-beaten omnibus while the policeman calmly
asked him questions and wrote down information on a
note pad. The air was routine, for the policeman was
proceeding as if this sort of thing happened all the time.
He was both efficient and methodical. Moreover, the
traffic flow had returned to normal, and passers-by (now
that the minor excitement of the moment had passed)
were continuing with errands that had brought them
out in the first place.

Yes, what H.G. was observing was just another performance of a modern (and mundane) ballet featuring a
good policeman who was ironically attempting to or-
chestrate chaos into a logical sequence. The coda to the
first half of the drama had just ended.

Act two began when a siren grew louder and louder,
eventually became ear-splitting and drowned out the
street noises. Then H.G. saw a shiny, red and white van
turn left off Van Ness and stop in the middle of Ellis
Street. A sign on the door read "Paramedic Unit 37,

SFFD." Two lithe young men in dark-blue uniforms leaped out of the vehicle and began attending to Stephenson. H.G. hurried farther up his side of the street to get a better view of their actions. First, they rolled Stephenson onto a chrome-tipped stretcher, then wheeled him to the rear of the van and lifted him up and inside. Their movements were graceful and choreographed. No wasted time or energy. No befuddlement or unnecessary dialogue. In seconds they were back inside their van, and while one spoke into a small metal device and simultaneously swung the vehicle around in a tight circle, the other affixed a mask over Stephenson's face, adjusted dials on metal cylinders, then began checking the victim's vital signs. The van sped away down Ellis Street, and the traffic responded to the siren, opening up before the vehicle like the Red Sea parting before Moses.

H.G. was overwhelmed. He recalled reading about the Crimean War where it was common for hundreds of wounded men to lie unattended for hours, even days. Those fortunate enough to find themselves in surgeries were either ignored or had their limbs hurriedly removed by overworked and undertrained doctors. Yet here, he had witnessed the functioning of a precise team, obviously very knowledgeable in the business of saving lives. My God, he thought, how wonderful and reassuring it must be for the people of 1979 to know that injury and/or loss of life was not viewed callously. That trained teams responded in minutes to victims of accidents with technology guiding the way. Surely the long-haired operator of the machine that struck Stephenson must be a throwback to an earlier twentieth-century man, a person not trained for the current sophistication of 1979.

Then he frowned and was momentarily confused. There was an irony here: Stephenson had been flattened by a product of advanced technology, then picked up and taken away (his life no doubt saved in the process) by a similar machine. One dealt death, whereas the other restored life. The scales were balanced.

"Whoosh," uttered H.G. A revelation, a discovery was taking shape in his mind. The machines, the dials, the push buttons, the communication devices, the detecting instruments, the lights, *et al.*, were *neutral*. Indiscriminate. Subobjective. The *operators* were the significant ones. Human beings. Walking, thinking, talking mind-body problems who could construct and fly a giant airship on the one hand, then shriek like a wild animal and commit a violent, irrational act on the other. Perhaps, then, the basic duality of human nature hadn't changed with eighty-six years of progress. Maybe the advent of science had only raised the stakes, so to speak, meaning that one either died faster or was saved more quickly. *Was* there really a new man? His sensibilities heightened by progress, his creativity freed by the machine, his rationality reinforced by technology? H.G. sighed. He was unequipped to answer those questions. He needed more time and more information to make an intelligent appraisal. Then he shuddered. He certainly hoped that the contemporary scales *were* tipped in favor of the new man governed by an advanced scientific rationality. But what if they weren't? What if the long-haired driver of the omnibus *wasn't* a throwback? What if—back there in his plush hotel suite—Stephenson had been right?

Stephenson. He was still Wells's first responsibility.

H.G. turned and timidly approached the black policeman who was at the corner of the intersection talking into a metal box. When the man finished, closed and locked the box, H.G. accosted him.

"Excuse me, sir, just where did they take that poor wretch who was struck by the motorcar?"

The policeman looked H.G. up and down, then frowned critically. "You know him or something?"

"Oh, no, sir. You see, I'm a newcomer here, and I was curious about the procedure used for such tragedies."

"The paramedics got him, and he'll end up at San Francisco General. Ain't it the same way in England?"

H.G. paid his taxi fare and got out of the vehicle in front of the main entrance to San Francisco General Hospital. The sun was setting and a cold fog was rolling in from the bay, but he just stood at the edge of the long walkway and stared. When he had first engaged the cab driver for the trip to the hospital, he had prepared himself for a marvelous sight; what he saw was completely unexpected.

The complex was vast, encompassing six city blocks and consisting of a dozen towering buildings. Yet, the structures were old and forbidding. They were painted a dingy red-orange which over the years had become stained with dirt and smoke. The shrubs and lawns between the buildings were brown with neglect. And around the entire area was a massive, black-iron fence, its bottom lined with old papers and other debris blown there by the winds. Behind the buildings was a twelve-story, brick smokestack emitting wisps of white steam.

H.G. shuddered. Instead of a modern-day cradle for the advanced arts of medical science, the place reminded him of a Victorian prison. It was, however, a hospital, for off to his left he saw a brand-new, oblong-shaped sign; against a white, internally lit background, cherry-red letters spelled out "Emergency." An arrow pointed around to the back side of the main building.

Another shiny, red and white van sped up the circular drive and went around the building following the arrow, so H.G. surmised that that was where he would find Stephenson. He quickly moved down the walkway and huddled inside his coat, for the wind was picking up, and the chill was much more noticeable.

In contrast to the hospital's main ingress, the emergency entrance was bustling with activity and thoroughly modern. H.G. sighed with relief and was reassured. Perhaps the front of the hospital was in disrepair and soon would be renovated. He pushed through the glass doors, and since he was more familiar with them now than the day before, he did not automatically reach for a brass doorknob.

The inside of the emergency-ward complex and out-patient clinic was a nineteenth-century scientific-romantic's dream. To H.G.'s immediate front across twenty feet of immaculate, off-white flooring was an island of brushed-silver lifts which several signs and arrows identified as elevators. With the flash of a light and the ding of a bell, one arrived, its cavernous doors automatically spreading. H.G. saw an attendant push an old man on a stretcher inside. The patient's complexion was as alabaster white as the linen that draped his cadaverous form. From the other side, an expressionless cleaning lady got on board with a cart of mops and buckets. The sweet odor of ammonia was unmistakable. The doors hissed shut. H.G. watched the flashing lights above; the lift descended four levels beneath the ground's surface. He briefly wondered.

He turned to his left. Across from the lifts was a "Reception and Information" center. The women behind the low glass partitions were all wearing starched white uniforms and hats. Regardless of age, their faces were serene, and their hair was coiffured. Some of them worked at small machines; the subdued hum and click of electrical energy was pervasive.

From the reception center, two wide, glistening corridors led off into the pristine bowels of the hospital. Stretchers came and went, but the condition of the patients was always ambiguous; there were no telltale signs; all was draped in white. Motorized wheelchairs buzzed along, too, causing H.G. to bubble with delight—whoever would have imagined that the incapacitated would be able to move about on an artificial source of energy? And then there were clusters of people, most of them dressed in the same style smocks, some white, some pink, some green, a few gray and even blue. H.G. quickly figured out that the colors indicated functions. That way in the haste of a serious medical moment, no one had to ask the others what their jobs were. How clever.

He bent over and touched the floor, then straightened up and ran his hand along a pastel wall. Yes, everything in the hospital was molded out of that same curious substance he had first encountered at the McDonald's restaurant. So smooth, so shiny, so soft, yet definitive to the eye. It must be the artificial lighting. He wanted to say incandescent, but he wasn't sure that the term would be correct, for the entire area was lit evenly and softly from overhead through large, rectangular sources. There were no shadows or black hallways from which one could hear the pitiful cries of patients racked with pain. Here, one could see everything! And there was music amplifying from boxes affixed to the ceilings. No agonized screams here!

H.G. smiled with pride. This, then, was the future he had predicted. This was what technology could do for mankind. These were the beautiful, sophisticated conditions under which one enlightened human being could help another.

And yet the facility was so vast. Were there that many sick and injured people? H.G. guessed not, for most of the humans he had seen so far were wearing uniforms and were obviously employed by the hospital. And that, too, was an encouraging sign, for it meant that there were enough doctors and nurses to administer the business of healing.

But the most remarkable fact of all was the absolute cleanliness of the hospital. For a moment H.G. was afraid to touch anything for fear of leaving some nineteenth-century bacilli where it wasn't wanted.

He recalled his brief stay at St. George's after his last and most serious tuberculosis attack, brought on by overwork and the collapse of his marriage to Isabel. They had placed him in a long, dismal ward that housed fifty other patients. The room was lit by four gas lamps, and since the high windows were never opened, the air hung heavy and stale. The dominant odor was a suffocating blend of excrement, bile, mildew and smoke. They had him on a lumpy bed with loose springs, wrapped in a plaster that had gone cold and soggy. Blankets were piled over him to break the fever that had consumed him for days. And when he coughed, excruciating pain would shoot through every nerve and muscle in his body. Then the doctor had come through and briskly examined the patients, ignoring the moans of the delirious, for there was nothing he could do that had not already been done. In 1892.

From that to this. Bright lights and starched linens. Music and hygiene. And not a sign, not a whimper of suffering anywhere. H.G. was overwhelmed.

"May I help you, sir?" asked a volunteer nurse's aide.

H.G. was momentarily startled to have someone break in on his thoughts, but he quickly recovered. "I believe an acquaintance of mine was brought here by two young men dressed in dark blue." He hesitated. "He had been struck by a motorcar."

"They'll help you at the desk, sir."

H.G. went to the reception center and patiently waited. Beyond the glass partition was a bank of television screens that showed corridors and various hospital rooms. A nurse sat before them pushing buttons on a console that changed the pictures. Occasionally, she made notes. H.G. was awe-struck. Why, a person could know instantly what was going on anywhere in the hospital just by pushing buttons! Think of the time and the lives that could be saved by such a miraculous device! Emergencies could be dealt with immediately. He grinned triumphantly. Stephenson had been short-sighted and wrong, for here television was employed for the public good. (Obviously, then, the images he had seen in the hotel room were shown to purge people of violent tendencies so that they could live up to the golden rule.) H.G. wondered if this form of communication were used all over the world. If so, great multitudes of people could instantly see what the others were doing and how the others lived. What a boon for rationality!

A statuesque blond nurse approached him and smiled. "What can I help you with, sir?"

"This afternoon an acquaintance of mine was struck by a motorcar and brought to this hospital. I'd like to find out the extent of his injuries and when he can be expected to be released."

"Certainly, sir. Can I have the patient's name and social security number?"

"His name is Leslie John Stephenson . . ."

She turned and worked the keys of a small electronic machine.

"But I'm afraid you've got me on the social security number."

"Date of birth, then?"

"I'm not precisely sure about that, either."

The nurse looked from the machine to H.G. "I'm sorry, sir, there is no Leslie John Stephenson registered here."

H.G. smiled patiently. "I don't think that he had any identification with him when he was struck by the machine."

"Then he'd be listed as a John Doe." She frowned, thought, then brightened. "Can you tell me where the accident occurred?"

"At the corner of Van Ness Avenue and Ellis Street."

She returned to the computer and typed in another message. Moments later there was a reply which she read to Wells. "Male, Caucasian, six feet tall, one hundred eighty pounds, brown eyes, dark-brown hair, dark complexion. Was admitted in a comatose state at 1613 hours wearing a pink shirt and light-blue pants."

"That's him! That's Leslie John Stephenson!"

"The official records list him as John Doe number sixteen." She smiled professionally.

"Can you tell me how he is?"

"I'm sorry. You'll have to speak with the patient's doctor . . . Mr. . . . ."

"Wells."

She wrote down his name, then pointed toward a corridor. "Why don't you wait in the visitors' lounge. The patient is being treated by Dr. Rodden. As soon as the doctor is off duty, I'll send him in to speak with you."

"Thank you." He turned and moved away.

Once past the island of elevators (he would never get used to that name), he found himself in the visitors' lounge. It was a large room decorated in shades of soft brown and beige, and considerably dimmer and quieter than the main part of the hospital. The floor was carpeted, and an abundance of plush furniture and reading material on tables awaited visitors. The music was louder here, and H.G. could distinguish a sweet (and bland) chorus of strings, a muted counterpoint of brass, then strings again, then brass, and so forth.

Yet, he was impressed. At St. George's the only provision for visitors was a damp stone room with one severe wooden bench against each wall.

He started across the carpet for an empty chair in the corner when he heard a curious sound. He turned and stared. Opposite the lounge on the other side of the corridor a man removed a can of something from one machine and then an apple from another! *Machines* that dispensed *food!* Good *Lord!*

H.G. was compelled to hurry over to the bank of machines for a closer look. Sandwiches reposed in the windows of one, fruit in another, soft drinks (whatever that meant) in a third, coffee, tea and hot chocolate in a fourth, and then a whole host of appetizing little snacks (the names of which were foreign to him) were in a fifth machine. Suddenly, he was very hungry, and so he returned to the sandwich machine, read the offerings, decided that "Ham and Cheese" was the most familiar and punched the button. Nothing happened. He frowned and inspected the machine more closely. Was there a procedure or code that had to be followed? A light flashed behind an opaque panel, and he read, "Insert Money." He blushed, fished in his pocket and pulled out a handful of coins. He deposited the required fifty-five cents and pushed the button. The machine groaned, whirred, returned his money and flashed another message: "Try Another Selection."

H.G. obeyed, but got his money back again, receiving the same terse information. Three more times he inserted his money into the machine, and three more times no food was delivered. His stomach growled and ached for sustenance. He felt faint and leaned against the machine until the unpleasant sensation passed.

He looked at the next machine in the line and frowned. He did not like fruit. Slightly annoyed, he moved to the snack dispenser and studied the offerings there. He rejected jawbreakers (the connotation made him feel weak), Life Savers (he was in good health), jujubes (they resembled medication of spurious origin) and toasted corn kernels (he had no desire to eat something that looked like the droppings of a small animal). All that remained were "Fritos" and "Hostess Twinkies." The latter appeared more nourishing, so he fed coins into the machine, pulled a lever and—lo and behold—out popped a Twinkie. He carefully unwrapped the little morsel and sniffed it. Visions of Mrs. Nelson's superb cooking came into his mind which were incompatible with the sweet and stale odor of the Twinkie. He sighed with disappointment, then shrugged and jammed the thing into his mouth. He chewed (not that rumination was necessary in this case), swallowed and did not feel satisfied or refreshed. If anything, his teeth hurt and twinged from the massive intake of processed sugar which had crystallized inside the Twinkie's white center of goo.

Ultimately, he settled for a cup of weak tea. He returned to the lounge thinking that the problem with the mechanization of food preparation and service was that there was no one to complain to. A waiter or a housekeeper could always throw out an unsatisfactory entrée and serve another, but none of the machines had been equipped with a "Take It Back" lever. Moreover, there were no "Compliments to the Chef" buttons to push, either. And given what the Twinkie was doing inside his stomach, H.G. concluded that such an addition to the machines would merely have been superfluous.

He selected an overstuffed chair, settled into it, then took a dog-eared *Reader's Digest* off the table. He was about to peruse this interesting little example of late-twentieth-century literature (popular, no doubt), when a white-coated doctor mouthing whispers of sympathy ushered three people of color into the lounge. H.G. put the magazine down and studied them with interest, for aside from photographs of American descendants of slaves, he had never seen black people before.

They appeared to be a family—in the Western, Judeo-Christian sense of the word. As opposed to the African. Although, upon reflection, H.G. realized that he had no idea what an African family was all about. His knowledge of the sociology of the dark continent was limited to the tribal system, which he distastefully compared to London's circle of private men's clubs.

He leaned forward, inspected the three more closely and saw no vestige of the jungle or the savannah in their behavior. They could have been any American or English family. The mother was graying, overweight, and was dressed in a shabby, dark-blue dress with white polka dots. The two young lads who assisted her across the lounge and into a chair were obviously her sons. The older one was tall, strapping and wore an outfit similar to Stephenson's new attire; he paced angrily while the doctor continued to whisper. The younger boy, in faded sweat shirt and brown pants, faithfully listened to the white-coated messenger of bad news. The mother began to cry. The doctor reached out and patted her shoulder. She pushed his hand away. He shrugged with embarrassment, apologized, turned and left the room. The younger boy consoled his mother, "Daddy's going to be all right. Don't listen to no doctor, Momma!"

H.G. continued to observe the family, distressed by their grief. He recalled etchings he had seen in American history books during his grammar school days depicting slavery. Yet, the African slaves had been emancipated the year before he was born. Why, then, did the image before him—set in this futurological hospital—seem so acutely historical? Did a different kind of subjugation exist in 1979? One which did not need the blatant implements of force to remain in control? Or was he romanticizing? There was only one way to find out. He would go over to the family and discreetly ask them if there was anything that he, H.G. Wells, could do to help.

He impulsively rose and started to approach the group when the older brother turned and affixed him with a stare. H.G. stopped short. The young man's eyes narrowed, his nostrils flared, and H.G. got the chilling sense that a barrier had just slammed down between himself and the black family. He searched the young man's face for an explanation, but the expression was cold now and full of murderous hate. H.G. wisely returned to his chair and pretended to read. An up-beat tune played from the speakers in blind counterpoint to the woman's moans of despair.

Thus, H. G. Wells unwittingly became a nervous

sociological stereotype of the late 1970s. Why had the young black looked at *him* with such a deep-rooted malice? *He* hadn't done anything to them *or* their father.

For the next two hours, H.G. waited in the visitors' lounge for Dr. Rodden to appear with news on the condition of Leslie John Stephenson. It was not a relaxing time, for every few minutes ambulances would arrive at the hospital. Moments later, relatives or friends would congregate in the lounge. Most of them (hence, the emergency patients) were black, brown or Asian, and H.G. saw in their eyes a hopelessness that left him depressed. With the exception of the hospital itself, he could have been in London's East End back in the nineties. The people looked the same. Technology hadn't helped these people. It mocked them.

The Chinaman with one eye who honed a knife on his boot. The gray-haired brown man who drank from a bottle in a paper sack. The young black girl—dismally swollen with child—who was badly beaten and waiting for assistance. The infant suffering from an unknown ailment left to scream, no one knowing why. The old woman, nearly blind, who did not know what they had done with her husband. The black man in the yellow suit and the orange derby who just waited.

Every one of them.

Shaken, H.G. left the lounge, acutely aware that in this small corner of 1979 a class system existed. He had always believed that progress would free men to practice good works. Now, he wondered, and it made him angry to be questioning his own convictions, especially since Stephenson had already done that earlier in the day.

He stormed past the island of elevators and went to the reception center.

"Yes, sir, may I help you?" The nurse behind the window was very pretty, sounded very bright, was obviously young and naïve, but what shocked H.G. was that she was black. She was not a modern slave; she was not downtrodden; she was not in the lounge waiting for news about a maimed companion or for treatment herself. What the devil was going on? If there was a rule book for this crazy potpourri of complexities, H.G. wanted very badly to have a look at it.

"Is there something wrong, sir?" She batted her long eyelashes in a practiced gesture of concern.

"Yes, there *is* something wrong. The nurse that was here before told me that Dr. Rodden would meet me in the lounge to discuss the condition of an acquaintance of mine."

"Dr. Rodden left the hospital ten minutes ago," she said apologetically.

"But he was supposed to speak with me!" H.G. exclaimed.

"I'm sorry. He won't be back on duty until the morning."

"Wait a minute!" H.G. exploded, turning purple. "You don't expect me to spend the night in that *lounge*, do you?"

"I'm sorry, sir, that's not my concern." She gestured to someone behind him. "Next, please."

Frustrated and helpless, H.G. turned and strode out of the hospital.

The cool night air was refreshing, and the fog softened the hard edges of the lights and muted the metallic traffic sounds. H.G. calmed himself, then started walking away from the hospital. When he got to the street, he wondered what he should do next, somewhat transfixed by the alien blinking of colored neon lights. Exhaustion came over him, so he sat down on the curb and tried to think out a logical course of action to follow. The first idea that crossed his mind was not a brilliant one; rather it was mundanely practical.

Get some rest.

Across the street were hotels, and their façades reminded him of nineteenth-century London. He hurried toward them, a homesick twinge in his empty stomach and several nostalgic tears running down his face. Then he angrily shook off those symptoms of self-pity. He didn't *need* a lot of internalized rubbish about the gay nineties and the good old days. What he needed was a decent night's sleep.

He entered the "Portrero Hotel & Rooming House (since 1929)" and started across a small lobby decorated with mildewing furniture and one sleeping black janitor. There was no one at the desk. He rang the night bell four times.

Five minutes later an ashen-gray black man shuffled from out of a dark hallway into the dimly lit area behind the desk. He rubbed his red eyes and pulled at the suspenders that held up his voluminous trousers over his otherwise bare frame.

"What you want, boy? Ain't no poon tang here no more, no sir. They all went uptown and took out business licenses when the new mayor got hisself elected."

"I'd like a room, please."

He put on a pair of rimless spectacles. "For the night?"

"My good man, what *else* would I want it for?"

The black man responded with a worn, yet timeless shrug, then placed a yellowing card and a pencil in front of Wells. "That'll be fourteen-fifty, please, sir."

H.G. dug into his pockets for the money, but all he found was a dollar-thirteen in small change. He frowned.

The black man blinked and waited. He was used to it.

Suddenly, H.G. grinned, for he remembered the traveler's checks he'd purchased from Amy Robbins earlier in the day. God, it seemed so bloody long ago! "Do you accept traveler's checks, sir?"

"As long as they ain't foreign."

H.G. chuckled at the unintended irony of the man's statement; he dug into his back pocket. Foreign, indeed! But now was no time to argue or make philosophic points. His body ached for a warm and soft bed.

The traveler's checks weren't in his pants pockets, so he reached into his coat. Ah, yes, a bed. No, a bath first. A hot, luxuriating bath. And then to bed.

Suddenly, he gasped and stepped back. His traveler's checks! He didn't have them! Were they lost or had he been robbed? He frantically went through his pockets again, but to no avail.

"Something wrong, sir?"

H.G. didn't answer. He turned and hurried out of the Portrero Hotel. Lacking a clear mind, an energetic body and the will to return to his first night's lair in the park, he went back to the hospital and once more entered the visitors' lounge.

Three small black children slept in the chair he once occupied while their fathers sat on the nearby couch playing cards. The other furniture was occupied, too. Beyond caring, H.G. lay down on the floor between the chair and the couch, and used a pile of the day's newspapers as a pillow. No one noticed; he could have been dying.

An ambulance shrieked home to the emergency ward, but H.G. did not lift his head. He—like the children—was learning; he could sleep anywhere.

An hour before her bedtime, Amy Robbins stood under the shower and let the hot spray loosen her neck and shoulder muscles, pleased that her life was her own. She had been free for a year now, in San Francisco—

the city of lights, restaurants and individuals—free to make her own way without compromise, free to say no, free to say yes, beholden to no one except herself. And she loved it. Against all odds, she had her own place, she was paying her bills and she didn't have to share a bathroom or a shower with anyone.

After a full ten minutes of muscle-relaxing pleasure, she made a languid turn, lifted her chin and allowed the water to fall directly upon her delicate face. She closed her eyes and smiled, then slowly raised her arms and leaned back so that the spray massaged her breasts and flat stomach. The routine irritants of the job were long forgotten; the tensions of the day melted. Life was good. Finally.

Refreshed, she turned off the water and stepped out onto a thick white carpet. The bathroom rapidly filled with the steam and scent of perfumed soap that followed her out of the shower. She leisurely dried herself, draped the towel over the side of the tub, then turned and reached for her robe, which hung on the door. Before she put it on, she looked into the fogged mirror and saw her own nude image softened and muted by the steam. She envisioned that she had just stepped out of an Impressionist painting. She was all pastels, and there were no shadows.

She left the bathroom and went down the creaky hallway into the living room of her one-bedroom, second-story apartment on Russian Hill. She crossed to her only expensive indulgence, the quadraphonic sound system, and put on a Viennese anthology of Mozart. Then she went into the kitchen, filled a crystal pitcher (a relic from her first marriage) and watered the potted plants in the apartment.

She returned to the kitchen, put away the leftover tuna salad, rinsed and stacked her dinner dishes. Chores finished, she poured herself a glass of chilled Chablis, padded back into the living room and curled up on the great, old sofa with that morning's *Chronicle*. The music swelled lightly and made her think of the one thing she truly coveted: a stone fireplace and the smell of burning oak. She smiled, dropped the paper on the floor, sipped her wine, leaned back and stared at the high ceiling. That would come. All in good time, and on her own terms. Right now she was enjoying the most precious gift of all—sweet solitude. Or was it?

The phone rang.

It was Harry, the junior executive with the leasing corporation. He wanted her to come down to this incredible Basque restaurant for drinks and frivolity.

"No, Harry, all I want to do is stay home."

He thought she was sick, offered his condolences and hung up.

She laughed, stretched, then settled back on the couch with a yawn and a smile. None of them really understood. It was as if empty rooms, place settings and beds assaulted their manhood. They couldn't stand for a woman to go about unescorted or to be alone. They could not feel the self-fulfillment of solitude.

Yet, she curled her toes under a pillow and reveled in it, for it meant that her world was her own. And— blessedly humane—she did not want others to have to depend on her. Never again did she want to imprison or be imprisoned as had been the case with her first marriage.

She got up, crossed the room and turned the record over. Then she went to her dining-room window and stared out at the trees, dimly lit from the street. She loved those trees; they were thin and delicate; they changed very slowly.

She returned to the couch for the last half of Mozart. She closed her eyes. Then, suddenly, her thoughts turned to that strange, naïve, almost helpless man, Mr. Wells from London. For the third time since she had left work. Why did his presence keep recurring in her mind? What was it about him? One moment he had seemed to be the archaic (yet debonair) lover, the next, he came across as an orphaned doll that needed dry cleaning. She did admit, however, that the combination could prove to be irresistible.

She wondered if he would call her as he had said, or if she would ever see him again. She shrugged, then burst out laughing, for she just remembered that poor Mr. Wells had left all of his traveler's checks at the bank.

Of course he would call again, and if she was still this curious and he didn't inquire first, she just might ask him what he was doing for lunch.

She drained her glass, yawned again, then got up and headed for bed. She stretched all the way down the hall, feeling drained and damned good. Ms. Amy Robbins was proud to be herself.

H.G. abruptly awoke to the smell and taste of stale newsprint. He lifted his head, blinked and saw that he had been sleeping with his face buried in the pile of newspapers. He cursed, then slowly stood. The lounge was empty, and bright sunlight shone in through the windows. He turned. The hospital seemed quiet and subdued. There were no crushes of people, no concerned doctors, frantic nurses or busy employees; not even the usual rush of sirens and ambulances. It was as if death and injury had to rest, too, and were waiting until the afternoon and evening (human frailty being more vulnerable then) to resume their normal pace.

He left the lounge and went down the corridor and into the men's room. He washed his face in a bright, porcelain sink and discovered that his two-day beard growth was somewhat noticeable. He frowned with displeasure, then sighed. Who would have thought to pack a razor on a trip through time? Then he sniffed himself.

"Whew."

Carrying a bottle of cologne along for the journey would not have been a bad idea, either. He frowned again, thought, then quickly removed his jacket, shirt and tie. He wet paper towels in the sink and proceeded to bathe himself. When he was finished with his torso, he gingerly lowered his trousers and shorts and washed below the waist. Then he redressed and smiled. A clean body made him feel civilized again.

As a final touch, he combed his hair with his fingers, then pushed and twisted his mustache into shape. He stepped back and regarded his countenance with admiration. He looked remarkably well given the lack of an adequate personal toilet.

He left the men's room wondering about the condition of Leslie John Stephenson. He hoped that the man would be well enough for the journey back to 1893. Then he cursed. How would he control Stephenson? How would he get the man back to the time machine? He wasn't a policeman, he was a writer and an inventor. Inventor? Ha! He thrust his jaw forward with determination. Then he'd bloody well just have to invent a way to handle his adversary.

He vigorously strode down the corridor, prepared to do battle at the reception center. He paused at the food machines long enough to purchase his morning cup of tea, swigged the lukewarm liquid down, then marched to the information desk. He forcefully asked to see Dr. Rodden. Much to his surprise, the nurse on duty was cooperative, and within minutes a harried, tired-looking man pushed through the corridor's double doors and approached him. A small plate on the man's long white coat above his left breast identified him as "Dr. A. Rodden. Staff."

"You wanted to see me?"

"My good man, I've been trying to see you for the past sixteen hours."

"Well, don't feel like the Lone Ranger. My wife's lawyer's been waiting for two and a half years." He emitted a dry laugh and started walking aimlessly toward the elevators like a man who never had time to catch up with himself. H.G. followed, scrambling to keep abreast of the foreboding M.D.

"Just what did you want?"

"A friend of mine is a patient of yours, and I would like to know how I can go about arranging for his release."

"See the cashier."

"Of course, but can you tell me if the man is in any condition to travel?"

"Sure. What's his name?"

"Leslie John Stephenson."

Rodden began flipping through medical charts on his metal clipboard.

"Although from what your nurses have told me, Stephenson has been registered as John Doe number sixteen," H.G. commented distastefully.

Rodden's eyes narrowed and he perused his charts more carefully. He stopped on a page, read it through, frowned and looked away. "Every so often—once a week, once a month—something unexpected happens around here for which medical science has no damned good explanation. This case was routine. We just wanted to look after him for a while." He sighed. "I'm sorry to have to report that the man died between two and four A.M. this morning."

SEVEN

"Dead?" H.G. gasped. "Dead?"

"I'm sorry."

"Can I see the body?"

"Wait a minute," said the doctor, suddenly suspicious. "Are you related to the deceased?"

"He doesn't have any relatives!"

"I'm sorry. I shouldn't have told you anything in the first place." He walked briskly away.

H.G. felt faint. He leaned against the wall of the corridor and used the railing (for convenience of the handicapped) to hold himself up. Remembering Mrs. Nelson's advice in the face of extreme stress (and bronchitis attacks), he forced himself to take six deep breaths. His head cleared, but he remained propped up by the wall, staring blankly at a rectangle of cool white light.

Stephenson dead? His life snuffed out by an alien mode of transportation? True, the chap had no doubt earned the full measure of a capital judgment, but he should not have died without first receiving a trial by jury. It was not a fitting end for an English gentleman, no matter how horrible his crimes might be. Killed by a motorcar, indeed! It was downright ignominious!

H.G. shuddered. The most ghastly thing of all about

the bizarre incident was the fact that Stephenson had died beyond his own time in a strange world where no one understood or cared that in this particular case the logical order of the universe had been violated. His cries of pain, his possible last-minute expressions of remorse had not been heard in 1893 London. Outside time, they had not been heard by anyone. The incident was more than unnatural; it was frightening. To be so alone, so totally lost in death. What would one's soul *do* on the eternity of a foreign time plane? There was no comfort to be taken in this death. None whatsoever. There would be no sighs of relief, either, for—outside time—the death had not occurred because the person did not exist. The ramifications were awesome, yet uncertain, and a great sadness came over H.G. What a brick to toss into the cogs of the Hegelian dialectic.

He stuffed his hands into his pockets, looked down and wandered along a corridor. He had been cheated. Stephenson was dead. He could not return home bearing the unholy grail. Justice would not be served. His own society would never know that their most base and vile member had finally gotten his comeuppance. God knows how long women would continue to walk the streets fearing that Jack the Ripper would materialize. And when H.G. did get home, he could not reveal his knowledge of Stephenson's demise, for they would think him insane. Alas, there would be no reporting of an extra-temporal, hence nonhistorical occurrence. The consequences were thus absurd because they would forever exist in one person's memory, and one person only. H.G.'s odyssey—which a short while ago he had considered to be a trip through time for the individual rights of man—had failed.

He continued wandering, and his shock passed, but the sadness remained. He remembered Stephenson, the university student, the athlete, the glib, cynical debater, the quick and charming young man who breezed through

Cambridge medical school. The surgeon, the healer, the aloof yet well-respected man. What if he *hadn't really* been Jack the Ripper? What if a mistake had been made or what if Stephenson had led him through time masquerading as a murderer? Was he, H.G. Wells, the butt of some fiendish practical joke? No, no, he told himself. Stephenson had not been fooling. There were no mistakes.

Well, then, so be it. What was done was finished. Leslie John—wherever you are—may you rest in peace despite your awful crimes.

H.G. sighed and straightened up. He saw that he was standing near the entrance to a large cafeteria full of people. The odor of hot food wafted out the door and assaulted his senses. He immediately felt weak, and saliva formed in his mouth. He read a placard by the door which announced that the daily breakfast special included two eggs, hash browns (whatever they might be), a rasher of bacon, English muffins, fruit cocktail and coffee all for only two dollars and seventy-five cents. He checked his funds. Eighty-seven cents. With stomach growling, he forced himself to turn and walk away from the cafeteria. Had he been home and in a similar predicament, he would have approached the proprietor of the inn and made some reasonable arrangement for sustenance, even if it meant sending the man a few shillings through the post later on. But here he had no credence or identification, and if he had learned one thing about the customs and mores of the people of 1979 it was that currency was king. Currency could get Jack the Ripper a suite at the Jack Tar. The lack of it could leave H.G. Wells neglected and starving in a pristine hospital corridor.

He rounded a corner, deep in thought. Logically, his primary goal now was to return to the Bank of England, explain that he no longer possessed his traveler's checks and attempt to get just compensation. But according to his rough calculations, eighty-seven cents would take him only about a half mile away from the bloody hospital and *then* what would he do? He hadn't the slightest idea. He might as well have been as far away from the Bank of England as San Francisco was from London or 1979 was from 1893.

He felt a rush of panic and would have gone berserk if he hadn't wandered around another corner and stumbled upon a bank of pay telephones. He stared. Coins clinked and indefatigable young men shouted into an electronic stratosphere about boys and girls, pounds and ounces, and sibling similarities.

A booth was open. He rushed into it, sat down, gazed at the telephone and for a moment wished that he could remove the plate from the front of the box and see what kind of machinery was inside. Instead, he read the instructions, deduced that he could afford to use the device, then removed the business card from his inside coat pocket and studied it. "Ms. Amy C. Robbins. Operations. The Bank of England, Ltd. 337 Sutter Street, San Francisco, California. 422-4316." Then he patiently recalled every detail of yesterday's conversation with Amy. He remembered that he had asked her to have lunch with him and that she had responded by referring to a telephone number on her calling card. The number in question, then, must be the seven-digit figure printed on the lower right-hand corner.

He glanced back at the telephone. But why were there *letters* on the push buttons? He thought hard for a few moments before sighing with resignation. There seemed to be no logical explanation. After all, "telephone" was spelled with a "ph" as opposed to an "f." What was the reason for that?

Suddenly, H.G. cursed his procrastination. Why was he hesitating? If he had the courage to push the time machine's Accelerator Helm Lever forward why was he balking at a telephone? Was he actually afraid of technology now? Perhaps so.

He straightened up. Had his mind slipped back to the Middle Ages due to some unknown and insidious energy field lurking in the Gaussian coordinates? How could he fear progress? That which possessed the key to the salvation of mankind? The telephone was a modern communication device that existed for public convenience and service. Very simply, people could talk to each other when they were miles apart. Business matters could be dealt with. News could be spread. Rumors squashed. Truths upheld. Thoughts and feelings exchanged. Intimacies shared. There might be millions of people between H.G. and Amy Robbins, yet no one else would know what they said to each other. Fear the telephone? Blasphemy! A priest might as well denounce the Pope.

H.G. removed the receiver from its cradle, placed it to his ear (as he had seen others do) and dropped his dime into the coin slot. Ding. Clink. Click-clack, crackle. Dot, dot, dot, dot. Rat-a-tat-tat. Click-clack. Crackle, crackle. Buzz. Buzz. More buzz. He pushed the buttons that corresponded to the seven digits on the card, held his breath and waited. There was another series of clicks, a static hush and then a ringing noise that sounded like a muffled bird call.

H.G. giggled with excitement.

"Bank of England, may I help you?"

"Marvelous," he inadvertently mumbled into the receiver.

"Bank of England, may I help you?" the operator repeated, slightly irritated.

H.G. opened his mouth to reply, then stopped. He had no idea what to say. He stared at the mouthpiece and was speechless.

The operator hung up on him.

Mortified, H.G. blushed, then muttered, "What bloody

nerve!" He put the telephone back onto its cradle, dug out another dime and rehearsed several lines for his next attempt.

He pushed the second dime into the slot and dialed again.

"Bank of England, may I help you?"

He took a deep breath, then forced out the words. "Hello, Miss Robbins, how are you this fine morning? This is Mr. Wells from London, that is, if you don't recognize my voice, but I'm sure that you haven't forgotten—"

"Sir, I am not Miss Robbins. Would you like me to connect you?"

"Why . . . certainly. Of course." He hesitated and his mind raced. The telephone system must be more complicated than he had originally thought. Lines must be multiples of hundreds and they must intersect with multiples of thousands and so on. The proliferation must be astounding. "Yes, please."

But the operator had already placed him on hold. He sighed, leaned back against the side of the booth and listened to an electronic symphony that he did not understand. Yet, the sounds were actually quite pleasing. He grinned, closed his eyes and tapped his foot to the irregular beat of the alien melody.

Suddenly, there was an amplified click. "This is Amy Robbins." The voice was muted, aloof, breathless, yet definitely *her*. H.G. felt extremely relieved.

He blurted out his memorized opening. "Hello, Miss Robbins. How nice you look this morning."

"Hello?"

"Hello." He grinned foolishly.

"Who is this?"

"You mean, you don't recognize me?"

"How *could* I recognize you?"

"We met yesterday."

"Is this *Frank*?"

H.G. scowled and blushed again. "No, this isn't Frank. You are speaking with Mr. Wells from London. *Remember?*"

"Oh, *yes*," she replied brightly, then emitted a girlish peal of laughter. "I was hoping you'd call."

"You were?"

"Well, not exactly. I *knew* you would call."

"You *did?*" He gasped, immediately fearful that some 1979ers possessed extrasensory perception. If she had been reading his mind from the beginning, he would be most embarrassed, indeed.

"Sure. Anyone who leaves fifteen hundred dollars in traveler's checks on my desk and doesn't call to find out where they are would be pretty strange, don't you think?"

"You've got a point." He sagged forward with relief. Thank God. She had his money. It wasn't lost, and he hadn't been robbed. Life would go on, and he would get home again—*after* a vacation in the wilderness. He smiled impishly. Everything was going to be all right.

"Mr. Wells, are you there?"

"Of course, I'm here."

"Did you hear what I just said?"

"Certainly, but that wasn't why I telephoned."

"It *wasn't?*"

"No, it wasn't. I *was* wondering if you would have lunch with me today."

"I'd love to." She sounded awed and quiet.

"Good, then. I'm absolutely delighted. May I call you Amy?"

"Yes."

"Where shall we meet, Amy?"

"Anywhere you like."

"Why don't we meet here?"

"What time?"

"The sooner the better. I'm famished."

"Come to think of it, so am I. Where are you?"

"San Francisco General Hospital."

"*What*? Is there something wrong?"

"There's nothing to be done," he replied calmly. "I'll explain it all when you get here."

"Are you sure that today's a good day for lunch?"

"My dear girl, I've never been more certain of anything in my entire life."

"Okay. I'll see you around eleven."

"And Amy? Would you be so kind as to bring my traveler's checks with you? It *would* save me a trip to the bank, and I *am* a little short of funds."

She agreed and hung up.

He left the phone booth feeling very good about himself. He ambled along and put the sirens and the urgent broadcasts for doctors out of his head. Amy was foremost in his mind. Her brown hair, her dark eyes, her delicate mouth, her curvaceous figure. It was amazing to him how quickly he had conjured up a mental picture of her purely on the basis of her voice transmitted by the telephone.

He passed the visitors' lounge and did not notice that once again it was filled with anxious yet hopeless minions of the neglected class; people who understood less about the world of 1979 than the visitor, incognito, from the nineteenth century.

Oblivious, he made his way out the doors of the emergency ward dreaming about his telephone conversation. He *had* to learn more about that method of communication. It was revolutionary; it was necessary; it was worthy of man. He burst out with a gleeful laugh.

"*Whoosh!* What a thought!"

Very excited, he hurried up the walkway, for he had just been struck with an idea. Telephone signals, he assumed, were transmitted by magnetic, electrical fields of energy—the *same* kinds of fields that powered his rotations through time. Therefore, he postulated, once he had a working knowledge of the telephone, it shouldn't be too difficult to adapt the device so that one could speak both into history and into the future. Telephoning through time! Speaking with dead relatives and unborn children. Querying Queen Victoria, the Tsar of Russia or a future leader of, say, the Chinese. How about *that* for the greatness and immortality of the human being?

"Whoosh, indeed!"

He was deep in thought picturing a telephone installed inside his time machine when he heard a horn toot several times. He turned and saw her waving at him from a sleek blue vehicle. He smiled, waved back and approached the automobile. Before he climbed inside, he read silver letters on the rear spelling "Honda Accord."

The interior of the machine was attractive and clean —nothing like the taxi he had ridden in the day before. He eased back in the seat.

"Oh, before I forget . . ." She smiled and handed him his traveler's checks.

"Thank you." He looked around. "What a lovely motorcar. Beautiful. Simply beautiful." He felt the dash.

"It's not exactly a Rolls-Royce," she said.

"No, it certainly isn't," he replied vaguely.

"Would you like to drive it?"

"I'm afraid I don't know how." He grinned dreamily. "But someday I'd like to learn."

"That can be arranged." She pulled away from the curb and began driving down the street.

Although he had learned a great deal about the fundamentals of driving from observing the cab driver the day before, he watched Amy's movements carefully. He definitely wanted to try his hand at the wheel before he went home.

" 'D' stands for 'drive' and 'R' indicates 'reverse'?" he asked.

She glanced at him with surprise. "Surely you've ridden in cars with automatic transmissions before."

"Not very often."

She laughed. "Ah, the British! So traditional." She gestured at the floor. "Look, ma, no clutch. Just a brake." She touched it with her foot. "And a gas pedal." She pressed it down all the way and accelerated up a ramp and past a road sign that read "Bayshore Freeway."

He leaned back and grinned with pleasure, thinking that linear speed definitely could become addicting.

"Herbert, what were you doing at the hospital?" she asked in more serious tones.

He frowned and looked away. "Oh, yes. *That.*" Then he briefly explained that Leslie John Stephenson had been accidentally struck and killed by an automobile.

"Oh, *no!*" She drove with her left hand, placed her right hand around his and held it tightly. "I'm *so* sorry!"

"So am I."

"Is there anything I can do? I mean, I know he was your friend, and I know—"

"He wasn't my friend."

"Huh?" She raised her eyebrows. "But yesterday you said—"

"He was no one's friend."

"I don't understand."

"I'd just rather not discuss it, if you don't mind."

"Oh." She took her hand away. "Okay."

He felt small. She didn't say any more, and very quickly the silence became heavy. He grew worried and did not enjoy the scenery, his first trip on a modern highway or the contagious rhythm of high-speed driving. Certainly, the death of Stephenson meant that now he could leisurely investigate 1979. He could be thorough and scientific. And if he survived his own archaisms, he could return to his own time with the vast knowledge of modern mankind.

But those thoughts didn't help. Here he was with a perfectly gorgeous young lady and he could not bring himself even to talk to her. He was embarrassed that he had cut her off so abruptly. He supposed that they would have a brief lunch somewhere and that that would be the end of it.

He sighed, looked out the window and tried to think of something pleasant to say once they arrived at their destination.

They parked and got out of the car. H.G. saw rows of small shops and markets; beyond were the masts and spars of a fishing fleet at anchor. Gulls circled, cried and dove. He felt very much at home, for aside from the architecture, he could have been strolling through the restful streets of Eastbourne. The smells and the sounds were the same. He breathed deeply and grinned.

"Ah, the waterfront!" he cried. "I love the seashore. How on earth did you know?"

She faced him, her eyes full of concern, her hands clasped in back of her. "Look, Herbert, I'm sorry about the way I acted in the car, but I've never really been very good when it came to things like death. If you don't want to talk about it, that's your choice and not mine. So, I apologize, okay?"

His stomach slipped, and his body surged with feeling. Before he knew what he was doing, he reached out, grasped her shoulders and pulled her close. His cheek touched her hair; she smelled clean and fresh—like the sea—with just a hint of perfume, just enough to make his knees sag and his hands tremble. She returned the embrace, and he felt her shiver slightly. He almost told her right then and there who he really was.

She took his hand and led him across the macadam to the canopied boardwalk that paralleled the small establishments of Fisherman's Wharf.

"Do you like seafood?" she asked gaily.

"Right now, I'd eat anything," he replied.

And so they entered Alioto's, and the maître d' seated them at a table by a large window that had a panoramic view of the wharf, the fishing fleet, the bay and the green mountains of Marin County. But what commanded his immediate attention, what he gazed at in awe was the Golden Gate Bridge. In his view, the massive twin towers, the suspension cables, the mile-long span stood as a monument to the infinite capabilities of man.

"*Magnificent,*" he exclaimed.

"It is a nice view, isn't it?" said the waiter who had been hovering near their table for several minutes.

"View, *indeed!* It's that *bridge!* It's both impossible and spectacular! I never could've *imagined!* The men who built it are geniuses, you hear? Pure geniuses!"

"Yes, sir," said the waiter, blushing at the show of overexuberance, yet managing a thin smile.

"My good man, how might one contact them and query them about their construction techniques?"

The waiter looked around, then replied discreetly, "I doubt that would be possible, sir, since the bridge was completed in 1937."

"Oh." H.G. stiffened and turned away from the window. "Oh, yes. Quite impossible."

Amy hid behind her menu and warily glanced at H.G. over the top.

"Would the lady and the gentleman care for a cocktail?" the waiter asked with a slight Italian lilt to his words.

"I'd love some wine," said Amy.

"A smashing idea," concurred H.G. He lifted his eyes to the waiter. "You wouldn't just happen to have a *grand cru* Chablis, would you?"

"Any particular *château*, sir?"

"I'd prefer a *château de grenouille*, vintage 1890, actually."

"I believe that the oldest *grenouille* that we have in the cellar is a 1976," he replied smoothly.

H.G. turned crimson at his faux pas, realizing too late that white wines turned to vinegar if aged for longer than three years.

"Could I interest you in a California Riesling, sir?"

"We'll try the 1976 *grenouille*, thank you."

"An excellent choice, sir." The waiter bowed slightly and left. H.G. got the distinct impression that the man would have said the same thing had the order been stale beer.

The wine was extremely good, but Amy did not have the courage to admit that she would have preferred the California Riesling. She ordered abalone, and he tried—devoured, actually—the scallops. The lunch was fun and the atmosphere perfect, although she began to suspect that there was something significantly wrong with the behavior and mannerisms of her companion. He kept questioning her about things that she had always taken for granted. And his references weren't quite right. They lacked the brevity and the salt that she was used to in the speech of other men. True, it could be merely the charm of an English gentleman. Or perhaps she had been in San Francisco too long.

He sipped his tea, then leaned back in his chair, delightfully sated, mind still buzzing from half a bottle of Chablis. He knew he was talking with too much flourish, but he didn't care. For the first time since landing in 1979 he felt completely at ease.

"Good?" she asked.

"My dear girl, the slight touch of crushed herbs, the

perfect blending of lemon and lightly salted butter, the thin, browned crusts—along with this exotic vegetable . . . I have never eaten a finer meal. And to dine with such a charming companion makes the entire affair a most pleasant experience, indeed."

"But then again, it's not McDonald's," she said with tongue in cheek.

He looked away, thought, then turned back. "No, it isn't." He was quite serious. "You're right."

She looked at him askance, sighed and poured herself the last of the wine. Was he putting her *on*?

"The view, that bridge . . . this is all too, too memorable."

"Herbert, are you an actor?"

He laughed. "Good God, no. If I were, I certainly would not be here." He laughed again, a faraway twinkle in his eye.

"Where would you be?"

"Oh, I don't know. Probably back in London, strutting across the boards of the Lyceum doing Addison's *Cato*."

"Addison's *Cato*?" she exclaimed with disbelief.

"Maybe not. Perhaps I'd fare better in *Lady Windermere's Fan*. I must tell you, though, I detest the theater."

"You like movies then?"

He was momentarily speechless.

"What's your favorite movie, Herbert?"

Right then and there he thought that she had finally caught him and for what seemed like the longest time could not think of a response. Finally, he decided that honesty was his only recourse. "I don't have a favorite movie," he said candidly.

"How perceptive you are."

He blushed at the compliment and immediately changed the subject. "My dear girl, how is it that a divorced young lady like yourself can make her way so easily in the world without a male companion?"

"Who said it was easy?"

"Well, I mean, you drive your own motorcar, you have a respectable position of employment, you live in a comfortable flat, no doubt."

"So I work hard. How does that make me any different from an English divorcee?"

"An English divorcee would go home to her parents in the country," he replied without thinking.

She laughed. "Either that's bullshit or you've been living in a cave, population under two hundred."

The words stung him. She excused herself to visit the ladies' room, and he certainly hoped that it wasn't for a breath of fresh air. While she was gone, he tried to sort out his thoughts. He felt cheap. She didn't know who he was, and until she did, he would feel like he was involved in an adulterous affair, for those things thrived on deception. He had to make a decision soon. Either he had to tell her about Stephenson and himself or he had to break it off.

Break *what* off? She hadn't asked him to become a suitor. Why the bald-faced assumption?

"Hmmm." Even though Amy Robbins had a good life, he sensed that she lacked something. It definitely wasn't men, for she attracted them. Rather, he perceived, it was what a *particular* kind of man could give her. A sudden thought struck him and he grinned. Could that person be H. G. Wells?

She returned to the table and smiled brightly at him. She had freshened up and applied new makeup, but the hint of red in her cheeks from the wine remained. She looked both ravishing and angelic.

"Tell me, Amy—"

"Oh, no. No more questions. You're avoiding me."

"I am?"

"Of course. All I've done is provide you with answers. I don't know anything about you."

"Why, that's absolutely ridiculous." With a nervous swing of his hand, he knocked over his empty wine glass.

"Are you married, Herbert? Is that the reason you're being so strange? Is that it?"

"Good Lord, no!"

"Well, then?"

"Well, then, what?"

"Are you sure you're not married?"

"Well, I was certain the last time I was home," he said lightly, then added, "But if I were, then I'd be paying my housekeeper, Mrs. Nelson, a decent living wage for nothing, wouldn't I?"

"Ah. You're *living* with someone."

"She occupies the upstairs bedroom off the kitchen along with pictures of her deceased husband. She is sixty-seven and makes the most delicious mint-flavored roast mutton I have ever tasted."

Amy laughed; she was relieved.

"The French poet Charles Baudelaire once said, 'Marriage is like a cage. Those who are inside want to get out, and those who are outside want to get in.' "

"You're divorced, then?"

"I told you that, didn't I?"

"No, you didn't."

"Oh." He blushed. "Well, yes, I'm divorced." He sighed. "I suppose that makes me unsuitable."

"For what? The priesthood?"

"I was unsuitable for that halfway through grammar school," he said ruefully.

"Just to remind you, I'm divorced, too, Herbert. Does that make me unsuitable?"

Suddenly very warm, he loosened his collar and wiped perspiration off his face with his napkin.

"Well? Does it?"

He supposed that it did when it came to the banns and vows of a proper marriage. One's bride should be Venus Urania—distant, unattainable, yet endlessly pursued and ultimately seduced on a celestial bed of white carnations. A divorcee did not qualify. He scowled because he knew that those thoughts were incompatible with his enlightened views on social change and scientific progress. But at least he did have the good sense to keep those thoughts to himself.

"No. But you're different. You're an American." He fervently wished that he had purchased a book on contemporary sociology before keeping the luncheon engagement with her.

"Cop out," she sung.

"I beg your pardon?"

"Never mind," she said. "Tell me what happened to your first marriage."

"I ran off with one of my students."

"You bastard," she said lightly. "Why?"

"I didn't want to be a suburban breadwinner."

"Now *that*, I can understand." She paused, leaned forward and gently touched his hand. "Do you still love her?"

"I don't know. I probably never really had a chance to find out."

"What went wrong?"

"I was at the university when I met her. She was my first love and . . . my first cousin."

Amy's eyes widened.

"After we were married, I didn't have a job or any money, so we took up chambers in her aunt's house, and auntie's little ceramics were all over the place. Knickknacks, we call them. There wasn't any place for me to sit, let alone write or tinker. We never talked. To make matters worse, when we went to bed, Isabel wouldn't even undress in front of me. Do you know that to this day I have never even *seen* her body? We weren't exactly David and Bathsheba, if you know what I mean."

She laughed. "Thank God you didn't have any children."

He was startled by her thought, then suddenly laughed, too, and the mirth was good, for he felt cleansed and worthy now. She was a child of the twentieth century and had told him that she had had liberal-minded parents, a wonderful childhood and a good education. Yet she had left college to spend two years in a marriage that was as empty and frustrating as his. Whereas he was the child of the nineteenth century and was forced to accept the concept of an angry God. He had had a wretched childhood, the family always bordering on poverty. The fact that he had even made it to the university was miraculous.

They were totally different. They might as well have been from separate planets as well as being from different centuries. And yet, they had ended up in the same place. Both had endured problems and failures. He sensed that they were equals; certainly, neither one was the product of a Utopia.

He looked at the bill for the lunch. $79.83. The price for the wine, alone, had been $55.00. He grinned. No, she was not a perfect human being. He wasn't, either. And at prices like that, they hadn't exactly eaten lunch at the Erewhon Restaurant in the Garden of Eden. The world, then, did not seem so alien.

They left Alioto's hand in hand.

"Do you have a previous engagement for this evening?" He slipped his arm around her waist and felt proud.

"Oh, no, sir," she teased.

"Shall we have dinner together?"

"Why not?" Her eyes sparkled.

"Why not, indeed."

"I must warn you, though, that you are not the kind of man that I normally go out with."

"Oh?"

"I've never met anyone quite like you before."

"I'll accept that as a compliment and meet you at your bank this evening, then?"

"Around six. Can I take you back to town?"

"No thank you, Amy. I want to browse awhile."

"Have fun," she called. "And don't hurt yourself."

He watched her cross the parking lot. He could tell from her stride that she was happy. When she kept turning around to wave, he discerned that she was touched by him. He grinned foolishly and knew that he should be afraid, but he was already looking forward to six o'clock outside the Bank of England.

Enough of that. He purposely turned away and lifted his head. It was time to throw off the idle and selfish thoughts of the romantic seeking a lover's caress. He could do that in any age. He objectively scanned the city before him and strode away from Fisherman's Wharf.

H.G. spent the entire afternoon at the San Francisco International Airport examining the current state of the art of winged flight. He would have stayed there for days, but he did not want to miss his dinner engagement with Amy Robbins, so he reluctantly climbed aboard an Airporter Coach for the ride back into the city. As the bulky vehicle pitched and yawed north along the Bayshore, he settled back in the plush chair and recalled what he had seen.

The most distressing discovery had been "airport security"—employed to combat a particularly ominous and vile phenomenon called "air piracy." And to think that just a few days ago he had predicated that crime would be eradicated in the late twentieth century. He had been wrong. Mankind's sense of morality had not kept pace with advanced technology. He would have to warn others of that fact when he returned home.

He shuddered. Thank God, Leslie John Stephenson would never have an opportunity to travel on an airship!

Then there had been the giant airliners themselves. He had watched them for hours, and his spirits had risen considerably. On the ground they had maneuvered like prehistoric pterodactyls gathering the strength to fly. But when they were launched a transformation took place. They leaped and soared into space—glistening in the sun and rivaling any celestial angel that William Blake had ever etched.

H.G. had tried to find out what part—if any—he had played in the development of the aircraft, but had been unsuccessful, airport security being what it was. Perhaps another day.

He climbed off the Airporter Coach at Taylor and O'Farrell, then briskly made his way through crowds of pedestrians to the Bank of England. He pushed a button on his digital watch and saw that he was half an hour early. He had enough time to learn more about his new environs, and hence appear less of a naïve fool in Amy's eyes. He impulsively grinned. If worse came to worst, he could always discuss aerodynamics over dinner.

He saw a newsstand across the street where men in suits browsed. He went over to the concession, hoping to find a pocket-sized history of the twentieth century. Instead, he found a day-old edition of the London *Times* for which he paid the grizzled and handicapped proprietor one dollar. Reminding himself not to be provincial, he tucked the newspaper under his arm (but in all truth, thank God *The Times* still existed) and continued to inspect the offerings.

He saw a magazine with an abstract design on its front and picked it up. It was titled *Scientific American*, and he flipped through it until he came to an article that captured his attention: "Wind Turbines—a Way into the Twenty-first Century."

The piece began by capsulating the depletion of oil and natural gas fields, the dangers and limitations of nuclear power (of which he knew nothing) and the impracticality of harnessing the sun in the next few decades.

It proposed as an alternative the use of wind to power the enormous electrical plants which were so necessary for the survival of modern civilization "as we now know it." The next page pictured wind-turbine systems already in use. The devices were short, squat and as unlike windmills as a cable car was an airliner. And yet H.G. understood. As opposed to something taken from the ground and burned, the wind *always* blew no matter what. Seafarers, for example, had been aware of the majestic and limitless power of the wind for centuries, H.G. told himself. And yet, so far it *wasn't* an integral part of this great, advanced technology? He was amazed and continued reading. The article concluded that mankind had to harness the wind in order to survive and progress. H.G. shrugged with disgust and replaced the magazine in the rack.

"I could have told them that eighty-six years ago," he muttered.

From another rack he lifted off a resplendent, opulent publication titled *Penthouse*. On the cover was the diffuse photograph of a scantily clad young lady, perhaps the most beautiful example of a female that he had ever seen. He stared, unabashedly meeting the eyes in the photograph, half thinking that they promised him something intimate. And they *did*! Great Scott, it was the opposite of experiencing Henry James, he told himself. One didn't want to skip a damned thing!

His hands fluttering, he carefully opened the magazine and looked farther. He came to a layout called "Scarlett," and almost buried his face in the pages. Talk about never seeing Isabel's body during two years of marriage! Here—in front of the entire world—was a hazel-eyed nymph with nothing between her and her readers except a pair of long white stockings! And *those* were discarded on the next page! He blushed, but could not stop staring at Scarlett. At first she was seen bathing and preparing to retire. Then she was on her bed, eyes closed, smiling, as if dreaming.

H.G. turned the page. Scarlett's right hand was between her legs now, her left upon her breast, her mouth open with self-induced passion. Then she was sitting up, looking surprised—as if someone unseen had stolen into her room. Her expression changed, and on the last page she was lying back, beckoning the reader to join her on the bed and taste her charms.

"Whoosh!" (And good-bye, Queen Victoria, wherever you are!)

H.G. realized that he was gazing at something for which he could be jailed back in his own time. The relaxation of censorship standards was obviously incredible. He definitely approved, but he couldn't fathom the change. If he weren't looking at the alabaster inner thighs of an exquisite young lass, he would not have believed it. His heart swelled with both lust for Scarlett and pride for whoever published the magazine. Why *shouldn't* a free man be able to admire the unfettered beauty of the female form? And if governments had finally stopped legislating morality, then maybe mankind *had* taken a giant step toward Utopia.

"You going to buy it or wear it out?"

H.G. jumped and turned. The proprietor of the newsstand was frowning at him from a wheelchair, his hands spread for emphasis. H.G. blushed, jammed the *Penthouse* back into the rack and moved away, fighting an erection that would not subside. He felt shameful and cursed himself. Why should he react that way? What the devil was wrong with nude and alluring women? *Nothing!* It was the Church, he angrily thought, the Church, mother, the environment at Up Park, the early school masters and the stifling effects of Victoria's reign. He must change his behavior; he must make his emotions as liberated as his intellect; he must free *himself* from the concept of original sin before he could even consider returning home to significantly alter the bumbling course of mankind's history.

Another time. Amy was waiting. And thank God he could finally straighten all the way up when she saw him, turned, smiled and waved.

She took him to the Ben Jonson for drinks and dinner, and he was delighted, for the decor of the restaurant was authentic Elizabethan London. And he was pleased to be inside a room where for once he was not faced with synthetic materials. The tables were actually made from wood, the carpets from wool, the napkins from linen, the silverware from pewter. (In fact, it was imitation pewter, but he could not tell the difference.) It made him unusually relaxed and comfortable to be in an environment that was real.

The food was excellent and made him proud that he was an Englishman. And since the gin was Bombay, he drank too much of it and waxed eloquent throughout the entire meal. With sweeping gestures, he spoke about the need to take a fresh look at John Stuart Mill's utilitarian notions, given the energy crisis and the drain on the world's natural resources. Wind machines weren't the answer—mankind needed to rethink its priorities and honestly admit that pleasure was its ultimate goal. And so on.

The only problem was that he laced his limited knowledge of 1979 with phrases and references that were a century old. He even commented, with a wild stab at sophistication, that the success of *Penthouse* was like what would have happened much earlier if post-Sedanist sentiment had prevailed.

That was it. No more. Despite his wit and charm, he

was driving her crazy. "Herbert, you're either an actor or an anachronism."

"I'm neither."

"Well, *something's* different about you! You're the most well-educated, well-read man I've ever gone out with, but where have you *been* for the past ten years?"

"Are you saying that I'm naïve?" he asked, blushing.

"*Oh, no.*"

He grinned and recovered. "Well, my audacity compensates for my innocence."

She laughed with delight, shook her head and gave him a look that was full of tenderness and admiration.

He knew then that he had already begun to court this girl in earnest and that his advances were working. He shivered with pleasure and felt warm all over. What he didn't know was that if she had not been interested in the first place, he might as well have tried to charm a mother superior in the order of St. Teresa. She chose her men now, having been chosen once in her life, which had been one time too many.

When they left the restaurant, H.G. fell silent—thanks to the sobering effects of several cups of tea and the realization that he was showing too much of his true identity. He felt a twinge of guilt that was stronger than the ones that had come over him during lunch at Alioto's. He knew that things had gone too far with Amy, and he wrestled with his conscience. What was he going to say to her? More important, how the devil was he going to say it?

They drove through the city, and a light mist began falling.

"Have you seen *Star Wars?*" she asked. "It just came out again."

"I beg your pardon?"

"*Star Wars.* Have you seen it?"

"Did you say star . . . *wars?*" He straightened up and

---

slowly turned to her, mind racing with questions that he was afraid to ask.

"Oh, come on, Herbert, will you quit putting me on? You know, the *movie!*"

"No," he gulped. "I haven't seen it."

"You *haven't?*"

"I've been rather busy."

"Boy, you really did need a vacation, didn't you?"

And so he found himself next to her inside a theater that was not as impressive as some of the great halls he had been to in London, although the seats were infinitely more relaxing. If nothing else, he thought flippantly, mankind has learned how to build comfortable furniture in the last eighty-six years.

The curtains parted, revealing, instead of a naked stage, a giant square of white that he did not comprehend.

"A long time ago in a galaxy far away," the entertainment began. A book projected on a screen? H.G. thought. Then he gasped and inadvertently ducked down below the seat in front of him, for two strange-looking air . . . No, they *weren't* airships, they were . . . *space* ships? Good God, they were firing at each other, and the sound was deafening! Who would have believed this after dozing through a staid performance of *The Importance of Being Earnest* with Isabel less than a year and a half ago? He peeked up over the back of the chair and saw the large ship swallow up the smaller one.

Amy turned and laughed at him. "Herbert, quit putting me on," she whispered. "You're worse than a kid."

H.G. composed himself and sat up straight, his eyes never leaving the screen. The magic of the film was overwhelming, the illusion so complete that he assumed his time machine had taken him into a future he never would have dreamed possible. Not that it was Utopian, either. Far from it. True, there had been the delightful little mechanical men who could think electronically, but what of the weapons, the ominous death star? Annihilation of worlds at the push of a button? The glorification of the evil side of human nature? Why, Darth Vader made someone like Jack the Ripper seem insignificant. After all, what were a few murdered courtesans compared to the destruction of entire cultures? Obviously, evil had not vanished with the dawn of a new age. Stephenson—damn his soul—may have been right.

H.G. sighed. He had glimpsed the future of the future and had seen how mankind could perversely turn progress into cataclysmic horror. Could he really have expected anything else? Perhaps not. But he *could* warn people against it.

Nevertheless, he was depressed, for the vision of the entertainment was twisted. The obsession was with how mankind in the future could use a fantastic technology to prolong oppression, enslavement and violence. That good had so blithely triumphed was not convincing to H.G. *Star Wars*, he opined, could have been written by Seneca.

Disturbed, H.G. left the theater numb. He kept his mouth shut and tried to smile and appear satisfied like other audience members.

"Like it?" she asked.

"It was interesting," he replied with deliberate ambiguity.

"Yeah. A little simplistic, but a lot of fun."

Simplistic? What did this girl know of? Were there *already* civilizations out there in space? He did not have the courage to ask.

"Maybe tomorrow night we can see something else," she said casually, then caught herself. "I mean, if you don't have any other plans."

He grinned. He didn't and he wouldn't. Obviously, she wanted to be with him, and that was the most reassuring thought he'd had since dinner.

She took him back to her apartment and nonchalantly invited him up for a drink. If he had not grown accustomed to her subtle directness, he would have been astonished, for never before had a female asked him anywhere.

Still, that was the most radical change in social behavior he had experienced yet. The freedom of a woman to take the initiative, which throughout history had been a masculine prerogative. He wondered how long the change had been the norm and what modern man thought of it. He would have to ask her. But later. This was, to use an image, her dance, and she was definitely in the lead.

He immediately liked the inside of her flat because it was old, yet had been remodeled to suit her tastes. Like the Ben Jonson, everything was real here—tables, chair, rugs, walls and bookcases. He didn't comment, but he sensed that some people in 1979 may not be all that thrilled with the fecund abundance of synthetic, imitative materials. He wondered, did that imply that there was a common fear of the future?

She took his coat and gestured at her couch. He sat down rigidly, uncertain and nervous in this, his first truly private encounter with a 1979er.

She returned with two glasses of chilled white wine, set them down on the table in front of the couch, smiled and asked him if he liked Mozart.

"I love Mozart," he replied, relieved that he would not have to comment on contemporary music.

A wall of sound came from across the room and wrapped around his senses. Surprised, he looked up and saw that she had engaged an electronic music device that obviously was the current version of the gramophone. Never had he heard such beautiful melodies— so crystal clear, so pleasing to the ears. He sighed, closed his eyes, leaned back and for a moment imagined that the entire London Symphony Orchestra was in the room playing for just him and her. He was transported, his nervousness swept away by the delicious flights of an eighteenth-century concerto.

"It's a quad system. Nice, huh?"

He nodded.

"I think I'll change. Look around if you want to." She left the room.

He got up to explore the flat and immediately saw a beige telephone on the floor next to a rocking chair across the room. He went over and carefully inspected it. He ached to dismantle the device, but he knew it wouldn't be cricket without asking Amy for permission first. Then again, just how did one go about phrasing such a question? Excuse me, may I have a look inside your telephone? No, no, that wasn't right. He sighed.

Finally, his curiosity got the better of him. He fished in his pocket, came up with a dime and used it—as he would a halfpenny back home—to unscrew the housing from the base. He lifted the cover off and grinned at the minute, complex circuitry. It reminded him of the time machine's RRL components which had been so difficult to assemble; except that all his wiring had been black.

"Whoosh!" What a deceptively simple idea! If one used colored wire to code the circuits, one eliminated the possibility of serious error.

"Beep! Beep! Beep! Beep!"

He gasped and straightened up. What was that noise? What had he done? He frantically inspected the telephone, but the beeping continued. In a panic, he quickly reassembled the device, but it was only when he finally but the receiver back onto its cradle that the noise stopped.

He retreated to the couch, took a large swallow of wine and calmed himself. Muck about with the technology of this age and it ends up shrieking at you, he muttered to himself.

She came back into the room, having brushed her hair

and changed into rather curious clothes. The shirt, a pullover, was common enough, but the other garment resembled a blacksmith's coveralls with a zipper that ran straight down the front. Interesting. Nevertheless, she looked ravishing, and thank the god of decorum she hadn't put on any more of her perfume.

She settled down into the pillows on the other side of the couch and tucked her toes under a cushion. Then she sipped her wine. She held the glass close to her lips and smiled at him over the edge.

They talked lightly of music and books, Amy being direct about what she liked and didn't like. H.G. was cautious if she mentioned something that he hadn't heard of, but once he got the drift of a particular philosophic view, he did allow himself to expand and expound. She was pleased, for he seemed genuinely interested in her opinions, which placed him apart from most of the men she knew.

"You know, Amy, when two people can communicate in an atmosphere like this without fear of malicious gossip, who needs marriage? Aside from religion, it's the most worthless institution I can think of."

She laughed. "Well, then, a woman would never have to worry about *you* proposing, would she?"

"My dear lady, I'm quite serious. I mean, I've never been able to understand—for example—why two people in love needed a marriage license before they could get into bed together." He spread his hands.

"Who says they do?" She smiled playfully. "As a matter of fact, who says they even have to be in love?"

He gave her a quick glance, then looked away and fooled with his mustache. "Well, I've published a number of articles on free love, but I'm not sure I'd go *that* far."

"*Free love?*" She laughed again. "I haven't heard that term since the eighth grade!"

"Oh, really? What would you call it, then?"

"What's wrong with 'The Sexual Revolution'? Or haven't you heard of that, either?"

Sexual revolution? My God, he thought, what did it *mean*? There were so *many* connotations. He grinned. "May I ask *who* is revolting against *whom*?"

"That all depends on the company you keep, doesn't it?" She replied in a low voice, then moved nearer to him.

He sat up straight. His head was buzzing again, and he didn't know what to do with his hands. Given her close proximity, he had no place to put them. Suddenly, he discovered his knees and hung onto them for dear life. There was a long pause.

"This has been a delightful evening," he managed to comment.

She nodded. "It's certainly nice to meet someone you can really talk to for a change."

"Isn't it? Especially when you share the same views."

"Who said I agreed with you?"

Surprised, H.G. raised his eyebrows, lifted his chin and listened.

"I mean, I don't happen to believe that religion is obsolete."

"You don't?"

"No, and I happen to think that marriage is a good way of keeping records. Especially if children are involved."

"Records? All they do is perpetuate bureaucracy."

"You're beginning to sound like an anarchist."

"You must be *joking*!" he ejaculated. "I'm a progressive socialist!"

"That's even worse," she said lightly.

He stiffened. "I *beg* your pardon?"

"What difference does it make? The corporations run the world, anyway." She paused. "Besides, you're one of the most charming men I've ever met."

"You're not exactly dull-witted, yourself."

She looked into his eyes, then slowly reached up and

touched his cheek with her fingertips. He melted back into the couch, uncertain about how to respond. Always when he had been with a woman before, he had been in command of the situation. Here, he wasn't sure of anything. The lights weren't even out! There was no way he could reach over and grab this woman and tell her that it wasn't wrong while taking her clothes off. They didn't have to be quiet; they didn't have to hurry; there were no time limits. He was not even sure that the furtive nature of sex existed anymore.

My God, what was he thinking of? For all he knew, sex was the furthest thing from Amy's mind. True, she had touched him, but the gesture was not a caress. It was probably meant as a sign of friendship and nothing more.

She finally looked away (Was there disappointment in her eyes?), and he regained the courage to speak.

"Well, I suppose that I should be going."

"Oh? Where are you staying?" she asked flatly, and he knew that he had said the wrong thing.

He smiled sheepishly. "Where am I staying? Nowhere, really." He blushed.

She sat up straight. "You mean, you haven't even checked into a hotel yet? Herbert, you've been here for two days!" She laughed and shook her head.

"I haven't had the time."

"But where's all your *luggage*?"

He grinned weakly. "I left rather unexpectedly."

She leaned forward and placed both her hands over his. "You are a *very* strange man. No, not strange. Mysterious."

Once again, he rose to the occasion. "Hasn't truth always been stranger than fiction?"

She stared at him again in wonderment, then smiled. The magic between them had returned. "You don't have to go, you know."

"I don't?"

"No. You can stay here," she whispered, her voice husky.

"I *can?*" he croaked.

"Herbert, will you *please* kiss me?"

She didn't wait for an answer. She embraced and pulled him down onto the center of the couch, her lips and tongue doing things to his mouth that he had never before experienced. Somehow, the kiss turned out both passionate and tender, despite the surprise nature of her sudden action. He tentatively began to return her caresses. She kissed him again and again, and each touch of her lips and tongue was more passionate and deeper than the time before. He shuddered and trembled. What was she *doing* to him? He felt as if his erection were going to burn a hole through his trousers; he crossed his legs. She maneuvered him onto his back and let her hair envelope his face and neck. Then she began caressing his chest, moving her hand in slow circles that gradually went lower on his body.

He became acutely aware of her hand when it reached his lower abdomen and began inching lower still *inside* his trousers and shorts! He was paralyzed with shock. This beautiful girl was not distant and unattainable; she was definitely interested in sex, for she was about to place her small, fragile and perfumed hand on his aching member! The last woman he had coupled with wouldn't even *look* at his penis, let alone touch it.

He became very nervous. This was not what he was used to; this was not the way it was supposed to happen. He had always insisted that both men *and* women were sexual beings, and that the act of love was a natural pleasure that should be shared equally. But, good *Lord*, who had ever heard of a woman seducing a man except in French novels?

Just before she was about gently to grasp his erection,

he extricated himself from the kiss, scrambled out from underneath her and sat up. (Once again, practice had defeated theory.)

Confused, she opened her eyes wide and stared up at him. "Did I do something wrong?"

She must be joking, he thought. On the contrary, she had been proceeding with more perfection than an angel in heaven, and he had been unable to cope with it. Shame-faced, he looked down and saw that a small stain had formed on his trousers, thanks to lubrication excreted by his Cowper's gland. He quickly covered the blemish with his hand and blushed crimson. "I guess I should be checking into a hotel."

"Don't you want to stay here?"

"I shouldn't."

"Okay, fine. I mean, if you don't like me or if you're all nervous and uptight about something, there's no point in you spending the night." She exhaled in a rush. "It's better to find those things out up front anyway."

"Right." He stood, took a step, then turned and looked back at her. He was trembling.

"Hey." She sat up, reached out and took his hand. "What happened?"

"I really can't explain."

"You're not gay, are you?" she asked with surprise.

"Gay?" He didn't understand.

"*Homosexual*."

He exploded with laughter, then abruptly stopped and thought. She was being serious; she did not understand that the problem was with his attitude, now obviously archaic. He frowned and sat down on the couch.

"Whoosh!" He had always considered himself a radical when it came to social issues, but in reality he was a hypocrite. His feelings toward sex had never really changed. He was a free-love advocate in name only. In the past, he had used the rhetoric to be fashionable and to convince reluctant women to submit without vows of marriage. Certainly, he had told them that they should enjoy sex, but he never really expected them to. And certainly, he had searched for a superb lover, but he had never expected to find her.

There was no doubt that Amy was a different kind of woman. Was *she* actually his Venus Urania? Or was he afraid to find out, afraid of his own sexuality?

He gulped, then turned and stared at her. She was pouting, and he had never seen her—or any other woman —look that way. Her face was flushed; her eyes were almost black; her lips were swollen and slightly parted. She was neither an animal nor a chaste goddess. She was a *sexual* young woman.

"Amy . . ." He felt a sudden rush of desire and lunged at her.

She lunged back. Soon, they were twisted and tangled on the couch, and *both* her hands were inside his trousers, and he was gasping with pleasure and trying to bury his face in the fullness of her breasts.

She extracted herself from him long enough to take him by the hand and lead him down the hall into her bedroom.

They made love several times in several hours and exhausted each other. She left the flower-printed sheets to luxuriate in a hot, scented bath while he lay back, stared at the ceiling and thought about the remarkable experience. He realized that he was still mired in Victorianism, for when they had first gotten under the covers, he had expected her to turn off the light and passively allow him to mount her missionary style. It hadn't happened that way. Instead, after she had lit candles . . . He blushed at the mere thought of the things that they had done, the pleasant sensations that they had shared.

Needless to say, the entire sequence of events added up to "equal" lovemaking, but now he was somewhat apprehensive. He had just joined the sexual revolution of the late twentieth century. He had been initiated, and yet he would have been satisfied with much less. True, he had written a few months ago that a female should enjoy sex as much as a male, but so *openly*? Without pledges of love and marriage? She had overwhelmed him, innocently taking pleasure as well as generously giving it back. For her to be so honest with her own sexuality . . . No, he was not apprehensive, he was frightened. Besides, he inwardly groaned, after this, how could he return to the nineteenth century and be happy with a "normal" sexual experience?

"Great Scott!" he exclaimed and sat up straight. What the devil was he doing sleeping with a lady of the future *anyway*? It was dishonorable! Certainly he could make no commitment to a woman who was perhaps one hundred years younger than he. He had to return to 1893 and get on with his life.

"Blast!" he muttered. He had no business breaking sexual bread with a lass who ultimately could expect nothing in return from him.

He groped for his shirt on the floor, then suddenly straightened up again. What if she didn't *want* anything from him in terms of a commitment? What if her sense of freedom extended far beyond the confines of her bedroom? Could she share her body with another as casually as she could indulge in a gourmet meal and a premium bottle of wine? Moreover, was *he* to be judged on such a basis as that? He frowned and blushed and lay back again, his hands under his head, his eyes staring at the ceiling once more. His conscience took a turn from guilt to jealousy. He genuinely *liked* her. He didn't *want* her coupling with some strange man on this bed or any other! He didn't even want to know about what she had done in the past. Yes, he wanted her to expect a commitment from him, even though he could not offer one. He sighed.

What a dilemma! To be removed a century in time from one's ideal lover. And if he did try to bridge the gap by revealing his identity, she would no doubt consider him insane; thus any chance for a serious relationship would be shattered, the pieces left to drift along the vast, alien emptiness of the fourth dimension.

His brain and eyes grew heavy with weariness. He rolled onto his side. His last thought for the night was that this lovemaking with Amy had been Utopian—a brief romp through the meadows of Eden. The only problem was that the apple had been eaten some time ago and the tree shaken bare of its fruit.

He slept deeply, but not well.

Something soft and light touched H.G.'s face, but did not startle him out of his slumber. There was a moist, gentle pressure on his lips that felt wonderful. Was he dreaming of her already? He must be. No one else had ever kissed him like that.

His eyes fluttered open, and he saw her delicate face above him. What a way to wake up! If every future morning promised this exotic return to consciousness, he might not ever go back home, or get out of bed, either! Come to think of it, he could stay here for the next thirty years and still unfailingly return to 1893. After all, what was past was past, and no one would know that he was gone until after he returned. He bubbled with laughter.

"Good morning," she said after breaking the kiss.

He looked up at her and grinned. "If you could fashion an alarm clock that felt like that, you'd make a billion pounds."

She laughed lightly, then gestured at the bedside table.

"I brought you some tea." Sweet-smelling steam rose out of a tall, blue and gray mug.

"Why, thank you." He rose up on one elbow.

"*And* the paper." She dropped the morning edition of the *Chronicle* beside him.

He picked up the front section and started to peruse it, then realized that Amy's pale-blue robe was open all the way down the front. He stared at her nude torso and willowy thighs. Then he swept away the paper that was between them. It floated into the air and fell to the floor, a confusion of stories and sections. He pulled her down beside him, kissed her and caressed her. She began to respond. He held her tightly. She pressed her body against his. He couldn't wait. He rolled on top of her, but was so eager that he failed to check his momentum. He kept right on going and fell off the bed.

Surprised, she rose up on one elbow and looked down at him. "Are you okay?" Then she began to giggle; she put her hand to her mouth, but could not suppress her mirth.

H.G. did not share her humor, however, for he was staring at the San Francisco *Chronicle*. He gasped and slowly shook his head.

"Herbert, are you okay?"

The jumble of flying newspaper had fallen open to a page-three story. The headline had captured his full attention. "GIRL FOUND MURDERED IN MASSAGE PARLOR. Police say 'Jack the Ripper' style slaying has no motive." H.G. slumped. He put his head in his hands and softly moaned.

"What's *wrong*?"

Dr. Leslie John Stephenson was alive.

EIGHT

Number 13 Nob Hill Circle was a stately, narrow and tall residence that recently had been renovated into five spacious apartments, complete with the latest in security systems to prevent the dangerous and unwanted from even getting past the hedgerow that surrounded the place. Freshly painted brown with a gray roof and trim, the structure glistened in the sun as it had done over one hundred years ago when first built.

On the top floor, a window opened as the building's newest tenant decided to let the crisp morning sea breeze into the beige and rust decor of his kitchen.

Leslie John Stephenson stood naked, leaning over the sink with his nose up to the window, smelling and tasting the good salt air. He turned, stretched and ended the movement by slapping his rock-hard belly. He put a pan of water into the built-in microwave range and waited a full thirty seconds until the water boiled. With another grin, he removed it and brewed himself tea. He took the cup and padded through his one-bedroom flat, not just furnished, but *decorated*. He loved the feel of the thick shag carpets on his feet, the look of the hanging chrome lamps, the splashes of pastel colors on the white walls, the contemporary furniture that was designed for sprawling instead of sitting. He smiled. The place was dark Victorian on the outside and opulent modern on the inside. He could not have chosen better living quarters to start his new life.

He set his tea on a glass table. Then he squatted by a Danish fireplace (the instructions had identified it as such), lit a long wooden match, flipped on the gas and basked in the instant glow. He settled into a chair in front of the fire, spread his muscular legs and let the heat warm his lower body. The uninhibited feel of being nude was exhilarating, for if his father had ever caught him undressed he had been immediately beaten. But that was past now. Yes, he was a new man in a new land. He sipped his tea and recalled how he had arrived on Nob Hill—high above exotic San Francisco—and how the final break had come.

The night before last, he had awakened in a hospital ward that housed nine other sleeping patients. After a brief, catlike inspection of the room, he had realized that he was being kept inside something called "Intensive Care Nineteen" and that *everyone* there, including himself, had been designated "John Doe." He had quickly crossed back to his bed, scanned his chart and discovered that he was number sixteen, was suffering from a concussion and was being held for observation. He had grinned, then, and almost laughed, for aside from a slight headache, he felt fine. He had been smacked and crushed by one of those modern hansoms that they called cars. And he had survived!

But there was more: he had heard a noise and ducked down behind his bed. After a moment, he had peeked over the top and seen a nurse push open one of the double glass doors, look inside, then leave. He had realized that he must leave the place before they discovered who he was. Wells was no doubt somewhere in the hospital trying to find him, trying to implicate him. He must disappear from the medical facility just as he had outfoxed Scotland Yard in the late nineteenth century.

He had straightened up, then looked at the chart of the patient next to him. The poor chap was suffering from emphysema. Stephenson had clucked his tongue and shaken his head, remembering that that particular form of lung disease was incurable. He had looked up and seen that the thin, elderly man was encased in a translucent, tentlike affair that rose and fell with his labored breathing. How marvelous, he had thought, inspecting the system of tubes and valves that led from the man's nose and mouth through regulators and finally to the oxygen cylinders.

The man was actually being kept alive by a mechanical device that governed his breathing, fed him an oxygen mixture and prevented infection. Remarkable!

Stephenson had retrieved his clothes out of the ward's common closet, quickly dressed, then gone back to his bed. He had taken his chart and switched it with that of the emphysema victim, then destroyed the poor soul's records and buried them in a waste receptacle.

Next, Stephenson had gone back to his life-sustaining oxygen system and admired it all over again. What enormous strides medicine must have taken in the last eighty-six years to waste this kind of technology on a nameless, old, dying man! Despite the dim light, he had read the rather simple instructions and traced the series of valves and tubes, then had checked the pressure gauges and indicators. He clucked his tongue again; the technician who had last calibrated the machine had done so incorrectly. The patient had not been getting enough oxygen. Stephenson had carefully adjusted the machine until it was working properly. He noticed that the emphysema victim began to breathe easier almost immediately. He smiled broadly.

Yes, he had been so taken with the automatic oxygen system that he almost hated himself for turning it off.

After he had left the hospital, he had gone back to the Jack Tar Hotel, retrieved his belongings, then checked out of the hotel. Then he hired a cab driver to take him through the city despite the late hour. They rode along the dark streets of the Mission District, and Stephenson saw trash and slime in the streets and gangs of brown youths strutting in the shadows, charged with bravado and evil. He observed drunks in doorways—half-living testaments to the god of human despair. There was also a profusion of policemen, which, he sensed, was all that kept this section of the city from being overrun by the denizens of chaos and anarchy.

They also had toured the Fillmore District where Stephenson witnessed similar monuments to the wretchedness of the human condition, only here the few people on the street were black, and the police did not hesitate to arrest them. As before: trash in the gutters was the decor here, and slime was the mortar that kept it from blowing into other sections of town.

He laughed gleefully. So the blacks were *still* enslaved, were they? And the nobleness of an Abraham Lincoln had all gone for naught. True, they had obviously made it out of the cotton fields, but into what? Like their eastern European counterparts who had gone to London to escape oppression in the late nineteenth century, these blacks had fled their rural chains only to be dumped into the bowels of a city and kept there by the invisible walls of a faceless ruling class.

Feeling triumphant, he had directed the driver to take him somewhere else. He had been right. The cornucopia of violence and crime that he had watched on the Jack Tar Hotel's television *was* a true barometer. Satan had not let him down. If anything, conditions here were worse than they had ever been in London's East End.

H.G. Wells had said that technology was the salvation and the redemption of mankind. What a simpering, incorrect fool he was! Technology hadn't erased urban blight, it had been used to *create* it! What delicious irony!

But, oh, Wells had been right about one thing: science was indeed a wonderful tool. The powerful few could use it to distance and shield themselves from the stench and anger of the masses. Stephenson was exhilarated. He really did belong—here, in 1979.

His tour had ended with a cruise down North Beach's Broadway. He had felt an instant affinity for the area. The lights were bright and gaudy, yet the alleys and side streets were dark. And the majority of small establishments advertised commodities of an illicit sexual nature! How simply smashing!

He gaped at several scantily clad ladies curved into doorways who beckoned passers-by in off the street. Yes, he definitely had to be near Broadway. Within walking distance.

He finished his tea and looked around his flat again. He had rented it within hours after leaving North Beach. Granted, the twelve hundred and fifty dollars for one month's rent was outrageous, but money was no object. In addition to his pound notes, he had three thousand pounds in gold in his money belt. If perchance he ever came up a bit short, he could always go back to the late nineteenth century and get more. Yes, Nob Hill was the perfect location for him. Such tranquility, such elegance, and only a mere six blocks away from Broadway. Hadn't *last* night's delightful crime proven the convenience involved?

He shuddered with pleasure, then sprang to his feet and headed for the bathroom. The time machine, he thought, what a simply *marvelous* invention. If one used it properly, one need never lack anything worldly at all. (Not that anything spiritual was worth a damn.) One need never even die! Why, the possibilities were staggering!

He went to the imitation-marble vanity, opened a drawer and took out the modern shaving cream and razor he had purchased just yesterday afternoon. Ah yes, the time machine! He looked up and smiled at his rugged visage in the wide mirror. *Imagine* the potential! In a matter of hours, he could be back in ancient Egypt, lurking through the palace antechambers, easily disposing of the guards with an automatic weapon, surprising Cleopatra in her boudoir. He could be assaulting and butchering her voluptuous body before Antony ever reached the shores of the Nile. A few minutes further along the fourth dimension, and he could be sodomizing Helen of Troy and cutting up the face that launched a thousand ships. Mary Magdalene could be his, too, raped and slaughtered before Jesus ever had a chance to save her wretched soul. But why stop there? Just a few centuries away, and he could violate and murder the simple peasant girl Joan of Arc, saving the British the trouble of a stake and a fire at Rouen, not to mention several thousand lives.

He leaned against the vanity, for the prospect made his knees weak. He envisioned all of history laid out before him like an obscure street in Whitechapel. He could pick any woman from any era; and when he had finished with her, he would have changed the course of human events. And what man had ever accomplished that? He could choose a queen or a princess. Isabella or Elizabeth, Catherine or Mary Queen of Scots. *Think of it!*

If only he had the special key that overrode the Rotation Reversal Lock.

He looked down and discovered that he had reached back into the vanity, picked up and was fondling the surgical knives that he had stolen from the hospital.

* * *

"I'll tell you what's wrong," said H.G., getting to his feet. "Dr. Leslie John Stephenson is *alive*, that's what's wrong!" He went to the closet, found his trousers and quickly put them on.

"I don't understand."

He picked up the newspaper and placed it in front of her. Then he went to the bedroom window and stared out, but did not appreciate the morning sunlight shining through the delicate trees and making shadow patterns on Green Street.

She quickly read the article but was still puzzled. "This doesn't say anything about Leslie John Stephenson."

"Of course, it doesn't!" he exclaimed. "The man obviously committed another horrible crime and then *escaped*! It's not as if he would leave a calling card, you know."

She came up behind him and placed her arms around him. "Would you mind telling me what's going on?" she asked gently.

He broke away from her and paced by the window. How much could he tell her? After all, she would need *some* explanation for his strange, agitated behavior. He decided to proceed as if the notorious Whitechapel murders had occurred just a few years ago. And—in his reality—they had.

"Amy, Dr. Leslie John Stephenson is actually a pathological killer who came to San Francisco several days ago. I am obviously here to apprehend the foul villain and see that justice is properly served."

"Oh. Then you work for Scotland Yard."

He cleared his throat. "Their interests *are* involved, although I am accountable only to myself, and Dr. Stephenson is totally my responsibility."

"It really doesn't matter who you work for." She could not hide the disappointment in her voice. "What's important is that you're not a writer or a world traveler at all, are you? And you told me that you were."

He was stung. He went to her, sat beside her and took her hand. "Amy, I wasn't lying to you! You must believe me!"

"Then if you are what you say you are, why are you—of all people—chasing a murderer?"

He groaned, heavy with the knowledge that he had unleashed Jack the Ripper upon contemporary society. "You might say that it is a personal vendetta."

"Did he do something to someone in your family?"

"No. The fact of the matter is that I allowed him to flee to San Francisco."

"How?"

"Amy, please. I can't explain just yet, but please give me your trust."

She laughed; his request seemed absurd. "First you tell me that this Stephenson is a traveling companion of yours. Then you tell me that he's dead. Now you tell me that he's alive and is a killer. And all because the newspaper says some poor prostitute was murdered." She paused. "If I hadn't actually seen him, I'd wonder if he existed or not."

"No one else but Stephenson could have committed that crime!" he interjected.

"Okay, okay, you've made your point."

"You'll trust me, then?"

She shrugged. "Why is that so important?"

"Amy, I might need your help."

"I'm not related to Sherlock Holmes, Herbert."

"You don't believe a word I've said, do you?"

She smiled. "Hey! I'm not involved in this, remember? So what does it matter?"

"Oh, blast!" He threw up his hands. "If only—"

"Herbert, if you're really convinced that Dr. Stephenson is responsible for this murder, why don't you just go to the police and be done with it?"

"I don't think they'd understand," he replied vaguely with a distant glint in his eyes.

"Oh, *damn!*" She had just noticed the time and discovered that she was far behind schedule.

"Amy—"

She scowled at him. "I'm going to be late to work! And I've never been late to work before!" She hurried out of the room.

He caught up with her in the hallway, turned her around and held her gently, but tightly. She resisted at first, then relaxed, for she could feel his concern, his need for another human being to understand. She didn't, but her sudden anger had melted away, and she sympathized with him.

"Amy, I—"

"Shhhh!" She placed a finger over his lips. "Don't say anything. None of this makes any sense to me right now, but that's not important. You feel genuine, therefore you are. And whatever you do, take care of yourself and don't get hurt. I'm a lousy nurse." She kissed him as she had done when she first woke him up. Then she turned, quickly went into the bathroom and closed the door.

He stared blankly at where she had been and heard the shower running. He grinned and felt a rush of emotion; he blinked and several tears rolled down his cheeks and into his mustache.

Stephenson found an English pub and restaurant several blocks away from his apartment. The place was not crowded. It looked like an establishment that catered more to a drinking clientele than a dining one. That was good to know, for if he ever got nostalgic, he could come in here some evening, sit at the bar and swap lies with the rest of the British expatriates.

Since he was famished, he ordered the most expensive

item on the menu and soon was brought a rib-eye steak, three fried eggs, a basket of chips, a plate of fried bread and a pot of hot tea. The main part of the meal was decidedly American, but after several bites, he wholeheartedly approved. When he finished eating, he pushed his plate away, then saw a morning newspaper on a chair several tables away. He picked it up, returned to his chair and while sipping his tea looked for a story that recounted last night's escapade. He was disappointed that he hadn't made page one, but that would come in due time. Besides, page three wasn't all that obscure, and he was particularly satisfied with the use of his infamous sobriquet, "Jack the Ripper." He grinned at the sketchy, inaccurate description of him that the black man at the massage parlor's front desk had given the police. He *loved* the accurate reportage of what he had done to the petite Chinese courtesan. It had been a pity that he hadn't had more time to work, but the blood had started to seep under the partition into the next cubicle. He had departed prematurely.

He chuckled upon reading the story's last sentence. "Police spokesmen refused to speculate about the murder, commenting only that 'no suspects exist at this time.'" He dropped the paper, leaned back in his chair and thought. According to hospital authorities, he was dead. Since he was currently a visitor in 1979, he didn't exist, either! His chuckle became a low laugh, and he couldn't ever recall feeling so secure. He had an omnipotent sense of well-being. Not only was he dead, he did not exist, he repeated to himself. Yet, he had never been in better health and he could render evil anytime he wanted to. The choice was his. Whoever struck his whimsical fancy.

What a truly remarkable position he was in. He pitied the San Francisco police, for there would *never* be any motives or leads, not to mention suspects. A Faustian delight at his power came over him. He was invincible—

protected by his keen sense of evil purely for the sake of evil.

He was about to leave when he overheard several customers speaking about crime. He listened.

"Did you read the story about Manson in the paper this morning?"

"Yeah."

"Think they'll let him out?"

"Not a chance."

"You know what really gets me? It costs the taxpayers twenty grand a year to keep that son of a bitch alive."

"Yeah," said the other. "And did you read about the other psycho that's running around out there?"

"No."

"Somebody killed one of them oriental massage-parlor girls."

"Boy, when the hookers ain't even safe, you *know* something's wrong."

"You better believe."

"Give us two more, bartender."

Who was this chap, Manson, that they were discussing? Stephenson wondered. He picked up the paper again and turned to the front page. The banner was "MANSON UP FOR PAROLE SOON." He avidly read the article, gleaning that "Charlie" was responsible for a whole string of brutal slayings.

What annoyed Stephenson, however, was the innuendo that Manson was the worst killer of all time. He didn't know who was (although it was an interesting question), but he certainly didn't think that the crown should rest on Charlie's head. What about Jack the Ripper's reputation? *So, Charlie's the worst of them all, is he? Well, then, maybe we should show the people of San Francisco who really is the greatest. Seventy-three stab wounds in someone's back is easy, Charlie. Wait until you read about what my little lancets can do.*

He rose from the chair, took his check and left the

dark room. At the cashier's out front where he paid the bill, he noticed that he was getting short of American currency. He frowned as he nodded good day and headed for the door.

He stepped out onto the sidewalk, squinted into the sun, then looked around to get his bearings. He wasn't that far from the Bank of England. Hadn't the delectable young lady said that he could exchange money anytime between the hours of ten and three? He had plenty of time.

He leaned back against the building and eyed the men that briskly passed. He appreciated their casual and debonair attire. He scowled as he recalled that the bloodstains had not quite come out of his only other outfit of clothes, now drip-drying over the tub in his Nob Hill flat. He must go shopping. He did not have *nearly* enough clothes for this time and this city. He had always prided himself on his dapper appearance and saw no reason why he shouldn't continue that standard in 1979. He must appear as the most ultramodern, the most expensive, the most sensual and exotic gentleman ever to slowly strut down The Broadway. He turned—his half boots flashing in the sun—and triumphantly started off toward the bank.

H.G. rose from Amy's dining-room table, went into the kitchen and poured his cup of tea down the sink. He'd already had five and his hands were beginning to shake. He glanced at page three of the newspaper—now worn and blurred—for the last time, then disgustedly dropped it into a wastebasket. Brooding, he went into the bathroom, undressed and methodically began to shave with her cream and razor. He ignored the small electrical appliances. This was his first real opportunity to marvel at the splendor of modern bathrooms, but he was not interested. He nicked himself with the razor because he wasn't used to the platinum blade, but felt nothing. He was preoccupied.

He stepped into a steaming shower and did not reflect on the plumbing of 1893. Besides, he was tired of gaping with awe at things. Shakespeare had written that cleanliness was next to godliness in the seventeenth century, so why get excited over a new generation of bathtubs and shower heads, anyway? Quite simply, he was standing under the stream of hot water because it relaxed him and allowed him to indulge his preoccupation fully.

There was no question about the newspaper article. A murder had occurred, and the depraved style *was* Stephenson's. True, an imitative killer was not out of the realm of possibility, but why now? The deduction was obvious: Stephenson was alive and free in a cosmopolitan city of the future just as Wells had feared. Questions came into his mind. Dr. Rodden had definitely told him that Stephenson had died two nights ago as a result of the motorcar accident. How could he be wrong? How could a hospital as advanced as San Francisco General be mistaken about a patient's death? Did they care who lived or died? Or were they so concerned with their technology that they had forgotten who it all was ultimately for? H.G. remembered the faces of those people in the visitors' lounge and understood their looks of despair. An irony existed.

Wait one minute, he thought, then frowned. Who was *he* to doubt a modern doctor and a modern hospital? Why was he so quick to assume that they had made a mistake? Maybe he, himself, was wrong. If Stephenson had been pronounced dead, then he was deceased, pure and simple. There was nothing to fear. After all, the brutal murder of women had not ended with the disappearance of Jack the Ripper from the nineteenth century. Therefore, the hospital and Dr. Rodden were right. Stephenson had died. The problem, then, was within himself. *He* was wrong; *he* was overreacting.

He dropped the soap, slipped while trying to recover it and almost wrenched his back. He cursed and let the soap sit on the drain between his feet. He *wasn't* wrong! He *hadn't* misread the newspaper! He knew that *somehow* Stephenson's death was a case of mistaken identity, and that the wily surgeon was on the loose in San Francisco. He had no proof; he just *felt* it, which made him angry because he did not like to rely on the inconsistencies of inductive reasoning. Yet, he had no choice. He must find Stephenson and find him quickly. He grimaced. He had no idea of even where to start looking. Moreover, he was not *deductively* certain that the object of his search was even alive.

He climbed out of the shower and began drying himself. Amy was right, too. He should query the San Francisco Police Department and offer them his assistance. He cursed again, beset by more apprehensions. If he told the police that he knew who killed the Chinese courtesan, but could not lead them to a suspect, wouldn't they suspect *him*? He couldn't tell them that Stephenson was Jack the Ripper and that they both had recently arrived via time machine! He didn't want to lie to them, either. He had never been any good at falsehoods. And what if—God forbid—they hooked him up to some electrical device that detected lies? They would undoubtedly learn the truth; they would question the thinking processes of his brain; they would not believe him still; and they would send him packing to an asylum. And there he would repose until he was old, gray and senile, and who the devil would write all those books with his name on them?

Better he not go to the police at all. Better he return home as quickly as possible, call on Mr. Hastings and resume his article-writing career.

"*Coward!*" he ejaculated.

He left the bathroom and stormed into the bedroom for his shoes and shirt. There was Amy, too, he thought. Could he leave her without an explanation? After he had found the holy grail of sexual delight and drunk deeply? Was he that ignominious a man?

He sighed. He could *not* leave 1979 without giving Amy an explanation, for better or for worse. That he had vacillated in his own mind was bad enough. Moreover, he could *not* leave 1979 without knowing for certain the fate of Leslie John Stephenson. And if he had to enlist police support in his search for the cynical surgeon, then so be it. He would risk self-incrimination, for he had to face reality (the time machine, notwithstanding) and his own creed of ethics. Stephenson was *his* responsibility and he must *do* something.

He strode into the living room and dialed the police, having gotten their number off a sticker on the side of the telephone.

"Sergeant Valentine speaking, may I help you?" The voice crackled electronically.

He slammed down the receiver, placed his head in his quivering hands and moaned. Just what the devil was he supposed to *say* to them? *Hello, this is H. G. Wells speaking, and I am a citizen of the nineteenth century. I am telephoning you today to warn you that Jack the Ripper is terrorizing your community. Could you please help me find him so that I can take him back to London and have him locked up in Old Bailey? I would certainly appreciate your kind and generous assistance.*

He fell back onto the couch and stared at the ceiling. Huxley had once said, *Tell the truth about science when it is either embarrassing or inconvenient, and you will discover that you will never have to worry about people doubting your word.*

Somehow, that didn't help.

When Amy Robbins rapped on one of the bank's glass doors with her car keys and was let inside by the security guard, she was embarrassed and hoped that no one would notice that she was twenty-three minutes late. Eyes down, she hurried for her desk. She sat down and began sorting through a stack of credit-card applications when she saw someone lean against her desk. She looked up, face hot with guilt, and could not hide the crimson hue of her complexion.

"You look *great*," said Carole Thomas, a buxom, keen-eyed lady who had just recently risen from the ranks of the tellers to become the bank's only other female officer.

"Oh hi, Carole."

"Something *happened*, didn't it?"

"What do you mean?"

"You're almost a half hour late."

"Traffic."

Carole laughed and nodded. "Where? Going in or coming out of the bedroom?"

"*Carole!*"

"Okay, okay, I won't pry. I'll just say congratulations. It's about time you met someone worth meeting." She started away.

Amy smiled and felt a surge of joy. "Carole?"

She turned. "What?"

"He's like a little boy and a grandfather all rolled into one."

"*Interesting.* Do I know him?"

"You've never met. I promise."

"Well, then, does he have a brother?"

"How should I know?"

Carole laughed. "A cousin, maybe? Look, I've got to run. Coffee later?"

"Sure. Hey—why don't you come over for dinner Friday night? You can meet Herbert."

"*Herbert*?" She rolled her eyes. "Are you sure you got the name right?"

Amy laughed. "Around six-thirty?"

"I'll be there. I wouldn't miss a look at a *Herbert* for anything in the world."

For the next half hour, Amy daydreamed about the night before. She felt warm and had no self-doubts. Her time with Herbert had been one of those momentous occasions when she knew that the feelings had been reciprocal. Even the mysterious scene with him this morning had not diminished her sense of well-being. Although, now that she thought of it, what *was* that scene all about, anyway? And really—just who *was* Mr. Herbert Wells from London? She sensed that when she did find out, she ultimately would be pleasantly surprised. Nevertheless—as before all things good—there might be a time of sorrow. It seemed the way of the world and the pattern of her life. Until then . . . She leaned back, placed her hands behind her head and let her mind drift back into her bedroom. She smiled.

Suddenly, she bolted straight up in the chair and stared at the clock across the room. What was she *doing*? The doors would be open in less than an hour, and she hadn't accomplished a *thing*! She grabbed all the papers out of her "In" basket and placed them in front of her, as if that would make them go away faster. Then she read a loan application from a Ms. Alexis Lynd who wanted to renovate a town house on Twin Peaks. The woman was an account executive for an advertising agency and had liquid assets in the sixty-thousand-dollar range. (Amy wished *she* did.) Application approved. And so it went. She attacked her work and had accomplished a great deal by the time the security guards unlocked the doors for the patrons of the bank.

She was concentrating on a report about fluctuations in world currencies, imagining the wails of Italian financiers as the lira continued to plunge, conjuring up the grins of sultans as the dinar tripled in value, when she felt a presence. She sighed, dropped her pen, pushed back from the desk and looked up.

"Yes, may I—" She gasped with a sharp intake of breath and almost put her hand to her mouth, but had the immediate presence of mind to hang on to the arms of her chair. Herbert was right! Standing before her in a poised slouch was Dr. Stephenson, the lean and dark Englishman who was supposed to be dead. He loomed larger than life, his deep-set eyes instinctively searching her face for weakness. She forced a smile and felt some color return to her face.

"Good morning, Miss . . ."

"Robbins," she replied automatically. Did his voice sound cautious? Did he suspect her reaction? Or was she being paranoid?

"Oh, yes. Miss Robbins. I hope I didn't startle you." He smiled thinly. "I would like to exchange more currency."

"Certainly."

He handed her a stack of pound notes.

She stared at them dumbly for a moment, thoughts racing through her mind. She opened and closed her desk drawer, then smiled again. "If you'll excuse me, sir. I'll check this morning's rate. It'll only take a minute."

"Take your time." He nodded imperceptibly and sat down.

She crossed the room, desperately hoping that her voice hadn't quavered. She went behind a row of teller windows, furtively grabbed a telephone and dialed her apartment. The five rings were maddening, but finally she got an answer.

"Herbert!"

"Oh, hello, Amy, dear, how nice that you should—"

"*Herbert, he's here!*"

A long, static-filled pause.

"For God's sake, did you hear me?"

"Keep him in the bank as long as you possibly can. I'll be there straightaway."

"But what if I can't?"

"Try." He hung up.

With a trembling hand, she hung up, too, then glanced back at her desk and saw that he was still sitting there. What she hadn't seen was that he had watched her make the telephone call.

She returned to her desk, chin held high, a smile etched upon her nervous features. She made a show of sitting down and arranging her clothes, as if movement would keep him occupied.

"One-point-seven-eight this morning, sir," she reported with forced enthusiasm. "That's better than when you first came in."

"Smashing," he replied in low, rich tones, continuing to lounge in the chair. His head was back and his eyes almost closed so that he appeared half asleep. Actually, he was brooding, his fingers twitching compulsively as he ran them back and forth over his lips.

She calculated the amount of money due him, then opened her drawer and slowly began counting out the dollars. She desperately tried to think of a ploy. She couldn't have a security guard detain him because there was no cause. That would only get her into serious trouble. Finally, she handed him the cash.

"There you go, sir."

"Thank you." He folded the money, pocketed it, rose and smiled at her.

She stood up, too. If she could just get him to talk.

Something. "Are you enjoying your stay in San Francisco?"

"Yes. Very much. Thank you."

"How did you like the Jack Tar Hotel?"

He frowned darkly; his eyes narrowed and glittered at her. Then he laughed derisively.

She realized her slip, gasped and placed her hand to her mouth.

"Miss Robbins, you wouldn't just happen to know a gentleman named Wells, would you?"

H.G. arrived at the bank five minutes too late and had to calm a visibly shaken Amy Robbins by tightly holding her hand across the desk and whispering reassurances. She was on the verge of tears, but controlled herself lest she call attention to herself.

"I'm sorry," she uttered. "I'm really sorry."

"It's quite all right, Amy. *Really.* I'll find Leslie John Stephenson. After all, he *is* only human." He hoped that his words sounded more confident than the way he felt.

She managed a smile. "You're so damned nice."

"Come on, then."

Amy made a quick phone call and learned that Stephenson had checked out of the Jack Tar Hotel yesterday, paid cash and hadn't left a forwarding address.

He might as well be dead, H.G. wryly commented to himself while he flagged down a taxi outside the bank. He asked the driver to take him to the police station, then sat back and blankly stared out the window. He took no pleasure in his ride through the city.

He was, however, quite simply amazed when he saw the size of the San Francisco Police Department. It was almost as large and forbidding as the hospital, although at least it was clean and freshly painted on the outside.

Uniformed policemen left the building in fours and fives, casually checked their weapons and other paraphernalia, then climbed into black and white vehicles waiting like cavalry horses and sped away. H.G. watched in awe. Never before had he seen so many police! And every one of them carried sidearms. It was as if San Francisco were at war against some rival state, only here—he thought it safe to say—the rival factions were within. An absorbing question crossed his mind. Were most San Franciscans criminally inclined, as Stephenson had opined in the Jack Tar Hotel suite? Was that why a city (even now) one fourth the size of greater London needed *regiments* of police to maintain the status quo? Or was the enemy the citizenry itself? And if that were the case, then America—at least the San Franciscan corner of it—had indeed become a totalitarian state. He frowned and pondered. If the land of the free *had* succumbed to some form of oppression, it certainly wasn't visible. He had detected no chains, no slavery, no one functioning against their will. No, no, he said to himself, there was no dictatorship here. He considered himself to be astute enough to recognize signs of *that* social evil. Unless people were controlled electronically. And if they were, then there would be no need for police. Still, why the vast numbers of men in blue?

"Whoosh!" He grinned. Of course! They were employed to assist the city's populace. That explained it.

He turned and started for the door, then stopped again. He frowned and rejected his positive conclusion. If they were good samaritans, he postulated coldly, then why did they carry weapons? He entered the building with a foreboding sense of melancholy.

He made his way to the Homicide Division with relative ease, correctly surmising that employees who directed him assumed that because of his conservative attire he was either a government official or a barrister. Once there, however, he became embroiled with a bureaucratic desk sergeant who wanted to know his name, address, telephone number, the precise nature of his business and to see his identification before he would even *consider* calling the lieutenant's secretary and arranging an appointment. Annoyed and ruffled, H.G. refused on all counts, then argued with the man, but got nowhere. So, he sat on the bench opposite the desk and decided to wait. He read through the newspaper and became knowledgeable of the political shenanigans of a certain Jerry Brown, governor of the state of California. The man was a master of gerrymandering and the red herring, he mused as he put the paper down and resumed glaring at the desk sergeant.

Three hours later, H.G. sighed and decided to relent. He told the desk sergeant that he had information concerning the identity of the "massage-parlor murderer."

"Well, why didn't you say so in the first place?"

Within five minutes, H.G. found himself seated on a red-leather couch inside an office. The walls were lined with plaques, degrees, photographs and other sundry milestones of one man's long career of public service. Behind a desk and staring out the window was Lieutenant J. Willard Mitchell, a graying but trim twenty-seven-year veteran of the force. His face had more wrinkles than a fisherman's; his skin was tougher than a prize fighter's. Occasionally, he would drink from a large mug and puff on a cigarette. His ashtray was overflowing. So were the stacks of papers on his desk. So was the amount of telephone calls that came into his office, making the electronic box beside his chair light up like a digital Christmas tree. As he regarded Mitchell, H.G. quickly understood that he was in the presence of a man who had seen it all, who had done everything, but didn't have the time to reflect upon one iota of it.

Mitchell suddenly swung up to a sitting position, picked up his telephone and pressed a button. "Ruth, hold the calls, will you please?" His voice had a slow and pleasant quality, making it seem like his thoughts were detached from the frenetic activity around him. "And tell Sergeant Ray to step in here, if he's got a minute."

Moments later, a man came into the room. He wore his hair shoulder-length. He was dressed in jeans and a colorful shirt open to his abdomen. Incongruously so, thought H.G.; first, he was a detective, and second, his face resembled that of a wise English bulldog. No doubt he, too, had had his share of experiences.

Ray took a chair across the room and regarded H.G. with a suspicion normally reserved for representatives of the mayor's office. He pulled a pen and note pad out of his pants and waited.

"Mr. Wells has some information on the murder last night, and I thought we should both hear him out. For the record."

"Which murder?"

"The one in the massage parlor."

"Oh, yeah." Ray made a note.

"Are you a U.S. citizen?" Mitchell asked H.G.

"No," H.G. replied. "As you can obviously tell, I'm from London. I'm here on a visit."

"First time in the States?"

"Yes."

"And yet you have information concerning a murder in the city of San Francisco?"

"Yes. You might say that I'm a citizen of the world," he added weakly. "I like to help people no matter where I am."

Mitchell leaned over his desk, folded his hands over a

mass of papers and forced a grin. "Fine. Now why don't you tell us what you came to tell us?"

H.G. cleared his throat and spoke in clipped, reserved tones. "I happen to know that the person responsible for the death of the Chinese courtesan is a man named Leslie John Stephenson."

"S-t-e-v-e-n-s-o-n?" asked Ray, furiously scribbling.

"No. Step-hen-son. The man resides in London. He is a Harley Street physician, approximately thirty-one or -two, six feet tall, one hundred eighty pounds I would guess, dark-brown hair and deep-set eyes."

"Check it out, Sergeant."

"Yes, sir." Ray left the room with the information.

Mitchell turned back to H.G. "How do you know this, Mr. Wells?"

"That's a bit hard to explain. As a matter of fact, it's impossible." His hands felt clammy and he rubbed them on his trousers.

"I see." The lieutenant thought a moment. "Are you a psychic?"

"I beg your pardon?"

"Do you have spiritual powers? I'm curious as to the source of your information."

"I have no supernatural gifts, Lieutenant! If I could reveal my source to you, I would do so gladly, but I can't. I've told you what I know."

Moments later, Ray returned and handed Mitchell several large, folded sheets. Then he excused himself and left the office. The lieutenant briefly studied the information before smiling tactfully at H.G.

"Well, I appreciate you coming in and sharing your insights with us, Mr. Wells. Where can we reach you in the event we need to ask you something else?"

"Is that necessary? It's rather awkward. . . . I've been staying with a friend. Must we involve her in this?"

"Only if we have to contact you. We're very discreet, believe me."

"Very well. I'm staying at 92½ Green Street and my friend's name is Miss Amy Robbins."

Mitchell nodded and put down his pencil. "Thanks for your time, then."

Suddenly, H.G. realized what was happening. He straightened up and spoke in a voice that was small but indignant nonetheless. "You're not going to do anything, are you?"

Mitchell could not help his knowing smile. He lit another cigarette. "I understand your concern, Mr. Wells. But ultimately, you're asking us to arrest a man for murder because you say he committed a crime. If we worked like that, half this town would be in jail."

"Are you doubting my word?"

Mitchell frowned, then picked up the information, scanned it again and began to read in a voice that had lost its pleasant quality and become flat. "U.S. Customs has no record of a Dr. Leslie John Stephenson entering this country, but he could have entered illegally. The British Government has no record of ever issuing a passport to a Leslie Stephenson, but he could've forged one. The London police have no record of a Leslie John Stephenson, and neither do Scotland Yard, the FBI, CIA, MI-5, Interpol or the Sûreté." He paused to drag on his cigarette and blow a smoke ring. "Finally, the United Kingdom's Bureau of Vital Statistics has no record of a Leslie John Stephenson." He allowed himself to scowl at H.G. "*Yes*, Mr. Wells, I *am* doubting your word."

H.G. was so impressed that he did not realize that Mitchell had called him a liar. "How did you get all that information so quickly?"

"Computers, Mr. Wells." He got up and went to the window. "We have them just like everybody else." He turned and gestured at the door. "Now, if you don't mind, I'm a very busy man."

"You're asking me to leave?" H.G. was astonished.

"Let me put it another way," he said kindly. "I've tried to be nice to you because you're a foreigner. Still, I don't appreciate publicity stunts or receiving false information! Quite frankly, Mr. Wells, if I wouldn't have to deal with your consulate, I'd have you locked up and held for seventy-two hours!"

H.G. stiffened. "I have not given you false information, Lieutenant!"

"The computers don't lie!" Mitchell replied sharply.

"My *good* man, do you mean to say that you would trust an electronic device more than the word of a gentleman?"

"Wouldn't you?" Mitchell grinned and held the door open for him. "And please, Mr. Wells, don't ever let me see you in this building again, okay? Cheerio."

Shaken, H.G. left and hurried for the exit. He bit his lip, disillusioned. He had gone to the police with a certain amount of hope and anticipation. He had never expected the experience to be so shattering. How could he remain optimistic about life in the future? Oh, certainly, they had cars and airships and telephones and television and an entire potpourri of electronic wizardry that did everything from drying one's hair to thinking for him. And yet, the technology had not freed mankind from crime; rather, man's inhumanity to man appeared to be on the rise. Why, if Lieutenant Mitchell's implications were accurate, crime was increasing faster than the police could control it!

He left the building, deep in thought. Was man incapable of keeping pace with science? Or had anyone bothered to find out? Or was it that the marvels of science did not serve all mankind, hence some reacted against it and committed horrible crimes? Or could it be that technology created its own form of alienation?

H.G. shuddered. He would have to answer those questions before he left 1979. For a moment, he wanted to cry. Would he have to *warn* people about the dangers of progress? Would he have to write that the future was a brilliantly lit, clean yet poisonous environment where one had nothing to look forward to? He clenched his jaws and turned his back to a sudden gust of cold wind. *Face it, H.G. Recognize it. You will write whatever is the truth and you will remain a champion of the intellect and the rational, no matter what.*

He began walking away from the police headquarters, head down, soberly looking at weeds that grew out of cracks in the concrete. All right, he thought, so there was no Utopia. So man couldn't handle technology right now. Who was to say that resilient and clever human beings of 2079 wouldn't straighten things out? Or 3079! He smiled. Perhaps he would take another flight along the fourth dimension and find out.

So, the San Francisco Police Department intended to do nothing about Leslie John Stephenson. He straightened up and threw back his shoulders. Then he would jolly well have to catch Jack the Ripper all by himself. And by so doing, he would teach them a lesson from the past, no doubt forgotten. He would show them—specifically Lieutenant Mitchell—that they should never take the word of a gentleman lightly.

Stephenson got off a cable car at Hyde and Beach streets after a most unpleasant ride. Despite the laughter and gaiety of the tourists, he hated the awkward little conveyance and cursed himself for impulsively hopping aboard. The car was *antiquated!* A buggering relic of the past. Slow and uncomfortable and inefficient. The experience reminded him of the many nights he had ridden the District Line and breathed the horrible fumes while crouched on a hard wooden bench, wondering if he would be accosted by the police. Yes, the cable car was nineteenth century, and it made him angry.

He paused to spit on the rear window of the car, then hurried away. He strolled along Beach Street, but did not appreciate the remarkable view of the Pacific, the graceful sea gulls or the brisk salt air. He wished for the fog and the night, disliking intensely the bright winter sun. The incident at the bank had left him deeply concerned. True, the fact that he did not exist in 1979 had put him in an ideal position. He could murder at will and not have to worry about leaving evidence behind. But the reactions of the young woman at the bank had been too obvious to ignore. H. G. Wells knew that he was alive, and that was a problem. Granted, Wells had always been inept when it came to physical confrontations, but the little man could not be discounted merely because he was unskillful with his feet and fists. Wells was clever and brilliant. He was a foe not to be taken lightly. An extremely formidable enemy.

Stephenson went up several flights of stairs and found himself in Ghirardelli Square surrounded by small, exclusive shops that had once been part of a chocolate factory. So Wells knew he was alive, did he? The only one who knew equalled the only one who could stop him. Certainly, he would have to rectify that. True, he was reticent to kill a male human being since murder was by definition a sexual act. Given the circumstances, however . . . Wait a minute! Maybe there was another way to deal with Wells. He didn't have to avoid the little scientist. He didn't have to worry about being tracked down and discovered by the man. Quite the contrary. He didn't even have to kill Wells. All he had to do was find him! And given this morning's episode at the bank, that shouldn't be difficult at all.

He remembered the large, heavy book in his Jack Tar Hotel suite that had been beside the telephone. Then he stalked the ells and recesses of the square until he found a telephone booth. He went inside and opened the directory that was chained to the shelf. What was the girl's name? The one who knew Wells? Robbins. Yes, that was it. He found the "R's," scanned the pages, then grinned with satisfaction. There it was. He memorized her address. He left the booth, strolled back into the square, breathed deeply and felt refreshed. He had absolutely nothing to worry about, for now he could resolve the problem of Wells. He could dispose of his unfinished business; he could pluck out the thorn in his side. Perhaps tonight. When the city was dark and thick with fog. Late tonight after she had gone to bed and in her revery would be ripe for surprise and unable to offer resistance. If he felt so inclined.

He smiled, fully confident again. Then he swaggered into a clothing store named (tastefully so, he thought) "The Body Shop." He saw the establishment was empty, a fact that surprised him. There was an abundance of contemporary haberdasheries; and the decor was mainly chrome and glass. Unseen speakers played modern music that made him want to dance without inhibitions. Indeed, this was no refuge for tails, top hats and waltzes; this shop *felt* like the future, and he was thrilled to be within its mirrored walls.

He selected seven colorful silk shirts with wide collars, balloon sleeves and fabric-covered buttons. He grinned. *Perfect* plumage for the here and now!

Then he saw her come into the room with a long curvaceous stride, tossing her head so that her hair flew like a thoroughbred's mane. She wore tight, bleached-muslin pants and a matching jacket-blouse left unbuttoned six inches below respectability. She had a pleasant face that was not beautiful; her mouth was a touch too wide, her brown eyes a little too trusting. Perhaps that was why he sensed that she lacked confidence. Then again, he could be wrong, for she stopped directly in front of him, placed her hands on her hips and did not shy away from his gaze.

"Hi, I'm Marsha. Can I help you with something today?" Her voice sounded husky, but had a cheerful quality.

"I'd like these, to begin with." He handed her the shirts.

"Hey, I *like* your accent!"

He grinned.

"Are you sure the size is right or would you like to try them on?"

"Oh, no, it's not necessary. The sizes are correct."

"All right." She went over to the cash register and left the shirts on the adjacent glass display case, then pirouetted and smiled. "Anything else?"

"Trousers. I'd like to have a look at some of them, if you don't mind."

"It's a pleasure." She led the way around a table and into an ell of the room where pants were stacked on shelves. He was acutely conscious of her behind and the fact that there were no lines beneath her pants. She wore no undergarments. His face became hot.

"These are all cut differently, so I better check your size and then you can try some on, okay?"

"If it's not too much of a bother."

"Hey," she said with a laugh. "It's my job." She looped a tape measure around his waist.

She was so close that he could smell her. The odor was clean, yet a trifle musty, as if she accepted that it was perfectly natural for women to perspire. The palms of his hands became moist; he felt himself stiffen slightly against the fabric of his trousers.

"Thirty-one." She kneeled and held her tape along the inside of his leg. She seemed to pause, and the moment froze in his brain. He couldn't tell if she was looking at him or trying to read the tape measure, but he could see all the way down her loose top past her breasts. His breath became labored; he could not control the twitching in his groin.

"Thirty-five." She rose, flashed him a bright smile, but gave no indication what she was thinking. "Any particular kind?"

He began looking through the stacks of pants. "Are you alone here?" he asked, his voice thick and guttural.

"The other girls are on a lunch break. Why?"

"I just wondered."

"Oh, I don't *run* the place, if that's what you mean. I just work here, and it's not a bad job. I get half off on anything I want."

She talks too much, he thought, as he selected a pair of jeans that had a small Union Jack sewn on one back pocket. He held them up and admired them.

"Want to try them on?"

He nodded.

She indicated a changing booth, and he went inside, stripped off his trousers and sighed with relief. His erection had vanished. Now he would be able to speak to the girl without stuttering. Now she would not know that she had touched the core of his lust and hate.

He slipped into the jeans. They were the tightest trousers he had ever worn, but they were not uncomfortable. He came out of the dressing room, went to the mirror, turned in front of it and loved the blatant fit and feel of the jeans. He was about to question the girl when he saw that she was looking at his crotch. He followed her eyes. The thin material actually *outlined* his private parts! He glanced up; she was still looking. He couldn't believe it. He knew that he had always been attractive to a certain kind of woman, but this genuinely surprised him because no self-respecting, nineteenth-century English shopgirl would *ever* look at a man that way. No matter what was in their hearts, they would never even *consider* such behavior!

Still, she stared! Why, she was behaving like the most obvious prostitute on Commercial Street! Obviously, social mores had changed considerably, and that fact was cause for excitement. Come to think of it, he had noticed while on The Broadway that courtesans in 1979 looked just like salesgirls or any other kind of woman. There seemed to be no special code of dress or behavior so that a gentleman might know if he were approaching a professional. Maybe there *weren't* any clear distinctions anymore! Perhaps all women responded like slatterns nowadays, even if some didn't receive money for services rendered. If that were the case, then he could solicit sexual favors from *any* female and not have to fear a response of outrage. Great Scott, he thought, how bloody marvelous. How simply smashing! Never again would he have to fear rejection or a lass—like his sister—who was overly eager and willing. He could treat them all like prostitutes. He could control them until that sublime moment when their barriers gave way and they acted like frenzied animals. Then he could take both their degraded lives and their noble virginities, for it wasn't *right* that a lady should enjoy the filth of a man or a father inside her.

He grinned at his dark countenance in the mirror. He must test his hypothesis.

He returned to the changing booth and quickly donned his other trousers. Then he came out and selected seven pairs of the jeans, all in different colors. He left the alcove and approached the cash register. She was there, boxing his shirts. When she heard him, she glanced up and smiled.

"Find what you like?"

He nodded and set the jeans down on the display case, his hands trembling with fear and excitement, for he could not find the courage to ask. He had *never asked* in his entire life. Furthermore, didn't he already have plans for the night? Wasn't he going to visit the Robbins girl, hence clear up the affair with Wells? He exhaled in a hiss. That meant that he had a perfectly good reason not to test his hypothesis. He frowned. He was rationalizing his lack of courage, wasn't he? That was no indication of the boldness that he expected of himself. After all, hadn't he tentatively decided to call on Miss Robbins *late* in the evening? When she was sleeping? He sighed. There was no conflict other than his own inner reticence.

She rang up his purchases and handed him two plastic bags thick with boxes. "It's been a *pleasure* serving you, sir."

The bill was close to three hundred dollars. He handed her a roll of bills, and when she gave him his change, their fingertips touched. He felt a surge of emotion that gave him all the courage he needed.

"Marsha?" His knees felt weak; his voice sounded strange. "I mean, that *was* your name, wasn't it?"

"Unhuh."

"I was wondering," he stammered thickly. "Did you have a previous engagement for this evening, or could I have the honor of calling on you?"

It wasn't that late, but the night was already black and cold. H.G. stood there drinking expensive gin—something he did not ordinarily do—and stared out the dining-room window. It was a time for contemplation, although his mind did not seem to be working logically. He was just gazing, and his brain recorded a still photograph. Nothing more and nothing less. He guessed that he must be tired, as he imagined classical heroes had been on the eve of arduous struggles. He sighed, sipped the gin and felt both leaden and giddy. The evening promised to be full of import and gravity. He did not want to think about it. If anything, he wished he were in his teens again, back at Up Park, cavorting with Melinda, the head cook's daughter, in the music room behind the harpsichord.

Playing cause and effect as well as Thomas Aquinas

ever did, he silently cursed his early interest in mathematics, for that really was where it all had begun—ending with the construction of the time machine and his rendezvous with Amy Robbins in 1979.

Then she came into the living room, fresh from a hot shower, looking gorgeous in faded jeans and an unbuttoned blue work shirt tied loosely at the waist. She dropped down onto the couch and gestured for him to join her. He grinned foolishly and obliged with a fleeting wish that both the past and the future would disintegrate, leaving him with this woman in this room for eternity. That hope realized would remove him from the responsibility, the mandate that lay heavy on his mind. But it was not to be so.

"Before I sit down, may I offer you a drink?" He smiled but inwardly groaned at the pedestrian manner in which he had started such a significant conversation.

"Sure."

"Neat or American?"

"*American?*"

"With ice."

She giggled, pressed her thighs together and curled her toes, anticipating and enjoying it. "Ice and Seven-up. Please."

"*Seven-up?*" His eyes widened and his free hand went to his mustache, a sure sign that he had been caught short. Seven-up? What the devil was that? he wondered. Some synthetic substance, or perhaps vegetable, that guaranteed that a person would rise at seven o'clock sharp regardless of what had happened the night before? The name made no sense.

"It's in the fridge. There's a six-pack on the bottom shelf."

He quickly translated "fridge," for the word was derivative of both "frigid" and "refrigerator," and he knew that she was referring to the electrically powered cooler in the kitchen. (Like the other devices that, a

1979er so nonchalantly plugged into the wall, he regarded the refrigeration appliance as a technological stroke of genius.) But the other noun that she had uttered left him feeling stupid. For an instant, his mind went blank. He was speechless, slightly swaying in front of her and looking off. Then he grinned.

"I know this is terrible," he said enthusiastically, "but I'm all sixes and sevens."

"Herbert, that's not terrible, it's *awful*!" She laughed.

"Well?"

"Well, what?"

"My dear lady, just what the devil is a six-pack?"

"Come on, you're putting me on! They have six-packs in London!"

"Under a different appellation, I'm sure."

"The Seven-up is in the six-pack of green *cans* on the bottom shelf—you *do* know what a *shelf* is, don't you?"

He bowed slightly and started for the kitchen, his eyes twinkling. "Of course. It's a geological phenomenon created by the erosion of winds or tides, generally found —but not exclusive to—the polar regions of the earth."

She stared after him, laughing and shaking her head, not quite sure whether he had a terminal case of naïveté or an overdose of charm. It didn't matter. Either condition would win both her heart and her hand.

He found the Seven-up and opened a can with relative ease. The effervescence reminded him of quinine water. He grew curious, sniffed the liquid, then tasted it.

"Hmmm." It was like sweet lemonade, only—to use a modern image—somewhat electrically charged. He took a large swallow and made the mistake of sloshing the stuff through his teeth. The resultant fizz bubbled through his nose up into his sinuses and down into his lungs. He gasped for breath, then was left coughing violently over the sink.

"Are you all right?" she called.

"It's nothing," he managed to reply after he'd cleared

his nasal passages. He wiped his eyes dry, then made her a drink. He put the Seven-up back into the refrigerator as if it were a can of nitroglycerin.

"Whoosh," he muttered. "Bloody Yanks'll drink anything."

He returned to the living room with the drinks, sat down next to her and frowned. He was reflective again, absorbed with the unpleasant task that lay ahead.

"How'd it go?" she asked softly.

"Not well. The police refused to cooperate."

"But why?"

"They didn't believe me."

"Didn't you show them your credentials?"

"You know as well as I that I am traveling incognito."

She sipped her drink and thought for a moment. "Why the secrecy, Herbert? I mean, really. It worries me."

He had a chance to tell her then, but when he looked into her open, concerned eyes, he could not bring himself to speak. He sighed and shook his head, released from the terror of the moment. "Believe me," he said glibly, "you have nothing to worry about."

"For sure?"

"For sure," he replied, thinking that the American vernacular sounded strange on his English tongue. "It is *I* who am beset with problems."

She nodded, uncertain about what he would say next. She was afraid, too, sensing love and not wanting it aborted at such an embryonic stage. She nervously ran her fingers through the long, sloping curl of hair alongside her face. "What problems?"

"You know. I have to stop Stephenson."

"You'll do it. You followed him this far."

"Only with great difficulty and some blind luck," he understated. "The man is a very wily fellow."

"I'll help you in any way I can, if you'll tell me what to do," she said brightly.

"You *will*?"

She slowly nodded. "I'd love to."

"It may be dangerous."

She smiled quickly and looked up at the ceiling. "I took a modern history course in college. And Robert Kennedy once said, 'Those who never dare to fail greatly never succeed greatly.' And that pertains to more than just your Dr. Stephenson."

"Ah, yes, Robert Kennedy. Irish chap."

She laughed and punched him lightly on the arm. "Will you stop it with your pretensions of ignorance?"

And then suddenly they were embracing and kissing tenderly. He held her tighter than usual for a long time. He felt her muscles relax and then her warmth.

"Amy. My dear. You're wonderful."

She pushed her head up alongside his, kissed his ear lobe, then whispered, "All I ask in return is that you be honest with me."

He fell back against the couch and felt the breath go out of him, but held on to her still. Then she sighed long and low, remaining content in his arms. Never before had he experienced such tender emotion. At the very least, they had become temporary partners and lovers, but who knew where it might lead? Perhaps they would hopscotch along the fourth dimension pausing to meet with her ancestors, then his. Maybe they would twirl in time and meet—*their* children? He blushed with delight at the thought and felt his mustache move against her cheek. Who knows? Maybe he would manipulate time so that they could exchange nuptial vows at a way station somewhere in the universe, and in attendance would be their parents, grandparents, great-grandparents, children and grandchildren. Why—Moses could officiate the ceremony, reading from stone tablets! Aristotle could be there, too, along with . . . Who was that man she had mentioned responsible for the admirable quote? A Robert Kennedy? He grinned and drifted back to the reality of her arms.

He considered their amorous alliance again, and the qualities each would contribute. He understood—although only unconsciously—that she was perhaps more capable than he. He was going to have to depend on her and hoped that he could return the favor with love and companionship. The partnership, then, was an equal venture, a union of two individuals on the same footing. Neither had experienced such reciprocity before.

He frowned and tensed slightly. She felt the change, rose and looked at him, her eyes and mouth questioning. He averted his head and sat up straight, a troubled expression on his face.

"Are you all right?"

"I'm not sure."

"What's wrong?"

"Nothing's wrong," he replied, staring across the room at a fern in a terra-cotta pot. The bloody hell nothing was wrong! His stomach churned. His hands began to tremble slightly. Amy Robbins was not just another girl or one half of an ordinary romp in the sheets. Their affair was no longer casual. Her offer of help and their subsequent embrace confirmed that fact. Although words and promises had not yet been exchanged, he knew that they would be very soon if he kept his mouth shut.

But since she trusted him already, didn't she deserve the honesty that she had asked for? Then he shuddered. He might never again have her arms around him and feel her lithe frame next to his. He might as well call her Juliet and admit that he had stabbed Tybalt without cause, then enjoyed listening to the man's death rattle. Yes, what he was about to say could shatter their emotional lives forever, and no trip on a time machine could repair that kind of damage. But she had to know.

"There's something I haven't told you," he said, quietly anguished.

She took his face in her hands and looked square into

his eyes. "If you're going to tell me that you lied to me before just so you could—"

"I haven't lied to you!"

"Let me finish." She paused. "If you're going to say that you're married, I won't believe you." She looked down. Her face was pale and her voice became distant. "And if you really are, then please don't tell me. Just leave and don't come back."

"For the last time, Amy, I am not married!" he exploded, then sprang to his feet and paced in the center of the room. "What do you think I am? A bloody philanderer?"

Puzzled, she stared at him as he walked in irregular patterns. "Well, if you're not married, what else could possibly be wrong?"

"I . . . I don't know how . . ." His voice cracked.

"Dammit, Herbert, will you *please tell* me?"

"I . . . I was born in Essex, London, on September twenty-first—"

"Oh my God." Exasperated, she exhaled in a long hiss. Then she glared at him. "So you're a Virgo. Terrific. I'm a Scorpio. Want to throw the *I Ching*?"

"*Amy!*" he cried with agony. "*I was born one hundred and thirteen years ago!*"

NINE

He must be joking, she thought, staring at him, amazed. He had made a big deal out of saying that he had something important to tell her, played around with her emotions and then said that he was *one hundred and thirteen*? And now—what incredible gibberish was *this*? He had arrived in San Francisco via a time machine that had been moved (while he was in mid-flight) from London as part of a traveling exhibition? And just three days ago he had been entertaining old friends in *1893*? What was that? In reality, he was chasing a killer who had used his revolutionary device to escape nineteenth-century Scotland Yard detectives? And he felt responsible lest this infamous villain wreak havoc in 1979?

There was one problem. The joke was not funny. It was the epitome of bad taste, given her commitment and her show of tenderness and love. Feelings she thought had been *shared*! This was no joke, it was a cruel prank, perhaps the cruelest of them all. She could recall only one other occasion when she had been treated in such a cavalier fashion. The last time her ex-husband had wanted sex, she had obliged, thinking that maybe there was hope for their failing marriage. He had misinterpreted her feelings, no doubt believing that she was just "letting him do it." The experience was thus quick, cold and, later, brutalizing. When she woke up the next morning, she found a twenty-dollar bill on her bedside table and a note asking for a divorce.

But this—this was horrible! What had she ever done to Herbert to deserve such treatment? Her astonishment gave way to confusion, and then she just felt deeply hurt, the ache settling over her, cutting through her, making her cold to the bone. Since her divorce, she had been wise to men, avoiding those who would trample her, respecting and liking those who responded in kind. And now—alas—along came this English swain with the broad mustache and the disarming smile. In just three days he had made her love him and now was deliberately destroying the emotion. *Why?* She had no idea, but more important, how was she going to get through this scene? She sighed inwardly and told herself to remain calm no matter what. She had always kept herself together by relying on inner strength. Now was no time to change.

There was, however, a limit to her threshold of pain. She could take no more of this little man rattling on about the fourth dimension. She slowly rose to her feet.

"Herbert?"

"Now that you understand, my dear," he said, unthinking, "I can tell you that I *hate* to be called Herbert. I am H. G. Wells, and I prefer to be addressed by my initials."

"H. G. *Wells*?" She hadn't been prepared for that.

"In the flesh and at your service." He grinned with pride.

"And Shakespeare's just around the corner, right?" She managed to laugh.

"I beg your pardon?"

"I think you'd better go now," she said, a slight quaver in her voice.

There was a hush. She saw his eyes open wide with

surprise, then dim as if someone had turned off a light behind them. He went limp.

"You don't believe me," he said dully. "For a moment there, I thought—" Suddenly, he approached her, his arms open wide. "Amy, you must—"

"*Please* don't come near me!"

He stopped and sighed bitterly. "I knew this would happen. I knew that telling you the truth would ruin everything, but you had to know. And I could no longer carry on the grotesque charade of being a modern, incredibly naïve Britisher, especially if we were—"

"If we were what?"

He sighed again. "Please forget it. Nothing matters anymore." He started for the door, head down, disconsolate.

"Forget what?"

He turned. "It's a damnable pity!"

"What's a pity? What are you *talking* about?"

"I don't know about anyone else in this room, but I happen to be falling in love with you!"

Surprised, she stared at him. Then she shook her head. She was astonished and bewildered. She did not know immediately how to respond.

And then suddenly he sank onto the couch in a paroxysm of sobs and covered his face with his hands. He angrily wiped away the tears and began to shout. "There is no God! *No* Supreme Being would *ever* create a human being and then allow this to happen to him!"

"Herbert, are you all right?" She wasn't at all sure about herself. The strength went out of her legs and she had to sit down. "Will you please tell me what is going on?"

He looked up, his eyes red, his face twisted with agony. "I just *did*! My name is H. G. Wells, and I was born in 1866, and I came here—not on a bloody airship—but on a time machine that right now I wish I'd never invented!"

She was no longer perplexed or hurt. Right then, she

realized that he was deadly serious, and she was perceptive enough to understand the ramifications. The man's imagination had replaced his reality, and it was absolutely chilling. She moaned inwardly and began to tremble.

"And I probably never would have landed here in the first place if Dr. Leslie John Stephenson hadn't stolen away in *my* machine! And *he* is no ordinary killer, my dear lady! Oh, no! I don't know how much of a history buff you are, what with your Robert Kennedys and the like, but the villain *I* am pursuing is a man they call *Jack the Ripper*!"

She gasped. Her eyes widened, and she clutched the arms of her chair. Fear came over her. The man's a nut, she told herself, and God knows what his reference to Jack the Ripper means! What would she *do*? She had never been alone with a lunatic before. What if he attacked her? She began looking around wildly for something to protect herself with. Her heartbeat pounded.

He rose from the couch. She was about to scream for all she was worth when he made a tired, effete shrug and turned away.

"It is of no use." His voice was low and sad. "I might as well try to tell this couch here that it is—like me—a perpetually moving swirl of electrons." Defeated, he slowly moved toward the door.

She sighed with relief and slumped in her chair. He might be a mental case, but it was clear that he was not going to harm her. As a matter of fact, the more critically she observed his behavior, the more *normal* he seemed. Why, if she hadn't heard his chimerical explanations, she could convince herself that he was behaving exactly like a rejected suitor, and she had seen a number of them in her time. Hold it, she thought and sat up straight. She had to play this out, for no man was going to get off that easily after spinning such an incredible tale.

He had his reluctant hand on the doorknob when she spoke.

"Wait."

He sagged and lightly pressed his forehead against the cool, enameled surface.

"Sit down."

He returned to the couch and gingerly perched on its edge, appearing to her vaguely reminiscent of a dog with a broken spirit who expected to be kicked. She leaned forward, placed her chin on her hand and contemplated him, searching for a sign, a clue, perhaps an omen. She was cool now that her fear had passed, but still she remained hurt and confused. She had loved him, she had offered to help him, and he had responded with utter nonsense for absolutely no reason. There just *couldn't* be any truth to what he had said; yet, she sensed that he was a genuine, straightforward person. What, then, was going on? She collected her thoughts and continued gazing at him, but no matter how she tried to work out the logic, she could not fathom what he had told her or why he had said it. Unless . . .

She gasped again. She had heard of UFOs and she really did believe that they existed. Was he attempting to convince her that he was from another galaxy? That he was an alien who had transmogrified himself into a small and infinitely lovable English gentleman? She shivered. If this were indeed an encounter of the third kind, then that meant that she had slept with a *creature!* God help her if his original form were that of an insect and she was pregnant! No, no, she told herself, it was too surreal. It wasn't even larger than life. *It just wasn't so. It was a total, elaborate, spectacular sham.*

She felt terrible again and wanted to cry, but would not allow herself the luxury. She forced herself to continue staring at him. Finally, things began to make sense and her thoughts seemed logical. She smiled grimly. First, this man was naïve and helpless. Second, she had made both spoken and unspoken commitments. Third, she had obviously frightened him beyond words. Fourth, since he could not accept her commitments, this was his demented way of extracting himself from a delicate situation. (Perhaps all he had expected was a one-night stand and had suddenly discovered that he cared for her.) Therefore, what he was really trying to say was that he was already spoken for. That was it, wasn't it? Pure and simple, no matter what he'd said before, he had a wife back home in a cottage near the seashore. He wasn't chasing a killer, he was probably collecting books for the University of Oxford's library. He undoubtedly had a flock of kids, too, and hadn't been out of the house in years. Too busy being a good father and provider. Of course. That had to be the answer.

"Why didn't you just say so in the first place?"

"I beg your pardon?"

"Why didn't you admit that you were married? What did you think I was going to do? Shoot you? I mean, face it. I've slept with married men before."

He blushed.

Aha, she thought. I was right!

"Whoosh!" He fell back on the couch. "The irony of it."

"What irony?"

"My dear girl, the irony is that someday I might be able to prove to you that I am the writer and inventor H. G. Wells, from 1893 London, but it seems that I'll never convince you that I happen to be foot-loose and fancy-free."

"Oh, come on, Herbert!"

"H.G.," he corrected her.

"All right, H.G., whatever! Since you're obviously not man enough to admit it, you might at least tell me why you concocted that bullshit story about spinning along the fourth dimension in a time machine! I mean, there must be a reason!"

"I would agree."

"Well, then?"

"It is the truth," he replied flatly.

"Ohhh, *damn* you!" She pushed back in the chair and stared at the ceiling. It seemed, or so she thought, that she was going to receive absolutely no satisfaction, let alone straight answers. There was, then, nothing to be done. She would have to ask him to leave, then pick up the pieces of her shattered emotions. "That's it, then. I'm sorry. Would you please leave?"

"What if I could *prove* to you that I am H. G. Wells? And that I recently arrived in San Francisco in a time machine?"

"That's impossible."

"Nothing is impossible, given the wizardry of science and technology."

"Look, just forget it, okay? Just forget it and lock the door on your way out." She turned away and closed her eyes tightly, but could not ignore the twinge of interest inside her.

"Listen, wasn't I right about Stephenson being alive? That was the truth, wasn't it?"

"Yes."

"Why didn't I think of it before?" he exclaimed joyfully. He turned to her. "Amy, I can actually prove to you that I am who I am!"

"Okay, okay! Just let me *think* a minute, will you?" She bit her nails—a habit that she had given up at age eight—and thought hard. Although she still did not believe him, she knew that one thing was certain: he was sincere. Furthermore, no matter what happened, she could not retract her feelings. They went too deep for that. Determination and endurance had always been among her better qualities. Was she going to opt for the facile solution this time?

She sighed. He might not be lying to her, but what he was saying was impossible. Yet, she had to see this thing through, she had to go with him every step of the journey if she were to make a proper, mature choice. Then—after he had presented his "evidence," so to speak—she would decide about the sanity and motives of her new lover. Until then, she would be suspicious, but loyal. So far, he had not betrayed her.

She got out of her chair. She was slightly dizzy and had to hold her head. Then she smiled. Her giddiness was not the result of emotional turmoil; rather, it was the product of a strange excitement that had seized her. What if he *could* prove his identity? If so, her predilection for him might turn out to be cosmic.

"All right, H.G. Prove it."

He turned, and she saw the strain in his face give way to a flush of relief.

"Do you have any tools?" he asked in an urgent voice.

"*Tools?*" She could not hide her amazement.

"You know, pliers, screwdrivers, wrenches, wire cutters, drills and the like."

"Yes, I have a few, but *why?*"

"And some oil. I'll need a can of oil, too."

At the corner of Fourteenth and Noe streets in a dour and uninteresting section of the city, Stephenson got out of a taxi, paid the driver, then walked briskly to the address she had given him. He suddenly shivered. His purple silk shirt beckoned rather than kept out the cold; he felt as if he were wearing a garment fashioned from ice. Tomorrow, he must purchase a good and heavy coat. Not anything as dreary as a wool Chesterfield, but rather one of those imitation-leather creations that the colored men seemed so enamored of.

He went up a steep flight of concrete steps and into the foyer of an old Victorian apartment building. The worn carpet was clean, yet smelled musty, and someone in the ground-floor flat had fried bacon several hours ago. His nose wrinkled with distaste, just as his eyes narrowed upon seeing the faded decor. He hated to be reminded of the nineteenth century.

He paused in the foyer long enough to scan the mailboxes for her name. Sure enough, there it was: "Marsha McGee: 37½ Noe Street." He turned and bounded up the stairs two at a time. If he hesitated now—on this, his first legitimate liaison with a woman—then he would bolt from the building and run screaming to The Broadway. He could not think about it. He had to trust his own animal magnetism. He did not want to pay for the postmortems he performed anymore. It would really gall him, given how far he had come.

Suddenly, he was there, staring at the numbers on the door. Below them was a peephole window and a metal knocker with the brass plating peeling off. He took a deep breath and rapped quickly on the wood.

"Just a second!"

He heard quick footsteps, and then the door was flung open (without a prudent look through the peephole window). He felt a pleasant rush of warm air.

"Hi. C'mon in." She was wearing jeans and a tight undershirt that emphasized her breasts and naked shoulders. Just brushed, her abundant hair shone, and he was reminded of a forbidden French postcard he had once found in his father's study called "Lady Godiva."

He entered her apartment hesitantly. Was he overdressed for the occasion? If so, she did not seem to notice; rather, she seemed pleased, even *happy* that he was there. She took his hand, led him across the bare wooden floor and pushed him down onto a splayed couch. It was the only piece of furniture in the room.

"Like a wine cooler?"

He nodded.

"Great, I've got a couple made up already." She went into the kitchen and returned moments later with two glasses. She handed him one, set hers on the floor in front of the couch. Then she went through what was once a double doorway into a darkened portion of the room that now served as her boudoir.

He saw her rummaging through a dresser (perhaps for a blouse to don?), then averted his head and tasted the concoction in the glass. It was a mixture of soda water, a peel of lemon and red wine. He was unimpressed, but the chilled liquid did soothe his dry throat. He smacked his lips with appreciation.

She came back into the room proper, hips curving as she moved, and went to the phonograph, which had been placed in the dormer bay window on the street side of the flat.

"You like Fleetwood Mac?"

"Quite," he uttered, vague but curious.

"Everyone I know goes for Linda Ronstadt in a big way, but she's just too sad for me. All those ruined love affairs and lonely nights. What a life." Then she laughed. "I could sure go for the money that chick's got, though."

She pressed a button on the record machine and turned up the volume to seven. The room was flooded with sound, and Stephenson instinctively jumped, making a quick move to protect his ear drums. He was sure that the music could be heard blocks away, yet she was swaying to the beat in the center of the room as if the level of decibels were the most natural thing in the world. He relaxed, and enjoyed the primitive rhythm and the high, sweet harmonies. The music did not have the grandeur of his favorite, *Ring of the Nibelungen* (which he had had the great fortune to see performed by the London Symphony Orchestra and conducted by the brilliant Wagner himself when he, Stephenson, was a first-year student at the Normal School of Science), but it was satisfactory. He smiled. It would do.

She sat down beside him, opened her left hand and revealed a hand-rolled cigarette. She lit it and inhaled deeply. The odor was unfamiliar to him; it wasn't tobacco, nor was it opium, which he had tasted in the squalid dens of the East End.

"It's some homegrown that I got from an old boy friend when I went back to Modesto to see my folks last month." She spoke directly into his ear in order to be heard over the music. Her close, hot breath made him shiver. She took another drag on the curious cigarette, then held it out for him.

He balked at first, then quickly figured that her gesture must be some modern refinement of the old American Indian custom of passing the peace pipe. It was, thus, a ritual of friendship and trust, and he laughed inside. He took the homegrown, imitated her and, after he had inhaled, collapsed with a series of coughs.

She giggled. "Oh, that homegrown! You gotta get used to it."

He recovered his breath, wiped away the tears in his eyes and nodded dumbly. A silent moment passed between them; there was only the music. He took a more conservative pull off the weed and passed it back.

"So what brings you to San Francisco?" she asked between drags, her eyes slitted now, her voice thick.

"The weather," he replied, suddenly light and giddy inside.

"The *weather*? Jesus, if I could afford it, I'd move to Honolulu in the morning."

He fell back onto the couch, closed his eyes and placed his hand on his forehead. The music seemed louder. His flesh tingled.

She lay back next to him. "Good stuff, huh?"

"I feel remarkable."

She smoked the last of the homegrown, snubbed it out on the upturned lid of a jar and then—much to his astonishment—swallowed the remains.

"I've always been a conservationist," she said wryly.

He nodded, but was unable to speak. He had no idea what she was talking about.

"What's it all about, anyway?" she said—not to him in particular—and stared at the bare walls.

"Life, I suppose," he croaked.

"Yeah, that's part of it, I guess, but you never really know, do you? I mean, sometimes I wonder, if you know what I mean."

He didn't, but he thought that he must understand, so he nodded again, slowly and with import.

"Hawaii is so far away and yet you can get there in just a couple of hours."

"I've never been."

"Neither have I."

"What's it like?"

"Oh, you know. What's this space like? I mean, we're into it, but what's it all about? It's the same there, for sure. Only warmer. But then again, maybe not. They have freak storms, too, you know."

"It must be nice."

"Let's go."

"We can't."

"Why not?"

"You have to open up the shop in the morning."

"Ah." She paused to take a long swig of her wine cooler and to reflect on the significance of his last statement. It seemed to linger in the air, blending nicely with the flights of Fleetwood Mac. "Limitations."

"Need not exist." His voice was thick and droll.

"To hell with them. All I want is to have a good time."

"That makes sense."

"I may never go back to work again."

"How delightful."

"And that may be what it's all about, anyway." She ran her hand lightly across his cheek. "You want some more wine before we leave?"

"Leave? Where are we going?" He frowned imperceptibly.

"I don't know. Somewhere."

"I'm surely not adverse to staying here, if it's all the same to you, Marsha."

"Hey!" She bounced up, suddenly full of energy. "I know!"

"What? Hawaii again?"

"No, no, we'll do that tomorrow."

"What, then?"

"Have you ever seen a porno flick?"

Amy parked in the empty lot that by day serviced the world-famous Japanese Tea Gardens. H.G. took her hand and led her in a wide circle around the back of the museum concourse. They made their way to the side door of the museum, from which he had first emerged into the future some three days ago.

Since the door was locked, he took a chisel out of the small bag of tools and began prying the metal face of the handle away from the door. When he had enough room to work, he inspected the bowels of the lock with a penlight. It was a sophisticated, cylinder dead bolt that would take some time to overcome, but would not be impossible. It operated on the same principle as the first pin tumbler lock did, invented by the American Linus Yale, Jr., in 1861.

He dropped to his knees, had her hold the penlight and began to dismantle the device. He became totally absorbed with his task and started to tinker. He took apart little nuances of machinery that he didn't have to, admiring modern man's advancement in the field of security. He came to a series of tumblers that interfaced, which meant that he would have to remove the entire bolt. With her nail file, he sawed through the machine screws that held the bolt plate into the door. Obviously, the bolt was flanged and could not otherwise be extracted. He began whistling a Mozart melody through his teeth.

"Shhhh!"

"Oh. Sorry."

"Will you hurry up?" she whispered frantically.

"This is not a mere wooden bar behind a castle door, mind you," he replied with a touch of sarcasm.

"Why don't you just break it?" She handed him a small hammer.

He spurned the crude bludgeon. "What do you think I am? A bloody Philistine?"

Before she could respond, he removed the cylinder, the door handles, then the bolt itself, which he held up in the light and inspected, as if he had just extracted an impacted tooth from someone's mouth.

Then they gathered up the tools and quickly slipped inside the museum's basement. After their eyes had adjusted to the blackness, he led her up to the first floor. Night lights were on, and H.G. was relieved that now he could see without difficulty. They were near the main entrance.

Suddenly, they heard the ring of footfalls coming in their direction. Amy looked around wildly for some place to go and threw her arms around him. Before he could react, he felt her pulling him and turned to see if she had discovered a hiding place. He gasped when he looked up, for she was about to yank him inside the *ladies' room*! Oh, no, he thought, not on your life!

He struggled with her, ignoring her whispered expressions of dismay. She finally gave up and pushed him away. The sudden change in momentum caused him to fall over backward, arms flailing at the air. He landed on his back, executed an awkward somersault and looked up in time to see the ladies' room door close behind her. He scrambled up and saw, across from Amy's cache, the sanctuary of the men's room. He ran for it on tiptoes and slipped inside just as a guard rounded the turn into the great hall.

H.G. hid inside a booth. When he heard the guard also come inside the bathroom, he climbed on top of the toilet seat and crouched. Cold, nervous sweat ran down his flanks. Then he heard a sigh and the static sound of a stream of urine hitting porcelain. He exhaled with relief. There was a great roar as the urinal was flushed, footsteps, a door opening and hissing shut, the faint echo of receding footfalls. H.G. crept to the door, stuck his head out and looked. He was momentarily startled, for he saw Amy directly opposite him, peering out of the ladies' room in a similar fashion.

They were reunited in the center of the hall, and despite her protests, he took her farther inside the museum.

They came to a rotunda. Suddenly, H.G. pushed Amy and himself behind a pillar. There was an information desk in the middle of the space, and the guard sat behind it, reading the newspaper and drinking coffee. They hid behind the pillar for what seemed like an eternity. Finally, the guard put the paper down, yawned, got up, nonchalantly crossed the rotunda and disappeared into a dark corridor.

H.G. nodded to Amy, and they continued on. Eventually, they got to the display room. He ushered her inside, and turned on the lights. Then they crossed the room and stepped over the rope barrier which during the day separated guided tours from the milestones in the career of the remarkable H.G. Wells. Beaming, he went to *The Utopia*. He patted its dull surface as if greeting an old friend and felt a surge of emotion. He yearned to be home again, enjoying a good read and a glass of claret in his study by the fire. He sighed. Another time, perhaps.

He went to the engine, lifted the hatch and looked

inside. The crystalline bars glistened like new and the stainless-steel gears still turned with ease. The insulation on the RRL circuitry was brittle, but still intact, and the ivory and diamond buffers had aged only in color. Metal rot had affected only thin sheets of casing. The critical parts were in splendid operating condition. He was pleased. He lubricated the connections, closed the hatch, straightened up and wiped his hands on a rag. Suddenly, he realized that Amy wasn't there. He hurried around the time machine and saw her perusing an old book atop a display case.

"What are you doing?"

She didn't look up. "How come you didn't like George Bernard Shaw?" she asked lightly.

Her question puzzled him. "You don't mean the drama critic for *The Times*, do you?"

She laughed. "Among other things."

"I've never even met the man!"

"Well, apparently you found him stuffy." She read from the book. " 'A dried-up, old vegetarian virgin who wrote for insomniacs.' " She looked at H.G. knowingly. "If, of course, you are who you say you are."

He jerked the book out of her hands and slammed it shut. He trembled. "Would you mind terribly much not doing that?"

"What's wrong?"

"I'd rather write the books before someone quotes me."

"I was only kidding."

"Well, I'm not. There won't be any point to my life if I know what I'm going to write and invent in the future." He dropped the book back onto the display case. "Blasted thing is nothing but an oversized epitaph."

He noticed that she was looking from him to some old photographs in another display case, comparing his visage to the black and white prints.

"Yes. The resemblance is uncanny, isn't it?"

She nodded, surprised and somewhat bewildered.

He went to the cabin door, kneeled down and pulled on a small ring handle. A prism-shaped device—covered with a fine, multicolored dust—came out of the time machine. He wiped it off and inspected it.

"What's that?"

"My version of a declinometer. It holds the magnetic variation steady during flight. In the process, it collects extratemporal residue and occasionally should be cleaned."

"Okay. Now tell me what it does."

"It keeps the machine from rotating into infinity."

"What's wrong with infinity?"

"It has no beginning and no end. So once you get there, you stay there."

"Why can't you get back?"

"Because there is nothing to get back from," he replied hollowly. "You become permanently frozen in a time warp."

"Oh," she said thoughtfully after a pause. She regarded him critically. "You certainly know a lot about this, don't you?"

He blushed and looked down modestly.

"*I* know!" she exclaimed, then snapped her fingers. "You heard about this exhibit, boned up on time machines, then brought me along because you were afraid to sneak in here and try it yourself! Right?"

He frowned. "Wrong."

"And you're not really H. G. Wells, you just happen to look like him, right?"

"Wrong again." He carefully pushed the prismlike device back into its housing, then climbed into the cabin.

She followed. "Hey, it's okay. I'll try anything once."

Miffed, he ignored her and frowned with disgust when he saw the dials on the control panel. The glass coverings were so smoked with age that it was impossible to read the facings. With a small screwdriver, he removed the covers and tossed them into the corner. They shattered with small, brittle tinkles.

"What are you *doing*?"

"Using my poor but immediate resources to correct a careless flaw in design."

He inspected the controls. Fortunately, the series of switches which activated and blended the engine's energy fields had been cast with porcelain, so they had survived the ravages of time. A drop of oil on each lubricated the brass springs beneath, making the switches easier to manipulate.

Soon he came to the Rotator Control, frozen in the eastward position. He cursed his lack of foresight in using a low-grade steel for this crucial handle, then dumped the rest of the oil over it. He tugged on it, mouthing Victorian obscenities. Finally, he tried to kick it loose. The Rotator Control did not budge. He turned to her, smiled weakly and spread his hands.

"At the present time, I am not equipped to repair the Rotator Control. Hence, we can go only into the future."

"Oh." She thought for a moment, then said flippantly, "So who wants to go back and change history?"

Once again, he ignored her remark. He gestured at the swivel chair. "When to, Miss Robbins?"

"Saturday," she said lightly. "Let's just go to Saturday. After all, I wouldn't want to lose touch now, would I? Or the *entire* weekend."

"Very well," he said politely. He turned and squinted at the dials, then very carefully set them with the aid of the small screwdriver. After synchronizing the cabin's clock with his digital watch, he finally straightened up.

"How long will it take?" She sat casually in the chair.

"To travel three days?" He raised his eyebrows. "Precisely one quarter of a second."

She laughed. "That's impossible."

"You don't think it works, do you?" he exploded.

"You just think that I'm a bloody, asinine fool who's mucking about with a useless relic of a museum piece, don't you?"

"I didn't say those things."

"You didn't have to."

He closed and locked the hatch, squeezed in next to her, strapped them in, then engaged the bank of switches. Then he cast a sidelong glance at her. He was redeemed and smiled grimly, for at that moment an expression of utter terror was on her face. She might as well have said, what if—by some miracle—this mad Englishman were right? He drummed his fingers on the mahogany arm of the chair while waiting for the familiar whine of the electromagnetic energy fields as they spun up to speed and interlocked.

"Well?"

Now it was his turn to be concerned, for no familiar noise was forthcoming. He turned off all the switches, then tried them one more time.

Nothing happened.

"There seems to be a bit of a problem."

"What?"

"It doesn't work."

"Damn." She sighed. "For a minute there I thought I was going to be the first real Alice in Wonderland."

He broke out into a cold sweat, suddenly struck with the horrible import of the moment. What if he were stranded out of his own time?

His face ashen, he quickly unstrapped them, sprang out of the cabin and ran to the engine. He glanced wildly at the displays around him, but they did not reassure him. The terrible thought crossed his mind that some-one *else*—perhaps Grinnell or even Preston—could have assumed his identity and continued his career! He lifted the hatch and began a close inspection of the engine with the penlight. His hands, however, were shaking so badly that the beam of light fluttered radically. He could not clearly see a damn thing. He moaned, then closed his eyes in an effort to calm himself. Suddenly, he pictured Mrs. Nelson. She was telling him to take seven deep breaths to relieve the stress, not understanding why he hadn't done it before. He obeyed and found himself once again collected. He coolly began investigating the electrical leads from the switches to the flywheel and the pulse generator. They were all in good condition. Then he wondered if his machine could traverse such a minuscule time differential of three days. It shouldn't make any difference, he told himself. Certainly, to have an engine operational for *exactly* one fourth of a second was cutting it close, but it was *not* beyond the capabilities of his design.

"I just realized something," she whispered into the compartment. "This is the most ridiculous thing I've ever done in my life!"

"If I were you," he countered matter-of-factly, "I would have thought that agreeing to have lunch with me was a much more serious mistake."

"Listen, don't you think this—this charade has gone on long enough?" She hesitated and nervously glanced across the room at the door. "Face it, this is insane!"

"Call it what you like."

"Can't we please get out of here? Any minute now someone is going to walk through that door!"

"My dear girl, I have no *intention* of leaving here until I discover what is wrong with my time machine," he said sadly, but with passion. "For you, the choice is a matter of trust. For me, the decision is cosmic." He continued working, his face and hands now black with eighty-six-year-old grease.

"I'm not going *alone!*"

"Suit yourself."

"Come on, H.G.! Let's go!"

He did not respond.

She leaned against the outside of the engine compartment, closed her eyes and bit her lip.

He worked his hand inside the reversal housing to see if any kind of debris could have lodged there. All seemed clean and clear and well lubricated . . . there were no burrs from friction . . . no foreign metal chips that may have stuck to the gear teeth. . . . Wait a minute! What the devil was that? Fingers moving like spiders' legs, he felt a cylindrical object that hung loosely, yet was attached. *That* did not belong there!

He extracted his hand, rummaged through his motley assortment of tools and found a hacksaw blade. He pushed the flexible steel into the housing cavity and laboriously sawed through the foreign object. There was a small clink when the thing finally fell into the housing well. He removed the blade, groped for the object, pulled it out and examined it in the flashlight beam.

It was a small, obscure lock.

He did not comprehend, for he was trying to remember something that he had done which had not yet occurred. "Now why in the devil would I have locked the engine?"

"What?"

"This was the reason it wasn't working." He held up the lock for her to see. "Some time ago the gearing ratio was locked so that it wouldn't turn."

"Why did you do that?"

He crawled up out of the compartment, closed the hatch and straightened up. "I'm not sure that I did. Since it hasn't happened yet, I'm not sure who put the lock on."

"Would you please explain something to me?" she asked. "How could you arrive here by time machine if the damn thing wasn't working?"

He grinned. "It *was* working . . . when I left."

She stared at him, unable to respond. She did not resist when he took her hand, led her into the cabin and strapped them both into the chair. She seemed dazed by the implications of his last remark. He engaged the switches. There was that characteristic low hum, and he was gratified and relieved. Since the "Ready" light was not working, he waited a full twenty seconds until he was sure that the pitch of the idling energy fields sounded right. Then he glanced at her, the ultimate question in his eyes.

She gazed back—astonished at the sound—then gulped and nodded.

His lips formed a brief kiss and he winked at her. Then he resolutely shoved the Accelerator Helm Lever forward until it locked in the flank position.

Stephenson had to clutch his knees to keep his hands off her as she drove back to her apartment. He kept glancing at her, wondering if she felt the same way that he did. The porno flick—as she had termed it—had been more than either of them had bargained for. It had involved the violation of a beautiful teen-age girl by a cult of desert-sun worshippers, climaxing with an orgy in homage to Satan.

He remained incredibly aroused. He wondered if he should touch her. After all, she had suggested the entertainment in the first place. No, no, better to let her make the initial move. He feared rejection; he feared surprised outrage. Observing was a long way from participation. He could not blindly accost this Marsha McGee, for she was obviously not a professional harlot. But, oh, how he *wanted* to place his hands on her!

"Well?" she asked. "Did you like it?"

How could I not like it? he thought. *It was brilliant, marvelous, a priceless work of art! A glossy black pearl to toss into the ugly eye of morality and womankind! I loved it!*

"I thought it was an extremely interesting and challenging piece of entertainment," he replied.

"Yeah, it got a little heavy in the end. I would've been satisfied with just some clean, good, old-fashioned sex. But I gotta admit, it really turned my head around."

When they were back inside her apartment, she replaced the Fleetwood Mac music with something called Alice Cooper. Stephenson did not understand the name, although he preferred the sound to that of its predecessor. She made them drinks and reported that they had smoked the last of the homegrown. She seemed surprised that he did not carry his own weed; or for that matter, drugs of any kind. Then she shrugged.

"I guess it's pretty hard to come through customs and security and all that with anything that gets you high."

"Quite true." He nodded.

She laughed. "I'll bet if they legalized everything no one would do it." Then she was up again and in her bedroom going through her dresser. She returned with a small vial of white powder and a tiny silver spoon, the handle of which had been sculpted into the form of a man and a woman engaged in a sexual union.

He grinned, for he recognized the substance in the vial to be cocaine, a stimulant that he had used liberally in medical school. He recalled with pleasure the incredible athletic feats he had performed under the influence of the drug. Once, he had come out of a scrimmage against Oxford carrying the ball and had trampled five of their best players while galloping the length of the field to score the winning points. He had, however, never permitted himself to indulge in the drug while on his sorties in the East End. He had always feared that the good feelings induced by cocaine would cause him to spurn caution in favor of reckless abandon.

"Like a toot?"

"Would you mean a spot?" he asked good-naturedly, trying to hide his excitement.

"Toot, spot, whatever." Her voice quavered with anticipation.

"It *is* cocaine, is it not?"

"High-grade. My boss brings it in on his boat and gives me grams for a song."

"Please, then." He bent his head forward expectantly. She shoveled, held a spoonful under his nose. He pressed one nostril shut and quickly sniffed. She did his other nostril, and he fell back against the couch, his blood racing, his head popping clear. He was unaware that a slight trace of white powder remained on his upper lip beneath his nose. He heard her sniff several times and gasp. She smiled at him and giggled. Her eyes sparkled. Then she leaned over him—her breasts pushing into his shoulder—and slowly licked the cocaine off his lip.

The gesture was so incredibly erotic that he was unable to move or respond in kind. She settled back on the couch and gazed at him.

"This has been a *wonderful* evening!" he exclaimed.

"Unhuh." She nodded.

"A delightful dalliance! A perfectly marvelous way for two extraordinary human beings to prepare for, ah—a time-honored moment?"

"Really."

"You know, Marsha, I feel that I have been in your shadow for ages now, and that quite suddenly you have turned to face me and acknowledge my presence."

"Whatever."

"Do you—do you wish that we honor our—celebrate *your* acknowledgment and *my* humble acceptance?"

"Unhuh."

"Then why don't we—" His throat went dry, and he was seized with a fit of coughing. "Excuse me."

He bolted up, fled into the sanctuary of her bathroom and closely regarded his image in the mirror. His breathing was shallow; his sinuses were draining; his teeth were grinding together. He suddenly realized that the cocaine he had taken was not pure no matter what she had said. There was some other chemical mixed with it that was twisting his thought processes. And yet, he felt so *good!* The drug, however, was not his dilemma, for he could handle *anything!* The problem was that he had *never* asked a woman for sex before; he had never made an advance without first making the perfunctory deposit of a gold coin. Even his romp with his sister (although he had not paid for it in currency) had been at her suggestion. He frowned and clenched his trembling hands into fists. This Marsha McGee was not a prostitute. Oh, she might be a wanton little slut by Victorian standards, but she obviously did not accept money. So bloody what? If she gave it away, she was a fool.

He sniffed, then swung out of the bathroom and slammed the door. He would just come right out and ask: would she like to rut with him? Fornicate? Copulate along with the ghoulish noise of Alice Cooper?

He came around the corner, his voice heavy and guttural. "Marsha . . ." He began. He stopped, then took out his pocketwatch and opened the lid, for he did not have to utter a sound.

She was lounging on the couch, one leg drawn up and thrown over the back, the other spread out on the pillows, its foot touching the floor and moving in small circles; her arms were behind her head, and her hair fell over them in the shape of a flower. She was smiling up at him impishly, because in his brief absence, she had removed all of her clothes.

In a quiet, chilling sort of way, he went berserk.

Amy felt unbelievably weak and drained. She lifted her head, opened her eyes and instinctively glanced at her watch. It read 10:23:45. Only a few seconds had passed since that terrified moment just before H.G.

pushed the awkward lever forward. Now he was standing over her, uttering triumphant and soothing phrases. He pulled her up out of the chair, and she leaned against the side of the cabin. The metal wall felt warm, and she thought that strange since she would have expected it to be cold. She also heard creaks and groans emanating from *inside* the plating; that seemed even more bizarre. She tried to remember what had happened after the lever had clicked and locked, but the passage of time had been so brief, so infinitesimal. She was vaguely aware of a mad swirl of bright colors and then a flood of blackness, but that was all. She knew *something* had happened, but wasn't quite sure what.

They left the time machine. Her strength returned, and she glanced swiftly around the display room. Everything seemed the same. He certainly appeared no different. What was he doing now, anyway? Inserting and turning a small key in a thing marked "RRL" over the door handle? Oh, well.

"Nothing's changed," she uttered hollowly.

"We only went to Saturday, remember?" He smiled generously like the Cheshire cat.

Was she the first real Alice? Had she actually jumped forward in time? She frowned, not wanting to believe, yet knowing that something had happened.

"What have you done?" Her voice was crisp and clear.

"Taken you to Saturday." He appeared perfectly relaxed; he was not tugging on his mustache.

"I have the distinct feeling," she said with a controlled edge, "that you haven't taken me anywhere."

"Oh," he replied casually. "You're in the same *place*. It just happens to be Saturday night right now as opposed to Wednesday night."

She wanted to say bullshit, but sighed instead, determined to let him play out his hand. Then she would sort it all out and come to both a conclusion and a decision.

"Come on," he whispered brusquely.

She followed him out of the exhibit to the door of the display room. She looked back once at the time machine and thought that she saw a faint, bluish glow dissipating around it, but wasn't sure. She dismissed the aura as a figment of her own psychological projection.

They left the room and moved cautiously along the dark corridor. Nothing had changed here, either, and she became increasingly skeptical. Did traveling only to Saturday mean that everything would appear the same? Perhaps—if there were a grain of truth to all this fourth-dimensional mumbletypeg—she should have opted for three years instead of days. Maybe thirty? Obviously, one did not age when time-traveling. Then again, who could believe this inimitable replica of the great H.G. Wells?

They came to the edge of the rotunda, and she remembered it well from what seemed like just a short time ago. The space was empty. She could hear the wall clock clack away the minutes as they remained poised on the periphery. Finally, he gestured and moved off to the right. She did not, for she had spotted a newspaper left folded on the information desk next to a cold cup of coffee. She knew that H.G. could not have staged that; she had been with him the entire time. Before he could stop her, she boldly headed for the desk. He saw her, reacted with a desperate wave of caution, but she was not to be deterred.

She reached the desk and scrutinized the newspaper. Section two of the morning *Chronicle* lay on top, and her eyes immediately went to the heading and the date.

"Saturday, November 10, 1979."

She gasped and lurched back. Was it *possible*? Had she actually traveled into the future? Oh my God, she thought, was it so easy to skip days, then return to one's own time and become a prophet? There was no doubting this fact! She had seen and read and comprehended a dated piece of the future! With a trembling hand, she reached out and touched the newspaper, then slid her fingertips down its surface. She looked at them and recognized the faint cast of black ink from the newsprint. Herbert had not been playing games; he had not been lying; she was surprised that he had had the patience to put up with her reticence; he was as true as Antony was to Cleopatra, as Romeo was to Juliet. She looked up—astonished, bewildered—and saw him cautiously approaching her. He *was* H.G. Wells, and she was certain that he loved her! She almost burst out with a whoop of joy, then obeyed his quick signal to control herself. She looked down at the newspaper again just to double-check. No, she was *not* deceiving herself; the date was the same. She sighed, then as an afterthought rummaged through the sections of newspaper just so she would know what the big deal was Saturday morning according to the gospel, *Chronicle*. She found page one on the bottom of the pile, took one look, looked again, then emitted a gasp that resembled a death rattle.

She sat down hard in the desk chair, her hand to her mouth, her body convulsing with fear. Waves of nausea swept over her. There was no need to look at the paper again, for that page would be eternally etched in her memory. She briefly fought for breath, then blacked out and slumped in the chair.

She awoke moments later. He was shaking her. She gazed at him, her eyes wide with terror. She trembled and whimpered with the grim knowledge of the future.

"What is it?" he insisted in a low, desperate voice.

She only had the strength to point. He followed her gesture, stared at the newspaper and exhaled slowly. His face became ashen, then turned crimson. She had never seen him so full of anger and determination.

"We shall see," he hissed. "We shall bloody well see about *this!*"

"What are we going to do?" she managed to utter.

"What else? Change the future."

He folded up the newspaper and stuffed it into his pocket. Then he picked her up and half carried her back to the time machine. As they went, she struggled to help him, despite her weakened condition. She knew she was alive and she wanted to prolong that precious gift forever. She did not know exactly what he was thinking or what he could do, but she definitely had destiny on her mind. She could think of nothing else as he assisted her into the cabin and—violently cursing—finally kicked the Rotator Control until it was free and they were thus able to journey into the past.

No, she would never forget that banner story: the San Francisco *Chronicle*. Saturday, November 10, 1979. "CAREER GIRL MURDERED. Fourth 'Ripper' Style Slaying Has Police Baffled." She had not read the story that accompanied the headline, but there was no mistaking the photograph of the victim and the identifying caption underneath:

"Bank of England employee, Amy Catherine Robbins."

TEN

When they reached the sanctuary of her apartment, he held her for a long time even though she seemed remarkably stoic. He knew that time-traveling just in itself had had a profound effect on her mind. That combined with the shock of the newspaper would have sent anyone else into hysterics. Amy was strong, he thought. And thank God for that. If there were a way out of their dilemma, he sensed that she would have to be strong. He shivered. Her life, now, was his responsibility. It was imperative that he stop the rampaging Stephenson. But *how*?

Finally, he felt her relax in his embrace. "Are you all right?"

She nodded, her head still buried into his chest.

"Want to talk?"

"I don't suppose you can tell me I just woke up after a horrible nightmare."

"No. I'm sorry."

She sighed. "Well, I'm not going to blame you for all this. I didn't have to get involved with you."

"I suppose we can always leave," he said, looking off, preoccupied.

"What?"

"I don't like the idea of retreat and I detest the

thought of leaving Leslie John Stephenson at large in this fine city, but if worst comes to worst we can go away in *The Utopia* before the time of your death. Or even on an airliner, I suppose."

"What are you saying?"

"Simply this—we avoid your murder," he said flatly. "And by so doing, we effectively change the future, *quod erat demonstrandum.*"

For a moment, she was excited. Then the light in her eyes faded and she sighed. "What if we can't change anything? What if it's hopeless?"

"Whoosh," he uttered, then got up and began pacing the floor.

"I mean, you've heard that old saying, 'What will be, will be.'"

He raised his eyebrows. "If you don't mind, I'd prefer not to hear a lot of rubbish about predestination. I happen to believe that man is capable of controlling his own destiny."

"I just don't want to die!" Her voice quavered slightly. She frowned and bit her lip.

"Amy, you are not going to die! Free will exists. And I have *already* changed the future by coming here on a time machine and meeting you."

"You're right." She sighed again. "I'm sorry."

He did not remind her that Stephenson had also changed the future by committing two grotesque crimes. H.G. scowled at the immense pressure he suddenly felt. He had to stop the villainous surgeon. He, H. G. Wells, was responsible! And he hated the passivity of just running away if the hour got too late.

Then he remembered that the newspaper from the future was in his coat pocket. He took it out, went into the dining room, spread it out on the table and studied it, hoping that the article would provide him with some clues as to Stephenson's whereabouts. It did not, but fortunately for his analytic, deductive mind, the story *did* recount Stephenson's heinous activities leading up to Amy's demise.

"Hmmmm." He skipped over the section about the oriental prostitute in the massage parlor, for that much he already knew. He read with horror and interest about what Stephenson had done to a rather pretty salesgirl named Marsha McGee. Other than Amy, however, most of the reportage was devoted to the death of someone named Dolores Clark who happened to have been the daughter of a prominent and wealthy black attorney. The girl's body had been found in John McLaren Park near a parking area between the lake and John F. Shelley Drive around 3:05 A.M. Thursday morning, November 8; approximately one-half hour after she had been murdered, police experts estimated. H.G. pressed a button on his watch. It was now 11:30 P.M. Dolores Clark would die in less than three hours.

Suddenly, he looked up from the newspaper and stared at the windows. An idea was taking shape inside his head. A marvelous idea: infinitely clear and simple and foolproof.

"Whoosh!" He got up and hurried back into the living room.

"What?"

"By George, I think I've got it!"

"You do?" Her eyes shone gratefully.

"According to Saturday morning's *Chronicle*, Dr. Stephenson has already murdered someone else. Her name is Dolores Clark and she will die in a matter of hours."

"All due respect—and I mean that sincerely—what has that got to do with me?"

"Everything."

"Explain."

"If we prevent that atrocity from occurring then your death will not occur, *non quod erat faciendum*."

"In other words, we head him off at the pass."

"Precisely."

"But how is that possible?"

"We know exactly when and where her murder will occur."

Wide-eyed, she stared at him for a moment and let the logic penetrate her brain. Then she slowly nodded and agreed. "That's—that's brilliant!" she whispered, then laughed, full of immense relief. "Everything's going to be all right, isn't it?"

"My dear girl," he replied with a casual affirmation of his most basic beliefs, "nothing is beyond the capabilities of man. All one has to do is think positively."

"You're absolutely amazing."

"How long does it take to get to John McLaren Park?"

"Twenty minutes. At the most."

"Just so we have plenty of time, why don't we leave at one-thirty?"

She nodded enthusiastically.

"In the meantime, I suggest that we rest. I, myself, want to be fresh for something as historic as a match with destiny." He sat down on the couch.

"What if we overslept?" Amy asked. She moved next to him so that her breasts pushed into his arm.

He chuckled. "You, a child of the present, are worried about oversleeping?"

"What's so unusual about that?"

"You have clocks that are run by the mighty, endless electron," he said expansively. "They don't lose time and their alarms are never stilled."

"Unless we have a power blackout."

"Oh." He gave her a brief, sidelong glance and felt stupid. "Yes. Of course."

"We don't have to sleep."

"How the devil could I sleep now?" he scolded. "My bloody eyes will be glued to the clock for the next two hours waiting for the damned electricity to stop!"

"I mean, there are other ways to relax." She placed her hand on his thigh.

"Oh. Hmm." He watched her unbutton her shirt and blushed with desire. She shook her breasts free, removed the garment from her shoulders, suddenly stopped and smiled. She squeezed her legs tightly together.

"I wonder," she asked.

"What?"

"When this is all over, we'll have to sneak into the museum again and try it."

"Try what?"

"Making love, silly! Can you imagine what it would be like if it were timeless?"

He gaped at her with astonishment. "What a simply marvelous suggestion."

Just off Broadway and Columbus Street was a nightclub and sometime discothèque. Its façade was a wall of imitation black marble crammed between two larger buildings and deliberately located on a narrow side street to promote the idea of an intimate and exotic hideaway. Other than the soundproof front door, the only break on the glossy black surface was a green neon sign, its letters drawn out into an elongated parallelogram.

"THE GREEN LIGHT BALLROOM" winked every thirty seconds, implying to those who cared that the inside of the club was an ultramodern lie, yet at the same time urging one to enter, pay five dollars for a mixed drink and find out for himself.

One who did not care was sitting at a small table in the center of the spartan room drinking gin. Leslie John Stephenson idly watched young couples—not necessarily heterosexual ones—dancing in front of the curtained stage. They moved in complex, quick patterns, jiggling and shaking. The men—some attired in flashy three-piece suits—twirled their partners as if they were dolls to be experimented with. Stephenson guessed that he was witnessing a modern minuet. The pace was no doubt faster than it had been in the seventeenth century, but he imagined that the cynical and decadent overtones were the same. Some things never change.

He sipped his drink, leaned back and sighed with appreciation. It was good to relax afterward. He chortled with satisfaction. The suggestive movements of the dancers reminded him of Marsha McGee swaying to the music in her apartment. Before.

He was flooded with vivid memories of the bestial sex he had enjoyed with her just a little while ago. He recalled with intense pleasure her face and how her expressions had changed. At first, when he had begun to beat her, she had reacted with a surge of passion; then, when she realized that the force of his blows had far exceeded the bounds of lustful exuberance, her eyes and mouth had opened wide with uncertainty. And finally, after he had hit her with his closed fist, her look was one of pain, terror and utter vulnerability, for she was naked, pinned beneath him, and he was inside her. She had started screaming, but moments later he had mercilessly slashed her throat and ended her life.

After he had performed his bloody ritual, he had cleaned up in Marsha's antiquated bathroom. Then he had left the Noe Street flat and taken a taxi to Russian Hill. He had gone to Amy Robbins' address, broken into her place and quickly discovered that she was not there. He had been surprised, for he had assumed that a working girl would have been in bed early, resting up for the next day's toil. He had been wrong. He had considered waiting for her return, then had grown nervous because he didn't like sulking about in a dark and alien flat. What if she didn't come home at all? Given the late hour, that was entirely possible. In fact, she was probably coupled with someone right now elsewhere in the city, the morals of these modern women being what they were.

He had left then, as quietly as he had come, cool-headed with the knowledge that time was on his side. So Amy Robbins was not home. He would come back tomorrow night. Earlier, perhaps, but he would return.

Then he had gone to the North Beach district of the city, discovered the Green Light Ballroom and now was thoroughly enjoying himself. His thoughts returned to the present.

The music ended and the dancers returned to their tables. A master of ceremonies came out onto the stage and spoke into a microphone. "Ladies and gentlemen, the Green Light Ballroom is proud to present for the first time in San Francisco, the Pet Killers!"

To mild, perfunctory applause, the curtains parted, revealing a band of lean and tall musicians dressed in black, their faces painted white, their lips purple. On a dais behind them was a silver cage. Inside it was a blond woman attired in a flowing chemise gown. Stephenson gasped at the sight and leaned forward with interest.

The band began with a complex oratorio that was titled "Blood Fever Blues." The room shook with the voluminous decibels, the cracks, crashings, whines and booms of the huge speakers. Lights flashed and glittered, and Stephenson was enthralled, for he could imagine that Satan himself would gladly make an appearance on that stage.

Midway through the long overture, the woman was released from the cage by a singer. He led her around by a leash. Other band members pushed her, screamed epithets at her. Some even slapped her. At the music's climax, they ripped off her gown, tied her up, then doused her with gallons of crimson fluid that Stephenson hoped was real blood.

As the guitars crescendoed with the final chords, the

singer pushed the woman to the floor, stepped on her, then pulled her across the stage and out of sight, leaving a dark-red trail behind her that was bathed in green light. Stephenson leaped up and began applauding vigorously and shouting for an encore while most of the audience sat in humorous or detached disbelief. The musicians, themselves, seemed surprised that one guest in particular would receive their first attempt at musical macabre so enthusiastically when even *they* wondered if they'd gone too far.

When the Pet Killers finished their inimical, if not unique, set for the evening, Stephenson was more excited than ever. The show had rekindled his desire. He thought, then laughed with delight. Why not? He hadn't done two women in the same night since September 1888. That had been a time when he had been anxious to demonstrate not only his virility but also (thanks to his class in basic surgery) certain other newly acquired skills. London had panicked then. So why not give the splendid city of San Francisco the same opportunity? With his practiced eye, he scrutinized the room for a sensuous young lady who might want to submit to his dark and primeval embrace.

"Would you like to dance?"

He turned. The girl kneeling on the empty chair behind him had not been there a moment ago.

"I'm Dolores." She smiled.

He was surprised and taken aback by her because *she* had approached *him*. Moreover, she was black, and he had never considered a woman of color as a sexual object before. He wasn't quite sure how to appraise her. She had exotic eyes, a pert nose and a lush, full mouth. Her body was not buxom as Marsha McGee's had been. Rather, this Dolores was petite and willowy, almost oriental in flavor. Her hair had been arranged into dozens of small braids, and the unusual styling made her appear to him a combination of the urbane and the tribal.

The attire was something to behold, too. She had on silk pajama pants which were tucked inside alligator-skin boots. Instead of a blouse, she wore a moss-tinted undershirt which advertised the club that they were patronizing. Her wrists were sheathed in thin bracelets that jingled when she moved, and her long neck was adorned with pearls deliberately tied askew.

Perhaps this black girl would be an interesting partner, he thought. And why not? They both would have been condemned in the nineteenth century for being together, but apparently that was no longer the case. He had observed and rather approved of the casual mixing of the races in 1979. It seemed areligious, asocial and out-of-step with Mother Nature, hence fitting to a Luciferian world. Therefore, wasn't it time that he participated? Besides, this girl projected sophistication and charm, indicating that she came from a wealthy background. She was definitely a step up from Marsha McGee, the middle-class shopgirl. That settled it, then. The ritual murder of a beautiful rich girl would bring out the police in droves; it would quickly raise the public outcry to a shrill and falsetto level. He would become important again, notorious, infamous. Worthy of Satan. He could not have made a better selection for his next victim had he chosen her on his own.

"I'm Leslie John."

He rose from the table and guided her down to the ballroom floor. They began to dance. He was hesitant at first, then closed his eyes so that he could sense the mood. He tossed his head back and became involved in the hard beat of the music. He moved closer to Dolores, twirled her back and forth, and imagined that she was a swaying, hooded cobra like the one he had seen at the Zoological Gardens in Regent's Park. The vision became extremely graphic: she alternated between the deadly reptile of the Kashmir plains and the houri, a beautiful, voluptuous, colored virgin—indigenous to the Koranic Paradise. Were those her fangs that were drawn back or her legs? His own dance became more frenzied, and he imagined that he, too, was a cobra. They were doing a mating ritual. Soon, they would entwine, exchange mutual strikes of passion and inject poison into each other.

He opened his eyes. When he focused, he saw that she was clearly and pleasantly surprised by his quick mastery of the dance. He emitted a small laugh of triumph. That was only the beginning. A celebration lay ahead.

Eventually, H.G. and Amy had drifted off to sleep, rocking in each other's arms, their odors mingling with their breaths—all to escape as one sweet, affirmative sigh in the face of adversity. Their dreams were secret, but the passion and love that they had shared made one thing certain: no nightmares would be dreamed in the house tonight.

Until the alarm rang.

They were both instantly alert and staring at each other. H.G. jerked his wrist between them, gazed at his digital watch and saw that the time was one o'clock. He sighed with relief, rolled over and punched off her clock alarm (the noise was music, and it seemed ridiculously inappropriate at that hour). They both got out of bed. She went into the kitchen to make him tea and herself coffee. He detoured into the bathroom, where he doused his face, not realizing or expecting how cold the water temperature got in the middle of the night.

"Blast!" he exclaimed, then leaped back shivering and cursing the god of extremes which obviously had not been affected by time. Right then he decided to take a hot shower in order to relax his tense muscles. He and Amy were well ahead of schedule.

He enjoyed standing under the warm water until he was suddenly nagged with self-doubt and worry. His ploy to stop the horrible Stephenson seemed so divinely simple, but had he let his unbridled optimism get in the way of Aristotelian logic? True, he had been the first man in history to conquer time, but that fact did not necessarily mean that he could overcome either destiny or cause and effect. Specifically, he could not explain the contents of Saturday morning's newspaper except by— what was the colloquialism she used occasionally?— "copping out" to predestination, and *that*, he was determined not to do. "Free Will" was a song that he had hummed ever since grammar school, in the tried-and-true tradition of all the great British thinkers. Forsake that ideology now? *Never!*

He lathered up with soap, then scowled again, inwardly cursing St. Paul, Thomas Aquinas and the entire bloody lot of the pessimistic yet brilliant Roman Catholic theologians. That didn't help, either, for the specter of the newspaper returned to his mind. How could he rationalize it? Dolores Clark had died and Amy had been butchered too. Those were/would be *facts!* How could he fight them? Was knowledge of the future worth a damn?

"Whoosh!" he exclaimed as a sudden thought struck him. Why hadn't it come to him previously? Of course! The entire basis of his fourth-dimensional methodology was that time spheres were geometrically stacked against each other like a massive pile of cord wood. All time was permanent in the universe; events continually occurred over and over again just as the atoms and electrons never stopped dancing in their perpetual swirl. (If time and events were not that way—if they were temporary as opposed to temporal—then travel into the past or the future would be absurd and of no consequence, for there would be no time, hence nothing to travel to.) And since time, events, causes and effects *were* permanent, that meant that Amy—and himself, too—were already dead somewhere in the universe. What they had discovered in the future, then, was an old event perhaps replayed innumerable times. Thus, the cosmic nature of what he and Amy were going to do was staggering! When he stopped Stephenson from committing a murder, he would be tossing a pebble into the mythic Sea of Tranquility. The ripples would travel across the universe and change everything in their path. When they reached the shores of Eternity, those same ripples would be a tidal wave, and they would shatter the predestined walls once and for all. Man would reign supreme.

He was not, then, just going to change a simplistic "destiny"; rather, he was going to replace an old time pattern with a new one. One newspaper had already been printed on Saturday, next. It would yellow and age with decay and fall from the cosmos, a petrified ash of what once was but would never again be. A second newspaper would take its place.

H.G. left the shower placid, a cosmic grin wrinkling his face. He leisurely dried his body, then began dressing. His thoughts turned inexorably to Amy, and he wished that he understood emotional patterns as well as he did logical, scientific or philosophical ones. Did he love her already? Since he had never really experienced what they termed "love," it was difficult to say. If the point became earth-shaking, however, he supposed he could (after a brief stop at 17 Mornington Place in the year 1893 for a quick chat with Mrs. Nelson and a few repairs to *The Utopia*) travel back to ancient Syria and observe David and Bathsheba to glean an answer of sorts. Yet, he knew that would not help, for the emotions were within him. Moreover, if he did truly love Amy and if she felt the same way, how would they solve the basic problem of being from different centuries? He had seen interracial mixes in 1979 and had accepted them as a natural and inevitable development in the great American experiment called "democracy." But an *intertime* mix? Theoretically, it should work, yet he was sophisticated enough to know that when it came to human relations, theory didn't mean a blasted thing.

He frowned. If only this Stephenson matter were over, he wished. If only it were finished, and he, H. G. Wells, had emerged victorious. Then he could indulge his feelings without fear that he had left something—a stone, perhaps—unturned. He sighed and managed a small, wistful smile. His thoughts returned to Amy. If only he could take her back home with him, for he knew that someday he would have to return to his own century and pick up the thread of his life. But she would never consent to such a radical uprooting, such a permanent move. No, he was certain that she would not go. After all, how could she be happy in the nineteenth century when she was happy here? How would she put up with Victorian ideals and standards? The ridiculous, fettering rules that he had fought every day just as a matter of principle? Not to mention the restrictions that his society placed on women. She would not be able to work in a position with any authority. Furthermore, not only was she a woman, she was an *American* woman, a bloody Yank. Why, just the accepted code of dress for ladies alone would send Amy rocketing back to 1979 just as fast as his device would allow. And if, in 1893, she ever expressed her attitudes with respect to men and the female sexual response, she would be denounced and publicly disgraced in every social circle that existed in greater London.

"Bah!" he exclaimed with disgust when he realized just how rigid his world was; a world that probably would not accept the most wonderful human being he had ever met in his entire life.

Yes, if he really *did* love her and if she ever did entertain ideas about going with him to 1893, he should convince her to stay here, in 1979 San Francisco. They would both be better off. Unhappy, but that would pass with time and the daily demands of existence. And if it weren't too painful, he supposed that he could arrange to time-travel occasionally; hop into the cabin, close the hatch and twirl forward into her arms. Ah, yes, that would be delicious; to steal away for the weekend or the Christmas holidays and to spend such rare moments with a lover eighty-six years removed in time! What delights! What exotic romantic interludes! And when he redesigned and improved *The Utopia*, why they could journey into the *distant* future together and examine the changes in the inimitable human condition. Who knows? Somewhere along the mysterious fourth dimension, they might find a real Eden where they might land and make their way hand in hand until they found the Elysian fields; both might forsake their home centuries for a life of eternal bliss.

He abruptly scowled and cursed himself. Such idle thoughts, such baroque flights of fancy did absolutely no good. Nothing was solved by that kind of wishful thinking. He must force himself to concentrate on the problem of Jack the Ripper.

He became worried again. What if—for some inexplicable, generic reason—he could *not* save Amy from Stephenson? What if he was wrong about the fallibility of Fate? What if—and he blushed at the thought—the Catholics had been right all along?

Amy was in the dining room, wearing loose and warm clothing, her hands wrapped around a steaming mug of coffee. H.G. came into the room, saw that she was dressed, and nodded.

"Ah, good, then. You're ready."

"There's tea in the kitchen."

"Why, thank you. How thoughtful." He went and poured himself a hot and stimulating cup. It seemed the wise thing to do before venturing out into San Francisco's cold mists. The fog would undoubtedly be thicker across the moors and reaches of McLaren Park, his own mythic Bosworth's field where so much was at stake for him and her.

He sat down next to her at the dining-room table, then checked the time. "I suppose we should be leaving soon."

"Why don't we review exactly what we're going to do first?"

He nodded, then gave his mustache both a twirl and a tug. The inevitable discussion about the inescapable. "All right. To begin with, we are agreed on things in general? Such as the police?"

It was her turn to nod. "If we call them, either they won't believe us or they'll show up and Stephenson will merely do his horrible thing elsewhere."

"Precisely. Hence, to rely on the police would give destiny an opening, wouldn't it?"

"Yes. And we can't alert Dolores Clark because she's with him and we don't know where they are."

"Therefore," he said loftily, "we proceed to the site of the crime. Now, according to the newspaper, the murder occurred"—he stopped and glanced up—"I should say, *will* occur, shouldn't I?"

"How about *won't* occur?"

"Ah, yes." He frowned and briefly started off. "At any rate, the event which is not going to occur happened at approximately half-past two. Hence, we should plan to arrive early." He smiled. "And then H. G. Wells, a man of thought, science, art and Utopianism, will become a man of action." He paused. "Shall we go now?"

"Just what do you intend to do?"

"Why, surprise him and stop the poor girl's murder! What else?"

"But how? We're not armed."

"I wouldn't want to be."

"I don't understand."

"My dear girl, when I confronted him before at the hotel, I cast the first stone, as it were. I stooped to his barbaric level, and I lost. He was right about one thing—violence is contagious."

"But there comes a time—"

"Look at it this way, Amy. The first man to raise a fist is the man who has run out of ideas."

"Very nicely put, but Stephenson is bigger than you, H.G., and extremely dangerous! What if you *do* run out of ideas? And words?"

He sighed. At that moment, he had. He thought critically about details that he had instinctively wanted to avoid, then spoke slowly. "There are two of us. And the intended victim, of course."

"And if worse comes to worst?"

"I suppose your motorcar could be considered a weapon. *He* would certainly regard it as such. And"—he concluded ruefully—"Dr. Stephenson's surgical instruments can be used against him."

She placed her hand over his and gave him a concerned, sympathetic look.

"None of that will be necessary, of course," he said in clipped tones. "Now. Shall we?"

They left her apartment three minutes ahead of schedule. They descended the stairs and went outside. He sighed, realizing that ultimately his faith in himself and his feelings for her were the most powerful weapons he had.

Before he got into the motorcar, he glanced over the top and saw that she was smiling at him, her eyes full of love. Good Lord, he thought, had she been reading his mind? He blushed and looked down. Certainly, he wouldn't mind revealing his feelings about her, but he wanted to wait until destiny had been defeated. It didn't seem cricket to make pledges on the eve of battle, for invariably such vows produced tragedy. Better to say nothing at all than to promise what might not be fulfilled.

He climbed into the Accord and settled himself in the seat. He glanced at her, then quickly looked away, for she was still gazing at him with a tenderness that until this point had been reserved for what she had termed "afterglow."

"I know," she said quietly.

They drove away. Out in the bay, a foghorn droned. Below in the city, a siren shrieked. Several blocks away from a well-to-do yard a basset hound responded with a mournful howl.

Leslie John Stephenson and Dolores Clark sat together at his table, sipping drinks, her right leg and his left pressed tightly together. Their heads almost touched so that they could talk low and still hear each other over the music. She smoked long, dark-brown cigarettes and blew the smoke past him. Occasionally, some would wisp up and fog her facial features, making her seem mysterious. That, he enjoyed.

"Ah, my dear Dolores," he said in rich tones. "Meeting you has been a sweet, albeit unexpected, pleasure."

She laughed. "Likewise."

"Are you enjoying yourself?" he asked, his eyes hooded.

"Unhuh."

"Well, then." He drained his glass and smacked his lips. "Shall we?"

"Shall we what?"

"Consider the remainder of the evening as an opportunity to improve on the beginning? Or, as an occasion

to celebrate the exciting, the unknown and the un-
charted?" He gave her a peck of a kiss and just a touch
of his tongue.

She shivered, leaned into him and emitted a small
laugh. "You talk like you dance."

They left the club, and after exchanging the necessary
banalities with respect to when, where and how, he let
her lead him toward her mode of transportation, which
turned out to be—like herself—sleek, black and elegant.
The name "Porsche 944" gleamed from the rear of the
machine.

He laughed as he slid into the snug capsule alongside
her slender frame and inhaled the fine, heady aroma of
rich leather that rose from the seats. Now he would let
this svelte young lady of color take him somewhere and
he would thoroughly enjoy himself. And, on the morrow,
he would return to 921½ Green Street, surprise Amy
Robbins and abduct her. She would lead him to the
inimitable little scientist, Wells. And if she refused to
cooperate? Then he would violate her and she would
die as all the others had before her.

But that was tomorrow. Now was time for Dolores.

He eased back in the plush seat, adjusted the fall of
his shirt and laughed again as she accelerated hard out
of the parking lot, hit the street in second gear and soon
was doing seventy miles per hour, the harsh, high echo
of the powerful engine disturbing the stillness of Pacific
Avenue.

He placed his left hand on her thigh and began
caressing her. With his right, he removed his pocket
watch and absently fondled it.

Amy and H.G. left Russian Hill and drove down
Jones to Market Street. Thanks to the late hour, the
traffic was light. She decided that they would arrive at

McLaren Park quicker if she took the freeway, so she headed for the Bayshore, expectant and deep in thought. The simple manner in which H.G. had explained things had made her suspect for a while. Then she had remembered that there wasn't an insincere bone in his body. Therefore, he was not holding anything from her; and if that was so, she had nothing to fear. She had racked her brain, trying to discover errors in his logic. But how could anyone question "A" exists and is followed by "B" and both are concluded by "C"? And face it, she told herself, if the man was brilliant enough to build a time machine, there was no reason why he couldn't stop a couple of murders.

She drove up an on ramp and steered south on the Bayshore, increasing their speed to a cautious fifty-eight miles per hour. No need to go *too* fast and risk a speeding ticket; that would be disastrous. And besides, they had plenty of time.

The closer they got to McLaren Park, the less apprehensive she became. They were going to do it, she thought, they were going to successfully change destiny! A bizarre excitement came over her, the likes of which she had never known before. It wasn't just the cosmic nature of their mission or foreknowledge of the future; it wasn't merely saving a girl's life and hence her own; it wasn't just foiling history's most notorious murderer, either. Rather, it was all those things and more: she had inexorably fallen in love with H. G. Wells. He was a great man. An author and inventor with few equals. She had never really thought in terms of an ideal mate before; she had no checklist of that sort, and she wasn't about to start one now. But to suddenly find that a person of his caliber was taken with her . . . She was awed. She felt stronger, more capable and confident than she'd ever been before.

Did that mean that she was no longer afraid of the enemy in this case? Perhaps, although to throw caution to the winds now would be foolish. It was just that she knew in her heart that they were going to win. Her fear, therefore, was no longer foremost in her mind. Determination and tenacity had replaced it. As long as she could trust H.G., she would defeat even Jack the Ripper. True love and a little bit of proper planning could conquer anything, including death. She smiled. They were nearing the exit for McLaren Park.

There was a loud bang.

At first, Amy thought that someone had fired a rifle or, perhaps more likely, had dropped a firecracker from a freeway bridge. Then she felt the car pitch, yaw and pull to the left and she knew differently. There was a hissing noise. The steering wheel shimmied badly. She fought to remain in control of the car just as she tried to ignore the swell of panic, the sick feeling that was building inside her belly.

"What the devil?" H.G. exclaimed.

Now devoid of air, the left front tire flapped wildly as the wheels still turned at high speed. Very quickly, the rubber was shredded by the rough concrete. The car veered farther left and scraped along the retaining wall that separated the north and southbound lanes. Amy jerked the wheel hard to the right and applied the brakes. The car fishtailed, its three good tires squealing, and finally stopped on the freeway's left shoulder.

She stared straight ahead, unable to move. Her heart pounded, her hands shook badly.

"*What's happened?*" His face was ashen. He knew that something had gone horribly wrong.

"We had a flat!"

"A flat? Can it be repaired?"

"We *have* to fix it!" She sprang from the car, went to the trunk and opened it. She grabbed the tool kit and jack, then struggled to get the spare tire out of its well. H.G. attempted to help her, but the spare seemed permanently lodged. It was as if the car manufacturer had carelessly neglected to make the well large enough and had thus unwittingly placed the tire in the enemy's camp. Finally, H.G. pried it loose and lifted it out of the trunk. He barked his shins on the bumper, howled with pain and dropped the tire. It started to roll across the freeway, and Amy had to chase it down.

Eyes wide with fear, she brought it back, laid it down, then began the tedious process of jacking up the car.

"What can I do?" he asked.

"*Nothing!*"

He looked around wildly. "If only there were a telephone! I could tell the police to go to McLaren Park! I could do *something!*"

"If you go down the freeway"—she worked rapidly and perspired heavily—"there's a call box on the side of the road every half a mile!"

"Right." He started off, then suddenly turned back to her, his hands clenching and unclenching. "I have to know! Flats! Do they happen often?"

"They *happen.*" She unscrewed lug nuts.

"Frequently?"

"I can't answer that!" She gestured at the ruined tire. "Look! It still has tread on it! It was still in good shape! I don't *know* why it happened!"

He stared at her a moment longer, then turned and hurried away.

She went back to the flat tire. She lifted it off the axle with a grunt and threw it to the side. She tried to place the spare on the axle only to discover that she had to jack the car up even higher for it to fit. She whimpered while pumping the handle and imagined that the blowout had been a sound heard along the entire length and breadth of the fourth dimension.

* * *

H.G. hurried along the shoulder of the freeway. Frequently, motorcars hurtled past, flashing their lights at him, their tires howling. He briefly imagined that he was on an alien planet surrounded by stampeding mechanical monsters. He felt extremely vulnerable, but doggedly continued on, his right hand using the wall as a guide.

A simple twist of fate.

Was that what it had been? Was there no explanation other than the helpless thought that destiny had indeed retaliated? And hence was omniscient? No, no, he told himself, let the priests think along those lines. Surely there was a logical way to account for the incident. The tire could have been cast from defective materials. The stress points could have been improperly tested. The tire could have hit something sharp on the roadway, a jagged rock, perhaps. There were innumerable explanations for the occurrence. After all, hadn't Amy said that flats *did* happen? Then he frowned. Yes, but why then? Why not before on the drive to Fisherman's Wharf? Or to the museum? And why had that particular tire gone flat and not one of the other three? He could not answer. He cursed his pessimistic speculations, his vacillations from the tenets of free will.

He was spared further self-doubt by a sign up ahead that spelled "Call Box." He sprinted the short distance, despite his consumptive history, quickly read the instructions on the yellow face and deposited the inevitable coin. (Unconsciously, he wondered how he was ever going to get along in the nineteenth century without this marvelous communications device.)

Eventually, he was connected to a desk sergeant in the Homicide Division of the San Francisco Police Department. He identified himself as a Mr. Wells from London and explained the emergency nature of his call.

"Would you repeat that, please?"

"Tell Lieutenant Mitchell that a girl is going to be murdered by the lake in McLaren Park at any moment! Please get there as soon as possible!"

"Your name again, sir?"

"*Wells!* W-e-l-l-s."

He hung up, turned and raced back toward the car. He had a sense of foreboding, but could not account for it. Had circumstances forced him to act against his will? Had he used the telephone or had destiny? Had there just been another simple twist of fate?

H.G. checked his watch as the Accord rocketed down Mandell Street, Amy at the wheel. The time was two thirty-five.

"We can still make it!" he shouted.

The car accelerated up a steep, curving hill, and suddenly they were inside the park, motoring through the black confines of a forest at top speed. H.G. could see the tension in Amy's face. Her jaw was clenched shut and her knuckles were white. Yet, she did not wax hysterical or say a word, and he admired her strength. He could only hope that he would be as strong when the time came. He sighed. If only he could have predicted the flat tire; if only they had left sooner; if only . . . He stopped and shook his head. There did not seem any way to know the variables as they were drawn closer and closer to the moment. And yet, if they were to emerge victorious from their confrontation with fate, it seemed imperative that they be aware of all the twists and turns. H.G. did not want either one of them to resemble Cuchulainn, that blustering hero of old Irish legend, the classic picture of tragic irony, who would go down to the shore every morning at sunrise to do battle with the waves of the Atlantic armed only with a heavy broadsword. He had not realized until he was a weakened, wasted old man unable to lift his weapon that the waves were endless and he was not.

H.G. shuddered and glanced out the side window. Perhaps he was too preoccupied with the struggle, the philosophic battle of wits with Clotho, Lachesis and Atropos (if one wanted to refer to the legend of another civilization). After all, there were human beings involved, too. Leslie John Stephenson was very much an active, conniving opponent. H.G. didn't know what the doctor had in mind, but he was certain that the so-called death of Amy was not by any means a random choice. It might just very well be the climactic event in a treacherous scheme that involved all three of them. If he hadn't consciously accepted the fact before, he did now. Amy was truly in jeopardy.

He frowned, pressed on the bridge of his nose and took several deep breaths. Amy turned her vehicle right onto John F. Shelley Drive and slowed down.

"Turn off your lights," he commanded sharply.

She did so.

"When you reach the entrance of the parking lot that services the lake, stop and let me get out. Then proceed slowly in the direction of a black motorcar. When you get close enough, use your lights as you would an artillery piece."

She gulped and nodded.

They went around a curve in the road and H.G. heard Amy groan with terror. The car stopped. Then she put her face in her hands and fell back against the seat. For an instant, he could not imagine what was wrong—until he saw a black and white patrol car stopped next to an automobile at the far end of the parking lot, its red, blue and orange lights flashing, its white searchlight blinking into the sky signaling for a helicopter. One policeman was frantically shouting into the squad car's radio. The other was down on the pavement, hunched on his hands and knees like a dog, retching out of control. H.G. heard sirens in the distance.

He knew then that they were too late.

ELEVEN

Somehow, Amy managed to maintain her composure for the drive back to Russian Hill. Once they parked in front of her building, however, she crumpled against the steering wheel. She began to sob, and her hands trembled so badly that she could not pull the keys from the ignition.

"Amy, it's all right! We won't be here!"

"You promise?" she cried in a whisper of panic.

"I promise! It's very simple. We'll just leave like we originally planned."

Still, she could not control herself. "I don't want to die," she moaned over and over. "I don't want to die!"

He took the keys out of the ignition for her, dropped them into his pocket, then helped her out of the Accord and up into her flat. He eased her down onto the couch. Beyond grief, she just huddled there and stared, like a catatonic, at nothing. He paced the floor, trying to concentrate on the evening's inexplicable turns of fate, trying to decide what they meant, trying not to be nervous about his failure to alter the course of human events. There had to be an answer other than the smug, Catholic concept of predestination. There just *had* to be! Then he sighed and cursed. There were no more Dolores

Clarks with which to test out a theory; there were no more margins for error; there were only fifteen hours left.

And then he went to her and held her tightly. He felt her pain. All of us know that we are going to die, he thought, but we can live with the absurdity of our own death because we don't know when it is to happen. Even most terminally ill patients can bear the knowledge that the end will come soon; but to know *exactly* when? H.G. winced. The misery she felt must be worse even than that of an innocently condemned man.

Suddenly, an idea began to form in his mind. What if they used *The Utopia* to go *further* ahead in time in order to discover a solution to their dilemma? He scowled. No, that wouldn't work, for they could time-travel a thousand years and still find out that they had *not* changed the future. Although that could mean merely that the future of record hadn't been altered yet. But how could he explain that to her when he could not even convince himself that traveling—say, to Monday—would be one iota more enlightening? No, their only hope was to stay in the present, dig in and grimly wrestle destiny with the strength of their own free wills.

What about the recent past? he suddenly thought. If he could not change history, then he could always relive the last few days over and over and permanently dwell on their Utopian lovemaking. No, that wasn't an acceptable alternative, either. He would always know in the back of his mind that he had perpetually eschewed a showdown with Stephenson and the Fates. That would be downright cowardly. Moreover, if he placed himself and Amy on such a temporal treadmill, he would be prolonging her life in limbo. And that would be absurd, for he would be *removing* her free will. The only acceptable choice seemed to be to remain on their collision course with destiny.

Suddenly, surprisingly, she spoke. "This is all so mind-boggling, H.G." Her voice quavered. "I don't feel in touch with reality anymore. Or sanity. You're the only thing that doesn't seem crazy."

He looked up and saw that the night had lifted; there was a gray fog outside the window. "It's dawn. You should get some rest."

"You're right, but I'm not sure that I can sleep."

"I could make you a drink."

"No. There's Valium in the medicine chest. It'll make me feel better, too. I'll get it."

He had gotten her a glass of water and watched her swallow two of the shiny pink things she had named Valiums. Then he had taken his own suggestion regarding the drink and was now on his second glass of gin, moodily staring out her bedroom window. He noticed that her face had regained its usual placid beauty and innocently attributed that fact to her normal stoicism and inner strength. He did not consider the drug she had taken.

He knew that she was gazing at him, but he did not return her look. Instead, he drank steadily and shrugged helplessly. He did not like to wallow in self-pity, but all of a sudden it just seemed so hopeless! He was exhausted, too, and could no longer think clearly.

She took his limp hand. "Hey. What happened to all your *joie de vivre*?"

"What's the bloody use?"

She frowned with surprise and confusion and briefly lowered her eyes.

"Who was I to think that I could change history? I mean, what *cheek*! A mere mortal who happens to stumble upon a heretofore untapped crystalline source of energy that can enable other mere mortals to hopscotch along the fourth dimension? I was lucky. So what?"

"So *what?* You're the only person since time began who ever *did* it!"

"But I haven't changed the scheme of things, Amy! I've failed to alter fate as we would have it!"

"That's not true! We're going to leave, aren't we? Doesn't that mean we *will* change history?"

"We're not leaving, we're running away, yipping like curs with our tails between our legs."

"What else can we do?"

"That's the point! Nothing!" He resumed pacing. "What difference does it make? The entire scheme was laughable from the beginning, anyway."

"Was it?"

"Of course it was! I am no god!"

"I wasn't aware that you believed in the supernatural," she replied coolly.

"I am not superhuman, then! Is that better?"

"Whew," she commented with a wave of her hand. "Can you imagine how insufferable you'd be if you were?"

"*Please,* Amy, I'm being serious!"

"You're being maudlin, and that's a bore."

"We are running away! We are leaving a hideous monster free to join all the other criminals in 1979."

"Tell me," she snorted with anger, "just what does Stephenson have to do with altering the course of human events, anyway? Other than being a rather notable menace to society? It's *my life* we're saving!"

Surprised, he turned. "What the devil are you getting angry for?"

"Because I never expected to hear this coming from you! I always admired your unfailing optimism, your devotion to the individual human spirit! And I never thought that I would hear H. G. Wells making a mockery of his own books!"

"What do *they* have to do with this, for God's sake?"

"They advocate free will!"

He turned away and peered out the window with a jaundiced eye, nervous about creations of his that he had not written yet. "Books? What good did they do? What good have any books ever done, now that you mention it?"

"You're making a fool out of yourself," she remarked flatly.

"What?" He turned. "How can you say that? The year is 1979! And men still commit atrocities! People still cheat each other! Lie! Steal! Harm! Hurt! Crime is rampant! Races and countries still oppress each other! The world reels through space as if no one on it ever thought of anyone but himself! As if the golden rule were still an embryonic idea, a figment of Moses' imagination!" He paused to take a breath. "And yet, if you and I were electrons we would have Erewhon at every corner with all of humanity abasing itself for our benefit and advancement!"

She looked at him with puzzlement.

"Don't you see? Mankind continues to make dazzling and miraculous progress in science and technology, and yet people are as badly off as they have ever been!" He flung his hand back flamboyantly and accidentally smashed it on the window. "And you talk of *books*," he managed to say through clenched teeth.

"Without yours, things might be worse," she retorted, not noticing his pain.

He averted his head and stared out the window again. He was angry that advanced technology had not, as a matter of course, created a new man right alongside all of its solid-state transistors and electronic chips. If *he* had been responsible for recent scientific developments, *he* certainly would have established a modern moral framework, too. Or was it that easy? After all, he had just lost. Had mankind lost, too? Before he had ever set foot in 1979?

"You don't have any more hope left, H.G.! You don't have any more courage!"

"What did you expect?"

"I expected exactly the opposite from you! Especially when we got close to the hour of reckoning!"

After an embarrassed pause, he managed to comment defensively, "Fighting destiny isn't easy, you know."

She blanched. Then she began to cry again, but honestly and in a dignified fashion. She lifted her chin and gazed at him steadily. "It may not be easy," she whispered. "But you better get used to it. Because I will not expect or accept anything less from you."

He gasped with surprise, started to reply, but could not. A silly grin took command of his facial features as the import of her last statement registered. Her remark had been both a challenge and a standard, and as such it had the ring of a permanent commitment. She had already affirmed her love for him, but neither of them had even attempted to grapple with the problem that they were from different centuries. Apparently—if he had read the conviction in her voice correctly—that was no longer an issue.

"You mean . . . ?"

She nodded.

"Good Lord," he said with awe. He took her hand. "Great Scott, what a marvelous ideal to have to live up to."

Suddenly, the world did not seem like such a hopeless, horrible place, especially if it were privy to the spiritual union of two souls from different time spheres. Maybe he couldn't alter destiny to suit his wishes. But she was right about one thing: he could not just abruptly quit trying; that was not part of his character. One could lose naïveté, one could bridle enthusiasm, one could temper impulsive idealism. Such was the process of becoming fully mature. One should not, however, make the mistake of scuttling determination and tenacity along the way. He recalled Huxley once commenting after one of his last lectures, a far off, yet steadfast glint in his eyes, *Lose your dreams and you will lose your mind, and life in kind.*

"I'd like to apologize for being less than myself. In your eyes."

He looked at her as if for the first time. Her eyes were open, warm, innocent, trusting. He touched her face and outlined the curve of her cheek with his hand as if memorizing it. He laughed with joy. *Time*? Why had he ever worried about that? What did time have to do with love, anyway? Nothing. Not in their case, at any rate. The fourth dimension would become their servant; they would use it to add adventure and romance to their love. He took her other hand and squeezed it tightly.

"What are you thinking?" she asked.

"That I am eternally yours."

She smiled. "I like that."

He looked off into the near and distant space. When the thought was complete, he turned back to her. "What was the term that the Bard once coined, my dear? Star-crossed lovers?"

She became radiant, even though she appeared to be very sleepy.

He chuckled. "Maybe someday I'll write about time-crossed lovers."

"I like that even better."

Lieutenant J. Willard Mitchell crossed the parking lot, got into the late-model, brown Plymouth sedan and lit his tenth cigarette of the day. It was not quite nine o'clock in the morning. He gestured at his partner, Sergeant Ray. The man started the car, and they drove away from McLaren Park.

Mitchell rubbed his weather-beaten face with a large hand as if that would relieve his worried exhaustion, which lay heavy and nauseous in the pit of his stomach. He had been up all night, and he had a feeling that it was going to be quite a while before he would be able to get a good night's sleep again. The press was beginning to rumble and clamor, and he didn't even have a suspect. He wasn't even close.

He stared out the side window with a jaundiced eye. First, there had been the Chinese hooker, Jade Chang. Then—just hours ago—the girl named Marsha McGee had been found by a neighbor who was going to complain about the loud music. And now this. A wealthy attorney's daughter. Murdered in her own car and then butchered. Blood everywhere. Mitchell shivered. He had never seen such vicious brutality before, and yet in all three cases there had been absolutely no sign of a struggle. From all indications, the women had been willingly involved in acts of sexual intercourse when the violence occurred. Maybe they had even expected entire evenings of carnal pleasure. The killer, then, would not be a recognizable, fiendish psychopath, Mitchell reasoned. No, this animal was smart and dangerous, for he had the ability to come across as a normal, passionate male. The lieutenant sighed and shook his head. Yeah, this guy made the Zodiac killer look like Robin Hood. Mitchell knew of only one other that could compare when it came to mutilating a corpse, and that was the hypnotic little madman now locked up in San Quentin, Charles Manson. He swore inwardly. This was all he needed five weeks before Christmas—a self-styled slasher. What should they call him? He mused sardonically. Sourdough Jack the Ripper?

Sergeant Ray turned left onto Bryant Street off Eighth and accelerated up the two blocks to police headquarters. When he pulled abreast of the main entrance, his gnarled face opened wide with astonishment. "Look!"

Approximately fifty members of the press corps waited outside the building. When they saw the car, they started for it en masse. Two local TV news "minicam" crews jockeyed for position, and one of their more aggressive newspersons violently shoved a rival camera operator to one side. The hapless technician stumbled and lost his grip on the shoulder mount of his Norelco. The sixty-five-thousand-dollar camera did a top-heavy flip and then smacked into the concrete pavement. Broken transistors spewed out of the ruptured case to lie alongside the remains of a twenty-to-two-fifty Canon zoom lens. The operator stared down in shock and the entire mob of reporters paused as if in sympathy.

"Christ. They're really out for blood."

"Take us around back."

"You'd think they'd had enough."

They parked in the motor pool and went upstairs to the homicide division. Mitchell shed his coat and tie when he finally got to his mahogany-paneled inner sanctum. His faithful secretary, Ruth, gingerly placed a steaming cup of coffee on his desk as if it were plasma.

"Thanks," he grunted gratefully, then lit a fresh cigarette. He swilled the coffee, sat down and stared out the window. Ruth left, but before Mitchell had a chance to think, Sergeant Ray slipped into the room and dropped another computer print-out on the desk in front of him.

"The fingerprints lifted off Dolores Clark's Porsche match those found at the Noe Street apartment," he reported soberly.

"Terrific," Mitchell replied with unenthusiastic sarcasm. "That means they also match the ones taken at the massage parlor."

As did the footprints, the blood traces, the bacteria, the sperm count, et cetera. Mitchell scowled and dropped the print-out into a wastebasket. There were no leads;

he did not have a shred of evidence. When all the data—fingerprints included—was programed into the department's star computer, there was no answer! Instead, they had received electronic confusion, and the computer (nicknamed "Sherlock") would print out "x's" and "o's," then shut down as if to cool its circuits.

Who had ever heard of fingerprints or a sperm count that didn't belong to anyone? Mitchell wondered. It was as if the computer were saying that the sexually perverted, twisted madman currently terrorizing San Francisco did not exist! The hell he didn't.

He was stymied. Flabbergasted. Perhaps he was getting old. Maybe he should retire and let some young Turk like Sergeant Ray take over. Maybe there were things that he was overlooking that someone newer and fresher might see right away. No, he wasn't ready to quit yet. Besides, his pride wouldn't let him, for he was in the middle of a very bad situation. He had always told himself that when he opted for that permanent "fishing trip," he would go out a winner.

The phone buzzed.

"Yeah, Ruth?"

"Are you busy, sir?"

"I wish I was." He grinned ruefully. "Come on in."

She entered. "Your calls." She handed him a telephone log sheet. On one side of the sheet was the time; on the other, the caller and any message. Since he hadn't been in the office since seven o'clock the previous evening, the list was impressive. He briefly scanned it.

"Anything interesting?" asked Sergeant Ray.

Suddenly, Mitchell bolted up in his chair and stared closely at the log sheet. "You remember that Mr. Wells from London? That curious little nut who called himself a citizen of the world?"

"Yeah?"

"He called to tell us about the Dolores Clark murder." Mitchell leaned back in his chair, dragged on his cigarette, blew a smoke ring, then allowed himself the luxury of a broad smile.

Ray grabbed the log sheet and studied it. He was puzzled and astonished. "At two thirty-*five*? That was before it happened!"

Mitchell nodded wisely.

"Jesus, Lieutenant! Maybe he was right about that Stephenson dude! Maybe this Mr. Wells really is a psychic."

"No. He's no psychic."

"Wait a minute! The computer said that *Stephenson* didn't exist. Just like the *fingerprints*!"

"Oh, he exists, all right."

"Who?" asked a confused Sergeant Ray. "Wells or Stephenson?"

"They're one in the same."

"Huh?"

"A psychopathic split personality."

"You lost me."

"The rational side comes into my office and says that he knows who a murderer is because he wants *us* to stop him from killing. Meanwhile, the insane part of this guy keeps on cutting up women. I think that this Wells is in reality asking for help. It's your classic case of Dr. Jekyll and Mr. Hyde."

"I still think he could be a psychic."

"Believe me, Sergeant Ray, he's no psychic." Mitchell snubbed out his cigarette. "He called before the murder occurred because he knew that he was going to commit it. He's our prime suspect."

Amy had fallen into a deep, drugged sleep.

For a long time H.G. sat beside her on the bed, monitoring her steady breathing, gazing at her delicate, relaxed features. He was awed by the tenderness that they had provided for each other. He was certain that he loved this girl now more than he had ever loved anyone or anything before. He vowed to himself that he would protect her and save her life no matter what. If he lost her, he would lose everything, including his own will to live.

He got up, went to her closet and took down a quilt that had been hand-sewn by her grandmother. He gently covered her with the old comforter as if he were shielding her with himself.

Then he left the bedroom and walked quietly down into the dining room. He stared out the bay window at the overcast sky and became edgy and restless. He frowned and began pacing. The grandfather clock across the room bonged once, reminding him that while he was moving around in limbo, destiny was steadily, inexorably coming closer.

"Blast," he muttered softly. He did not like the idea of leaving. It seemed a full-scale retreat in the face of adversity. And he didn't care how insurmountable the odds appeared, it irked him to run from something. It was not in his character to avoid conflict and confrontation, hence he was uncomfortable with himself. He grimaced. To lose fairly and squarely was one thing, but to give up? To concede defeat? No, he told himself, it was more than merely running. It would mean that Stephenson would win by forfeit. He would remain at large, free to carry on his career of dastardly atrocities. Definitely, this was one defeat which would not be more triumphant than a victory. True, Amy's life would be spared, but he, H. G. Wells, had not lived up to his responsibility. He had told the cosmos that he would bring Leslie John Stephenson back to the nineteenth century to face justice. He had not done that; what was worse, he no longer actively intended to.

"Whoosh," he exhaled in frustration. Then he glanced at his chronometer and pushed a button. It read precisely half-past eleven. He still had approximately six hours left. That should be time enough to do something, he thought. As opposed to passively waiting. Dalliance did not seem worthy of him, Amy Robbins or *The Utopia*.

Suddenly, he had an idea. He raised his chin at a defiant angle and grinned. Why not? Certainly, it wouldn't take that long—an hour or two at the most. He must try, he told himself. Yes, he must. To give up now would be to drown the hopes for an enlightened mankind in the Sea of Tranquility. As Huxley had once said, *Above all, a man must be true unto himself; if not, then he becomes vanquished and can be true to no one.*

If to no one else, he owed it to Amy.

H.G. left the flat, his mind perfectly fresh and clear despite his body's lack of sleep. He knew precisely what he was doing, although he was not certain why he was doing it. Was destiny pushing him around with an invisible hand? Blindly forging its own way even though H.G. held the crucial high card of foreknowledge? He didn't know, he *couldn't* know.

Determined, he stepped off the curb and flagged down the first available taxi going down Jones Street slow enough to stop.

"Where to, sir?"

"The San Francisco Public Library."

It seemed like a perfectly reasonable idea; perhaps even a possible solution to their dilemma. He was going to the library to find out if the legendary Jack the Ripper had ever been caught. If he had, then that meant that he, H. G. Wells, had successfully taken the villain back to 1893 London and remanded him into the custody of Scotland Yard. Such knowledge, H.G. deduced, would have tremendous bearing on what final course of action he chose for this evening.

He got out of the cab at the corner of Hyde and McAlister streets and paid the driver. He was pleased to be within the vicinity of a library again, and the size of the building impressed him. He briefly recalled the many hours that he had used the library in South Kensington as a refuge during the advanced stages of decay that had infected his first marriage.

He quickly entered the library and requested every book on the infamous killer who called himself Jack the Ripper. After an agonizing, twenty-minute wait, an assistant librarian returned and placed a stack of approximately fifteen volumes in front of H.G. He took the books and hurried into a far corner of the large reading room. He spread the books out on a long wooden table, then sat down and began reading.

An hour later, H.G. slammed shut the last of the books and cursed low, under his breath. He dropped his head despondently and for a long time just stared at the grain of wood that was the table.

"I failed," he said out loud.

He looked at the book again and reread the inescapable conclusion. *Jack the Ripper was never found, never captured and never identified. To this day, his identity remains one of the great, unsolved mysteries in the history of crime.*

"Whoosh," he muttered. What did that mean?

Quite simply, that events had obviously occurred as it now seemed like they were going to occur. Destiny had triumphed. H.G. and Amy had fled and Stephenson was left free to prowl the twentieth century. Or, H.G. could have stayed at the apartment and confronted Stephenson and *then* lost. In that case, Amy would die as reported in the newspaper. He sighed. Fate wasn't cruel, it was horrible; a cosmic fiend that stood behind the force of evil.

He raised his eyebrows. There was a third alternative. What if he stayed and confronted Stephenson and *Amy* lived? Of course! He would send Amy away and *he* would stay! Why hadn't he thought of it before? Then he frowned and looked at the book again. ". . . one of the great, unsolved mysteries in the history of crime." He, H. G. Wells, had not taken Jack the Ripper back to the nineteenth century. Therefore, if he *had* defeated destiny, then Stephenson had been vanquished in 1979. And H. G. Wells was responsible.

But how? He was physically incapable of subduing the man! That much he already knew! And he did not possess a weapon! He never had; he abhorred violence.

Suddenly, he gasped, for he just realized what he was going to do next. His hands shook and his face was ashen. He slowly stood and shuffled for the great oak doors. He was going to leave the library. He was going to pursue the only acceptable alternative left open to him.

He was going to purchase a pistol.

"Sam's Pawn Shop—Instant Cash" was located east of Market Street near the Greyhound Bus Depot. Although only blocks away from the library and the civic center, here the complexion of the city was radically different. There was debris and grit in the streets, despair and resignation in the lifeless eyes of those who happened to be up and about. The buildings needed painting and the air tasted heavy and foul with fumes.

These facts troubled H.G., but he tried not to think of them as he stood at the counter and patiently waited for the proprietor to take the pistol out of the display window. When he had left the library, he had gone in search of a sporting-goods store. Ironically, he had remembered that it was Leslie John Stephenson, himself, who had mentioned that anyone could buy a weapon in this, the so-called Utopia of 1979. All one had to do was find a sporting-goods store. Well, apparently pawn shops sold small arms, too, H.G. thought, along with a little bit of everything else in the universe. He stood there, staring into the dark, almost black recesses of the shop and saw relics caked with dust that had not even been conceived of in 1893. A technological scrap heap, he mused. Worn and faded monuments to the future capabilities of science hanging unnoticed and unused in deep shadows. He wondered what functions they had once served. And if this were the end for these futurological antiques, then why had they been built in the first place? He moved deeper into the shop for a closer inspection, examining an "RCA High Fidelity tape recorder—only $12.50." The material spelling out the name was cracked and discolored.

As other relics took on shape, texture and color, he imagined that the human race might end up right back where it started. Like this, in a cave; man, with his *objets de précision* hanging on the wall, deprived of the sun, and the wind and the rain. Mankind, with its penchant for rushing in where angels feared to tread, had created a mindless, disrespectful technology already. Who knew what synthetic monsters man was capable of creating in the future? Monsters which would quickly control and devastate the earth's surface? Were computers, in fact, the beginning of such a debacle? His prophetic thoughts were interrupted by the proprietor.

"Eighty bucks."

"Seems reasonable enough."

The man shrugged. "This day and age I wouldn't be caught dead without a piece." He whistled faintly. "But that's just me."

Although he had to force himself, H.G. reached out, tentatively picked up and inspected the pistol. It was, according to the tag, a .38-caliber Smith & Wesson special. He could feel and smell the light coat of oil that covered the weapon's surface. His hand began to tremble, and the pistol felt like it weighed a thousand pounds. Never before had he touched a firearm; never before had he *not* wanted to tinker with a mechanical device. He hated the snub-nosed, malevolent example of man's inability to be rational; the steel-blue symbol of man's inhumanity to man; the tempered icon of Ara, the goddess of vengeance; the precision instrument that paid homage to the out-dated morality of the Old Testament. He detested the pistol. It stood for everything that he abhorred. He moved to set the weapon down on the counter.

Something stopped him.

What about Amy and his love for her? Which was ultimately more important? A matter of his principles or her life? Certainly, he could be true to himself and save her, too. Or could he? The tension in his gut increased. He sighed. He would never resolve those questions. There wasn't time.

Suddenly, his heart began pounding and he shuddered. For all of his revulsion for the handgun, he was surprised to find that now it actually felt quite good nestled in the palm of his hand. He hefted it. He felt calmer; a sense of well-being came over him. He was astonished. He could not imagine what had possessed him! To enjoy handling an instrument of death!

"Like the feel of it?"

He did not respond.

"Here, let me show you how it works."

Twenty minutes later, H.G. left the shop, the special in one coat pocket, a box of ammunition in the other. He moved slowly along the dismal street and tried to convince himself that everything would be all right. Despite his purchase, he was worried. He felt his positive, idealistic stance slipping away. Was he losing his grasp over himself? Was he becoming a minion for the bloody Fates with no mind of his own? Come to think of it, what had possessed him to go to the library in the first place? True, his reasoning had seemed clever at the time. If he had discovered that Jack the Ripper had been caught, then he would have been much less apprehensive. Such was not the case, however; and as a result, he was going to shoot an ex-classmate for the good of humanity, past, present and future.

Suddenly, he stopped walking. What if he couldn't go through with it? What if, at the moment of reckoning, he was *unable* to pull the trigger and slay the Goliath of Fate? That thought had never occurred to him! He clenched his jaws; he slipped his hand inside his coat and grasped the pistol for support. Of course he could fire it! He could do anything in order to save the life of Amy Catherine Robbins. He resolutely strode forward.

Amy stirred. Although not awake, she half rose from the bed. As soon as her body felt cold air, she fell back, rolled into a ball and snuggled in the comforter. How nice. H.G. had covered her up. She was warm. Toasty. It felt so good to be warm. To sleep. Everything was fine. And when she was done resting, H.G. would take her away and they would live happily ever after. But she had to sleep first. It felt so good to sleep. She dreamed.

It was a pleasant time, one of the many tranquil moments of her childhood. She was on the boat at the lake, drifting through the summer, her arm dangling over the side, the water caressing her fingers. The sun was setting behind the pine and birch on the shore, making the surface of the lake golden. A warm breeze blew. The water lapped against the side of the boat and made a comforting, sloshing sound. The boat rocked gently, and for a moment she was in her mother's arms, then a lover's. The world was perfect; the joy was endless. She sighed then, completely secure. She had always been a highly tolerant, strong child. Moments like these were why. Her existence was placid. Her life would be a smooth drift through the golden waters of the cosmos. Her thoughts would always be free from worry; her flesh would always be caressed by cool water and warm breezes. She was an eternal child of the universe; Amy, the goddess of Tranquility.

Someone was calling her from the shore. The boat turned and she opened her eyes and could see the dock. H.G. was there and he was waving at her and smiling. She felt a surge of joy and was surprised. She had not expected him. Obviously, her lover had been able to take time off from his search for truth and goodness and come up to the lake to join her for the holidays. Now every day would be a holiday. Yes, that was him on the dock, and he wanted to be with her now. Together they would laze through the universe, a union of blissful perfection.

She should get up and bring the boat around and sail to the dock so that he could get on board. Yes, that was what she would do, even though she did not want to disturb her own peaceful revery. She looked up. The boat no longer had a sail; it had vanished. She shrugged. She would row. She reached out languidly and her hands found the gunwales, but the cold metal eyelets held nothing. The oars had vanished, too. She sighed. What to do? Nothing to be done. She missed her lover so.

The breeze became stronger, and the boat drifted farther away from the shore. H.G. got smaller and smaller; he receded into a dot, and no longer could she hear him or see him waving. She thought that maybe she should leave the boat. Dive over the side and swim to the dock. He would reach down and help her up the ladder and they would hold hands and laugh and gaze at the horizon. But wasn't it too far to swim now? she wondered. And the boat had drifted farther away still. Did she know how to swim? Or had she forgotten?

She decided that, regardless, she had better try to swim to shore. It was then that she discovered that she could no longer move. She laughed inside. It didn't matter anymore.

Suddenly, the breeze became a gale. Waves crashed against her boat. The gentle lapping had become loud, insistent banging on the wood of the craft. She wished that it would stop, for the afternoon had been so pleasant. She never wanted it to end. As Amy, the sacred one, she commanded night not to fall.

Still fast asleep, she pulled her pillow over her head.

H.G. wandered down Mission Street, his coat sagging from the weight of the pistol and the ammunition. He walked through six more blocks of the industrial slum before he realized that he was not going to find a taxi in this part of town. He turned west on Fifth Street and headed back toward the center of the city. He sighed as he plodded along and was depressed. The gloom of the area had finally gotten to him. He understood, profoundly so, that almost one hundred years of technological development and scientific progress had not improved life for most people. Humans still had to live and work in antiquated, dirty, unsafe environs. And, as he had exclaimed to Amy just hours ago, the evil side of human nature appeared to be on the rise. (He, himself, had just purchased a pistol.) Did that mean that Stephenson, the champion of perverse cynicism, would emerge victorious even in his own death? Would the arch villain score the final, mocking points in their debate with his own mortality? Would he play Mephistopheles to H.G.'s Dr. Faustus?

H.G. shuddered. He couldn't speculate about that. He just had to keep reminding himself that he would do what he had to do for the love of his life.

He would, however, have to seriously rethink his idealistic opinions when he returned home. It did not appear, he admitted, that man had been freed from despair by the mighty power of the electron. It seemed, God help mankind, that technology had freed the human animal so that he might become more dangerous and inhumane, instead. For example, a man on horseback could hurt others if he didn't look where he was going. Put the same man in a motorcar that harnessed power equivalent to an entire herd of the equestrian beasts, or at the controls of an airship, and one did not have to think very hard to conjure up the result. Stephenson was correct. It was a common occurrence in the news. An acceptable part of modern existence just as the stench of rotting flesh had been to those who had lived with the plague.

Did that mean that H. G. Wells, inventor *extraordinaire*, was suddenly advocating a return to a way of life that existed prior to the Industrial Revolution?

"No, damn you!" He said out loud to his alter ego.

All I want is for the juggernaut of science and technology to push human civilization toward a workable value system, a pervasive golden rule. Something that mankind has always wanted and now—because it has unlocked the doors to eternity and the universe—can achieve. All I want is to see a few examples of that kind of progress so that I may return to my humble, primitive century relieved and not have to spend too much of my precious time worrying about and warning others of Armageddon.

He sighed and shook his head. His mind cleared of its lofty cogitations. His eyes focused. He was standing on the southeast corner of Fifth and Market streets. His digital chronometer told him that it was half-past two in the afternoon. He still had plenty of time. He decided, however, that he should get a cab and go back to Russian Hill and Amy Robbins. She would no doubt want to pack a few things before he sent her off, and she would be angry if he let her oversleep. Also, he would probably have to spend some time arguing with her in order to get her to leave without him. Being the generous, concerned person that she was, she would be more worried for his safety than her own. He grimaced. Convince her, he would. He had to. His plan was *truly* foolproof this time. He would send Amy off in her Accord before the sun set—*hours* before the supposed time of her death. She would never be in jeopardy. Then he would take up root in the rocking chair, squarely facing the door, .38 Smith & Wesson special ready to fire. When Stephenson came through the door, he would pull the trigger and end the man's twisted existence.

What if something unexpected happened? What if he was overlooking another surprise? A thunderclap? Another ironic yet simple twist of fate? He shuddered again. After all, right now *he* was pursuing a course of action, a sequence of events that *she* had not anticipated. He felt a twinge of guilt. He had not told Amy that he was going to leave. Obviously, he could not have once she had fallen asleep, but still, his actions seemed a breach of trust. Especially when he had touted his honesty to her all along. If she woke up and found him not there, she would have good reason to become furious. She might even panic.

"Whoosh!" How callous of him. At the very least, he could have left her a note. And what if the unexpected *did* occur? He frowned. He couldn't think about that anymore; he couldn't rack his brain over *every* possibility in the complex chain of cause and effect. If he did, he would end up like Hamlet; he would still be here on this street corner conjuring up alternatives while Leslie John Stephenson was mounting the stairs at 92½ Green Street.

He reminded himself that he was now H. G. Wells, a man of action. Jaws fixed, he stepped off the curb and impatiently waved at passing taxis until one finally pulled over and stopped. H.G. climbed in the back and gave the cabby the address. The driver moved back into traffic and accelerated north on Market Street.

H.G. sighed, leaned back, then discovered that his hand was resting accidentally on the pistol inside his coat pocket. He jerked it away and scowled; he was more depressed than ever. It seemed as though this taxi were taking him further and further away from a part of himself that he did not want to lose: his optimistic views on the human condition. And how could he seriously champion rationality any longer when here he was with a pistol in his pocket? It would appear that no matter what happened, the inimical surgeon had won the battle of philosophies. H.G. stared out the window and felt small. How could he worry about an innocent population, how could he consider justice when the world he found himself in seemed so much more inherently evil than the one he had left? He had encountered no bastions of morality, none even *falsely* conceived. Rather, his observations had told him that the world of 1979 was vastly more conducive to a Jack the Ripper than it was to, say, a savior. Wasn't he, himself, walking testament to that fact? A peace-loving, law-abiding human being now actively planning to kill someone?

He suddenly began to weep.

What a terrible position for a man to be in, he thought. He had been forced to compromise his principles, to betray his *raison d'être* for the one he loved. *Man is the cruelest animal*, Nietzsche had once said. *Unto himself*, H. G. Wells added. He was utterly disconsolate.

His weeping became sobs, and his thoughts muddled. All that was left was Amy. He had to be with her as soon as possible. Now. Especially now. It seemed urgent. He was suddenly possessed with a longing that became unbearable. He straightened up and grabbed the back of the driver's seat.

"Can't you go any bloody faster?"

His outburst surprised and startled the driver. The man gulped, nodded and pushed down on the accelerator. The taxi responded sluggishly, but eventually was lumbering through the city's streets at a good clip.

They came to the intersection of Jones and Green streets. "Thank you. Thank you very much," said H.G. He paid the cabby, sprang from the taxi, skipped around its side and hurried down Green Street. As he headed into the small cul-de-sac, he grinned and seemed joyfully relieved to be so close to Amy. And just moments ago, he had been so despondent. How mercurial were the emotions of a man in love, he exclaimed to himself, then laughed. He was here! He would be with his beloved Amy in just a few seconds and they would emerge victorious. They would be the first two human beings in the history of the universe ever to defeat destiny on earth, its home turf.

He slowed down and stopped by one of the boxed trees on the sidewalk in front of her building. Before going inside, he briefly glanced at a strange sedan parked on the street, then paid it no heed. Amy was waiting! He had to hold and reassure her!

He ran up the outside steps, burst into the foyer and was about to race up the flight of stairs to her door when four large, steel-like hands grabbed his arms and shoulders. He was violently jerked back through the foyer, out the front door and tossed onto the hard concrete of the sidewalk. Dazed, he tried to rise and recognize his assailants, but he was never given an opportunity. A hard, polished boot connected with his midsection, and he went down again and smacked against the box that held the tree. He flailed his arms and turned and opened his mouth to scream Amy's name when something heavy and flexible smashed into the back of his head. The world went gray then, and his body limp. He felt himself being roughly jerked up and tossed onto the backseat of the strange sedan that he had noticed just moments earlier.

Then the motorcar was moving, turning, accelerating. He was overcome with an attack of nausea, for he was helpless. He was being forcibly taken away from Amy during her ultimate hour of need.

TWELVE

Leslie John Stephenson stirred in the dark-brown sheets of his king-sized bed. He stretched his lean and hard body, tightened his muscles, then emitted a loud yawn and relaxed. His eyes popped open and he realized that he had awakened with a smile on his face. He raised his head to look at the clock on the dresser across the room. Fifteen minutes past three. My, wasn't he the slothful one, lying around until the middle of the afternoon! Especially when he had to prepare for this evening's work and resolve the business with H. G. Wells. He chuckled and refused to be hard on himself. After all, enjoying two women in the same evening could put a strain on a man. He wasn't as young as he used to be, either. And the police had gotten to McLaren Park much sooner than he would have expected. It was as if they had been called! He had been surprised and had to slink away through quite a large forest just like a fugitive in an enemy country. He hadn't gotten home until seven o'clock in the morning, and he had been exhausted.

"Even angels of Satan have to sleep sometime," he said to himself.

Whistling, he swung his naked frame out of the bed, went into the bathroom and stood under a hot shower.

It had been worth the exhaustion. The seduction and murder of Dolores Clark had been the most profoundly satisfying sexual occurrence that he had ever experienced. Completely naked, she had been astride him with her back to his chest, her dark, glistening body moving wildly; she had been moaning, but gradually those sounds had become shouts, frantic pleas for release. He had groped for his knife, found it, then climaxed with a frenzy while driving the blade into her belly time after time. He did not clearly remember what he had done next, so great had his passion been, so utterly complete his satisfaction.

He took his ritual cup of tea in front of the Danish fireplace and watched the afternoon, winter sunlight shining through the large stained-glass window across the living room. He thought about H. G. Wells and laughed. The little scientist was probably going crazy reading the accounts of the murders in the newspapers, realizing that his time machine was responsible. Yes, Wells was no doubt still tenaciously attempting to track him down. He laughed again. What delicious irony! Wells was going to find him very shortly, only not quite in a way he would suspect.

Stephenson poured himself more tea from the silver service on the glass table next to his chair. He automatically sucked and chewed on his lower lip, relishing his classic yet rococo scheme. His actions would be liberating; they would leave him unfettered and unthreatened. He would have a time machine at his beck and call; he would be invincible; he would be one step closer to the proud embrace of Satan, the Supreme Originator.

He sipped his tea, then suddenly realized how composed he was. His flat was quiet and peaceful, too. Such tranquility inspired verse. He went to the secretary desk in the corner, sat down and began to compose a poem.

> Why, true love belongs to brutality,
> Said the King with keen mentality.
> Come, come, my queen, my dove,
> Let us quench our thirst for love.
> I am yours forever, she nodded and vowed,
> To be done away with, killed, or ploughed.
> For a lass must understand the reality
> Which saith, "True love belongs to Brutality."

He threw back his head and laughed and laughed at the rhymed couplets. He was delighted with his quick, off-the-cuff creation. He jotted it down for eternity, then shivered with pride. While the poem had been written quixotically, it nevertheless had a lightness, a fandango rhythm, a voice that was positively tongue-in-cheek. And yet, he had sacrificed none of his important thematic material. Yes, this piece of verse was definitely worth posterity. He would have to arrange for its publication. After all, he was sure that his composition would rival anything Shelley had put down in *The Cenci*.

He quickly dressed, then left his flat and hurried down the steps of Nob Hill Circle to Mason Street. He wanted to purchase an exotic knife before the night got under way. He felt extremely good and well-rested. Maybe— if he had time—he would stop and enjoy a light supper before proceeding to the flat occupied by Amy Robbins. He smiled. Surely Satan had blessed him.

Suddenly, he exploded with laughter. Maybe he *was* Satan! Had the prophecy finally come true? Was he, Leslie John Stephenson, the personification of the devil? Perchance a compilation of a billion years of the dark side of man? He grinned from ear to ear, for he certainly hoped so. But he wasn't going to dwell on it, he was going to prove it.

Evil for the sake of evil!

He turned into the traffic. No taxis appeared in the next onrush of vehicles, so he struck a pose that he had already witnessed many times in 1979, stuck out his thumb and waited for a lift. He hoped that whoever gave him a ride would be someone he could exploit.

The smaller of the two men drove the sedan slowly down Jones Street as if on a languid tour of the city. The other was turned, looking over the back of the seat and hefting the .38 Smith & Wesson special, a bemused expression on his face.

"You're making a mistake!" H. G. Wells shouted. "A horrible, terrible mistake!" The handcuffs cut painfully into the flesh of his wrists. "A girl is going to be murdered back there, do you hear me?"

"Nice piece. Where'd you get it?"

"Why don't you read him his rights?"

"Yeah."

"Will you please *listen* to me!" H.G. sobbed hysterically.

"You have the right to remain silent—"

"Please!"

"And the right to an attorney of your own choice."

"For *God's sake*, man!"

"You are hereby warned that anything you say may be used against you in a court of law."

"You don't understand, do you!" H.G. screamed.

"Listen, dude! If you don't quit screaming at me, you ain't going to be able to talk much longer! Do *you* understand *that*?"

"Or care," H.G. added softly. He stared out the window, his mind racing with ominous, fateful, cosmic questions. He knew that he was helpless, yet he had to stay in control, he could not let his mind snap or all would be lost.

They finally got to police headquarters and drove around back to a loading dock where several uniformed officers lounged, smoking cigarettes and joking with each other. A sign overhead read "JAIL" and H.G. knew that he would have the dubious privilege of entering the building via a door reserved solely for prisoners. They pulled him out of the sedan and led him toward the building. No one took any particular notice. The little inventor could have been anyone—rich man, poor man, beggarman, thief. He was routine.

As H.G. was propelled through the door, he managed one last look behind him. The shadows were long, and he wished desperately that he could read his watch, but it was on his wrist behind his back.

Time, now the most cherished gift of all, had been stolen by those who would enshrine justice and enforce the law.

"I am no criminal!" he exclaimed, but no one listened.

He fell into a state of torpid shock as they led him down a green corridor to an elevator. He was made to board, and the machine slowly descended. He became numb and bewildered. His thoughts were heavy; he was filled with a great sadness. He realized that if he had been totally honest with Amy and told her his intentions, he probably would not be here now. At the very least, she would have accompanied him. The worst that could have happened was that they *both* would be in police custody right now. As it was, Amy was alone— waiting for him to return. And he wasn't going to unless he could convince the police that he was an innocent victim of circumstances. He could only hope that Amy would have the sense to leave her apartment. If she dallied, thinking that she should wait for him, she would be greeting Dr. Leslie John Stephenson instead. With that thought, he straightened up, screamed with panic and threw himself at the elevator doors. The larger detective grabbed him and hurled him against the far wall of the elevator. His back hit and then his head snapped hard into the metal facing. He slid down the wall to the floor. The detective impassively helped the little man to his feet and steadied him.

Then the elevator stopped and its doors opened. H.G. was led to a desk at a caged window, and he recognized that the officer behind it was a sergeant, hence a man of some authority.

"I demand to see Lieutenant Mitchell!"

"He'll be along, by and by."

They removed his handcuffs. Then they handed the sergeant H.G.'s pistol, his newspaper, his traveler's checks, his precious digital chronometer and everything else in his pockets. As a final indignity, they took off his belt, and he reddened, thinking for a moment that his trousers would fall off.

"My good man!"

"We wouldn't want you hanging yourself now, would we?"

And then he was fingerprinted and photographed and it took such an agonizingly long time. Everyone was so casual, and H.G. wondered if all these modern police ever did was laugh at each other's tasteless jokes, smoke cigarettes, discuss women and comment on "the Raiders," whoever they were.

He was led to a cell. He realized with sudden horror that he was not immediately going to be given a chance to explain. He would not be able to save Amy's life! "Please, there isn't much time! I must see Lieutenant Mitchell!"

"You hot to confess or what?"

H.G. pulled away from his captor and made a hapless break for the door. He was caught before he could get outside. They twisted his arms to the breaking point, propelled him back across the room, hurled him into a tank and slammed the door.

H.G. was alone. He got up off the floor and looked around. The cell smelled faintly of urine and bile. He put his face in his hands.

"No," he moaned. "Oh, God, please, no!"

Lieutenant Mitchell was doing what he usually did when a murder investigation made him nervous. He was enjoying a leisurely dinner at Rocca's. For some reason, food calmed him and removed the nauseous feeling in his stomach brought on by exhaustion. If he ate slowly; and that, he had.

He finished his dessert of vanilla ice cream, then sipped his third cup of coffee, lit a cigarette and reflected. There was really nothing else he could do but wait. Sure, the press was howling, but they always did. The D.A. and the commissioner had the good sense to be unavailable for comment; they let him and the chief handle it. That was what made Mitchell's job worthwhile. The politicians respected his track record and left him alone.

He scowled and sighed. If only this one were over, though. Then he really might entertain thoughts of retirement or certainly a vacation. He grinned and felt much better. The meal had removed his tension. He checked his watch, left a healthy tip for the good service, then left the restaurant. He drove back to police headquarters.

When he walked into his office, he had no sooner turned on the lights and hung up his coat when the phone rang. He quickly lit a cigarette, inhaled deeply, then punched the flashing button. "This is Mitchell!"

"Where you been, Lieutenant?" asked Sergeant Ray. "I've been trying to get ahold of you for a couple of hours!"

"What's up?"

"We got him! Officers Spector and Scheff apprehended the suspect entering the building at 921½ Green Street."

Mitchell felt a wave of rapture pass over his body, giving him goose bumps. News like that made it all worthwhile, and once again, he was fiercely proud to be a cop. "You can tell Spector and Scheff to pick up their sergeant's stripes."

"You bet, sir."

"You can lift the rest of the stake-out around the girl's place, too."

"Yes, sir."

"Didn't I tell you I had it figured right?"

"You sure did, Lieutenant. He wanted to be caught. That's where he was staying, all right."

"He didn't harm her, did he?"

"Who?"

"Amy Robbins. The girl who lives in the place where you nailed him."

"She wasn't there."

Mitchell sighed. "I sure as hell hope that she doesn't turn up dead somewhere." He took a hard drag on his cigarette. "Where you got Wells now?"

"Downstairs in the slams."

"I want to talk to him."

"I'll set it up right now, Lieutenant."

Mitchell grinned. "Oh. One more thing, Sergeant."

"What?"

"You still think he's a psychic?"

The afternoon had been replaced by evening, and Amy's apartment was dark and quiet. Still, she slept, although the drug had begun to wear off. She was warm, encased in the comforter. Her mind lingered on the threshold between dreams and memories, and she was secure in the tranquility produced by that mental state.

The old grandfather clock in her living room bonged six times with a muted, brass chime that hung in the air for a few seconds, then dissipated.

She woke abruptly and sat up straight, her eyes wide and unblinking. For a moment she didn't know where she was, since the drug had left her senses groggy. She gasped. It was dark! She swung off the bed and looked at her window. It was night outside! She peered at the clock above her bed. *Six*? There must be some mistake! What was she still doing in her apartment? She was immediately conscious of her pounding heart.

She ran to the door and turned on the overhead light. The illumination reassured her for the moment, and she instinctively felt herself to make sure that she was all right.

"H.G.," she called tentatively. "Don't you think it's time we got out of here?"

She walked lightly down the hall to the bathroom door and rapped on it. "H.G.? It's awfully late," she whispered, trying to keep the urgency out of her voice. "H.G.?"

He wasn't in the bathroom. She frowned and reminded herself that she had a strong character and plenty of self-control. She peered down the hall and saw that the rest of her apartment was dark, too. She shivered, and the tremor ran from the back of her neck to her toes. She grew afraid and strained to listen for a noise— *anything*—that might forewarn her of danger. There was nothing except the very faint sound of a stereo coming from across the street. She did not move a muscle; her body tingled, every nerve feeling the vibrations in the air. What was out there? Anything? Something? She gulped and felt a sudden rush of panic. She took a deep breath, sighed and remained in control. Then she forced herself to think and instantly felt better.

Of course. H.G. had inadvertently fallen asleep, too. Probably on the couch in the living room because he hadn't wanted to disturb her. She relaxed somewhat. Sure. That was it. After all, he had been up all night. Well, then, she'd better wake him, and they'd better leave in a hurry. The hour was fast approaching, and she could not afford to indulge in false yet comforting thoughts which told her that it could never *really* happen to her.

She tiptoed down the hall as fast as she could go without making noise. She paused at the edge of the living room and strained to see into the blackness, but all she could make out were vague forms.

"H.G.?" she whispered insistently. "H.G.?"

She waited for several minutes huddled against the wall. She hesitated, deathly afraid to cross the room, yet knowing that she must. Eventually, she could no longer bear the sound of her own breathing. She *bolted* to the couch.

"H.G.! Wake up! H.G.!" She was leaning over the sofa and feeling for him, but all her hands found was the cold fabric of pillows in the darkness. *He was not there! He was gone!* With a low whimper of fear, she backed away from the couch, then whirled around fast lest someone grab her from behind. She stumbled blindly toward the foyer, imagining that at any second a gloved hand was going to close around her throat. She hit the wall; her hand fumbled for the light switch and turned it on. She slowly turned, her chest heaving, and surveyed the room. Her lower lip quivered spasmodically; she was about to come unglued. She gulped, shut her eyes tightly, took a deep breath and shook her head. No. She was not going to fall apart. There wasn't time. She was going to control herself.

She straightened up, then glanced back and made sure

that the front door was locked. She hurried to the couch and found her sneakers where she had left them just hours before. She put them on and laced them. Where had he gone and why? When had he left? What had happened while she so blithely slept? If she hadn't firmly believed that he was trustworthy and reliable, she never would have allowed herself to take the Valium and go to sleep in the first place! She frowned. He, himself, had insisted upon total honesty between them. Now she realized that he had not been honest with her. He had left the apartment and had not told her and her life was in jeopardy.

She quickly went down the hallway into the bedroom. She took her coat out of the closet, put it on and turned off the light. *Why?* Why had he left? She stopped, leaned against the doorway and sighed. She shook her head. She could not think that he had betrayed her.

Every move he had made, every action he had taken had been for her benefit. Thus, there was no reason to doubt him now. She could only hope—fervently so— that he was all right. She wiped away a lone tear, a simple expression of longing to be by his side. Suddenly, she gasped. *What if something had happened to him? Something awful, something horrible and painful? What if he had been unable to give her an explanation? What if he had been forced to leave the apartment?*

The grandfather clock bonged once, telling Amy that the time was now six fifteen. The sound was the same as it always had been, but now she associated a chilling, ominous finality with it. The noise shattered her pretense of calm. Her heart pounded faster. She hurried to the window in the dining room and peered outside, hoping that maybe she would see him coming for her. The street was empty. Her hands were shaking.

She must leave.

She had to get out. Now. She grabbed her wallet off the dining-room table and ran for the front door. In the foyer she remembered her car keys; she stopped and fumbled in her pockets, but did not find them. She frowned and turned. Had she left them on the sofa? Or put them in the desk?

The room was harshly lit and barren except for the clock on the rear wall. H.G. sat at one end of an imitation-wood table in a chair similar to the one he had first experienced at McDonald's. Three times he had patiently explained who he was, where he was from, how he had arrived in 1979, what he was doing and the immediate danger faced by the love of his life, Amy Robbins. Three times Lieutenant Mitchell—baffled by Wells's rational and sane sincerity—had shaken his head in disbelief and asked H.G. to start again. Three times a police recorder at the other end of the table had silently, inconspicuously worked the face of a small keyboard and taken down the bizarre tale.

Mitchell chain-smoked and paced in the center of the room, but remained calm and detached. He had questioned thousands of suspects in his career and in due time almost all of them confessed if they were guilty. He was, moreover, a patient, thorough man. He turned. "Let me see if I've got this straight." He raised a finger and looked at H.G. with a blank expression. "Your name is H. G. Wells and you came here on a time machine called *The Utopia* and you're chasing a Dr. Leslie John Stephenson who you insist is Jack the Ripper."

"You've got it, Lieutenant." H.G. nodded furiously. "That's absolutely correct. I could not have phrased it more succinctly myself."

"Do you realize how ridiculous that sounds?"

H.G. stared at his interrogator. For a moment there he had thought, wishfully so, that Mitchell was going to accept his explanation and cooperate. Obviously, that was not the case. The sick feeling in the pit of his stomach returned.

The black hand of the wall clock jumped forward. H.G. glanced at it, then wiped sweat off his ashen face with a trembling hand.

It was 6:17 P.M.

He moaned and leaned forward. "For God's sake, Lieutenant! There isn't much time! Please! Save the girl!"

"I already have, Wells," Mitchell replied coldly. "Her and a lot of other women in this city."

"In forty-three minutes, Leslie John Stephenson is going to walk into her flat and murder her!"

"Leslie John Stephenson doesn't exist and never did."

"What are you saying?"

"Stephenson is you and you are him. Half of you wants to kill women and then cut them up. The other half is sickened by such behavior and wants to get caught." He grinned. "Congratulations, Wells. Your half finished first."

H.G. gasped. "No! You've got it all wrong! You must believe me! *Please! There isn't much time!*"

The lieutenant emitted a dry laugh. "I don't know about you, Wells, but I've got all night. Now why don't we try again? From the top?"

H.G. twitched in the chair and wanted to bolt for the door, but knew that he wouldn't get far. He tried to calm himself so that he could explain a fourth time, but was unsuccessful. He shook badly all over. When he tried to speak, his throat would close, and he would convulse in a dry retch.

Mitchell observed his prisoner's behavior and then left the room without a word. Moments later, he returned with a pitcher of ice water and a glass. He poured some and handed it to Wells.

H.G. gratefully drank. The gagging sensation left him. He looked up at Mitchell and nodded with thanks.

"Now. Would you like a smoke?" Mitchell held out a pack of Camels. "Would that help?"

"No," H.G. replied hollowly. "I have told you the truth. So help me God."

Mitchell sighed, then lit one for himself, straddled a chair next to the recorder and rested his chin on its back. He scrutinized H.G. thoughtfully. Someone rapped on the door. "It's open." Mitchell's eyes never left H.G.'s face.

Sergeant Ray entered the room with a large, sealed manila envelope which he carefully placed on the table in front of Mitchell. "These are his personal effects."

"Anything interesting?"

"Yeah. This." With his other hand, Ray gave Mitchell the .38 Smith & Wesson special and the box of ammunition.

The lieutenant released his breath in a long hiss, brusquely examined the weapon, then casually tossed it onto the table. It made a loud and rude clatter. He ground out his cigarette and rubbed his wrinkled face. Then he affixed Wells with a jaundiced eye and gave him a knowing look. "They didn't make thirty-eight specials eighty-six years ago, Wells."

"You've got it wrong, Lieutenant! I purchased the weapon just this afternoon so that I might defend Miss Robbins! I was going to apprehend the foul miscreant, Stephenson! I was prepared to shoot him, if necessary!"

Mitchell laughed. "You'll have to do better than that. A whole lot better."

H.G. closed his eyes and took a deep breath. He gritted his teeth and clenched the arms of the chair until his knuckles were white. Cold, nervous sweat dripped and ran down his flanks. He *had* to remain calm; he *had* to control himself. He *had* to use his logical mind and think of a way out of this. He feared that if he became hysterical they would take him back to a cell and that would be the end of it. He had to keep the lieutenant here and somehow he had to convince him. "Please, Lieutenant," he said softly. "The girl, Miss Robbins—"

"I've got another theory, Wells." Mitchell got out of the chair and resumed pacing. "None of the women you murdered resisted. As a matter of fact, all of them were engaged in sexual acts just prior to their deaths. Why? How? Very simply, they were under duress. You had a gun at their heads. *This* gun."

H.G.'s eyes widened; he could not immediately reply. He was filled with terror, realizing that this clever yet methodical police lieutenant already had enough evidence to send him to prison! The man's theories were solid; his arguments were perfectly logical. But there wasn't a shred of truth to anything that he was saying! There must be a way to convince him otherwise; there must be a way to save Amy's life in the short time that remained.

"Let's see what other bits of evidence you were carrying around, Wells." Mitchell moved to the table. He ripped open the manila envelope and dumped out its contents.

"Please, Lieutenant! Forget everything I've said, all right? Just forget it! You must save Amy Robbins!" He shouted. "Why can't you at least send one of your men over to her flat to protect her? If you don't she is going to die at seven o'clock!"

But Mitchell wasn't listening.

Instead, the lieutenant was looking at an edition of the San Francisco *Chronicle* which he had removed from the manila envelope. He gazed at the picture of a very pretty young woman named Amy Robbins and read a headline about another murder.

"Jesus H. Christ," he whispered to himself. He could not fathom what he was seeing; he did not know what to make of it; never in his twenty-seven years on the force had he ever encountered anything quite so bizarre. The newspaper was dated November 10, 1979, and was purported to be tomorrow morning's edition—something which wouldn't even be printed for another eight hours or so. He rubbed his face furiously, scowled at Wells, then handed the newspaper to Sergeant Ray. "What do you make of this, Sergeant?"

"Yes, that's right!" the little Englishman shouted. "Take a look at it!" He turned toward Mitchell, a glint of hope in his eyes. "It proves my innocence! It proves what I've been saying, you fools! Now do you understand what I've been telling you?" He glanced up to the clock. "It's twenty to seven, Lieutenant! You've got exactly twenty minutes! *Now* will you send someone over to protect Miss Amy Robbins? So that she does *not* end up a statistic on the front page of that blasted newspaper?"

Mitchell ignored Wells. "What do you think, Sergeant?"

"Jesus, I don't know." His gnarled face was pale. "Maybe we should send somebody over to her place. I mean, did you see this box up at the top?"

"What box?"

"One-hundred-to-one shot pays off big at Bay Meadows," he quoted, then glanced at Mitchell. "What if this thing is for real, Lieutenant?"

"Of *course* it's *real*!" H.G. exclaimed.

Mitchell could see that his partner was shaken, for he kept glancing at Wells as if the man really might have supernatural powers of some kind. The lieutenant snorted derisively. "You're not looking at a psychic,

Sergeant Ray! You're looking at one of the sickest killers you've ever seen!"

"Yes, sir, but the date. What about the date?"

"For Christ's sake, Sergeant, use your brain! Haven't you ever heard of novelty shops where they print fake newspapers?" He gestured at Wells. "This guy is so twisted that he concocted a newspaper story about his next victim!"

"Yeah." Ray nodded sadly, still distracted. "Payoffs like that only happen to people who are retired or unemployed, anyway."

H.G. was astonished. He blinked his eyes repeatedly and pressed his hands into his temples as if fighting for control. "You mean . . . you mean you don't even believe *that*? An example of futurological history?" He waved at the newspaper. "My God, man, what more could you possibly *want*?"

"The truth."

Mitchell saw his prisoner rise up in his chair, his entire body coiling for an explosion. He tensed himself.

Then, suddenly, Wells sagged and went limp. Tears streamed down his face and his lips quivered. "I'll make a deal with you, Lieutenant!" he cried.

"You're in no position to make a deal."

"If you'll send someone over to the flat of Miss Robbins and save her life, I will confess to anything that you like."

"I'm not interested in copping a plea, Wells. I want the truth."

"What the hell, Lieutenant," Sergeant Ray interrupted. "What can it hurt? I mean, if that's all he wants. Why *don't* we send a car over?"

Mitchell sighed, then shrugged. "Yeah. You're right. Then maybe he'll cooperate. Right, Wells?"

H.G. nodded.

Mitchell glanced at the sergeant. "Go ahead." Ray

left the room, and then Mitchell swung back to H.G., his eyebrows slightly raised, an expectant expression on his face. "I'm listening."

"I killed them all," H.G. croaked, his voice choked with relief. "Every last one of them."

Amy had looked in her desk, she had looked in the kitchen, she had looked in the bedroom and the bathroom. Everywhere. She had gone through her coat pockets a dozen times. The car keys were nowhere to be found. She went to the desk one last time and forced her eyes to search every space as if a grid. Still no keys. Desperate, she emptied all of the desk drawers on the table and sorted through the contents. Nothing. She ran back into the bedroom and did the same with her dresser drawers. She searched the entire place again, her stubbornness driving her. The grandfather clock bonged once more.

Six forty-five.

She had fifteen minutes left. That was all. She was not going to drive away from 921½ Green Street, she was going to run away. That eerie feeling crept up her spine, making her shiver, urging her to leave *right now*. She hurried down the hallway and crossed the living room. She was about to open the front door and flee when suddenly she froze and emitted a sharp gasp. She placed her hand to her mouth and stared, for she had just heard a clicking noise in front of her.

The doorknob was slowly turning and the lock was moving right along with it.

She lurched back, her eyes wide, her head shaking "no" over and over again. Some primeval instinct for survival inside her took control and quelled her scream of terror. Her mind suddenly became crystal clear and immediately aware of the options that were open to her. There was no chance for her to escape, given the absence of a rear exit from the apartment. And she could not very well attempt to leap out of a window, for she heard the lock snap free. There wasn't time! Any second now and the door would open and he would be inside! She spun around, and slipped inside the foyer closet with just moments to spare.

She released her breath in a low hiss, then reached behind her and grabbed the clothes-hanging bar so that she would not faint and fall. When the blood returned to her head, she carefully worked her way behind the unused coats and dresses that she had always kept hanging there. She squatted on the floor. Physical control left her. She began shaking; her breath came in gasps; she felt incredibly cold all over; and her heart pounded so hard that she was sure that the sound could be heard in the living room. She bit her lower lip to try to stop from shaking.

Then she heard him out there—moving around slowly, quietly, catlike, professional. He was *early!* She screamed inside. *Early!* In the newspaper story, the coroner had reported that the murder had occurred between seven and seven-thirty. Well, the coroner was *wrong!*

She screwed up her face, attempting to prevent a sudden rush of tears. She tightened all her muscles against the sobs and convulsions that swept over her body. The result was that she sounded like she was dying.

The fear was awful—worse than the actual event, she was certain. Her skin crawled, anticipating a flood of light, a madman's chortle, a strong hand in her hair, a sudden jerk as she was upraised, and then a searing pain as a knife slashed through her throat and moments later cut open her abdomen. She twitched spasmodically. She moaned low. She feared that her mind would snap and that she would burst out of the closet and throw herself at his feet, begging for release, screaming for sweet death.

The expectation of pain stopped her and enabled her

to control herself. But she was left with one horrible question: Did one feel the pain forever? Did the moment of anguish repeat itself in terrible, dialectic cycles through eternity? How would she know?

Somehow, she found the inner strength to close her eyes and pray with dignity to a supernatural being that she had accepted only casually before.

He pushed the door closed with his gloved hand, then carefully slipped the surgical knife that he had used to unlock her front door back into its sheath inside his polished half boot. He moved quickly across the foyer into the living room, his lithe and powerful body crouched low, ready for the unexpected. He paused, his eyes darting around the flat. He saw nothing, straightened up and relaxed a little. Then he checked out the dining room and kitchen. After that, he inspected the bathroom. Finally, he crept into the bedroom, halfway hoping that he would find H. G. Wells and the girl coupled passionately, unable to stop even though they both recognized the chilling incarnation of death. He sighed. No such luck. Instead, the room gave him the impression that a thief had been here before him. He frowned with puzzlement, then grinned. He rather liked the look of chaos about the room—the sense of disorder and turbulence.

He turned and walked back down the hallway through the living and dining rooms and into the kitchen, a small, satisfied smile on his face. He was alone.

This time, he would wait, although he did not think it would be long. The girl had left the lights on, which told him that she was only out for a short while. Maybe dinner, perhaps, since he saw no dirty dishes in the scullery. He rummaged in the cabinets and found the bottle of Bombay gin. He grinned again. So Wells *had* been here! Then there would be no problem. Certainly the girl would know where he was if he was familiar enough with her to visit her flat. Maybe they would return together. Wouldn't that be a pleasant windfall? His task would certainly be made much simpler.

He poured himself a glassful of gin, then returned to the living room and seated himself in the stuffed chair. He sipped the drink, sighed and chuckled. Everything was going just as he'd planned.

He removed the exotic Spanish knife, his latest purchase, from its sheath tied to his left leg. He admired the glint and curve of the blade. It was fifteen inches long and fashioned from hard Toledo steel. Granted, it would be no more or less effective than his surgical knives, but it *looked* worse. And that was important given the significance of the evening. He must ensure that he would be in the strongest position possible. After all, he would not be bargaining with an idiot. He smiled. Although if Wells already did have strong feelings for the girl, he would be more likely to make a fool of himself. Stephenson laughed. That would be absolutely marvelous.

Perhaps the matters of his infinite freedom, his eternal reign as the human prince of darkness would not be so difficult. If he won tonight, he, Leslie John Stephenson, would be liberated forevermore. No longer would he have to worry about being doggedly pursued by a determined, nasty little harbinger of positivism. No longer would he have to fret about a possible discovery. No one would know. He could commit atrocities and evil at will, and the time machine would be to him as fire was to the venerable God of War. Satan would rule. No longer would there be any self-righteous pretenders to the throne. No longer would there be any questions. And Leslie John Stephenson would become the eternal angel of the apocalypse—riding the fourth dimension—

dispensing death and pain and sorrow and misery and maybe even pestilence arbitrarily, absurdly, on a whim, a notion, an impulsive passing fancy.

Enough of dreams and fantasies, he told himself. Needless to say, they would all be realized soon, and the evening would be a milestone. But first, he must concentrate on the physical act of surprising and capturing Amy Robbins. He drained his glass and sighed with appreciation. He rose from the chair and silently crossed the room, moving around the couch and into the foyer. He turned off the light, then stepped back from the door and adjusted his eyes to the blackness by blinking them rapidly. Gradually, forms and shapes once again took on definition and size.

He heard a noise from the street and grinned. No doubt that was Amy Robbins. He absently fingered the blade of his Spanish knife, his breath coming quicker now.

A small, muffled thud.

He whirled around and frowned. Had that noise come from the front door or elsewhere? Had his senses deceived him? *No! There had been another noise!* Was someone already *here*? *Inside* the bloody flat? He turned a complete circle in a crouch, his knife at the ready, his heart pounding, his body tense. A tremor of fear passed over him. He began to perspire. He strained to see the slightest movement; his ears listened for the slightest noise; his skin was aware of the vibrations in the air. Slowly— very slowly—he continued to turn.

Suddenly, he focused on the foyer closet. He hadn't looked inside that cupboard when he had first come in, had he? Was someone lurking in there?

He took a deep breath, licked his lips and raised his knife. He began to move forward, but only a few inches at a time. He did not want to create any unnecessary noise. He crept closer and closer to the closet, his breath coming in a low hiss. He reached his left hand out for the door handle and with his right raised the knife higher still.

"I killed them all!"

After that, the pretense had dissolved, the shred of self-control had broken down. H.G. had fallen forward on the table and had begun to cry with relief. He realized that his behavior was embarrassing, undignified and demonstrated a lack of strength, but he could no longer hold back. If Amy was still in her apartment, the order that Mitchell had given might very well save her life. That was the most important thing in the universe right now. Therefore, he did not care about a show of emotion. After all, what was *that* when juxtaposed with the scheme of the cosmos, anyway? What was that but an infinitesimal part of the life and love that he was sacrificing himself for? What was *he* without *her* but a tragedian outside time?

Enough ethereal thoughts and speculations, he told himself; there *was* a postscript to his most recent turn of events. He had hopelessly complicated matters by making a confession. He sighed. Very soon he was going to find himself in prison, unable to be with Amy. Furthermore, he would not be able to use *The Utopia* and escape this current world of contradictions and inequities. Yet, he did not view his dilemma as hopeless. Amy would be out there fighting for him. She would marshal proof of his innocence and get him released.

He smiled optimistically through his tears. Yes, he would eventually settle with Mitchell and the police. Somehow. His sacrifice would not be in vain. In the meantime, if it still was not too late, had he not scored another telling victory against the forces of Fate?

Mitchell had left the room then, only to return moments later with a steaming cup of coffee. He had seated himself, lit a cigarette and continued with his interrogation, asking detailed questions which were difficult for H.G. to answer since he was not used to fabrication.

Finally, Mitchell sighed, rubbed his weather-beaten face for what seemed like the thousandth time and scowled at Wells. "You killed them all, huh?"

"How many times do I have to say it?"

"Then how come you don't know how much Jade Chang charged per trick when she was alive?"

"Money means nothing to me, my good man."

"What kind of car did Dolores Clark drive?"

"A . . . a black one."

"What kind?"

"I'm not interested in motorcars, either."

"What color were the seats?"

"Red," H.G. guessed, then smiled cleverly. "After I got through with her."

Mitchell scowled. "What did you have to drink at Marsha McGee's place?"

"I don't recall."

"You don't recall."

Exasperated, H.G. straightened up. "I've already confessed, Lieutenant! What the devil do you want?"

"The truth."

Before he could resume questioning, the door opened. The inevitable Sergeant Ray slipped into the room as if pursued. His thick face was chalk white, full of fear and worry.

"There's a phone call for you, sir," he announced in sorrowful tones.

"Take a message."

"I think you should answer this one, sir." His voice was almost a whisper. He gave H.G. a sheepish, sidelong glance, half sympathetic, half in awe. Mitchell followed his look and quickly paled.

H.G. gasped and stood up. "Is she all right?" he asked, trembling. *"Please tell me! Is she all right?"*

Mitchell gestured to the recorder and he left the room. Then the lieutenant went out, closing the door quietly, refusing to look H.G. in the eye. No answer was forthcoming.

H.G. knew then that his beloved Amy was dead.

THIRTEEN

Lieutenant Mitchell leaned on one of the dining-room-table chairs for support and stared out the window at the lace trees, their delicate leaves intermittently lit by the flashing red and blue lights of the six squad cars on the street below. He had been sick only once before during a homicide investigation. That had been seventeen years ago when he had witnessed what a cuckolded husband could do to his wife with a .357 Magnum at close range.

This one was worse. His first thought before collapsing with nausea had been that he had just seen the ultimate in human bestiality. And his cloud of tobacco smoke had not prevented the fetid smell of coagulating blood from bringing on the attack. But that had passed, and now he wondered. What kind of human being was capable of committing such an atrocity? He grimaced. If there had once been a soft spot in his heart for the agonized criminal, supposedly twisted by society, there was no longer.

"Lieutenant," whispered a uniformed officer. "Are you all right?"

"Don't ask stupid questions," he replied quietly. He

forced himself to go back into the living room where his old and reliable team was going through the motions of a thorough investigation. They, too, were horrified; their faces were frozen in expressions of shock. The entire room had been sprayed and splashed with blood—as if the murderer had used various and sundry parts of the victim's body as paint brushes. There was not one item which had not been stained red; conversely, there was not one part of the deceased's form which had not been defiled and mutilated in some way.

The photographers finished and looked to Mitchell for instructions. He waved them out. The technicians completed their taking of blood samples, their swift yet methodical sweep of the apartment for evidence. And finally—thank God—the coroner's deputies, who normally were the first to be done, finished placing in plastic bags the parts of the corpse. It had been an exploration of the macabre for them, a devil's treasure hunt. They had had to refer to an anatomical chart to make sure that they had not left anything behind.

Mitchell remained in the apartment after everyone else had left. He wanted to sear the violent tableau into his brain, for he had been dead wrong about the murder suspect in this case. He had to rectify that. He remembered the other victims—the Chinese whore, the salesgirl and Dolores Clark. Each one of those murders had been stylized, almost staged; a sense of joyous evil had pervaded them. But, here, there was a difference. The killer had been frenzied, angry and frustrated. There had been no control to the mutilation. Preliminary reports indicated that there had been no sexual contact prior to the murder. The killer, then, must have been surprised in some way, Mitchell concluded. Something must have gone wrong.

He started down the stairs. So what? Maybe a dog barked. Maybe a neighbor dropped by unexpectedly.

That still didn't change the fact that he was no closer to a suspect now than he had been days ago. He realized morosely that his theory about Wells and the murders was completely logical, yet totally wrong. By the same token, he didn't buy any of that garbage about time-traveling, either. It just couldn't be true! The only possible conclusion he could reach, then, was the one held by Sergeant Ray. Wells was a psychic. There was no other way he could've had foreknowledge of at least two of the murders.

He came out onto the sidewalk and saw a crowd of news reporters surge against the cordon of police that surrounded the building. The immodest, inevitable cacophony of questions shouted at random began.

"Was there another murder in this building, Lieutenant? *Officially?*"

"Yes, there was."

"Was it anything like the Dolores Clark killing?"

"It was similar."

"Do you have any suspects yet?"

"No comment, gentlemen."

"Was the victim a prostitute?"

"No, she was not a prostitute. If you want more information, you'll have to wait until next of kin are notified. Now, if you'll excuse me, gentlemen?"

"The neighbors say somebody named Amy Robbins lived up there! Is that who it was, Lieutenant?"

"I am not *sure*, gentlemen!" He turned and glared at them. His voice began to quaver. "There was no way for me or anyone else to identify the corpse! It was *beyond* recognition, you understand, gentlemen?"

H.G. was huddled in the corner of the small room staring at tomorrow's newspaper still on the table. The headline was true; the prophecy had been fulfilled. He had his coat wrapped tightly around him and violently shivered even though the temperature hadn't changed. He had lost. Inevitably. Amy was gone. He was alone. Eighty-six years from home, and no particular desire to return. It did not matter that he had not beaten destiny. It did not matter why their carefully laid plans had gone awry. It did not matter why the police had so stupidly intervened and then failed to act quickly enough. Amy was dead. He would never hear her speak again or feel her touch or sense her warmth or see her eyes. The latter was the most painful. He could envision her face and her eyes as he had gazed at them just that morning, dreaming of sharing Elysium with her. Her beautiful eyes would haunt him forever; she had been his responsibility; her death would lie heavy on his soul. And *that* mattered. And so did the fact that Stephenson was still running loose in the city of San Francisco. H.G. vowed to himself right then and there that he would stay in 1979 until he found the infernal, heinous doctor and extracted revenge.

Yes, vengeance, by God! And the devil with justice!

That philosophy of remedying social ills was neither consistent nor quick nor brutal enough. Not when it came to the memory of Amy Robbins. He would never stand idly by and watch Stephenson get sentenced to life in prison or even the gallows. He wanted to kill the villain with his own hands and make *him* feel some of the pain that he had inflicted upon Amy.

Suddenly, H.G. doubled over and sobbed. He felt so empty and cheated. *Why* had he even bothered to play with Fate? Why hadn't he insisted that they just leave when they first knew? Or was that just how cruel time really was? He, H. G. Wells, had unlocked the passageways of the fourth dimension. Perhaps there always had been a hidden irony to his discoveries and subsequent invention: that the past and the future had been permanently preordained and could not be altered no matter what. Hence, a person who traveled forward in time and returned to his present would be swollen with the knowledge of the future (whether good or bad), yet would be unable to impart that knowledge to anyone! At the very least, no one would believe him, as if that mattered anyway. Helplessly, he would watch the human condition plod toward whatever ultimate fate awaited it.

Moreover, that was precisely the reason why he, H. G. Wells, could not go back along the fourth dimension and resurrect Amy Robbins. To relive three days with her over and over they had already dismissed as the height of absurdity. And to leapfrog over her death would be more than tantamount to running away and avoiding reality; it would be living in limbo and begging the existential question. True, she would be alive, and they would have each other, but how long could their love hope to last if she knew that he was ultimately responsible for her terrible death? If she knew that she could never choose to return to her home hour and live out her natural life? And how could he love her when all the cosmos knew that he, the extratemporal mischief-maker, had failed to save her life?

Foreknowledge, then, was trifling at best, poisonous at worst. Long ago, the die had been cast, the Fates had been sealed. And what did that say for a paradise on earth? How did that speak to a Utopia? Not to mention progress through science and technology! All of those light-headed, naïve notions were worthless! False! They might as well be a fine layer of dust on the futurological scrap heap of human civilization, for they meant nothing.

The devil with optimism, then! Down with ideals! It is all going to end up however it was first conceived! With all of the universe laughing at the butt of the

*cosmos—the human animal—who has just enough sense
to realize with horror what is happening to him and
not enough intelligence to do anything about it.*

Amy is dead. God help us all.

He wiped his face dry with his handkerchief, cleared
his throat and looked up and around through red-
rimmed eyes.

Lieutenant Mitchell had come into the room and was
just standing there, staring at him. "You're free to go."

H.G. slowly nodded.

"I want you to know that I'm sorry. I'm truly very
sorry."

H.G. rose from the chair and collected his things—all
except for the pistol, which had been confiscated. He
dropped the newspaper from the future into a wastebasket, then walked out the door.

"Can I offer you a lift somewhere?" Mitchell called
after him.

The former little torchbearer for idealistic thinking
replied over his shoulder without turning. "You don't
have a conveyance that could take me far enough away
from this place, Lieutenant."

H.G. walked away from police headquarters and soon
was swallowed up in a light fog. He paused at an intersection and tested the wind with his nose. His posture
had imperceptibly changed. No longer did he stand perfectly straight with the look of an Anglican choir boy.
He was slightly crouched, instinctively ready to turn, his
slitted eyes matching his profound shift in mood and
conviction.

A small gust of wind picked up some debris (Styrofoam cups and plastic sandwich wrappers) from beneath
parked cars and blew the stuff away. H.G. nodded as if

nature had affirmed his new stance. The litter would no doubt eventually filter down to a slum. The meek shall *not* inherit the earth, he mused. Only its garbage.

He hailed a cab at Mission and Sixth, although he did not immediately know where he would go. Then he sighed and shrugged helplessly. Who was he to think that he could outsmart a master criminal such as Leslie John Stephenson? Let alone find him. What did it matter, anyway? Amy was gone, and he had no stomach left for the late twentieth century and its potpourri of imperfections. He was sick of 1979.

He told the cab driver to take him to the science museum in Golden Gate Park. Yes, the devil with it all. He would admit defeat, climb aboard his time machine and return home to a more genteel time. Upon arrival, he would remove THE UTOPIA from above his cabin door. He would obliterate the words (and hopefully the concept they stood for) by melting down the brass plate and tossing the slag into the Thames. Then he would pick up the pieces of his life and get on with the cruel banalities of existence.

They crossed Market Street and drove west on Geary when suddenly H.G. felt a twinge of emotion in his gut. He decided that he wanted to return to Russian Hill for one last look. A remembrance of what seemed like a distant past. He felt compelled to return, as if to remind himself of what once was and what could have been. True, all that would be there was a building, but it had been *her* building. Yes, she was dead now, but the very least he could do was say good-bye. The least he could do was pay his respects.

He told the driver to turn right on Van Ness and let him off at the corner of Green Street. Once there, he paid the cabby, then trudged up the street toward Russian Hill. He moved like an automaton, his shoes scuffing the sidewalk, his eyes open only for obstacles that might be in his path. His mind was sealed from any more speculation concerning free will, predestination and knowledge of the future. His face had taken on an embittered cast, his muscles hard against the cold night air.

Leslie John Stephenson stood in the shadows of a massive hedgerow between two large houses just up the hill from the cul-de-sac. His spot was safely secluded, yet he had a view of Green Street below. He also had Amy Robbins and she was alive. One of his hands held her by the hair while the other rested on her shoulder, clenching the Spanish knife. Its blade was against her throat. She quivered like a bird in the paws of a predator and was silent.

He watched and waited. He did not speak to her for there was no need. Rather, he was lost in his own thoughts. The evening had not gone as he had anticipated. He had found Amy Robbins in the cupboard in the foyer and she had given in without resistance once she had seen his exotic knife. But then the *other* girl had come into the flat without knocking, announcing brightly that she was sorry that she was a little bit late. The girl had seen the knife at Amy's throat and had become petrified with fear. It was that split second of inertia that had saved him. He had clubbed Amy Robbins unconscious, grabbed the other girl and slashed her throat without ceremony. Then he had gone into a frenzy.

He frowned and cursed himself. There had been so *much* blood this time. If only he had not lost control, despite the surprise visitor. If only he had not given in to his fury and wallowed in it. He could simply just have slain the girl and let it go at that. Then he *still* could have stayed in the flat and proceeded as he had originally planned. But after he had finished with the girl's corpse, Amy Robbins had regained consciousness and had begun screaming. He had silenced her by brandishing his knife, but the damage had been done. Someone had undoubtedly heard the shrieks; hence, he had been forced to flee with her.

Once safely away from the building, he had threatened Amy Robbins with death and subsequently learned that she had indeed been expecting Wells to show up at her apartment. Therefore, Stephenson had returned to Russian Hill after the police had departed and taken up his vigil. He just hoped that the bargaining with Wells would not be difficult. Whatever happened, he must control himself. Any more self-indulgent, indiscreet behavior and he might find himself in serious trouble. He inadvertently twisted and tightened his grip on her hair. She moaned with pain and sagged. He grinned, full of hatred for all the females of the species.

And then he saw the little scientist shuffling along the north side of Green Street. The man appeared depressed and was moving aimlessly. He stopped across the street from the girl's building and stared up at the darkened windows of her flat. Then he put his face in his hands and slumped against a boxed lace tree on the sidewalk.

Stephenson grinned again. The upcoming transaction might just be easier than he had originally thought. Perhaps he had overestimated the brilliance and cleverness of H. G. Wells.

He prodded the girl with the point of his knife. They went down the hill to the side of an old Victorian mansion on the cul-de-sac. He stopped. He did not want to step out of the shadows yet, for he would risk detection. He couldn't call out, either; however, he would have to get Wells's attention. He thought for a moment, then chortled. He took one hand out of the girl's hair, removed his watch from its pocket and snapped open the lid.

The light French lullaby began playing, its flights of melody softened by the mist, but audible nonetheless.

Stephenson saw Wells lift his head, listen for a moment, then approach with a quick and curious, yet cautious stride.

At first, H.G. thought that the music was coming from inside someone's abode, then realized that that was unlikely given the late hour. Perhaps someone had left one of those radios found in motorcars going. He peered into the open window of a squat vehicle with a canvas top that resembled a beetle.

"H.G.!"

He whirled around and gasped. Someone had called him and the sound of the voice was agonizingly familiar! Was he hearing some hallucination induced by travel along the fourth dimension?

"H.G., I'm over here!"

Amy was alive! With a hoarse, inarticulate cry, he rushed toward the side of a house, anticipating her warmth and the feel of her winsome frame against him.

"Amy, oh my God, Amy! Are you all right?" And then suddenly he stopped short. *They* had stepped out of the shadows. H.G. saw that the fiendish Stephenson had her with a knife pressing against her throat. She was held up mainly by the strength of the villain's hand in her hair.

"Amy! My God." He stared, unable to believe his eyes. "But who . . . ?"

"He murdered Carole," she croaked. "Carole Thomas, my friend from work. I'd invited her for dinner." Her voice faded, but she managed to continue. "You were right. The newspaper was wrong."

"A mistaken identity!"

She nodded and began to sob quietly.

H.G. rose to his full height and glared up at Stephenson. His chest swelled out. "What the devil do you want?"

Stephenson chuckled. "Surely you must know. The special key that overrides the Rotation Reversal Lock circuitry. It's what I've wanted all along. Give it to me and we'll call it quits."

H.G. gasped. "How did you find out about that?"

"How else? From the diagrams in your rather spartan Mornington Crescent laboratory. Given the close proximity of Scotland Yard's finest, however, I did not have the time to ask you for it then."

"What makes you think I'll give it to you now?" he queried, naïvely so.

"Would you like to watch Miss Robbins die?"

H.G.'s eyes widened; he began to tremble. "She isn't part of this! This is a struggle between you and me!"

"The heroic doesn't suit you, Wells," Stephenson replied contemptuously. "Your voice lacks timbre and your stature significance."

"My God, man, be reasonable!"

"I'm being perfectly reasonable. It's just that I can't have you following me through eternity like the venerable Flying Dutchman now, can I?"

H.G. did not respond, for he was looking at Amy. His eyes found hers and recognized the utter terror in them, the dismay, the longing to be free from a most horrible ordeal.

"Yes, lovely creature, isn't she?" Stephenson slowly drew the flat of the blade across her neck as if caressing her. "It would be a shame if I were compelled to harm her because of your reticence."

H.G. looked up at his adversary with hollow eyes. He was choked with emotion and unable to speak. He waited for either a surge of anger or a flash of brilliant deductive logic so that he might turn the tables on the monstrous fiend. Neither came to him.

"But we're wasting time," Stephenson remarked casually. He placed the tip of the knife to her temple. "Give me the key or I'll kill her."

H.G. slumped. He really had no other choice. When it came down to deciding whether he wanted carte blanche to the cosmos or to be with the one he loved, it was no contest.

"You'll release her, then?"

Stephenson exploded with laughter. "Of course, Wells! Hasn't that been the drift of my remarks since this conversation began? I'm proposing a simple, businesslike trade that I believe will be mutually beneficial for both of us."

"You promise?" he asked in stentorian tones.

"You have my word as a gentleman."

"All right. I'm agreeable." He sighed with relief. "Let her go and then I'll throw you the key."

Stephenson chuckled. "No, no. My mother was rather an atrocious woman, but her many failings did not include raising a mentally deficient son." He paused. "Throw *me* the key. *Then* I'll release the girl."

"On your honor?"

"As a gentleman."

H.G. dug into his pocket and pulled out the small key that overrode the RRL. For a moment, he inspected it wistfully. He remembered fashioning the key with his own hands. At the time he had not realized what colossal, immortal powers he was infusing into such a small piece of metal. *C'est la vie.* A human being was more important than a bloody machine any day, no matter how spectacular the technology was. And he wasn't quoting Huxley, he was quoting himself. Then he tossed Stephenson the key. It clinked on the concrete in front of Amy. Stephenson quickly scooped it up with the knife hand, pocketed it, then tightened his grip on Amy's hair and once again placed the knife to her throat. He grinned at Wells and backed across the sidewalk toward the street.

"There's just one thing, my dear fellow. Candidly, I'd have expected you to notice by now that I am not a gentleman."

H.G. gasped and staggered back. He never could have imagined that he could have been deceived so simply and at such a frightful cost! Was this the end result of his moral stance, his own honesty and trustworthiness? His implicit belief in the word of a gentleman? It could not be so! Or were the Fates—now that they had him down—determined to teach him a lesson? It did not matter. He did not have time to think.

"Please, let her go! She is not part of this!"

Stephenson chuckled. "Oh, but she is, my good man, she most certainly is. Forgive me for being so slow in diagnosing the condition, but you are in love with her, are you not?"

"All *right*! So what if I am?"

"Then she should be denied the gift of life so that you may grieve for her."

"*No, wait!*"

The doctor laughed. "Relax, old chap. Calm down. I am not going to murder her before your very eyes. True, I may not be a gentleman, but I do have taste. So do not trouble yourself. Really. Excessive worry is not good for the liver. Suffice it to say that she will meet her maker somewhere along the fourth dimension after we have both had a chance to relax and enjoy each other's company."

Enraged, H.G. shouted at him. "You won't get far! I'll telephone the police!"

"Do what you like, you little fool." Stephenson laughed, then opened the door to the beetle-shaped motorcar with the canvas top.

"H.G.!" Amy cried with ominous despair. "He took her keys, too! He's got Carole's car!"

Then Stephenson forced her into the driver's seat and made her start the engine.

H.G. ran for the vehicle, screaming, but it was already pulling away from the curb. He grabbed onto the rear bumper. The acceleration jerked him off his feet and he ended up sprawled on the pavement. He looked up in time to see the red taillights of the little motorcar turn at the intersection, then disappear from view.

With a groan, H.G. got to his feet. He ran to her apartment building and went inside. He realized that telephoning the police might be a futile gesture. If they had been too late twice already, why not a third time? Still, he must, for there was nothing else he could do. He crossed the foyer and vaulted up the stairs to her flat.

The door was locked.

He sank down onto the stairs and put his face in his hands. Of course. There had been a murder. It was probably standard procedure. He cursed himself over and over. God, what had *possessed* him to trust such a perfidious villain? Why had his natural instinct been to accept Stephenson as a gentleman? Especially when he knew of the man's horrible crimes? He sighed. The deceit merely confirmed what H.G. had learned about human nature in the past five days. He was a fool, a cretinous idiot. Then he began to sob. Never before had he been so utterly disconsolate. Gone was the love of his life. Gone was his machine, *The Utopia.* He was hopelessly mired in a year and a time that he wished he could block out of his memory.

He had been tricked, beguiled like a simpleton, humiliated. He was angry, too. How could he *possibly* have given up the key?

Suddenly, he straightened up and gasped. Key? He fished in his pocket and extracted the ring with keys that

Amy had used to operate her Accord. His mind raced wildly. Of course! He could follow them! It did not matter that he had never driven a motorcar before. He understood the principles, he had seen them driven, he had had their operation explained to him more than once. Moreover, if millions of average twentieth-century human beings could do it, then there was no reason why one logical and rational nineteenth-century human being couldn't do it too. Besides, in this particular case, necessity precluded the matter of choice.

H.G. hurried from the building and jumped into the Accord parked out front. He quickly scanned the controls, then nodded with conviction. He inserted the key, turned it, and the engine sprang to life. He grinned and turned the steering wheel back and forth just to test the feel. He touched the accelerator, then put the motorcar into gear. It leaped forward and smashed into the rear of the vehicle in front. Glass tinkled. He remembered and placed the shift on the "R." The Accord zoomed backward and slammed into the car behind. More glass tinkled.

"Blast," he uttered.

Windows opened and lights went on. Irate people began screaming about their cars. Finally, H.G. pulled hard on the steering wheel while simultaneously manipulating the gearshift. The car lurched out of the parking space into the street. He turned it in a wide circle and grazed three parked vehicles on the other side of the street. He turned the wheel back and forth, then pressed down on the accelerator, assuming that like the Helm Lever in the time machine one had to be definitive. The Accord rocketed toward the intersection and flew across Jones Street.

Fortunately, the hour was late and there was no traffic, for by the time H.G. had reached Van Ness Avenue he had driven through six stop signs and sideswiped a dozen more parked machines while weaving from one side of the street to the other. Amy's car had sustained considerable damage; it looked like it had been through a meteorite shower.

H.G. turned south, but jerked too hard on the wheel and found himself going perpendicular to the roadway, aimed at the sidewalk. He cursed and swerved back to the right, but not before plowing through a line of trash cans. He cursed again and gradually manuevered back to the correct side of the street. He realized that he must manipulate the controls conservatively or he would never make it to the science museum. He motored slowly and steadily the rest of the way down Van Ness without incident.

When he reached the Geary Expressway, he managed an awkward right turn, but overcompensated and flattened a "Yield" sign. The engine began to tick, and he feared that he had damaged it in some way. He was also afraid that if he didn't hurry, he would be too late. He increased speed. His steering became jerky again, and the battered Accord once again swayed back and forth, listing like an abused ship in a typhoon. Since the road was straight, H.G. was all right until he found himself descending into a tunnel. He became apprehensive and stiffened his grip on the wheel. The vehicle veered into the wall, bounced and scraped against the concrete time after time.

He pulled it to the left and did the same thing against the other wall.

"Great Scott," he exclaimed and inadvertently pressed down on the accelerator. The motorcar responded instantly and shot out of the other end of the tunnel. H.G. hung on for dear life, his face ashen, his heart pounding, his eyes riveted in front of him. The Accord, its suspension system ruined, angled hard toward the right. H.G. used all of his strength to bring the nose of the car back to the left. Nothing happened. Horrified, he saw that he was heading for a telephone pole. He steered farther to the right to avoid the obstacle, bounced over the sidewalk, crashed through a brick wall and flattened more trash cans before finally getting back onto the roadway. He cursed the machine for having a mind of its own, realizing that, as Huxley had once said, *somewhere and sometime, mankind must draw a line in the sand and make his stand against technology.*

Despite the damaged vehicle, H.G. somehow made it to Park Presidio Boulevard. He turned left onto the wide street, not seeing that, unlike other streets he had traveled on, this one had a swath of green right down the middle.

"What the devil!" he ejaculated.

The Accord leaped the curb, crushed several small trees, blasted through a hedgerow and tore up the lawn. The motorcar shimmied and squeaked down the island as if it were about to explode. H.G. frantically pulled on the steering wheel and maneuvered the machine back onto the pavement. He was, however, going the wrong way on a one-way street, but did not realize it until he was inside Golden Gate Park. A car was coming the other way, horn blasting. H.G. froze, then forced himself to act. He jerked hard to the left. The Accord vaulted across the street and narrowly missed the oncoming car. It jumped the curb, spun around twice, then rolled down a slight hill and finally—mercifully so—came to rest on its roof in the middle of a pond in the Japanese Tea Gardens.

Dazed, but unhurt, H.G. scrambled out of the ruined vehicle and did not understand the implications of its resting place. He brushed off his wet clothes, then sloshed to shore. Once he got his bearings, he looked off through the dark fog and saw the faint outlines of the science museum. He grinned triumphantly and began running for the building.

He got inside via the same basement fire door through which he had so innocently entered the twentieth century five days before. He hurried up to the main floor and raced toward the display room. He was sickened by the dead security guards he encountered: one had been slain in the great hall, the other, surprised and stabbed in the rotunda. Neither had had a chance to defend himself.

Finally, he was inside the display room just in time to see Stephenson prod Amy into the cabin of *The Utopia* with his knife. He turned, waved at H.G., then climbed in after her. With an outraged roar, H.G. rushed after them, but before he reached the time machine, Stephenson slammed the door in his face and locked it. H.G. pounded on it helplessly. He tried to dig his hands under the door, a plate, anything, but the smooth, metallic surface had been so carefully planned, so painstakingly built that he could not even manage to slide a fingernail under a rivet.

The engine! He could sabotage it!

He raced around behind the device, grabbed the hatch-cover handle and pulled. It didn't budge. Then he remembered that for obvious safety and security reasons he had designed the hatch cover's interior latches to automatically lock once the cabin door was closed. He slumped to the floor and put his face in his hands. He had wanted to be completely protected from the outside world while time-traveling.

Right now, he hated his brilliant, meticulous brain, for no one could interfere with the flight.

Once safely locked inside, Stephenson temporarily released her and turned away to once again familiarize himself with the controls of the time machine. She threw herself at the door, her hands frantically reaching for the handle and the lock. She felt him grab her shoulder, spin her around and take her chin in his hand. Angry now, she bit through the flesh of his hand to the bone. He howled with pain, raised his arm and tried to stab her. She blocked his intended blow, then moved closer to him and with all her strength brought her knee up into his groin. He screamed and dropped his knife and grabbed his crotch with both hands. Writhing with pain, he half turned away from her. She pursued, attempting to claw at his eyes, but he flung her off with one, powerful backhand. She slammed into the side of the cabin and her head bounced off the hard steel.

Dazed, she tried for the door again. He hit her in the belly with all his weight behind the blow. She collapsed, unconscious.

When she awakened, she felt extremely cold. She heard him breathing heavily and moving about the cabin clicking switches on and off and moving levers. Gradually, her head cleared. She was doubled up on the floor. Her naked stomach was now badly bruised from the incredible force of his large fist. *Naked*? She tried to rise, only to discover that he had used her blouse to tie her hands behind her. She moaned softly. He turned and approached her. Although cramped, he seemed perfectly fine, despite her knee to his groin.

Grinning, he kneeled beside her, inspected her face, then used his surgical hands to probe and test her intimate parts. Face it, she told herself, she would die soon. Violently. He would use her body first; no doubt, in a variety of ways. If only he would not prolong his bizarre ritual. That was all she could hope for. Then she turned her thoughts to H.G. He was safe. Thank God for that.

He twisted her face into the light, and she found herself staring into his narrow, deep-set eyes. They were the devil's eyes, she thought. Small and wicked. Mad.

"Your hair is not black like hers," he commented. "And your skin is not creamy enough." Then he smiled and nodded. "But you're closer than any of the others. By far."

He straightened up and reached down for her. He picked her up without effort and placed her astraddle him in the chair. She felt the harness being strapped over them both, and she began trembling. The switches were on! The Time-Sphere-Destination-Indicator was set for the year 2000! She heard his interminable breathing in her ear. He whistled. His arms came around her and his hands rigidly grasped the Accelerator Helm Lever. With a joyful shout of triumph, he shoved the bar forward until it locked in the flank position.

Nothing happened.

Suddenly, H.G. lifted his head. He frowned and cocked his ear toward the time machine. Strange, he thought, the engine wasn't making any sounds at all. Therefore, Stephenson hadn't left yet. Why? He quickly scrambled to his feet, then gasped as the realization came over him. *Of course* Stephenson hadn't left yet!

When he and Amy had returned from their journey to Saturday, he had replaced the small lock on the central gearing wheel, effectively preventing the pulse generator from transmitting electrical starting power to the engine!

He was not sure why he had done it—other than feeling the need to indulge his suppressed belief in superstition and the supernatural. In other words, he had placed the lock there originally, so he must have had a good reason. Perhaps his deductions had been concerned with the sanctity of the universe. Whatever, he had no doubt feared that someone *else* would place their irresponsible hands on the Accelerator Helm Lever.

He remembered his thoughts when they had returned from Saturday. Then, he had worried about the fact that before the trip he had cut through the bar of the lock. He had shrugged off the concern and replaced the little device anyway. He had realized that since it would be hanging in the path of a gearing system, the engine would not work, regardless. He grinned. In this case, then, the mere physical presence of an unsophisticated foreign object near the heart of his machine meant that both he and history would have a second chance.

He heard the cabin door unlock with a great clank and saw it slowly being pushed open. Then Stephenson pushed Amy through the hatch, the knife to her throat. He followed.

"As you can see," Stephenson stated coldly, "she is still alive and in one piece. *Presently*."

H.G. was filled with relief and gratitude, but did not show his feelings. A plan was beginning to form in his mind as he realized that he, too, could use deceit to his advantage.

"The only question is, Wells, how long will she remain in that condition?"

The tenacious little scientist studied his adversary and did not respond. His expression was blank, impassive.

"Either you fix this infernal contraption or I'll kill her right now."

"If I repair the machine, you'll kill her anyway," H.G. replied flatly. His voice did not betray his pounding heart or his dry throat.

The villain smiled cleverly. "Maybe I will and maybe I won't." He lounged against the side of the time machine, still holding Amy. "There are two ways to look at it, my dear fellow, depending upon how one views the human condition. You can repair the device thinking that your good deed will be rewarded in kind. Or, you can perform the good service fearful that the worst will happen anyway. Would you agree with my assessment?"

H.G. nodded slowly.

"Regardless, then, you really have no choice, do you? Unless, of course, you're more callous that I thought."

"You're right."

"H.G., no!" Amy screamed. "Don't do it!"

Stephenson laughed. "He has to repair it, my dear girl, for he is hopelessly in love with you. Isn't it marvelous how weak the human heart is?" He turned to H.G. "Go on! Fix the blasted thing!"

H.G. shrugged helplessly. "But I have no tools."

Stephenson reached down, removed the surgical knife from his half boot and tossed it. The instrument clattered across the floor to H.G. "That's the best I can do."

"H.G., please!" she cried. "I'd rather die!"

H.G. picked up the knife and went to the engine. He lifted the hatch cover, then got down onto his back and pushed his head and torso into the engine compartment. He did not need the knife—or any tools, for that matter —to remove the small lock from the central gear wheel. All he had to do was insert his arm into the reversal housing, twist his wrist the wrong way, bend his fingers back in the other direction and, presto, the lock was in his hand. The engine was free to function. Then he took a deep breath and studied the complex wiring. His eyes narrowed. He clenched his jaw with determination. Yes, the time machine would work all right, but not in the way that Stephenson suspected. H.G. raised the villain's knife.

"Just what the devil is taking you so long?" Stephenson demanded.

H.G. slid out of the engine compartment, got to his feet and closed the hatch cover.

"Well?"

"It is done."

The doctor grinned. "Thank you, Wells, you're a jolly good sport." He took a guinea out of his pocket and flipped it to H.G. "Keep the change, old boy."

He turned and began to push Amy inside the cabin. She moaned fearfully and tried to resist.

"Why did you fix it, H.G.?" she screamed. "*Why?*"

"Because he's a simpering, callow fool who believes in the golden rule!"

Stephenson violently shoved her halfway into the cabin. Despite the prod of his knife, she continued to resist. Finally, he got her all the way inside, but in so doing he lost some of his momentum. His watch chain became tangled around the door handle. He automatically turned to extricate himself and inadvertently let go of his hostage.

Amy bolted free of the time machine.

H.G. was surprised by the sudden turn of events, but recovered quickly and rushed the cabin. Stephenson saw him coming, emitted an oath, then slammed the door and locked it. Caught outside, his pocket watch swung from the handle; the lid had popped open and the French lullaby played.

H.G. banged on the door, then realized—once again—that his attempts were futile. There was nothing he could do. A low hum emanated from *The Utopia*. Inside, Stephenson was no doubt preparing for flight. H.G. cursed, then looked down at the absurd little pocket watch playing music. Suddenly, he gasped and stiffened, for below he saw the ring handle for the declinometer. He grabbed it and pulled the prism-shaped component out of the machine. He dropped it, then backed away from *The Utopia*, afraid to contemplate what he had done. He saw Amy, still in a state of shock. He quickly untied her and then they embraced tightly. Her supple body shuddered as the tension left her. She began to sob. Her cries gradually became whimpers of joy. He imagined that he was hearing a celestial symphony, a celebration of everything that was good, a song of life.

He was crying, too, for he knew that Amy was finally safe. There were no more deceptions. The moment was real and true.

They moved away and stood back across the display room from the time machine, trembling in each other's arms and silhouetted by the intense blue energy field that surrounded *The Utopia* as the engine gradually warmed. He held her tighter and caressed her face and hair. She had stopped sobbing, her attention drawn to the time machine much like the enthrallment one could see in the eyes of a lower primate held spellbound by the lights of an automobile. He, too, stared at the spectacle in awe. He heard the hum of the engine reach its familiar pitch and level off, indicating that speed had been achieved. A faint, red glow blinked intermittently from behind the small, opaque cabin windows, and H.G. knew that very soon now Stephenson would make his cosmic leap into the fourth dimension. The aura around the machine became whiter, then swirled into translucent patterns. H.G. held his breath with anticipation. Would *The Utopia* explode? He truly did not know what to expect.

Suddenly, the engine growled as if straining against itself. There was a clunk, then another hum, more high-pitched than before. Everything was dazzled by an intense explosion of light that seemed too powerful to have originated from anything except a celestial source.

A long, agonized scream emanated from the cabin of the time machine in spite of the soundproofing. A terrible, elongated wail that echoed through the universe, gradually dying out like a comet falling forever beyond endless horizons.

A long silence.

From the top of the cabin, a wisp of smoke rose, then

slowly dissipated along with the bluish cast that surrounded *The Utopia.*

After leaving the museum, they retreated to the smoky haze of a warm and intimate bar that had no windows which might serve as portholes for the imagination. They had both seen enough to last a lifetime. Or so H.G. told himself at that particular moment.

And in time, the inevitable questions were asked and answered.

First, Amy had wanted to know what H.G. had done after she had finally gotten away from Stephenson. H.G. explained to his exhausted yet enraptured companion that once she was safe, he could jerk the prism-shaped declinometer out of his machine. Inside the cabin nothing at all was affected; hence, there was no way Stephenson could fathom that he was about to embark on a journey which would never end.

"Oh," Amy exclaimed. "Then you sent him to Eternity."

"Exactly." He smiled and nodded.

"Does that mean that he's dead?"

"I don't really know, my dear." He sipped a gin and bitters. "And I'm not really sure that I want to speculate, other than to say that Dr. Leslie John Stephenson is no doubt permanently stuck outside of time."

"*Permanently?*"

"Of course. You remember. Once you arrive at Infinity, you cannot return, for there is nothing to get back from. Ever."

"But what about your time machine? It's still in 1979."

He smiled. "Quite true. When Stephenson asked me to fix *The Utopia,* I realized that all was not lost."

"I don't understand."

"I really didn't have to fix anything. All I had to do was remove the lock which I had placed on the engine earlier. But while I was under the machine, I cut part of the RRL circuitry with the villain's knife."

She gasped, her eyes wide. "You were planning to follow me!"

"Fortunately, I was spared that ordeal due to the man's ultimate carelessness."

She laughed joyfully. "Go on."

"When I pulled the declinometer, he went to Eternity *without* the machine. If part of the RRL circuitry had not been already cut, *The Utopia* would have gone with him. I was lucky."

She shook her head, her eyes full of astonishment. "You are amazing."

"Thanks to this." With a sheepish and magical grin on his face, he reached into his pocket and took out the small lock that he had removed from the engine's central gearing wheel. He chuckled and reminisced. The tour guide who had first encountered him in 1979 had been correct: the time machine *had* never been known to work, although the poor man never would have guessed in a million years that the reason why not was an infinitely simple, drop-forged bicycle lock.

H.G. emitted a long, luxurious sigh. He hefted the lock in his hand and speculated about how the principle of matter rejuvenation actually functioned when one was traveling into history. (The bar of the lock was cut *now*: it would be whole then—eighty-six years in the past; but if only it were placed, say, on the control panel, hence being left inside time and exposed to the swirling vortex of high-energy rotation.) Suddenly, he grinned broadly.

He finally knew that he, H. G. Wells, had actually been the one who had originally placed the lock on the machine when he got back to the nineteenth century. And he knew why, too. After the cosmic ordeal that they had both been through, he realized—profoundly so—that no one must ever use his time machine again.

"So then what do we say about Dr. Stephenson?" she asked, her eyes wide.

He shifted in his chair. "According to history, no one ever really knew what happened to Jack the Ripper." He raised both his eyes and his glass and toasted the skies. "And they will never find out, either, my dear."

"You know what," she said, her voice full of awe. "I just realized something."

"What?"

"I'm in love with an older man."

EPILOGUE

Unlike Leslie John Stephenson, the fate of H. G. Wells and Amy Robbins became common knowledge. Far more common, perhaps, than either of them desired, although neither was ever known to complain in public about the questionable virtues of fame and fortune. What happened—briefly—was this.

When H.G. eventually returned to 1893, he took a consenting Amy with him. Since they arrived within minutes of his original departure—thanks to his precise calculations—Mrs. Nelson was not surprised that he had come home so soon. As a matter of fact, she never really was sure whether or not he had left. Especially since she hadn't had a chance to find the envelope containing the fifty pounds and his letter of explanation in the basement. She was not particularly amazed by the digital watch he wore; she assumed that he had created it in his laboratory. She was, however, shocked by the presence of Ms. Amy Robbins and flabbergasted that such a pretty young lady would dress in such a bizarre fashion. But, like most good and true English gentlewomen, she stoically accepted the news from H.G. that his female companion, most recently arrived from America, would be moving in for the duration. Besides, Mrs.

Nelson and Amy quickly became fast friends and, on rare occasions when alone, they would share mild outrage at the inconsiderate nature of the adult male of the species.

Needless to say, London society was utterly scandalized that H. G. Wells and a woman from the notorious city of San Francisco were living together under the same roof. As a result, the articles that he was obligated to pen for the *Pall Mall Gazette* became even more popular. His readership avidly looked for erotic tidbits from the radical who was living in sin and enjoying it. Demands on his time became heavy, for he had begun his first novel. But he never forsook his daily bicycle ride through the city, now accompanied by Amy. And if the weather was good, they spent Sunday afternoons boating on the lake in Regent's Park. If not, the two of them invariably could be found in the library of 17 Mornington Place by the fire, sipping wine and reading to each other.

H.G. had returned from his sojourn a wiser man. His vision of the future was more skeptical, and hence realistic. No longer did he blindly trust the proponents of science and technology, for he realized that they could be morally bankrupt. Moreover, he understood that during his eighty-six year hiatus many of their dazzling creations had been employed to devastate societies and annihilate human beings, sometimes for no reason at all. Furthermore, he had seen that an advanced technology could effectively crush people if they themselves allowed it to happen. He had seen that man was dangerously close to becoming a slave to the artificial, automatic world that, ironically, he had created for his own power and convenience. Therefore, if Techno-Utopia ever did become a reality, the possibility existed that it would ultimately serve only itself.

H.G. had no answers, failing a return to organized religion. He could only dedicate his life and work to making frequent eloquent pleas for rationality. What was it that Huxley had once said? *It is a fact that men must control science and occasionally check the inevitable advance of technology. What is even more important, however, is that they must control themselves according to the designs of reason if they are to avoid a final solution of no quarter.*

Amen, H.G. had finally added.

With unfailing devotion, Amy helped him finish his book, and shortly thereafter *The Time Traveler* was published. It created a sensation in literary circles, although not entirely a favorable one, and instantly became a best seller. One critic was prompted to report that the work deserved serious attention because of its "fantasized, yet penetrating insights into the future of mankind."

And what of H.G.'s cosmic battle with destiny? He never did claim superiority or even victory. He preferred to let the matter rest alongside the notes on his desk and other philosophical riddles. Suffice it to say that Herbert George Wells and Amy Catherine Robbins were married in 1895 and lived happily together in a state of mutual tenderness for a good, long time.

Dell Bestsellers

A novel of terror aboard the President's plane, as one desperate man holds the passengers and crew at gun point, high over the skies of America!

"The right ingredients. A top notch yarn."   *Pittsburgh Press*

A harrowing flight to the brink of disaster!

AIR FORCE ONE

by Edwin Corley
author of *Sargasso*

A Dell Book   **$2.50**

(10063-1)